TORN IN TWO

SAINT VIEW SLAYERS VS SINNERS
BOOK 2

ELLE THORPE

WWW.ELLETHORPE.COM

Copyright © 2024 by Elle Thorpe Pty Ltd

All rights reserved.

No part of this book may be reproduced in any form or by any electronic or mechanical means, including information storage and retrieval systems, without written permission from the author, except for the use of brief quotations in a book review.

Editing by Studio ENP

Proofreading by Barren Acres Editing

Cover photography by Michelle Lancaster

Cover model: Christopher Lynch

Original cover design by Elle Thorpe Pty Ltd

Discreet cover design by Emily Wittig Designs

V: 2

For Shianne.
Without you, my audio books would take so much longer and have so many more mistakes. Thank you for all that you do.
Elle x

1

KARA

Dirt filled my nostrils.

Every time I opened my mouth to scream, it was all I could taste until I coughed and choked, trying not to swallow it down. My muscles froze with each clump of soil hitting the wood just inches above my face.

From the tinny speaker I'd been buried with, my husband's teachings played in an endless loop.

"Women need to be reborn when they have sinned. They need to prove their worth. Prove that the evil can be leached from their souls."

The box around me was tiny. I wasn't tall but I barely fit, my legs twisted painfully. Once they'd filled my grave, no air would seep through the cracks and crevices letting in the dirt.

How long could a person live, buried beneath the ground?

It couldn't be long in a coffin this size with my panic stealing great gulps of air, my brain unable to calm enough to stop.

Josiah was going to get his wish.

I was going to die with his godforsaken words ringing in my ears.

"Are you sure about this?" a muffled voice asked from somewhere above me. "This is…shit, man, this is a lot."

"Just fucking do it!" a second voice snapped. "You heard his words. Women need to be reborn to cleanse their souls of their sins! Put your foot on the motherfucking shovel and do what you were told to do. Stop questioning me!"

Their voices were too muffled to recognize, my fear too thick around me to think clearly.

Hayley Jade had already lost one mother when I'd taken her from Shari's home. Now she was going to lose another. Had I even told her I loved her? I'd been so wrapped up in worrying about her refusing to speak, and hating myself for not knowing how to connect with my own daughter, I hadn't even said the words she should have been told every day.

That she was loved. Special.

Safe.

I'd never been able to promise her that. Not after running from Josiah. Not after my sister had been murdered and everything pointed toward me being next.

At least it was only me in here. I could only thank the Lord that Hayley Jade was with her Aunt Rebel and cousins, surrounded by men who would protect her, the way I couldn't.

She'd be okay. Rebel would raise her as her own.

Tears leaked from the corners of my eyes at the thought of never seeing my daughter or older sister again. But at least they'd have each other.

The makeshift coffin lid bowed beneath the weight of the dirt, the men arguing back and forth. The recording mixed with their words, all of it becoming a confusing mess I couldn't make sense of. Another shovel load of earth forced the flexible plywood to squash my nose and kiss my lips.

Fresh panic speared through me. Frenzied, I kicked and fought and punched, but it was no good. Everything became harder, sharp movements growing sluggish and weak, sleepiness creeping up on me like a shadow I couldn't escape.

My brain battled to block it out. To fill my memories with something happier. Something worth fighting for.

Hawk.

Hayden.

I'd found happiness and hope in their arms. It had been barely a glimpse of what I could have had, and it had been sweet, but it had disappeared in the face of Hawk's lies.

I hated him for lying about Hayden's death, while simultaneously loved him for teaching me how it felt to be desired.

I hated Hayden for holding me captive, but then being so kind and sweet I'd spent five years secretly in love with a man who could never be mine.

The wood groaned, trying to keep the load from collapsing on top of me. My chest squeezed with pain from lack of oxygen.

With my last breath, I screamed.

Screamed for Hawk.

Screamed for Hayden.

Screamed for me.

2

HAYDEN

"She's not fucking there, Chaos!"

I stared at Hawk, the smug grin falling from my face.

Kara was supposed to have met me at the back gate to the Slayers' compound. The plan had been rushed, no thought given to the details or what came next when all I'd been able to think about was that she was here, and five years had done nothing to dull the connection between us.

It had reignited, hot and hard, a bond not just born of physical attraction but of shared trauma. My heart had always been linked to hers in a way I'd never been able to find with anyone else. In a way that couldn't be forgotten, no matter how much I might have tried.

I'd thought nothing of following her into that cinema bathroom. Locking her in a stall with me. Showing her I was alive and I wanted her.

I'd always fucking wanted her.

But she was with Hawk, and Hawk hated me with

every fiber of his body. Slayers vs. Sinners. That's how it had always been in Saint View. Him on one side, me on the other.

He was never going to let her go without a fight. But I'd asked her anyway. I'd asked her to meet me. Run away with me.

And that's where I'd been when Hawk found me and dropped the goddamn bomb that Kara had a cult leader husband and a club full of Louisiana bikers trying to take her home to him.

Against her will.

Over my dead body was I losing her again. I didn't care if it was me against fifty. They weren't taking her anywhere.

She didn't know it yet, but she was mine.

She'd always been mine.

"Then where the hell is she?" I stared at Hawk, praying he had the answer.

He dropped the gun to his side and shook his head. "I don't know."

That wasn't fucking good enough.

I strode to the van Luca had left on the side of the road. It had the logo of an Italian restaurant printed on the side, but not ten minutes earlier, the back of it had been filled with women. Women I'd freed because fuck Luca. He might have been my boss, and this might have been my way inside the Slayers' compound to meet Kara, but I wasn't helping Luca traffic women. Not anymore.

I'd been young and stupid and desperate enough to fall into that trap once. It had led me to Kara, but I wasn't doing it again.

I'd ram the fucking Slayers' gates down if I had to.

Something inside me delighted in the thought, after what they'd put me through the last time I'd been inside their compound.

I gunned the engine as Hawk jerked open the passenger side door and glared at me. "Where the hell are you going?"

"I've been watching the road ever since I left the theater and haven't seen anyone leave. Unless someone managed to get her out on foot, she's still in there somewhere."

Hawk glared at me. "They could have taken her out on bikes. Cut through the woods in any fucking direction."

He was right, but I had to hope that wasn't the case. It would take hours to send a search party out that far. "Well, we ain't going to know by standing here, are we? So get in or get out. I don't care. But I'm going to find my girl."

Hawk let out a string of expletives as I damn near ran him over, but he gripped the doorframe and, through sheer willpower, dragged himself inside the moving vehicle. "Not *your* girl. My fucking girl. And God, I hate you. You could have at least let me get in. I probably just ripped something in my shoulder."

"Decide faster next time then," I growled back, attention firmly on the road, tires kicking up dust. "Or work out more so you aren't so precious."

Hawk flipped me the bird. "I work out plenty."

I was aware. I'd seen him naked not all that long ago, when we'd both had the unpleasant experience of being strip-searched at the local police station. Hawk was all tanned skin and rippling muscle that had been hard not to look at.

Shame his mouth and shitty attitude ruined everything else.

"Then quit your whining." I pushed my foot harder on the accelerator, the van eating up the miles of what felt like the world's longest driveway to get to the Slayers' gates.

Hawk gripped the "holy shit bar," his ass bouncing up and down on the seat with the force of the van traveling at pace over the uneven road. "You know you're a dead man if you step foot inside those gates, right?"

I gritted my teeth, staring down the imposing gates as they rose in front of us. "Then I guess I'm a dead man."

Hawk braced himself on the dashboard. "Stubborn prick. Slow the fuck down. You're going to kill us both."

"Need speed to get through those gates. You said yourself, your brothers aren't going to unlock them and roll out the red carpet for me."

Hawk's knuckles were white. "Jesus fuck." The van lurched over a pothole. "Who knew your driving was so bad? Stop, you idiot! Trying to ram your way through ain't going to get us anywhere except in a mangled wreck or airlifted to the hospital."

"You should probably put your seat belt on then. Because I'm not stopping." I meant every word. Screw Hawk and his club and their stupid rules. "My woman is in there."

"She ain't your fucking woman!"

"Well, she sure as hell isn't yours either." We were driving too fast, but I couldn't take my foot off the accelerator. Not when everything inside me demanded I get to

Kara. "Now, you gonna get your boys to open that gate, or do I have to kill us both?"

He glared at me. "Ain't no way I'm going to Hell holding your hand. It would be just my goddamn luck to get stuck with you for the rest of eternity because we died on the same day." He stuck his head out the window, waving his arms and hollering at whoever was on the gate. "Get them open! Get them open!"

I flashed my lights and slammed my fist down on the horn. My heart pounded. All I could think about was getting to her. I didn't care about anything else. Not the Slayers' gate or the van or me or Hawk. All that mattered was her.

Everything else was just collateral damage.

I'd seen the video of men surrounding her while she danced. Touching themselves while they watched her. It wasn't much of a leap to assume that right now, they were doing a whole lot more than just looking.

Bile rose in my throat.

Hawk's attempts at drawing attention our way failed. The gates didn't open. No guard wearing a Slayers' jacket stepped from the shadows to stop us.

I braced myself for the hit. For the spray of shattering glass and the scream of twisting metal. Waited for the pain I knew would come.

It would be worth it.

Hawk jerked the wheel, sending the van into a spin on the dirt road.

It had the desired effect of stopping me from ramming down the gate, but the g-force of the spin and the fact Hawk hadn't listened when I told him to put his seat belt on, sent him flying into me.

His head collided with mine and we both groaned, the van coming to a stop with Hawk practically on top of me.

"Have I mentioned today how much I hate you?" he moaned.

Pain radiated through my skull, centering behind my eyes as the world stopped spinning and came back into focus. "Get off me and open the gates, and maybe I'll spare you the details on how much the feeling is mutual. Why the hell did you do that?"

With some shoving from me, Hawk peeled himself off me, but it wasn't without a glare of indignation. "Are you seriously giving me shit right now? I probably just saved your life."

"We would have been fine."

"Those gates are reinforced, dickhead! You would have killed me. And fuck, even if you'd only killed yourself, I don't want to be the one who has to tell Kara that."

He was such a hypocrite. "You were willing to kill me for stepping through the gates a minute ago, and now you're worried for my safety?"

Hawk grimaced, rolling the shoulder that had slammed into me when he'd slid. "Yeah, well, it's a confusing feeling to hate someone and yet also apparently need to keep them alive because..."

He clamped his lips together.

"Because Kara loves me."

He said nothing.

But I knew I'd hit the nail on the head. "And you love her, and you don't want to see her hurt. That about sum it up?"

"Her taste in men sucks if that's true." He got out of

the van and moved to the entrance. Still rubbing at his shoulder, he reached for the control panel that would presumably require a pin code. Then stopped and leaned hard on one of the gates.

It swung open.

It hadn't been locked at all.

I rolled my eyes and called out the open window, "Seriously? It wasn't even locked? We could have been down there by now!"

Hawk turned around. "The gates are never unlocked. Never unmanned." He poked at the panel and shook his head. "It's completely dead. The entire security system is down."

I twisted my fingers around the steering wheel at the tone in his voice. "What does that mean?"

He shook his head and got back into the van. "Not only could anyone have gotten out, anyone could have gotten in." He swallowed thickly. "The cops think there's a serial killer. One who goes after sisters."

I shook my head, trying to make sense of that. "What has that got to do with anything?"

"Kara's sister was murdered a couple weeks ago."

My blood ran cold. "So not only are we up against an entire chapter of bikers who apparently want to drag her back to her abusive husband and his whack-job cult, we also have to worry about some serial killer potentially inside the gates?"

Hawk looked over at me. "As well as none of the Slayers killing you on sight."

"Or you stabbing me in the back. Which we all know is more likely."

Hawk sighed and then held out his hand. "Twenty-four-hour truce. I fucked up with Kara in letting her think you were dead. And you're right. I love her and I want her back. Killing you will only make her hate me more. The last thing I want to do is cause her pain."

I wasn't an idiot. Hawk was the way I got inside without being shot on sight. He'd grown up on this land and he knew it, even in the dark. I didn't. He was my best bet at finding Kara, as well as staying alive long enough to take her home with me.

I took his hand, shaking it. "Did we just become best friends?"

It would have almost been funny if shots hadn't interrupted, the cracking boom of a gun piercing the night air.

3

HAWK

"Leave the van!" I shouted to Hayden. "Those shots came from the woods. We're going to have to go in on foot."

I wasn't waiting for him. We had rules about guns within our boundaries. Nobody was permitted to use one without some sort of very good reason, and the punishment was harsh for breaking the rules. It was to stop drunken Friday night arguments over a pool table from turning into a shootout. When everyone was armed and nobody's moral compass gave a shit about ending a life, we had to have some sort of guidelines or we'd have no members left living.

The prez was the only person permitted to fire a bullet and walk away without question. So either War or Riot was getting trigger-happy, or somebody else had found a reason to send a bullet into the night air.

All I could think about was someone taking Kara from me. But imagining someone forcing her onto a bike to take her back to her husband, or putting a rope around her neck and drawing it tight until she couldn't breathe was useless.

No one was hurting her.

Shouts came from ahead, muffled by the blood rushing in my ears and Hayden's heavy footsteps crunching through the undergrowth behind me.

A second gunshot splintered the night, this time louder. Closer.

I doubled down, stumbling on the uneven ground, catching myself on the trees as I fought my way through the scrub in the darkness, no time to stop and turn on flashlights.

A figure stepped out of the darkness, and I pulled my gun. Moonlight caught the Saint View Slayers' emblem on the back of his jacket before I needed to question whether I should shoot.

"Ice!" I recognized the prospect's fair hair and slim build. "Did you find her—"

A bellow from somewhere up ahead cut me off. "Hawk! This motherfucker has buried your woman alive!"

My blood ran cold.

The sound Chaos made behind me was something between a shout of anger and a moan of agony. I let go of Ice's shoulder and sprinted for the clearing ahead, Chaos at my side, both of us bursting out of the trees at the same time.

Riot, president of the Louisiana chapter, was on his hands and knees, scooping dirt from a hole.

Not a hole.

A motherfucking grave.

Beside it lay two dead bodies, both in Slayers' jackets,

one a Saint View original, one with a Louisiana patch. Their blood seeped into the ground, spreading out around them like halos.

"What the fuck have you done?" I yelled at Riot, staring in horror at Ratchet's dead body, lying completely still next to Thunder's. I didn't need to check their pulses to know they were both dead as fucking doornails.

Behind me, Ice let out a string of cuss words, but it was Hayden who caught on quicker than any of us. He skidded to a stop at the edge of the grave and peered over the edge.

He's buried your woman alive.

Riot ran a hand through his hair, gripping the back of his neck in dismay. "I heard her scream. It was weak, but I heard it."

"Kara!" Hayden and I shouted in unison.

There wasn't a sound.

He stared at me in horror. "How long has she been down there for?"

It had been hours since I'd lost track of her at the party. Terror coursing through my veins, I shook my head. "Too long. Way too fucking long. Get her out!"

Frantic, I scraped my fingers through the dirt, hauling it to the edge of the hole and then up, spilling half in an attempt to remove the soil. Over and over we did the same thing. Ice grabbed the shovel while Chaos, Riot, and I dug with our bare fingers. Other members found their way out of the woods and into the clearing. If they questioned what we were doing, I didn't hear it.

All I could think about was getting this fucking dirt off her so she could breathe.

And that we weren't going to be fast enough.

Something inside me snapped. Some floodgate that had been holding in everything I felt for the curvy brunette.

I was so fucking in love with her, and she was going to die, all because I'd lied to her. If I'd been a better man, an honest one, maybe she would have chosen Hayden, but at least she'd be in his arms, breathing and healthy, instead of suffocating beneath the earth.

I couldn't stand it. The realization made me want to claw my face to pieces.

"Women look to us for guidance. They are lost sheep, while you are their shepherd. It is your job, men of the Lord, to guide them to their rightful place. To teach them how to behave and how to honor the Lord by honoring the men the Almighty made in his image."

"Wait, wait. What is that?" Chaos asked, clearly hearing it too. "A recording?"

A scream of frustration and agony ripped from my chest. We could wipe serial killer off the suspect list, at least for tonight. "That's her psychopath husband's podcast." I'd searched for it when Kara had mentioned it, and there was no mistaking Josiah's smarmy voice, luring men in with promises he couldn't fucking keep.

There was no way she was dying in that hole with his words the last thing she heard. I refused to let that happen.

I threw myself in.

Boards beneath my feet cracked.

I stared up at the others.

I didn't need to voice what we'd all heard. We were nearly there.

I tore into the remaining dirt, my nails catching on

the cheap wood, splinters spearing through my fingertips as I tried to get a hold. "Give me the shovel!" I shouted at Ice, who obediently handed it in.

I fit the shovel head to the corner of the box and stamped down hard.

A satisfying crack came back to me. There was no room in the hole to get decent leverage to pry the nailed-down box open, but fucked if I was going to let that stop me. I stomped on the shovel again, deepening the crack.

The attempt split the lid enough that I could fit the shovel head in and pry up one side of the lid. Dirt slid back down the sides of the hole and into the box I'd made.

"The sides are going to collapse!" Chaos shouted. "Get back!" He shoved Riot and Ice away from the edge. "Hawk! Get her out!

If the side collapsed and filled in the hole again, there was no way we were getting Kara out in time.

Hayley Jade would be without her mother.

I wasn't going to be the one to break that kid's heart again. Or my own.

I fit my fingers into the thick crack I made, flinching when they touched her skin.

A knot formed in my throat, but I forced it down, wrenching the wood with everything I had.

It splintered. Came away in my hands. I fell back against the edge of the hole, pain shooting through my back at the force of the impact, but none of that mattered.

She had air.

"She's not breathing!" Hayden shouted, the flashlight on his phone bouncing off Kara's face.

I scrambled onto my knees, her body yielding

beneath my weight. I hated that I was crushing her, but bruises wouldn't matter if she was dead.

Her face was covered in dirt. I picked her up by her shoulders, shaking her hard and removing the soil from her face at the same time.

Her head flopped around like a rag doll.

Hayden reached for her, but there was no time to get her out. I laid her back down, ignoring his shouts and the reaching hands of Ice and Riot and the other members who crowded around, watching on, trying to help.

The entire world boiled down to her and me.

The weight of her life in my hands.

The only woman I'd ever fallen for, lifeless unless I could get her back.

I didn't give myself time to think or feel. On autopilot, I turned her head. Cleared her mouth.

The faint thump of her heartbeat met my fingers. "She has a pulse!"

But that didn't mean she was breathing. Hayden had been right.

I tilted her head, pinched her nose, and breathed for her, forcing my air into her lungs until they expanded.

Above me, Riot shouted for someone to get an ambulance, but we were way out in the woods. It would take any ambulance twenty minutes to get out here. Twenty minutes Kara didn't have.

"Come on, Little Mouse," I whispered, releasing my hold on her nose to see if she'd breathe again by herself. "You aren't fucking dying in this goddamn hole with Josiah's bullshit in your head. I won't fucking let you. Breathe."

Her chest didn't lift.

"Hawk, please," Hayden pleaded. "I can't lose her."

My heart ached at the sincerity in his voice. Not just for him, having to watch her so lifeless, but for me. Hayden hadn't seen Kara in years, and yet he knew exactly what he wanted. What she was to him.

Everyone knew he loved her and how she felt about him. We'd all seen it in the way she'd defended him, despite the shitty things he'd done. I'd downplayed it as Stockholm syndrome, all while knowing it was more than that. It was why I'd been so damn scared to tell her the truth, knowing whatever the bond was between them, it was stronger than anything I could try to compete with.

I'd had her in my arms for weeks. Had her naked in my sheets. And all I'd done was make her come. I'd been too fucking gutless to tell her the truth. To tell her I wanted more than just what was between her legs.

Wanted her for her.

I pinched her nose again and breathed two short breaths into her mouth before releasing her nostrils.

I glanced up at Chaos.

"Please, Hawk," he begged softly. "I'll do anything."

Fuck. I'd held a gun to the guy's head no less than thirty minutes earlier, and I'd been fully prepared to pull the trigger.

Now I was watching him break in a way that stirred up memories I had spent a long time trying to bury.

The memory hit me hard.

"Hawk, please! Save her!"

It was another man's voice in my head. Another set of eyes that pleaded with me to save the love of his life.

No matter how much I hated Hayden, nobody deserved to lose their soulmate. Not him.

Not me.

Neither of us was losing her tonight.

Hades could go to Hell alone. None of us were following him.

I pinched her nose again and pleaded with her, my lips barely above hers. "Come on, Kara. If you aren't going to breathe for me, I get it. I never deserved you in the first place. But maybe you'll breathe for him. He's right fucking there. You just gotta open your eyes."

I didn't care who she wanted. Only that she wanted it enough to live.

I forced more air into her lungs.

She jerked beneath me. A gasp for air followed, the sound pure joy to my shattered heart. "She's breathing," I bit out, fingers shaking as I rolled her onto her side and stroked her back.

A cheer went up around us.

Which was so out of place when there were two dead bodies and a whole lot of questions that needed answering.

4

GRAYSON

The group of men gathered around on cheap folding chairs looked as ordinary as any. If anything, they were perhaps more average than the regular Joe.

A clever disguise common with men like them.

None of them wanted attention, and styling yourself as normal as possible was the easiest way to do that. They wore jeans and T-shirts and sneakers. Their hair was brown or blond or black and styled with regular, off-the-barber-shop-wall cuts. Nothing special. They could have been suburban dads. Tradesmen. White-collar office workers. Truck drivers.

You'd pass them on the street and never give any of them a second look. They were underestimated every day by almost every person in their lives.

A dangerous mistake to make.

But one only I knew about.

The group didn't have a fancy name like Alcoholics Anonymous, though it worked in much the same way.

There were some differences, like meeting when a member called, not at a set time.

But if that phone rang, then we went. All of us.

Well, all but one.

I sighed, noting the empty chair Trigger's absence left. I still set it out for him whenever the group descended upon my home, but it hadn't been used in a long time.

"He's not coming, Doc," Whip commented idly, following my line of sight. "You know he's not."

I forced myself to nod. "I know. But there's always a tiny part of me that hopes he will."

Whip stirred sugar into his coffee. "You're going to give yourself an ulcer worrying over him."

He was right about that.

I glanced over at Torch, X, and Ace, the three of them chatting quietly amongst themselves while they waited for the toaster to pop and deliver their breakfast. These meetings always seemed to get called early in the mornings, and I understood why.

Nights were hard for men like them. The darkness outside whispered seductively in their ears, and it was when temptation was highest. The morning brought regrets.

So I always kept a loaf of bread in the freezer, just in case I suddenly needed to feed the four of them toast.

Five of them, if Trigger had come.

But there was no point waiting for him. Whip was right. He didn't care if he was breaking the number one rule of the group. Which was if that phone rang, you answered it. You showed up for the others. Because then one day, when you needed them, they'd be there for you the same way you'd been there for them.

Trigger had pissed all over the one damn rule I'd set, and he didn't give a fuck.

I lifted my arm to glance at my watch and then whistled at the trio still slapping peanut butter on their toast. "Let's go, guys. I've got work this morning."

To their credit, all three politely nodded and brought their plates to the circle I'd set up in my living room. All four of them looked expectantly at me.

I grinned. "Really? We're going to start with me?"

X eyed me. "You could have called this meeting as much as any of us."

The second rule of the group was when someone needed a meeting, we called for it on a private number. Nobody actually answered their phones. There was no need to, nobody but the six of us had those numbers. But a call on those specific phones meant at the top of the hour, we would meet to talk. And that meant *all* of us talked, not just whoever was in need the most.

In an attempt to gain their trust, I'd started participating in the group as much as running it.

There were things on my mind. Things that seeing another strangled woman on the table of a morgue had brought up. The marks around her neck had been the same as the ones around my wife's neck years earlier.

Maybe it was a coincidence. Plenty of killers strangled their victims.

But I couldn't rule out that the person who'd killed my wife and my sister-in-law might also have killed the woman lying dead on that table.

And that Kara could be next.

I wasn't going to say that to these men though. Or the one so notably missing from the room.

So I shrugged and lied, "Nothing to report here. Just work. The gym. Hockey. All pretty boring."

Ace tilted his head to one side, studying me. "You're lying. Something is up with you."

X nodded in agreement. "You're being cagey as fuck."

Unlike most of my patients, who were so self-involved I could have strapped on some fake boobs and sung Dolly Parton songs without them noticing, these guys understood people and human behavior in the same way I did.

My understanding came from years of study.

Theirs did too. Only none of them had cracked a book or attended a lecture. Everything they knew came from the way they studied people.

Psychopaths were good at that. Watching. Waiting. Learning all sorts of things about their victims before they attacked.

I found them endlessly interesting.

"I've shared as much as I want to share for today." I set the boundary firmly. "Whip, how about you?"

The big man cracked his neck and then rubbed at the spot with his thick fingers. "Working on a new target. Haven't decided if he's the one yet."

"Straight off the prison release list?" X took the question out of my mouth.

Whip shrugged.

I squinted at him. "If you're going rogue, you need to tell me. Let me run some checks on whoever it is."

Whip stared at me. "They ain't good people, Gray. I promise."

"Even still, I want a name. You want someone added

to the list, then we all have to agree. That's how this works."

Torch chuckled and flicked his cigarette lighter. "Whip wants to keep his new toy all to himself."

Whip flipped him the bird. "Can you blame me? If I put his name on the list you'll probably set his fucking house on fire."

"Come on, Dad!" Torch mocked, ribbing Whip for being the oldest of the group. "Just a little blaze. Nothing crazy."

We all knew he hadn't chosen Torch as his group name for no reason. The man was a complete pyromaniac and thought nothing of setting fire to a house while his victim slept inside.

Though he'd admitted many a time that he preferred to block off the exits and hear them scream.

Whip turned to me. "I'll tell you, but you keep him off the list so fire fingers over there doesn't get to him before I do."

I nodded, passing my notepad and pen to the older man and watching him scribble a name across it.

X leaned over to try to sneak a peek, his chair legs lifting off the floor.

Whip shot out one hand so fast X didn't even see it coming until he'd fallen off his chair.

I hid a laugh as he grumbled and got back up, shooting Whip a dirty look in the process.

Whip just rolled his eyes at me as he handed me back my notepad. He was probably only in his early forties, but he was the unofficial father figure of the group. Anyone else shoving X off a chair like that probably would have ended in a murder, but X, Ace, and Torch all tolerated Whip's grumpy old-man moves.

He'd earned the right to put them in their place, and we all knew it.

I focused on the younger man with the snake tattoos covering his entire body. Even with a sweatshirt on, they were visible creeping up his neck and across his knuckles. "X, you want to talk?"

"About my bruised ass?" he snarked.

"Or about how you've been lately?"

He pulled out a cigarette and leaned over so Torch could light it.

Any excuse for the man to create flame.

X inhaled and then blew out the smoke in a long plume. "Got my hands dirty last night." He glanced at me. "Thirty-seven on the list, by the way."

I noted that down, not remembering the name of the person in that slot, or the reason they were there, but I felt no remorse. If they were on the list, they were on it for a reason. They were either a rapist, a child molester, a granny basher, a prostitute killer, or had committed some other crime that had landed them in our sights.

I couldn't care less about the man who lay dead somewhere, probably buried in a shallow grave in the woods or tossed off the Saint View bluff. But I did care about the man sitting across the circle from me.

Watching him more closely, I noted the way his leg bounced, just the tiniest amount, like he was actively trying to control it and not quite getting there. "You're triggered," I suggested softly.

X snapped his gaze to meet mine. "I'm fine."

"You know you're not," Ace disagreed. "You're twitching. You never fucking twitch."

X took another drag on his smoke. "Fine. What the fuck ever. I can't stop thinking about the blood spilling. Every person I walk past I think about slitting their throats and setting free the crimson river..."

"Very poetic," Whip said dryly.

Torch faked a yawn. "Who cares? Just do it. See what happens."

I groaned internally and shot him a look. "Don't say things like that. That's not helpful in this space, and you know it."

He sat up a little straighter, suitably abashed. "Fine. X, don't kill people on the streets, okay? Stick to the list."

It wasn't the worst advice, and sometimes, I had to take what I could get. Nobody had ever claimed a support group for psychopaths would be perfect. But these men had found their way to me one by one or were sent to me by Trigger. They came to these meetings, not because they wanted to give up their vices altogether. It was almost impossible for a true murderous psychopath to change who they were at their core.

But these men were trying to channel their urges in more productive places.

And I was trying to help them.

I pointed a pen at X. "I agree with Torch. Focus your energy on the list. Or go cold turkey for a month."

All four of them gaped at me like that was the most ridiculous suggestion in the world.

Whip shook his head. "Asking him to go cold turkey for a month is like asking a man to give up sex."

"Or breathing," Torch added. "Fucking hell."

I sighed. "Meetings then. Every time you think you're going to slip, you call us instead." I sternly focused in X's direction. "*Every* time."

He gave me a nod and held his hand up like he was a Boy Scout. "I will not poke knife holes in the skin of an innocent just to see how they bleed."

I squinted at him. "Really?"

He grinned. "You're the one who likes affirmations."

I gave up and turned my attention to Ace, knowing I had to wrap this meeting up so I could get to work. "What about you?"

He shrugged. "Shot my neighbor's rooster yesterday."

The entire room broke out in a cacophony of shouts.

"Oh, you are messed up in the head." Whip's disgust was written all over his face.

Torch rolled the wheel on his lighter so fast it made sparks. "This makes me real fucking unhappy, Ace. *Real* fucking unhappy."

"You can't fucking kill animals, you psychopath!" X shouted.

Though wasn't that the kettle calling the pot black?

This was exactly why I'd first agreed to start working with men like this. The way their minds worked was endlessly fascinating. There was barely a blink when X had talked about running his blade into another human being or when Whip had admitted to stalking another target, an unapproved one at that. But Ace kills a rooster…

"Humans are all pieces of shit," Whip explained. "Even the ones not on the list. None of us are innocent. We do bad shit. Lie. Cheat. Steal… Litter."

I hid a laugh at him throwing in littering with the rest of the list.

"Animals though," Whip continued. "They don't know any better. They don't do bad shit." He glared at Ace. "Killing them is messed up."

Ace huffed out an irritated sigh. "The little fucker got into my yard and chased me! What was I supposed to do?" He reached into his duffel bag and pulled out a clear plastic bag.

His neighbor's dead pet was inside.

"You see the claws on that thing? He was gonna rip my eyes out!" He tossed the bag in my direction. "Here. Thought you could eat it. You're on that Keto diet thing, aren't you?"

I stared down at the dead bird on my lap and then around at the group of men all watching me.

Clearly, we still had some work to do.

5

HAYDEN

I was going to die.

At least the clearing, awash with pink and gold as the sun rose, was a pretty place for it all to end.

"Does somebody want to tell me why the fuck we have two dead members and a Sinner in our compound?" War roared from the middle of the crowd, his gaze centering on me. He pulled his gun. "What kind of fucking death wish do you have, Chaos?"

"Don't shoot him," Hawk said with reluctance from the bottom of the hole where he was monitoring Kara's breathing. His tone was anything but convincing, as if he did kind of wish War would put a bullet through my head. "At least, not until Kara's out of the woods."

War dragged his gaze away from me and onto his VP. And then to Kara, lying in the hip-deep hole on her side, so deathly quiet in the midst of the drama surrounding her.

War dropped his gun and knelt at the edge of the hole. "What the fuck happened?"

He'd been late to the party, but somebody else was going to have to fill him in.

I focused on Hawk, hating it was him down there and not me. It had taken everything inside me to not shove him out of the way and take his spot.

But I knew exactly how good Hawk was with anything medical. He might not have had a degree in anything, but he knew what he was doing. I was alive as walking, talking proof of that. I didn't know the first thing about checking pulses or doing CPR.

I was completely useless to Kara right now, and as much as I hated to admit it, she needed him in this moment more than she needed me.

That hurt like fucking hell.

"Can we move her yet?" I asked him. "She needs a hospital."

War glared at me. "Hawk knows what he's doing. She doesn't need—"

"She does," he interrupted. "She does need a hospital. She needs X-rays or something to check her lungs and make sure she hasn't inhaled dirt. I can't do that here."

War nodded. "Shit. Okay, yeah. I'll get the club van."

Hawk went to nod, then screwed up his face and shook his head. "Chaos has a van. We'll take her in that."

Surprise punched through me.

Clearly, it caught War off guard too.

Both of us were plain shocked when Hawk gathered Kara up in his arms, lifted her, and then held her out to me.

He glared at me when I didn't move. "Fucking take her, Chaos. I can't get out of this damn hole carrying her."

Shit. I crouched at the edge of the grave she'd nearly

died in and took her from his arms. The breath whooshed from my lungs. Just hours earlier she'd stood right in front of me, eyes bright, skin pink with health. Now she was barely conscious, her body a dead weight in desperate need of medical attention.

"Hayden," she mumbled, her voice raspy, like she'd been screaming.

"It's me, baby. I got you." I stepped toward the woods, the van abandoned somewhere beyond.

Hawk whistled sharply. "This way, asshole."

I didn't argue with him. Hawk might have been lacking in a lot of areas, his personality in particular, but this was his territory.

So I shut up and followed him, clutching Kara close and keeping pace with Hawk, who slow jogged through the trees.

It was easier than the trip in, despite the addition of Kara's weight. Anything was easier than blindly running through the woods in the darkness.

Hawk opened the sliding door on the van and closed it after me when I got in. There were no seats, the back designed for deliveries, so I sank to the cold metal and put Kara on my lap. She curled in on herself, resting her head on my shoulder and closing her eyes.

I didn't like the sound of her breathing. It seemed too shallow and wheezy, and she winced with each inhale.

"Hawk," I said, a low warning in my tone.

He glanced back at us in the rearview mirror. "Yeah, I know. I can hear it too. I'm driving."

All I could do was hold Kara close and pray she'd be okay until we got to the hospital.

*H*awk pulled up outside the ER with a screech of brakes and the blaring of his horn. "Can we get some help out here!" He got out of the van and slid the back door open.

Kara's breathing was barely a rasp. I wasn't even sure if she was just exhausted or unconscious.

I got us out and met the attendant running out with a gurney.

He took one glimpse of Kara's dirt-covered, vaguely gray skin and put his fingers to her neck, checking for a pulse.

That's how fucking dead she looked, even though her chest did rise and fall with shallow breaths.

"She has a pulse and she's breathing," Hawk barked out, gripping the side of the gurney and pushing it toward the hospital doors. "Now move!"

I grabbed the other side, helping it along.

"She was unresponsive for an unknown period of time," Hawk continued. "And she might have inhaled dirt. A lot of it. So make sure you do whatever the hell checks you do for that."

The attendant nodded, repeating the information to the medical professionals as we entered the hospital.

One of the male doctors looked at her and then at us. "What happened to her?"

Hawk, who had been full of confidence, barking out orders a second ago, froze.

I knew what he was thinking. He'd ditched his MC jacket while he'd been driving, but if we told these people the truth, that she'd been buried alive, the police were inevitably going to ask us where.

Hawk and I were both known to the cops. It wouldn't take them long to get a search warrant for my house. The restaurant. The Slayers' compound. Wouldn't be long until someone found a trace of what had happened out there.

Or the dead body of a biker. There had been a couple to choose from.

I could dump Hawk in it pretty bad right now. Luca, too, which he would deserve after he'd tried to use me as his pawn, once again. The cops would surely find some sort of evidence at both the restaurant and the Slayers' compound, but my house was squeaky clean since I'd been out of the game so long.

I could walk away into the sunset with Kara and Hayley Jade. Maybe we'd send Hawk and Luca a postcard from wherever we ended up, addressed to the Saint View jail where they'd both be seeing out their days.

My gaze met Hawk's. His expression was full of anger and indignation, and maybe even some resignation.

But then he ran his hand over Kara's forehead so tenderly, and I remembered the way he'd brought her back to life. My stupid fucking tongue wouldn't form the words to dump him in it. "We were at a party," I told the doctor. "She got too close to the edge of a small cliff and ground gave way. She didn't fall that far but brought some dirt and soil down on top of her."

The doctor swore beneath his breath and barked out a lot of medical talk to his team around him.

I didn't understand a word of it but I looked at Hawk,

who nodded at the doctor's commands. He didn't argue. If what the doctors were doing was good enough for Hawk, when he clearly loved Kara so much it had changed his whole personality from abrasive, rude jackass, to tender, attentive boyfriend, then it was good enough for me.

"One of you her husband?" a nurse asked, jotting notes down while the team rushed Kara through the corridors.

"I am," I lied quickly, knowing that with a serious health complication, only immediate family would be let in. Fucked if they were keeping me away from her.

Hawk shot me a glare that was so full of malice I was surprised it didn't wither me to the spot. "I am," he growled.

The nurse glanced between us, confusion etching her forehead into lines. "You're both her husband?"

Hawk looked ready to punch a hole through my face, but he grit his teeth and answered, "That's what we said, isn't it?"

The woman stopped us at the door, forcing us to let Kara and her medical team carry on without us. She tapped something on her iPad. "Noted. Go take a seat over there somewhere, and I'll come get you as soon as you can see her." She pointed to some chairs that formed a small waiting room.

Neither Hawk nor I moved, both of us standing there, peering through small rectangular windows on the door until Kara was out of sight.

The nurse's gaze danced between the two of us. "So just out of interest, you're..." She cocked her head to one side, considering her words. "If it's sister wives for women...does that make you brother husbands?"

The way the color drained out of Hawk's face at the mention of the two of us being husbands would have been funny if Kara hadn't been lying on a gurney somewhere, struggling to breathe.

"Your homophobia is showing, husband." I ignored the woman's question and passed him to move toward the seats.

He ignored the nosy nurse as well, shoving me instead until we were out of her earshot. "Fuck off. I don't hate you because you love the dick. I hate you because you are one."

I rolled my eyes, slumping into a seat, no idea where he'd gotten this idea that I liked men from, but more than happy for him to pick a fight because it beat remembering the sickly color of Kara's skin. I had no problem with Hawk assuming I was into guys. But clearly, he did. "No? You're saying your balls didn't just suck right up into your body at the mere thought of me fucking you?"

His gaze met mine.

And for the briefest of instants, it wasn't disgust I saw there in his expression.

It was white-hot fucking heat.

It hit me too. That same rush of attraction I'd felt when we'd been stuck in jail together for a night.

"Don't talk about my balls, Chaos." Hawk scrubbed a hand over his face. "I'm dirty and tired and probably in shock. The last thing I want is you traumatizing me some more."

The hospital bustled around us, our conversation made private by the dull hum of machines beeping, medical conversations, and beds on wheels being moved up and down the corridor.

"Because you're not a homophobe? Right. Gotcha." I was tired and dirty too. I hadn't slept in twenty-four hours, and he wasn't the only person sitting here nursing a new mental scar from seeing Kara buried beneath the fucking dirt like a corpse. So fuck him if talking about his balls was easier than thinking about the fact Kara could have stopped breathing again, and neither of us would even know it until some doctor walked out here and decided to drop a bomb.

The thought had me clenching my fingers around the plastic armrests so tight my knuckles ached.

His hand fell away, and he glared at me. "Because we both know you'd rather talk about my dick, right? About how fucking much you want it?"

I raised an eyebrow. Talking was better than silence. I couldn't stand the way the silence whispered this was my fault. If I hadn't come between Hawk and Kara earlier, none of this would have happened. Sure, she probably would have been naked in his bed, but at least she would have been protected. Happy.

I would have been miserable, but look where being selfish had gotten me? I was miserable anyway.

Poking at Hawk's barely disguised bi-awakening at least stopped me from thinking about anything else. I sank my head back against the wall and stared at the ceiling. "That how you're trying to play this one? That it's me who wants it? Okay, sure, let's talk that out since we have nothing better to do." Neither of us had a phone or a book or anything else to pass the time. "Tell me how I want it?"

Hawk recoiled. "What?"

I snorted at his horror. "Yeah, come on. Tell me how I want it. In my mouth? Or in my ass?"

I glanced over at him.

My breath quickened at the expression he tried to cover.

I sat up straighter and shook my head. "Nuh. No fucking way. You actually were seriously just thinking about that, weren't you?"

He sank down in his chair, crossing his arms over his chest. "And you weren't?"

I shook my head. "Nope."

It was such a fucking lie.

"You weren't thinking about the way my dick would taste, Chaos?"

I glanced around the room. It was nearly empty, only an older man asleep in a chair at the far end and a younger couple who were engrossed in their phones. Nobody was paying either Hawk or me any attention.

All of a sudden I was thinking about what his dick would taste like.

I'd been playing, poking at him to get a rise, but the thought of getting on my knees for him was suddenly all I could see. "I'm really fucking tired if the thought of your dick in my mouth is getting me hot."

He leaned in and lowered his voice. "How about my dick in your ass then?"

I wasn't even sure if we were joking anymore or serious. Only that heat flushed through me so hot and fast that I stood to get a paper cup full of water, from a dispenser on the other side of the room, before my cock could get all the way up like it was threatening to.

I stood there for a good few minutes, drinking the

water and pretending to read a pamphlet from a holder on the wall. My brain wouldn't even register the words. They swam in front of my eyes, my brain just focusing on getting my dick to behave.

For once in his life, Hawk had nothing to say. When I returned to my seat, we fell into an awkward silence, both of us refusing to look at the other.

All I could think was I must have inhaled some dirt or something as well, because my chest was tight and my heartbeat raced at the very idea of Hawk wanting me like that.

6

KARA

*L*ight pierced the darkness, only for it to sting my eyes and force them closed again. The noises around me added to the confusion, and the ache in my chest cemented the feeling of dying.

If this was the afterlife, I'd clearly not made it to Heaven because it hurt. Everything hurt so damn much.

I let my brain coast on the pain, memories focusing into sharp details then drifting away just as quickly.

Hayley Jade. Rebel. Hawk. Hayden.

Cages. Coffins. Josiah.

His face was there in the darkness, a terrifying demon of a figure that made me never want to close my eyes again.

I sat up gasping, this time determined to keep my eyes open. I didn't want Josiah in my head.

"Take your time," a gentle, vaguely familiar voice soothed. "You're okay. Do you know where you are?"

I blinked rapidly, trying to make some sense of the

scene around me. It was all so bright, and for a tiny second, hope filled me.

Hell wasn't light and bright like this. Maybe my sins had been forgiven.

"Heaven?" I asked through cracked lips.

The man chuckled. "I hope not, because the food here is pretty awful."

He sat on the foot of the bed, his smile soft and his eyes kind. "You're in the hospital. Do you remember me?"

I focused on his neatly styled hair and the brown eyes behind his glasses. "You made me an elephant."

Grayson grinned. "I did. Want me to show you how I make roosters?"

"Maybe some other time." I grimaced as my lashes fluttered closed, Josiah's face there, forcing them open again.

Grayson's smile fell away. "I'm a bit worried about you. You get dragged out of here by some Slayers' thug. And now you're back with injuries that make me and the rest of your medical team pretty unhappy."

Embarrassment crept up my neck. "I'm sorry. You really don't need to worry about me." This man was a doctor. He was probably busy saving lives. Nobody needed to be concerning themselves with me. "Is he here?"

"Who? The MC thug?"

I nodded. "Hawk."

Grayson's mouth flattened into a worried line. "I'm told he and another man are out in the waiting room. Apparently they both claim to be your husbands."

My fingers took up a violent shake. I didn't know why Hawk was claiming himself to be my husband, but if

Josiah was out there, I wasn't safe and I needed to run. From both of them. Hawk might not have abused me the way Josiah had, but he was a liar.

And now he was sitting out there with the man who'd forced me to marry him, only to spend years terrorizing me for not being able to produce a child.

I ignored the wheeze in my chest and pulled the oxygen tubes away from my nose. I reached for the drip in my arm, ready to yank it out.

Grayson caught my fingers. "Don't do that. It'll just mean they have to stick you again, and you're already hurt enough."

I fought with him, fear wrapping its way around my body at the very thought of being so close to my husband. It would only be a matter of time before he sweet-talked his way in here. Josiah was the ultimate charmer. It was how he convinced once sane, rational people to believe the lies he fed them. "Let me go. I can't be here. If Josiah's found me, I need to run."

Grayson's eyebrows furrowed together in confusion, but he pinned my hands to the bed and looked me in the eye. "Nobody is going to hurt you in here. You're in the hospital. There are multiple locked doors between here and the waiting room."

His calm words did nothing to temper the rising panic inside me. It choked my throat, cutting off the air, until I was yelling, desperate to get away. "It's not enough. He'll get to me. He always does!"

Grayson didn't flinch at the screeching tone. "According to your notes, your husbands in the waiting room are Hayden and Hawk. There's no mention of a Josiah."

I slumped, the fight going out of me instantly. Soft hospital pillows caught me. "Oh."

Grayson gave me that same smile from earlier as he let go of my wrists. It bordered on playful and lit his entire face, though the worry didn't leave his eyes. "How many husbands do you have exactly?"

I sighed, letting him fit the oxygen back to my nostrils. "Only one. And of the three of them, the one I'm legally married to is the only one I never want to see again." Though Hawk wasn't high on my list of people I wanted to see right now either.

Grayson settled back at the foot of my bed. "Want to tell me why?"

I shrugged. "Josiah's not a very nice man."

Grayson jotted that down on his notepad, which reminded me that the last time we'd met, he'd said he was a psychologist.

His pen slid across the paper resting on a clipboard. "Talk to me about cages."

I froze. "Why?"

"You were talking about them in your sleep."

He looked up, his gaze remaining neutral, even though I was sure mine was anything but. He didn't ask me twice. Or try to change the topic in the face of it clearly causing a reaction in me. He just waited patiently. "Take your time."

I'd done such a good job of forcing myself to forget that even now, when I tried to bring the memories to the forefront, my mind resisted remembering. "I can't," I whispered.

I hadn't even told my sisters about the cages. Nobody knew but me and Josiah.

Grayson nodded and put his pen down on the white blanket covering my feet. "You don't trust me. I get that. Why should you? We barely know each other. But I only want to help." He smiled again, and it was so simple and pure. "It's kind of my job."

"I don't have a good track record when it comes to trusting men," I admitted.

"How about I tell you my experience with cages then?"

If it was anything like mine, I was sure I didn't want to know.

But Grayson didn't wait for me to answer. "My parents dumped me in foster care when I was pretty young. I can't really remember how old I was, but old enough to remember them and know that they didn't want me."

"Oh," I said softly. "I'm so sorry."

He shook his head. "I'm not sure I was even that mad to begin with. They were shitty parents, and foster care was a chance at having a better life. I think I even remember being excited." He laughed, though it held a bitter edge. "That was before I realized how truly awful human beings can be. My foster parents made my biological parents seem like saints."

The pain was so clearly etched into his expression that I hurt for him. "I can relate," I said quietly, more to myself than to him.

He glanced up at me. "Your parents too?"

I picked at the skin of my wrists nervously, not wanting to speak badly of the people who'd raised me. I'd been brought up to respect my elders at all times so I'd never said a word about my parents' betrayal, always focusing my anger on Josiah.

Yet, it had been them who'd allowed it. Them who'd brought Josiah into my world then failed to protect me from him. They'd *given* me to him to use and abuse in any way he saw fit. They'd watched me walk around in that veil for years and never lifted a finger to help me.

They'd never even realized the bruises and trauma that veil had hidden.

I didn't understand that. Protecting Hayley Jade was all I'd ever done, even though giving her away had broken my heart. I couldn't raise her in a house with a monster, so when Josiah had wanted her gone from his home, I'd done what I'd thought right and let her go without a fight.

When Josiah had threatened her life again, I'd run with her.

I'd protected my child, even though my parents had never protected me.

A tear dripped down my face. "My parents sold me to my husband. Forced me to marry him."

Grayson nodded. "Mine locked me in a cage whenever they went out. Which was a lot. They'd go out for half the night, drinking and doing drugs and who knows what else. They locked us all up while they were gone so they wouldn't have to pay for a babysitter. Said we'd steal from them if we weren't in the cages. Sometimes, even after they came home, they left us there while they passed out or partied some more."

I put a hand over my mouth to hide my gasp.

Grayson looked me in the eye. "Is your story really any better?"

I wished I could say it was. "He used it as a punishment. He said I needed time alone with the Lord so I could understand why I wasn't being granted the child Josiah wanted so much. It was supposed to be my time of repentance and a place of solitude." I shuddered at the memory of the cage door slamming after Josiah had thrown me inside. "But it was a cage in a basement and a punishment for embarrassing him."

There had been so many punishments, in so many different ways. Rape. The cage. Spending hours and hours on my knees on hardwood floors. They were only the tip of the iceberg. He'd continued finding new ways to hurt me every month my body hadn't done what he wanted. Like he was searching for the perfect punishment that would wake me up into producing an heir for him.

Grayson picked up his notepad again. "And those men outside. Hawk and Hayden. You swear to me neither of them are your husband?"

I shook my head quickly. "They're nothing like him." I said it with absolute certainty, even though others might have disagreed. Hawk had lied. Hayden had held me captive.

But nobody had ever been as good and sweet to me as the two of them. Nobody had ever made me feel as safe. As wanted.

Grayson steeled me with his dark-eyed gaze. "Then how are you so hurt right now, Kara? If it wasn't them who hurt you, then who did?"

I was telling the truth when I replied that I honestly had no idea.

7

HAWK

"Hawk!"

I started, my thirty-five-year-old back protesting at the uncomfortable seated position I'd been sleeping in and my shoulder aching like I'd torn a muscle or two digging Kara out of that grave. My ass was numb, and War's sharp shout was enough to drive pins into my brain.

War, Bliss, and Rebel all stood in front of me, their eyes wide.

"What?" I stretched painfully. Fucking hospital seats.

"They're just wondering why I was letting you sleep on my shoulder," Chaos said dryly.

I jerked, realizing my arm was still pressed against his. "No, I wasn't."

"Um, yeah, you were." Rebel pointed at Hayden's shoulder. "Had your head on him and your face pressed into his neck like you were inhaling him."

I scowled at her, but my gaze quickly moved to War, who wasn't anywhere near as gleeful as Rebel had been at the chance to tease me about something. War looked vaguely murderous. Bliss just seemed concerned. And very, very pregnant. How the hell she hadn't popped that kid out yet was beyond comprehension.

I got up quickly. "Sit down, Bliss. That baby is gonna tip you over."

She didn't complain, groaning as she lowered herself into the seat, which I was grateful for because it drew some of the attention away from me.

I glared at Chaos and muttered, "Could have woken me up, asshole."

"I tried. You sleep like you're dead. And you snore."

"I do fucking not."

He raised an eyebrow. "And drool. I have a wet patch on my shoulder now."

Oh, fuck this guy. I hadn't slept in more than twenty-four hours. So I was tired and fell asleep on him. Didn't mean I wanted to go to bed with the guy.

I shoved my hands in my pockets, not wanting the reminder of what Chaos and I had been talking about earlier before I'd apparently taken a little nap.

Thinking about fucking his mouth and his ass sent another hot flush through me that I wished would just piss off. He was hot. So what? I wasn't into guys. Anyone who didn't think him attractive would be lying. He had his dirty-blond hair scraped back into a tie at the nape of his neck, and he was filthy from digging in the dirt with me, smudges all over his cheeks that only made his blue eyes pop. His T-shirt clung to his pecs and abs, but I only noticed them because I was forever working on my own, so I paid attention to them in other guys. Didn't mean I wanted to get them naked and go down on them.

Except my idiot brain wouldn't stop conjuring up images of Hayden doing exactly that, and it was really starting to irk me.

I wanted Kara.

Kara with her full tits and sweet, curvy ass.

"Any news?" Rebel anxiously peered past me through the windows in the doors to the treatment rooms and wards.

I didn't fucking know because I'd been asleep. We all looked at Chaos.

"Not much," he said reluctantly. "Only that she's stable and talking. They wouldn't let me...us...see her."

Rebel drew her mouth into a determined line. "They'll let me. Unlike you two, I'm family."

I didn't bother telling her that we'd tried claiming we were her husbands in order to get in. To be fair, that probably hadn't helped our case. I doubted anyone believed we really were brother husbands.

Though my sleeping on Chaos's shoulder had probably raised some questions.

I left Rebel to go yell at the nurses, and turned to War, a million questions playing over in my head. "What the hell happened last night?"

War glanced at Chaos, wary distrust in his eyes. "I'm going to walk five steps that way to talk to my VP. I'm going to leave my woman right there beside you because she's exhausted, and if you want to live to see Kara, you'll not only not lay a finger on my old lady, you'll also make sure nobody else does."

Bliss rolled her eyes at War's little speech of dominance and waved him off impatiently. "Stop hovering. He's Liam's brother. He's not going to hurt me." She turned to Chaos and held out her hand like they were at a business meeting. "I'm Bliss. Forgive me if we've met before." She pointed at her bump. "Baby brain is real."

"Bliss, you do remember he shot me in the leg, right?" I complained.

Rebel glanced over from the nurses' station. "Can you blame him though? I think about shooting you daily."

Chaos chuckled.

Rebel shot him a look. "Don't you be getting your giggle on. Bliss and Kara are a whole lot nicer than me. I wouldn't trust you as far as I can throw you."

War dragged me across the room before I could conjure up a comeback for the pipsqueak who was forever a thorn in my side. She was lucky I actually also liked her, because she was a permanent, attitude-filled, pain in my neck. If she was going to pick on Chaos too, I could be down with that.

War positioned us so he was watching Hayden and Bliss chat, but I already knew Chaos wasn't going to pull anything.

He'd had all night to try and he hadn't.

I couldn't believe I'd fallen asleep on him, though my right side was still warmer than my left from where I'd been cuddled up to him.

Fucking mortifying.

I scrubbed a hand over the back of my neck. "What the hell happened out there last night?" I asked again. It had been a madhouse of bodies and clubs and Josiah's fucking voice playing down a speaker.

War let out a long sigh. "I don't know. Two dead. Ratchet from our crew, Thunder from theirs. Riot says he saw Ratchet put a bullet in Thunder. Riot was the one who put Ratchet down for breaking club code and killing another member. He was within his rights to do so."

"That's bullshit! Ratchet wouldn't have shot the guy for no reason if they were working together. Something else had to have happened."

War shrugged. "They're both dead, so all we can do is guess."

I forced myself to say the words I didn't even want to think about. "Which of them put Kara in that hole?"

War shook his head. "Thunder was their contact with the Ethereal Eden group. He was working directly with Josiah, so it makes the most sense that it was him. All that shit about her having to be buried to be reborn..." He shuddered. "Creepy fucking cult."

"Thunder was a piece of shit," I mused. "Never liked that prick, and Riot has piss-poor judgement when it comes to prospects. He never should have patched that guy in, let alone let him handle a job like that." I shook my head. "Ratchet was a good guy. He didn't fucking deserve this."

"Didn't deserve it if he was innocent," War said quietly. "There's every chance it was him who took Kara out there. For all we know, Josiah's people got to him and paid him off to get to Kara." He shoved his hands deep in his pockets. "Or they were working together. This reeks of a two-person job. That grave was deep, and they had to have carried Kara and the coffin out there. That's too much for one person unless it was planned really damn well."

Anger rose inside me at the reminder of someone putting Kara in a box, closing her in, and burying her beneath the ground. I suddenly didn't give a shit which one of them it was. "They can both go to Hell."

War didn't look like he agreed, but what else was he supposed to do? The only other person who'd been there when shots had been fired was Riot. He was the Louisianna club president. He'd been all over Kara earlier in the night. Maybe that had been part of his plan to lure her away.

But unless we wanted to start a war within our own club, we couldn't accuse Riot of something like that. Not without a hell of a lot more proof than just my best guesses, which were likely tainted by the jealousy that still threatened to destroy me every time I remembered Riot giving Kara drinks, and the dirty way his gaze had undressed her without her permission.

"The security system was down last night when Chaos and I came in."

War ran a hand over his face. "We were in church, and everyone else was in the clubhouse to keep Riot and his boys in check. Their chapter is so much bigger than ours, and the vibe was so off, with them just turning up out of the blue. I don't even know if there was anyone on the gate. I'm sorry, man. That's on me. My head isn't in the game right now." His gaze slid to Bliss again.

A sharp whistle cut through the room, and Rebel glared at me and then at Chaos. "The nurse here says Kara's *husbands* can go see her."

Chaos shot up off the chair like a rocket, then nodded at War, as if handing back custody of Bliss's protection.

Fucking brown-noser.

I used the moment to push ahead and get to the nurses' station first.

Rebel was like a tiny little bottle of soda that had been shaken up and was ready to burst. "Husbands, my ass," she mumbled. "I just want to see my sister."

The tiniest twinge of guilt plucked at heartstrings I didn't know I had. I slung my arm around Fang's girl and drew her in so I could talk in her ear. "Just let me have this one, pipsqueak. You *want* to see her. I *need* to. She was damn near fucking dead when I pulled her out of that hole, and I've never been so scared in my entire life as I was trying to get her to breathe again. Let me have this." I swallowed hard. "Please."

She glanced up at me in surprise, like perhaps she, too, hadn't realized I had a heart that had apparently only started beating for Kara.

She nodded once. "But don't be too long!"

I kissed the top of her head, and she shoved me away. "Ew, God, Hawk. Get away. You smell like a sewer."

I sniggered as I followed the nurse down the hallway, Chaos so close behind me I was aware of his every move. He smelled no better than me at least. Both of us in dire need of a shower.

That I refused to think about, because if I thought about us both needing to get clean, then I was going to get hard, and that was fucking messed up when the only place I actually wanted to be was at Kara's bedside.

The nurse stopped at the doorway to the room and gestured for us to go inside. "The doctors are just finishing up with her. You can go in."

I froze two steps in the room.

Kara was swallowed up by the large white hospital bed and walls. She had oxygen tubes in her nose and more lines plugged into cannulas in her hand.

But she was alive. "Hey, Little Mouse," I managed to choke out.

Kara's eyes met mine, moved to Chaos, and then eventually came back.

"Get out, Hawk," she said softly, but with an edge I'd only heard from her in the last twenty-four hours.

Chaos glanced at me in surprise, and damn if I didn't want to punch his stupid face in. I knew it was unfair and Kara's rejection now was my fault. Saving her life didn't mean she owed me her forgiveness.

But I'd earn it.

"Hawk, leave. Please." Kara's eyes filled with tears, her voice a wobble.

Her fingers twitched, and I wanted to believe it was because she was fighting the urge to reach for me, and not the urge to curl them into fists.

Chaos cleared his throat. "Kara, he saved—"

"I don't need you talking to my woman on my behalf," I seethed at him. All the hurt and anger and fear that had been sitting like a rock in the pit of my stomach swirled to life. I logically knew it was misplaced, but I wouldn't take it out on Kara, and laying the blame squarely on my own shoulders was asking too much when all I wanted to do was cross the room, pull her into my arms, and tell her that I fucking loved her.

The last thing I needed was Chaos being all fake nice to get brownie points with her. The very thought pissed me off so bad I could barely see straight.

Whatever truce we might have called for a few hours was over. He could go to Hell.

I stared at her, so broken and bruised, and I wanted to kill someone all over again. Thunder. Ratchet. It didn't matter which. If I could have made them deader than dead for what they'd done to her, then I would have in a heartbeat.

I strode to Kara's bedside, ignoring her demands for me to leave, and took her chin between my fingers.

She stubbornly jerked out of my grasp.

"Look at me, Little Mouse."

She did. I'd expected fire in her gaze. Anger.

But when I saw the pain there, the hurt I'd caused, I realized I'd been hoping for the easy way out and she wasn't going to give it to me.

Good for her.

I was fucking proud of her for letting me see how much I'd upset her. Her anger had never bothered me. But hurting her...that was fucking inexcusable.

"Just go, Hawk. I can't do this with you right now."

I swallowed down the lump in my throat. "Fine. I'm going. But only as far as the corridor. I'll be here to take you home when they let you leave."

She ripped my hands away from her face and then wrapped her arms around herself. "No."

I squinted at her. "Fine. I'll get Fang or War—"

"I'm not going back to the compound."

I froze. "What the hell does that mean? Of course you are. It's your home."

She stared at me miserably. "It's not my home. It's my prison. I can't go anywhere. Can't go shopping. Can't see my sister. Hayley Jade can't go to school."

We'd talked about this at dinner the night before... shit, had that seriously only been last night? It felt like a lifetime ago. Like we'd been different people who'd had that conversation across a little table in a shoddy Saint

View diner. She'd told me the compound had become a new sort of prison.

And I'd become her jailer.

"We can fix that," I promised her. "Whatever you want to do, you can."

As long as someone went with her. But that wasn't going to help my argument, so I zipped my lips to keep the words from spilling out. "Kara, that cabin is your home. Hayley Jade is happy there." I'd thought they both were.

She shook her head.

Anger made its way through the regret. She was so fucking stubborn when she wanted to be. I threw up my hands in frustration. "Where then? Where the hell else are you going to go, Kara? You can't go to Rebel's place, all beaten and bruised the way you are. You'll scare the shit out of the kids. You can't go to Bliss's place. She's about to have a baby any day. They need time to be a family. The only other place is the compound."

Kara's shoulders slumped.

I almost hated she knew I was right. I didn't want her to not want to come home. The idea was killing me that she didn't want to come back to the club. Back to me.

Chaos cleared his throat. "She can stay at my place."

Kara looked up at him in surprise.

At the same time I growled, "No. Fucking. Way."

Kara snapped her head in my direction. "This isn't your decision."

"Like hell it's fucking not!" I lost a grip on my control at the very thought of her being out in the middle of the Saint View slums, only protected by Hayden fucking Whitling. She'd be a sitting duck for his enemies, as well as her own, and probably mine too. "You think Josiah is going to give up after one attempt at getting you back? Chaos can't protect you!"

"He did before," she said softly.

Oh, her fucking Stockholm syndrome was going to be the death of me. "He held you against your will, Kara! That is not the same thing!"

Anger flashed in her eyes. "You have no idea what happened between us all those years ago. No one does but him and me."

I ground my molars. "He has you as brainwashed as Josiah did."

"Watch your fucking mouth," Chaos swore at me. "I get you're mad. And you're scared—"

Oh, that was fucking rich. "I'm not scared. She's just not going with you."

Kara's face flushed with hot red anger. "Fine, Hawk. I'll come back to the MC. On one condition."

Something loosened in my brain, relief flooding in. "Anything."

She pointed at Hayden. "He comes too. You give him a room at the clubhouse so I can see him whenever I want."

"What?" I practically squawked. "You want me to let a Sinner stay at our clubhouse?"

Even Chaos looked wary. "Kara, I..."

"So it's a no?" She glared at me, challenge in her eyes. "You'll let me stay there. You'll protect me. Give me whatever I want. As long as what I want isn't him. Is that about how it goes?"

It was the truth. I didn't want to admit it, but it was.

But the bigger hurt was what she wanted wasn't me. With him in the picture, I was out.

Clearly, I had to let that go. Let her go. I couldn't make her come back with me.

Hell, she'd gotten hurt on my watch, so maybe Hayden really was the better choice.

I gave in. "If you really want me to let you go, Kara, then go. Go live your life with him. I hope he makes you happy."

The worst part about the whole thing was, when I walked out the door, I truly meant it.

At the end of the day, I wanted her and Hayley Jade's happiness more than I wanted my own.

I'd fucking grown up. Pulling the woman I loved from a hole in the ground and breathing life back into her had forced a change I hadn't known I'd wanted.

It was a shame it was twenty-four hours too late.

8

HAYDEN

My phone buzzed insistently as I strode through the now familiar hospital corridors, winding my way along the path I'd taken every day to Kara's room. I took the phone from my pocket and swore at Luca's name flashing on the screen for what had to have been the fiftieth time since he'd left me on the side of the Slayers' road with a van full of women I was supposed to deliver.

"Go to Hell." I sent his call to voicemail, just like I had all the others.

I hadn't listened to a single message he'd left, nor did I have any intentions of pushing "play" on the one that came in now.

I'd made a massive mistake getting back in with Luca, and I wasn't even surprised it had all gone sour. Part of me had known it would.

I paused outside Kara's door, cracking my neck and breathing deep so I didn't bring any of the black cloud surrounding me into her room.

I twisted the handle and was met with a beaming smile on the other side.

My heart squeezed at the sight of her sitting up in bed, tube- and wire-free, color back in her cheeks, and so damn happy to see me.

Whatever I had going on with Luca failed to exist when she looked at me like that.

I'd had days of sitting in her hospital room just watching her sleep, or trying to stay out of the way while nurses and doctors came and went. But today she seemed good. Healthy. "Hey, gorgeous." I moved my way around the bed to her side and kissed her cheek. "You feeling okay?"

She grinned, but then her smile faltered. "They said I can go home today."

I widened my eyes, excitement kicking up inside me. "Shit, really? That's fantastic. Star patient, you are."

She laughed. "I don't know about that. I've been in here for days."

"Still a rock star to me." I sat on the chair next to her bed and picked up her hand, threading my fingers through hers.

She stared down at them. "I'm not going to hold you to it."

I squinted at her. "Hold me to what?"

She dragged her gaze up to meet mine, and damn if there wasn't something magnetic about her eyes. Something that made me want to stare at her for hours, because she settled something rough and uneasy that had lived inside me for half my life.

She rubbed her thumb along the back of my hand. "Staying at your place. With you."

I gripped her chin between two fingers, refusing to let her turn away. "I've had to be apart from you for five years. You think I want to go even one more night not under the same roof as you?"

She sucked in a shaky breath. "We barely know each other. And you're asking me to move in with you."

She was right. But I didn't fucking care. "I know enough."

She shook her head, worry creasing her forehead into frown lines. "We don't even know the most basic things. Like what's your favorite food? I don't know."

I was a jackass but I laughed at her.

She screwed up her sweet face and slapped my arm. "Don't laugh. It's not funny. I'm serious. What's your favorite food? I can't do much else, I'm not qualified for anything, but I can cook for you. If I know what you like."

I shifted my grip on her chin to cup her cheek and then slid it to the back of her neck, holding her still and leaning in so we were eye to eye.

She fell silent and I pressed my forehead to hers. We sat there for a moment, connected, breathing, until she didn't seem so panicked.

"I know you're the strongest woman I've ever met," I said softly. "I know you'd do anything for your daughter, because I watched you fight for her all those years ago. I know you're kind, and sweet, and that you protect the people you love." I breathed her in, skin tingling every place we touched. She was so fucking warm. So alive. So here in my arms that I couldn't believe my damn luck. "I don't need to know your favorite food, Kara. I know your heart."

A little of the tension fell out of her shoulders, and

she twisted her fingers in my shirt. "I don't understand you," she whispered. "I don't understand why I feel the way I do when you're around."

Neither did I. But all I knew was I didn't want it to stop. I wanted it to have a chance. I wanted her in my home. My bed. My life.

I wanted to kiss her so fucking bad it hurt, but I didn't want our first kiss to be in a damn hospital room.

"Come home with me, and when you're fully healed, we'll get Hayley Jade." My stupid heart squeezed again at the thought of the dark-haired girl I'd seen with Hawk that day at my restaurant. About how I'd felt years ago when I'd found out her name and realized Kara had named her for me. "I want you," I whispered, saying the words I'd wanted to say to her years ago. "I have nothing of value to offer. My home is a piece of shit. I have no money. No job." At least not anymore, after what fucking Luca had done. "I don't know your favorite food. Or hers. But I'll learn. I *want* both of you."

A tear dripped down her cheek. "Okay."

If I hadn't been in a hospital, only separated from other patients by flimsy green curtains, I would have cheered. It took everything in me not to slam my lips down on hers. "For the record, my favorite food is pizza. I'm pretty basic like that."

Her smile was so blinding it short-circuited my brain, ruining it for anything other than making her happy. She smiled up at me like I'd just made her whole day by admitting I had a thing for greasy carbs with too much cheese.

When I hadn't been watching Kara heal, I'd been cleaning my shitty apartment, hating that I lived in such a dump. I wasn't even a particularly messy person. But the apartment was old and dingy, and even though I'd scrubbed the tiled floor on my hands and knees, it wasn't much better than when I'd started.

My fingers shook as I unlocked the door and held it open so Kara could enter. "We'll get something better," I promised her. I didn't know how, with neither of us having a job, but I would. I'd be the man she needed me to be. I'd step up and make her a home. Take care of her.

But guilt plagued me. I'd been part of the most traumatic events of her life. I'd been part of the reason she'd fled back to her parents' home for that trauma to continue in a whole new way.

I owed Kara more than money could buy and I knew it. I didn't think for a second I was worthy of her, and yet that connection between us refused to allow me to let her go.

Kara gazed around the small space. The tiny living room and kitchen were barely bigger than her hospital room, the bedroom only big enough for a bed and little else.

But if Kara saw the cracked tiles in the bathroom shower, or the dirt in the carpet that no amount of vacuuming would remove, she didn't say anything.

Instead, her eyes lit up at the furry trio that all ran to her like she was goddamn Snow White calling her woodland friends.

The traitorous kitten assholes ignored me completely,

winding their way around Kara's legs, meowing for her attention.

"You didn't tell me you had pets!" She smiled up at me with that happy smile I wanted on her face at all times.

"I'll go buy you more if you keep looking at me like that."

She laughed, crouching to pet the kittens who were growing like weeds now that someone was actually feeding them daily. "I rescued them," I told her. But I didn't tell her from where. No need to remind her of that hellhole I'd kept her in.

The guilt slammed me hard and was made even worse by her acting like I'd hung the fucking moon just because I'd saved a few kittens.

Hawk had accused her of having Stockholm syndrome. Of forming feelings for her captor that weren't real.

The idea left me so damn cold inside I refused to pay it any attention. I desperately wanted to believe she was here because the connection between us was real. And not because she was traumatized.

"I always wanted pets," she confessed. "Small, huggable ones like this. We have cows and sheep and chickens at the commune. Some horses that we weren't allowed to ride for fun because they were to be saved for work." She lifted one of the fuzzballs and stroked her fingers over his head and the back of his neck. "What are their names?"

I shrugged. "I just call them all Cat."

She laughed and shook her head. "You can't do that!"

The kittens were obsessed with her. One had crawled into her lap. The one in her arms had fallen asleep. The third was insistently demanding her attention with tiny mewling noises. None of them had ever cared quite that much about me. It was like they sensed the good in her.

It was hard not to. I did too.

I put down the bag Rebel had grudgingly packed for her and dropped off at the hospital. She'd been about as happy about this new living arrangement as Hawk had been.

"Can I get you anything?" I asked Kara. "Tea? Coffee? Water? Snacks? A roast dinner?" I grinned at her. "Okay, maybe not the roast because the kitchen here is pathetic."

She shook her head quickly. "I should be the one getting that for you." She glanced over at the kitchen that was really nothing more than a hotplate and a sink. "Oh."

"I do most of my cooking at the restaurant," I admitted.

She smiled softly. "Snacks are always nice."

I pointed at the couch. "Go sit. Relax. Put a movie on. I'll get something together and join you in a second."

She hesitated, watching me pull lunch meats and cheeses from the refrigerator. There was chocolate and a range of different types of crackers in the cupboard. I might not have been able to cook for her, but that didn't mean I was going to dump a bag of Doritos into a bowl and call it good either. I had every intention of making sure she ate well while she was here. I'd find a way to make her whatever she wanted.

I didn't want to remember the way Caleb had withheld food from her and the other women when he'd forced me to keep them hostage. I'd snuck them in as much food as I could when he hadn't been around, but it had never seemed like enough.

"I can do that for you," she said awkwardly. "Truly. This is a woman's work."

I paused in the middle of cutting up a salami.

"That's what I was taught," she said quietly. "At the commune, women do all the cooking. We serve the men."

I'd already heard enough about her commune and the people who lived there. The more I knew about them, the more I wanted to drive out there, find her goddamn husband, and put a bullet through his head.

Which was saying something because I'd vowed years ago when I got out of the gang life that I wasn't going to be that sort of man anymore. I didn't want to terrorize or kill people. I didn't even own a gun these days.

But that didn't make me want to hurt her husband any less. It would take me no more than thirty minutes to find someone in Saint View to sell me a gun. I could be at Ethereal Eden's gates before sunrise.

But as appealing as that sounded, it all meant leaving Kara here alone, and I wasn't doing that. "Your only job is to sit your sweet ass down on that couch and eat all of this food."

A tiny smile lifted the corner of her mouth. "I can do that."

Damn straight she could. "Remote is on one of the armchairs."

She sat and picked it up, studying it for a second. "Don't laugh at me, but I have no idea how to use these things. I haven't watched TV in years."

I brought the tray of food over to her, dragging a side table closer so I had somewhere to rest it. I took the remote from her and showed her which buttons to press. "I'm never going to laugh at you for not knowing something. There's plenty of shit I don't know." I'd spent my entire life feeling dumb because my older brother was smart and good at everything. He'd never tried to make me feel bad, but I had anyway. I sure as hell never wanted to make Kara feel like that because she'd grown up sheltered from the real world. Her innocence only made me want to protect her more.

I flinched at a crash outside in the hallway, and Kara and I both looked to the door.

"What was that?" she asked.

"Nothing," I assured her. "Walls are thin, and people around here aren't super considerate of their neighbors. It can get noisy. Sorry."

She shook her head. "Don't be. There's nothing wrong with where you live."

But there was, and the crash outside the door had me jumpy. I'd never much worried about security, knowing I could take care of myself if the need ever arose.

But I'd never had something as precious as her to protect before.

I left her scrolling through romantic comedies on Netflix and got up to subtly check the lock on the door.

I'd buy another one tomorrow. Though no amount of deadlocks would stop someone if they tried kicking the door down. The thought left me cold. I moved to the windows and pulled on them all, making sure the locks were engaged. Why hadn't I rented a place with bars? One well thrown rock or brick, and anybody could get in here. Why hadn't I ever paid attention to this before?

Because I had no belongings of value, and I didn't care half as much about my life as I did about hers.

"Movie is starting," she said softly.

I jerked my head up from where I was inspecting a broken lock.

I hated the concern on her heart-shaped face.

"I'm safe here," she told me firmly. Like she wanted it to be true.

I wasn't one-hundred-percent sure I believed her. Hawk's warnings about her people being out there searching for her played over in my mind. They'd gotten to her at the Slayers' compound, where there were fences and state-of-the-art security. These people weren't messing around. They had connections.

The memory of Hawk lifting her from the ground, not breathing, nearly buckled my knees.

She watched me carefully and then stood, crossing the room to me so she could take my hand. "Just come sit."

Her fingers wrapped around mine was everything I'd thought about for years. Warm and sweet. I would have followed her anywhere.

I sank onto the couch, pulling her down next to me. She landed with an oof, and I wasted no time in closing the gap between us, putting my arm around her shoulders and drawing her into my side. Our thighs pressed together, and she settled into the crook of my arm, her head resting on my shoulder.

Like this was where she was always supposed to be.

She pressed "play" on the movie, but I didn't watch it.

All I wanted to watch was her.

She ate the food I'd prepared. She giggled at the love interests on the screen.

I leaned over and touched my mouth to hers before I could even think about what I was doing.

She jerked away sharply, and my heart stopped.

"Fuck." I dropped my arm. "I'm so sorry. I shouldn't have done that..."

But her expression wasn't what I expected. She seemed surprised, but her lips were gently parted, and her gaze roamed my face, lingering on my lips like she wanted me to do it again.

So I did. I leaned in, slower this time, giving her every chance to stop me.

When she didn't, I pressed my lips to hers.

She wriggled onto her knees and wrapped her arms around my neck, kissing me back.

My chest tightened so much I could barely breathe for wanting her.

I kissed her slow, lips brushing over hers gently before taking the kiss deeper, opening my mouth and encouraging her to do the same.

She whimpered in my arms as our tongues met and I held her tight, fucking loving the way her full tits crushed to my chest. I ran my hands up and down her back, the knitted fabric of her long-sleeved top fuzzy beneath my fingers.

I ached to feel her skin, the heat radiating from beneath her clothes so damn tempting, but I refused to rush her.

We kissed, exploring each other, my fingers greedily wandering over the curve of her hips and her ass. Her long skirt did nothing to hide the body she had beneath, and every touch of her increased the desperate need growing inside me.

"Kara," I whispered on her mouth before I could lose myself in the feel of her. "We should stop."

She shook her head, her lips still touching mine. "Don't."

I groaned again, pushing her back so she was laid out on the couch beneath me. I held my weight off her, balancing it on my hands and knees, all while joining our lips again because I couldn't get enough.

There were shouts in the hallway, and I tensed at the thought of someone out there. Though I lived on the ground floor, so there was always someone out there.

I'd never cared before. But now it was all I could think of.

"Hayden," she whispered.

I dragged my gaze back to her and wondered why I'd ever left it. The pink in her cheeks was the prettiest thing I'd ever seen, and I buried my face in her neck, kissing and licking the soft skin there until she moaned.

She twisted her fingers into my shirt and dragged me down on top of her, her legs spread, one off the couch so I could fit between her thighs.

I'd expected her to be meek in bed. Inexperienced. I hadn't expected her to raise her hips, seeking contact with the ridge of my erection.

I ground it against her, our clothes in the way but the feeling of her soft core at my cock addictive. I wanted to strip her naked. Bury my face between her legs. Lick her until she came and then do it all over again until she'd had so many orgasms she couldn't see straight.

I kissed her instead, hungry for the taste of her, craving the feel of her hands in my hair, and her hips raising to meet mine.

"I don't want to hurt you," I whispered over her lips. "You just got out of the hospital."

She stared up at me and shook her head slightly. "It hurts more when you stop."

I never wanted that. I grazed my hand along the outside of her thigh, daring to gather her skirt up with me as I went until it was rucked up around her waist and her simple cotton panties were on display. I groaned, loving the sight of the wet spot our make-out session had created. I wanted to have her soaked right through the cotton covering before I took it any further.

Wanted her so wet I knew exactly how much she liked what I was doing to her.

She caught my hand, drawing it to her core. "Touch me."

Her breaths were needy pants that matched mine. I ran my fingers along the edge of her underwear, inching them to where she wanted me most.

Three sharp thumps came from the front door, hard enough to shake the entire frame.

I froze. This was no accidental noise made by the neighbors.

"Chaos!" Luca shouted from the other side of the door. "I'm done with you not answering my calls. You owe me ten women. So unless you want me to start with the sweet little thing you picked up from the hospital this afternoon, I suggest you don't leave me standing out here waiting."

I'd been so damn worried about Kara's people finding her, I hadn't even considered the real danger came from me.

9

HAWK

TEN MINUTES EARLIER

I'd been sitting outside Chaos's shitty apartment building for hours, watching him and Kara through the cracked blinds of his ground-floor apartment. I was fully aware I was a loser. As pathetic as a stupid high school kid with a crush, who followed girls around when they didn't even know he was alive.

I'd turned full-blown stalker because sitting at the clubhouse, knowing she was out in the world unprotected, was more than I could handle.

So I'd sat on my damn bike, getting a numb ass, and turning Peeping Tom like the perverted creep I was.

They were just fucking sitting there. Watching a movie or something.

But he had his arm around her, and every part of me wanted to storm in there and rip it off her. Shove him across the room, up against a wall.

I closed my eyes for a second, the idea of being chest to chest with Chaos, our faces too close, coming into view.

Kara watching from the other side of the room as he undressed me. Stripped his clothes. Forced me down on my knees and demanded I take his cock.

My dick twitched behind my jeans.

I groaned, squeezing my eyes tight and pushing out the idea.

It didn't help when I opened my eyes and he and Kara had changed positions, him lying over the top of her, her skirt around her waist and her panties on display for the entire fucking street to see.

Who was I kidding? There was nobody out here but me. I was the only asshole watching the woman he loved get railed by the guy he... Fuck. I didn't know what Hayden was. Or what I wanted from him.

Only that I couldn't stop thinking about the things he'd said at the hospital. About the idea of me fucking him.

I watched him grind over Kara, and the jealousy was there, hot and fast, the desire to storm in there and rip his hands off my woman.

Only when I waited a minute, watched the way he kissed her, the way her body responded to his touch so sweetly I could practically hear the way I knew she would be moaning, the jealousy disappeared.

Leaving desire in its place.

My dick got hard, and this time, I knew it wasn't just for Kara.

"Great," I muttered. "Just fucking great."

I was the biggest fucking hypocrite. I'd given War such a hard time when he'd fallen for a guy.

I'd known all along that part of it was me projecting

my own unresolved feelings about the idea of men fucking men.

It wasn't done in the club. We'd grown up with fathers and their friends who used words like faggot and fairy. I'd had my first woman shoved at my dick when I was barely old enough to get it up.

Nobody had ever asked me if a guy might have gotten me harder.

I hadn't questioned it either. Just shoved down the occasional realization that when I was watching porn, sometimes I watched the guy just as much as the woman.

It wasn't that I liked the thought of them more. But that I knew what having a woman on my cock felt like. I knew what her touch did to me, and sure, I liked it. I'd fucking loved Kara's body wrapped around mine and the feel of her curves against my skin.

I fucking loved *her*.

But I'd watched men fuck on TV screens. I'd watched men dance at strip clubs.

I'd thought about letting Hayden fuck me.

It had turned me on.

As did the thought of having Kara watch. Or of having her in between us, both of us impaling her, feeling Hayden's cock nudged up against mine, both of us inside her pussy.

My balls ached with the desire building inside me.

I needed to go home.

I couldn't sit out here watching them anymore. This was fucking torture.

I started the bike, not caring the damn engine was loud, and steered it down the shitty Saint View street Chaos called home.

I paused at the end for a sleek gray Porsche, the driver's profile visible through the windshield as he took the corner. He lifted a hand in greeting, and I did the same back because it was instinct, and something about the guy was familiar.

I rode along the backstreets of Saint View, puzzling over how I knew the guy until my thick-as-rocks brain finally puzzled it out.

I spun the bike around so fucking fast I nearly gave myself whiplash. Within a minute, I was back on Chaos's street and dropping my bike on the road outside his apartment, not giving a fuck if I ruined the paint.

Luca Guerra would be buried six feet under before he got anywhere near my woman.

I ran across the sparse lawn, sending my boot against a security door that didn't live up to its name because it crumpled beneath the force of a single kick. Seriously? This was where Hayden wanted Kara to live? He had to be fucking joking.

I paused at a T intersection in the corridor, turned about and not sure which direction Chaos's apartment was.

"Chaos!" Luca shouted. "I'm done with you not answering my calls. You owe me ten women. So unless you want me to start with the sweet little thing you picked up from the hospital this afternoon, I suggest you don't leave me standing out here waiting."

The red haze that dropped down over my eyes was instant.

So was the way I pulled my gun.

On silent feet, I moved along the corridor, finger over

the trigger, rounding a final corner and taking aim at the back of Luca's head, right as Chaos opened the door.

I paused. I was a decent shot but not perfect, especially not at this distance.

He might have shot me once upon a time, and maybe I owed him a bullet, but the fact I might miss Luca and hit Chaos instead had me freezing, finger shaking.

Chaos's gaze slid to me.

Held.

When I didn't move, he turned back to Luca.

Chaos's eyes darkened. "You so much as come near her and you're a dead man."

Luca laughed, the sound uncharacteristically bitter.

I didn't know the guy well, but from what I'd heard, he wasn't fazed by much. His control over his emotions was exactly what made him deadly. He was sharp as a tack. Slick. He never missed.

But today that had slipped because either the guy wasn't as good as his reputation had led me to believe. Or he was downright distracted.

He leaned in, so he was all up in Chaos's business. "That's a lot of talk for a man who claims to be out of the game. You gonna throw yourself back in by killing me? Wouldn't that cause a scandal?"

"I'm not killing anyone," Chaos said, his voice full of steely determination.

"No?" Luca sniggered. "So you're planning to give me ten new women to replace the ones you let go?"

Chaos practically closed the gap between the two of them, so they were eye to eye.

Luca's sharp intake of breath was audible, even from where I was standing. His breathing quickened, shoulders rising up and down with the force of nervous intakes of air.

It would be nothing for Chaos to lean in and kiss him. For him to lay his mouth across Luca's and plunge his tongue inside, kissing him the way he...

The way he should have fucking kissed me.

Something inside me screamed in irrational jealousy. Which was all I seemed to feel these days. But unlike when I'd seen Chaos with Kara, this time it didn't give way to wanting Luca to join us. It only fed the rage I was trying to keep a hold on.

"No," Chaos murmured. "I'm not killing anyone. But I'm not going to stop him either."

His gaze flickered in my direction.

Luca spun around.

My finger pressed down on the trigger.

The shot exploded from the gun, damn near deafening in the hallway. The doorframe exploded into shards of wood and plaster dust.

Chaos yelped like an injured puppy. "Jesus fuck, Hawk!" He clutched at his arm, inspecting his torn sleeve, the thin trail of blood trickling down from his bicep, and then turning around to inspect the bullet lodged into the wall. "You fucking shot me! It went right through my damn arm!"

The bullet had barely nicked him. But my fingers shook, adrenaline pumping through my blood.

Luca glanced between the two of us, suddenly more unflappable now than he'd been a second ago when it had seemed like Chaos had been going to make out with him.

I trained my gun on him again, fighting the wobble in

my arms, and he just raised an eyebrow. "You aren't the best shot, Hawk. Do you really want to try that again? He's got a woman inside, you know?" He clapped his hands together gleefully. "Oh, of course you know! It's the one he stole from you, right?" He leaned on the wall, completely ignoring Chaos and the blood seeping through his fingers where he clutched the graze the bullet had given him.

Kara peeped around from behind Chaos, who tried to hold her back, but she shoved him out of the way to get a better look at his arm.

She gasped at the hole in his shirt and then at me, still holding the stupid weapon I was clearly out of practice with. "Hawk!"

I didn't say anything. I was too fucking mortified.

Not a feeling I was very experienced with, and it had me reeling. As did the sight of Chaos bleeding and the realization I'd been inches from putting that bullet into his chest.

Accidentally.

Fuck, my aim needed some serious work.

I lowered the gun. We all fucking knew I wasn't shooting anyone with Kara standing right there.

"The neighbors have probably called the police," Kara murmured.

Chaos and I both knew, in neighborhoods like this, the residents were used to all sorts of disturbances outside their doors, and it was a hell of a lot safer to mind your own business.

Luca chuckled. "Shall we try again? I admit some fault. Perhaps my greeting wasn't as polite as it could have been."

"You don't fucking say," Hayden growled. "I owe you nothing, Guerra."

Luca tutted beneath his breath. "Now see, that's where I disagree. You cost me a lot of money the other night. But I can let that go. The real problem is that you haven't shown up for work since, and we're opening in a few days."

Hayden stared at him. "You don't seriously think I'm coming back to your restaurant?"

"*Our* restaurant," Luca corrected. "You have a partial ownership, don't forget, and your name is on the window. Have you paid any attention to your Instagram account lately? It's not so little anymore. People are getting excited for your food…and for…uh…dessert." His gaze slid to me. "Do tell War and fam that I'm sorry for the sex club competition, but I'm sure he'll take it as a compliment. Maybe we can cross promote sometime?"

"Maybe you could walk barefoot across hot coals all the way to Hell?" I suggested instead.

Luca laughed like we were old friends reconnecting, which couldn't be further from the truth. "You're a funny man, Hawk. Is that what Chaos likes about you? Or do you have…other assets he likes more?"

Heat rose up the back of my neck again. Fucking Guerra. He knew everything, though the showdown that Chaos and I'd had on his restaurant security cameras had probably clued him in on where to poke.

He pushed off the wall, his gaze on Hayden. "I'm going to let this all slide, as long as you show up and do the job you're contracted to do. You don't have to like me. Nobody does, but I'm a good business partner. You live in a shithole. We both know this isn't where you want your woman and that girl of hers growing up. We all know your dream is Sinners and what we're doing there."

"Dreams can change," Hayden said bitterly.

Luca patted his cheek condescendingly. "Fine. Come to work and hate every minute if you prefer. I really don't fucking care." His voice lowered an octave. "But you're in this, Hayden. There's no backing out now. You think it would matter if Hawk had put a bullet in my back just now like the cowardly bastard he is?"

"I could try again if you like?" I growled.

Luca ignored me, his stare solely for Chaos. "If I go down, there's a second in line. And a third. And a fourth. Nothing changes." His gaze switched to Kara before coming back to his chef. "You're in and you know it. Especially since you've got something to lose now, don't you?"

Rage ripped through me. I raised the gun again, everything inside me desperate to pull the trigger, even though I knew I couldn't.

Luca put his hand up, palm facing me without even looking in my direction. "Hold your fire, Quick Draw McGraw. I'm going." He strolled down the hallway toward my gun like he didn't have a care in the world. He dropped his voice to a whisper as he strolled past. "Keep your boy in my good books, Hawk. Neither of you will like what happens if he doesn't show up for work this week. I want him. And I don't know if you've noticed, but I generally get what I want. One way or another."

A possessive surge of jealousy coursed through me, hot and hard. In an instant, I grabbed Luca's arm, hauling him in close, talking in his ear while staring straight at Hayden, even though my voice was low enough he couldn't hear me from the other end of the corridor. "I'll be sure to remember that the next time he asks me if I want him on his knees or on his back."

Luca stiffened beneath my touch.

A sly smile spread across my face because he'd just confirmed his weak spot.

He liked Hayden.

Too fucking bad. This guy was a woman-trafficking piece of shit, who Chaos might have been dumb enough to get into bed with in a business sense, but fucked if I was letting someone close to Kara do anything more than that.

"See," I whispered to Luca while staring down at Kara and Hayden watching us silently. "I get what I want, too."

And apparently what I wanted was them.

Both of them.

10

HAYDEN

Hawk whispered something in Luca's ear, Hawk's smile turning smug at the way Luca wrenched his arm out of his grip and stormed off down the hall.

Hawk waved his fingers daintily at Luca's back and called out, "Don't let the door hit ya on the way out! Wouldn't want to get any Saint View filth on that expensive jacket!"

The exit door slammed, and Hawk's smile fell, his gaze landing on my arm.

Blood dripped through my fingers and down my forearm. It wasn't a huge gush, but enough it fell onto the already stained carpet of the hallway.

"You happy now?" I growled at Hawk. "I shot you. You shot me. We even?"

Hawk sighed, putting his gun into the back of his jeans and strolling down the hallway like all hell hadn't broken loose in the ten minutes before. "I didn't do it on purpose, you know."

The throbbing in my arm made me grouchy. "No? You're seriously just that bad a shot? I find that hard to believe."

Hawk eyed me. "Believe it, okay? I'm great point-blank. Don't often need to shoot anyone from a distance. You want me to look at it?"

"No," I said quickly.

Kara nudged me gently. "Let him. You need stitches. He's good."

"I am." Hawk's arrogance rolled off him as thick as Luca's expensive cologne.

"So modest," I grumbled.

"Do you want me to fake modesty or go get the first aid kit from my bike?"

I lifted my hand to peer at the wound. It wasn't that bad. I'd definitely had worse cuts just from horsing around in the backyard with Liam when we were kids. But it did need stitches, and the last thing I felt like doing after being at the hospital for days was going back there. We'd spend hours waiting for a non-urgent injury like this.

I gave in. "Go get the kit."

Hawk, clearly pleased with himself, strutted off down the hallway like his shitty aim wasn't the whole reason we were here in the first place.

With my non-injured arm, I pulled Kara in and kissed the top of her head. "I'm so sorry," I murmured, holding her tight. "Are you okay?"

She nodded against my chest, wrapping her arms around my waist. "I'm fine."

But as much as she tried to hide it, trembles racked her body.

She wasn't fine. She was fucking terrified.

And I didn't blame her. We'd gone from making out on the couch to getting shot in the space of a minute.

Luca and Hawk were both right. It wasn't safe for her here. I needed to go back to work this week, and what was going to happen then? She couldn't just stay here alone. Even if she somehow convinced me she could, we both knew we could never bring Hayley Jade here.

This was a fucking mess, only made worse by Hawk strutting back with a suture kit and apparently not a problem in the world.

He paused at the sight of us, my arm wrapped around Kara's shoulders, but to his credit, he hid his jealousy well.

Not well enough for me not to notice, but it was a good try.

He held up the kit and shook it in my direction. "We gonna try doing surgery in the hallway or you going to invite me in?"

I reluctantly stepped aside, knowing he was right, but at the same time embarrassed to have him see my shitty place. Not that the MC was luxury by any means. But at least it was secure.

I knew when Hawk walked into my apartment, all he would see was how I couldn't keep Kara safe here and I was a fucking idiot for even trying.

For once, though, Hawk didn't run his mouth. He just looked over at Kara, his gaze turning gentle as it ran all over her body. "Are you okay?" His voice was softer than I'd ever heard him before.

She nodded. "Hayden, though…"

Hawk turned his attention to me. "Sit down."

"I'll stand." I didn't even know why it was instinct to argue with him. It just was.

"Fine. Whatever." He put his suture kit on the kitchen counter and then went to the sink, squirting a thick dollop of liquid soap onto his palm before scrubbing them together and rinsing them off. From the kit he pulled gloves and an antiseptic wash. He shoved my torn shirt out of the way and unceremoniously squirted the fuck out of my arm with the stinging liquid.

I hissed, gritting my teeth.

Hawk grinned while he prodded at the wound. "You can cry if you want, you know? I'll judge you, but if you just want to let go of those tears…"

"Hawk…" Kara warned.

He grinned at her and then went back to cleaning the damage he'd done to my arm. "It's not so bad. Five or six stitches should do it. Might not even scar and mess up your tattoo."

I didn't really care if it did. A lot of those tattoos had been inked years ago, when I was angry at the world and everyone in it. Having a bullet pass through one of them was maybe symbolic of a life I wanted to leave behind.

One that I could never seem to escape from though.

I changed the subject as Kara positioned herself on a kitchen stool in between us. "So how is it the VP of the Saint View Slayers MC can't shoot for shit?"

He shrugged, loading up an injection of something. "I never learned."

"I find that hard to believe. Didn't your old man raise you in the club? I'm surprised you and War weren't shooting things from the day you were born, just preparing for a life of crime."

He poked the injection into my arm none too softly.

I probably deserved it. I was goading him. It was distracting me from the pain in my arm, and the worse pain of realizing I needed Hawk's help. In more ways than one.

Hawk pushed down on the syringe, delivering what I really hoped was anesthetic and not some drug that was going to have me dead on the floor so he could run off with Kara alone.

Something in me knew he wouldn't, though. He'd had his chance to kill me. More than once.

I might have even deserved it.

When my arm went numb, the throbbing pain from the wound disappearing, I knew I was right.

Hawk threaded a needle with some sort of medical fishing line and poked it through my skin. "Our dads tried. War's a decent shot. I just ain't." He peered at me over the top of his thread. "But War can't sew up a wound for shit, so who would you prefer here right now?"

I didn't mention the fact if it had been War here, with his better aim, I probably wouldn't be the one bleeding right now. But if Luca Guerra had been bleeding out on my doorstep, we would have had a whole lot more problems than whether my tattoo would still look right with a scar through the middle of it.

"Can you tell me what you're doing?" Kara asked Hawk quietly.

She watched Hawk intently, like she was taking mental notes.

He jerked his head. "Come over here so you can see better. If you can get my phone out of my back pocket and turn the flashlight function on, that would be helpful too."

She slid off the stool and slipped her hand into his back pocket, moving around Hawk with the familiarity of two people who knew each other's bodies well.

Jealousy surged within me at the touch of her hands trailing across his back and ass. At their heads so close together, the two of them huddled over my arm and Hawk explaining the process to her, Kara nodding and soaking it in like it was the most interesting thing she'd ever learned in her life.

"Are you still going to volunteer at the hospital clinic?" Hawk asked her.

Kara's reply was quiet. "I want to."

"I'll still volunteer with you. Even if you're living here. I'll still volunteer so you aren't alone."

She didn't look up. If anything, she studied my arm even harder so she didn't have to make eye contact with either of us. "Just because you pulled me out of a hole and showed up here tonight, doesn't mean I've forgiven you."

It was suddenly like I wasn't even in the room and it was just the two of them.

His voice went soft, verging on tender. "Please, Kara," he whispered. "I'm so fucking sorry. About everything. You don't have to forgive me. I get it. I blew any chance of that. But I can keep you safe. Just let me do that. Please."

A younger version of myself would have given in to the jealousy that curdled my stomach, watching the two of them together. I would have demanded I could protect her too.

But tonight had proved I couldn't be everything she

needed.

She needed him too. Considering he was stitching me up yet again, apparently, she wasn't the only one.

So I swallowed my fucking pride and through clenched teeth, I said her name.

When she turned her attention to me, my heart could have exploded with how much I wanted her. How much I felt for her. How much that connection between us demanded I do anything for her, even if that meant I didn't get what I wanted.

"You should let him go with you." I swallowed down the bitter regret building in my throat. "And I think you should go back to the clubhouse too."

Hawk jerked his head up to stare at me, but I ignored him, focusing on Kara.

Her eyes were so damn huge. "You don't want me here?"

I cupped her cheek, guiding her face so she wouldn't misunderstand what I was saying. "The only danger out there isn't from your people. You know now who I'm involved with. Luca is right. I can't just walk away from the restaurant. It's not that simple. I don't even know I honestly want to. I know I can make Sinners amazing. But there's no denying that Luca isn't a good guy, and this won't be the last time he tries to make me do something I don't want to do. It won't be the last time he threatens you to get to me."

"What are you saying? You don't want to see me anymore?" Her question was a broken whisper.

"It's not that. It's never that, Kara. Fuck. I haven't even thought about another woman in years because all I can think about is you. If I was half the man I want to be, I would walk away and let you live a life that isn't tainted by everything I do."

"I don't want that." She reached out, clutching her fingers to my shirt like she was expecting me to walk out the door. "Please. Stay. Stay with me. Meet Hayley Jade. I can't keep running. I need to just sit still for a minute and catch my breath."

I wanted to give her that quiet place where she could just be at peace. I just didn't know how.

Hawk cleared his throat, glancing at me and then at Kara. "I want you to come back to the MC. I know shit went down in there, but that's over now. Riot took his boys home to Louisiana with a promise to cut ties with Josiah and Ethereal Eden. He actually said to tell you he was sorry. First time I think I've ever heard that prick admit he fucked up. But the point is, they're gone. And Ratchet is dead. We've got the security back up and the place locked down for as long as it takes for you to feel safe there again."

She shook her head. "I can't go back to that cabin. They were in there, Hawk. They took me from my bed."

My fingers clenched into fists at the thought of anyone doing anything to her against her will. I'd been the man who hurt her like that once before, holding her in that shitty house. I'd had no choice, but it didn't matter.

I should have gotten her out anyway. I should have put her first.

I wouldn't make that mistake again.

"Go with him," I told her. "I'll still be here. I'll still see you..."

That connection between us screamed at the very

thought of leaving her. Of not having her right here beside me every day. I didn't understand it, didn't even want to. All I knew was that it would be agony to let her go again, but I'd endure it for her.

"You don't have to go back to the cabin. I'll make a room for you in the clubhouse," Hawk offered. "You'll be in the room right next to mine."

She looked at me. "I can't—"

But Hawk was done hearing it. "You can. And you will—"

Kara tried to interrupt with protests again, her fingers wrapped in my shirt and her gaze desperate.

I was sure my heart was tearing right down the middle as I tried to convince her this was the best thing for everyone. Even though I knew that with her back at the clubhouse, it would be nearly impossible for us to have any sort of relationship. I couldn't see how it would work. I couldn't go there. She couldn't come here. If I asked her on a date, she'd probably show up with the Slayers in tow, like the Secret Service trailing around after the president.

Super fucking romantic.

Hawk raised his voice and spoke over the top of both of us. "And Chaos will take the one on the other side."

We stared at him.

For so long it clearly pissed him off. He threw his hands up. "Well? Either of you want to say yes?"

"Yes," I said quickly, even though I had no idea how the hell this would work when the Slayers all hated my guts, and I was one-hundred-percent sure Hawk had not cleared this with any of them.

But the idea of having her between me and him, of

seeing her every day, and knowing there was someone there for her during the nights I'd be at work, settled something that had been raging inside me.

Hawk was giving her back to me. Clearly not out of the goodness of his heart. I was sure he didn't give a flying fuck about how I felt.

Kara obviously had the same doubts I did. "Why would you do that? The other men at the club, they won't like it. All they know of Hayden is he was your enemy. That he shot you. That he's opening a club that will rival the one Bliss runs. They'll call you a traitor. They'll question your authority. You'll get your way because you're VP and War's best friend, but why would you do that? Why would you bring the hate of the entire club down on you like that?"

She'd just said everything I was thinking. Just way more eloquently.

Hawk let out a frustrated sigh, his gaze piercing when it caught hers. "Fucking hell, woman. Don't you know I'd throw myself off a building for you?" He put down the needle and gave her his full attention. "Don't you know I'd endure any of the bullshit coming my way if it meant you have everything you need? I love you enough to give you him."

She sucked in a shocked breath. "Hawk..."

He shook his head, red staining his cheeks behind the scruff of his beard. "Don't say anything. I didn't mean to tell you that here. I just..." He switched his focus to me. "Your arm is fine. We're done. Just...just fucking bring her home, okay?"

All I could do was nod, not that he saw it. He was too busy packing up his kit and walking back out the door.

11

KARA

If it were even possible, the Slayers' gates had somehow become even more imposing in the week I'd been away. Or maybe it was just the fact I was now approaching them in the passenger seat of Hayden's truck.

"They're going to lock me in the basement," he mumbled. "This is such a bad idea."

"They won't," I said, voice full of a confidence I didn't really feel.

Unless I thought about how I trusted Hawk with my child and so trusting him with Hayden's life was no different.

If he said Hayden would be safe here, then he would be. I had to believe that. I'd heard the sincerity in Hawk's voice when he'd said he loved me. He wouldn't hurt me by going back on his word.

It didn't stop my palms from sweating when Hayden stopped the truck outside the gates and Ice appeared from the shadows, a shotgun held in one hand.

"Kara?" he called out.

I rolled down the window. "It's me."

He lowered the gun and came to my side of the truck, peering in. His face relaxed into a smile. "Hey. You don't look dead anymore. You doing okay?"

"Much better, thank you."

He grinned, but then his gaze slid past me to the bags in the backseat holding all of mine and Hayden's clothes. Ice's eyes darkened in Hayden's direction. "You're a brave man. There's a whole club full of hate waiting for you down there, you know that, right?"

"I don't want any trouble," Hayden said quietly.

Ice shrugged and opened the gate for us. "Your funeral, brother."

I glanced nervously at Hayden as he nodded once and then urged the truck through the gates.

They closed with a metal-against-metal clang that sent a shudder down my spine.

He reached over and took my hand, squeezing it. "Listen, if they give me shit, you don't try to stand up for me, okay? If there's a fight, don't get in the middle. I've earned whatever is coming to me. You just let them go. I can take whatever they dish out. You hear me?"

I wanted to argue. Wanted to assure him none of that would happen.

Except we both knew we were walking into a lion's den, and while the lions might like me, they all had the scent of Hayden's blood on their minds.

I didn't think I could agree not to help him if push came to shove though. So I didn't make a promise I couldn't keep.

Hayden parked the truck at the end of a row of bikes,

and we both got out, him shouldering our bags, leaving me only the smallest of them all to carry.

I led him to the doors and pulled them open.

The entire club waited on the other side. All the guys. Their wives. Rebel and Bliss's partners who weren't part of the club.

Everyone fell silent, their gazes all on us.

It was Hawk who moved first, pushing his way from the back of the room with Hayley Jade in his arms.

My heart skipped a beat at seeing her sweet face, even though she quickly buried it in the side of Hawk's neck.

I touched a hand gently to her back as Hawk leaned down to take the bag from my hands. He lowered his head, brushing his lips across my cheek. "Welcome home, Little Mouse."

Despite myself, a thrill raced down my spine at hearing him use that nickname again. At having him so close his warm breath coasted over my neck, reminding me of the way his tongue felt every time he traced patterns there.

Despite how angry I was at him, my body still reacted in the same way it always had.

Hawk turned around and faced the room. "Quit gawking at them! I don't give a shit how any of you feel about Chaos being here. This ain't a fucking..." He shifted Hayley Jade in his arms. "I mean, a *fudging* democracy. If you don't like the decisions War and I have made, feel free to show yourself out the door."

Nobody moved.

Nobody looked very happy though.

Rebel and Bliss came to my side. Rebel picked up my hand and squeezed it, staring up at Hayden with unabashed interest. She cocked her head to one side. "Well, I'll give it to you, Sis. You like the pretty ones, don't you? All cleaned up and not reeking of mud, I can see the appeal."

"We're right here, Roach," Vaughn called from the couch where he sat between Kian and Fang.

All three of them were staring at Hayden like if he dared to so much as glance at Rebel wrong they'd be on him in a heartbeat. Bliss's guys were no better. Vincent or Scythe, I couldn't tell which, stood to one side of the room, absentmindedly turning over a blade in his fingers. Nash and War nursed drinks at the bar, all of their gazes fixed on Hayden.

I wasn't sure if this was going well, or very badly. But nobody had pulled a weapon, so that was a start.

With a bright smile, Bliss hugged me. "It's going to be okay. Some of the guys changed rooms, and we moved all of your stuff up from the cabin. Hawk set up the room next to yours—"

War interrupted. "Hawk might want to tell Kara about that himself."

Bliss clapped a hand over her mouth, her eyes going wide. "Oh, of course. I'm sorry. I got overexcited."

Confused, I shook my head questioningly at her. "What's going on?"

She smiled. "He's really sorry for whatever it is he did. I'll let him show you, but just know he's been working nonstop since you agreed to come back."

She moved away to War's side, who seemed much happier to have her in arm's reach.

Hayden cleared his throat and held his hand out to War. "I appreciate you having me here."

War stared at his hand and then up at his face. "You haven't earned that handshake yet. Offer it again in a few weeks when you've proved you aren't a threat to anyone here, and I'll gladly shake it. But right now, you're a fox in my henhouse. For reasons I can't possibly comprehend, Hawk went to bat for you, and that's the only reason I'm allowing it. But it's against my better judgment. So you want me to shake your hand, earn it."

Hayden's mouth twisted into a grim line, but he dropped his arm and nodded. "I will."

It was on the tip of my tongue to defend him, but Hayden had asked me not to. So I bit my tongue, even though it killed me. This was War's club, and he only had the best interests of the people who lived here in mind. That included me and my daughter. I could hardly begrudge him that.

War jerked his head down the corridor. "Your room is the fourth on the left. If you're smart, you'll stay in there until everyone has had some time to process this."

Hayden nodded once and kissed the top of my head. "I'll see you in the morning, okay?"

He walked away, taking a room halfway down the hallway. It left two doors between his and Hawk's. Probably a good thing to have some space between them.

The rest of the room went back to their conversations and pool games now the entertainment was over. I found Hawk watching me, still holding my daughter. She had her head lying on his shoulder.

"She's tired," he confirmed when I approached them.

I nodded.

"You want to help me put her to bed?"

I stared up at him. "You do that?"

He shrugged. "Me or Queenie. Rebel if she's here. She's missed you though."

My heart ached at the lie. Hayley Jade wouldn't even look at me. She was more comfortable with anyone else. But I wouldn't let that always be the case. I'd healed. And Hayley Jade needed to know I was still here. That I'd struggled to find myself, to work out how to help her, but I wasn't ever going to give up or love her any less. "I missed you too, Hayley Jade," I said quietly. "I'd love to tuck you into bed, if that's okay?"

She raised her sleepy head and stared at me with those eyes that haunted my dreams.

My heart nearly broke in two when she nodded.

Hawk ruffled her hair gently. "That's my girl."

I could have melted into a puddle with all the feelings those three words sent through me. If seeing her in his arms wasn't enough to defrost the ice that had formed around my heart with Hawk's lies, those words would have done it.

He went to the door next to his, hand resting on the knob. "This isn't finished, but I've been working on it for a while. The cabin only had one bedroom, and even if she slept down there with you, I wanted her to have a room of her own up here..."

He'd picked the room closest to his.

My heart squeezed painfully as he opened the door to reveal pale-pink walls and a white iron-frame bed covered with a pretty quilt. There was a small wardrobe filled with Hayley-Jade-sized clothes, and a shelf full of books and toys. A couple of Barbie dolls lay abandoned on a thick rug that covered the scuffed-up floorboards beneath, evidence she'd already been playing in here earlier in the day. All the rooms here had their own bathrooms, and Hayley Jade's had a fluffy pink bathmat with matching towels hanging from the rails.

Hawk knelt beside the bed to lower my tired child to her pillow. He tucked her blankets around her. Her dark eyes watched him intently.

"Time for bed, Hay Jay." He leaned over and switched on a nightlight sitting on the bedside table.

Hayley Jade shook her head stubbornly.

He stared at her for a second, something silently passing between them. Then he sighed, as if he'd understood whatever it was she'd been saying with her eyes. "Seriously? Again?"

I frowned, not sure what he meant by that, but a wide smile split her angel face, and she nodded.

He glanced over at me and then squinted at the little girl. "Your mama is going to laugh at me if I do that."

Hayley Jade turned her eyes to me.

I stepped forward, perching on the edge of her bed and put my hand over my heart. "I promise. Whatever it is. I will not laugh."

I meant it. Whatever was going on here was clearly important to her, and if it was important to Hayley Jade, then it was important to me too.

Hawk groaned. "Fine. Fine. But you two tell anyone else..."

I gave Hayley Jade a wink and drew my fingers across my lips, miming the closing of a zipper.

She giggled.

Hawk started singing beneath his breath.

I glanced over at him, surprised, and he just shook his head, continuing on with the song I didn't recognize. It wasn't one of the church songs I'd been taught as a kid, and I had a very limited knowledge of popular music from my time on the outside, but it wasn't a song I recognized from then either.

But I didn't need to know the words to enjoy the deep, husky sound of Hawk's voice.

He was singing to my daughter, and clearly not for the first time. Her small body relaxed into the soft mattress, and her dark lashes fluttered closed while Hawk sang the strange song about shimmering lights and Heaven or Hell.

I listened to every word, and when he finished, Hayley Jade was out, her breathing soft and regular, sung to sleep by a biker who everyone thought was heartless.

But I knew better. I knew his heart. The true essence of who he was. Even if he didn't show it to anyone else, he'd shown me. And he'd shown my girl.

He rocked back on his heels and stood, jerking his head toward the door. We both tiptoed out, and he closed it behind me with a soft snick.

"What was that song?" I asked him. "A lullaby?" I knew what that was, but I was unfamiliar with them. If my parents had sung to me or my sisters as babies, I didn't remember.

He cleared his throat and rubbed a hand across the back of his neck awkwardly. "Uh. Not exactly. I don't know any of those. It was 'Hotel California' by The Eagles."

That didn't mean anything to me, but Aloha overheard and snorted on his laughter.

Hawk shot him a look that promised death by a thousand tiny cuts if he didn't shut up, but Aloha ignored him and started up his own warbled version of the song.

Hawk just steered me to the door between Hayley Jade's and Hayden's. "This is yours."

I gasped when he opened the door to reveal a clean, simple space. The bedding from the cabin had been brought up and covered the large bed. My clothes hung in the closet, and the en suite had some sort of sweet-smelling reed diffuser sitting on the bathroom counter, next to a fluffy towel and my toiletries.

"This was Gunner's room..." I stared at Hawk wide-eyed. "I can't just take it from him."

Hawk leaned against the doorway. "He's not here much anymore anyway. He was happy to give it up for you."

I was sure that wasn't true and Hawk had probably used his rank to get his way. But I couldn't deny that here with Hayley Jade was where I needed to be. I'd spent weeks hiding in that cabin. Hiding from her. It wasn't big enough for all of us.

All of us.

Me. Hayley Jade. Hayden.

And Hawk.

Something warmed inside me at the thought of the four of us. It was ridiculous, when Hayden and Hawk were ready to kill each other at the drop of a hat, and I hadn't forgiven Hawk for what he'd done.

But he was making it really hard to hold a grudge.

He pushed off the wall and nodded at me. "Sleep tight, Little Mouse. You're home. Where you belong."

12

KARA

I poked my way around my new bedroom as the sounds of the party outside dissipated. There was a baby monitor on my dresser that showed a real time video image of Hayley Jade sleeping soundly in the room next door. I picked it up and watched it for a moment, checking the rise and fall of her chest as she breathed slowly and deeply, content in sleep.

Wandering into the bathroom, I took a shower, lathering up my skin and hair with fruity-smelling lotions Hawk had picked out for me, and then wrapped myself in a thick towel, drying off.

Then I pulled on panties and an oversized cotton shirt that hung mid-thigh and got into the big bed that someone had neatly made.

Had that been Hawk too? He'd proven himself oddly domestic and was clearly capable of tucking in sheets.

The clubhouse fell silent, and I wondered what Hayden was doing on the other side of the wall.

But an hour later sleep still hadn't claimed me, and

when I got out of bed and left my room, it was Hawk's bedroom door I found myself in front of.

I didn't knock.

The door could have been locked, but it wasn't, the handle twisting beneath my grip.

In the darkness, I slipped inside.

The lamp flipped on, and I found myself staring down the barrel of his gun.

He blinked, then flopped back on the bed. "Jesus fuck. I could have shot you. I thought you were Chaos, sneaking in here to stab me in my sleep."

"He wouldn't do that."

Hawk rolled onto his side to put the gun beneath his pillow, showing off strong arms and a rib cage full of black and gray tattoos. "Yeah, well, don't mind me if I don't take your word for it."

I traced my gaze over his body, my head full of all the sweet things he'd done. The way he'd stitched up Hayden. The way he'd sung for my daughter. The way he'd made me a home and welcomed me back into it when the first one had been tainted with bad memories.

Something flickered in Hawk's eyes. "What are you doing in here?"

"I never actually said thank you. You did all these sweet things—"

"Don't fool yourself into thinking it makes me a nice guy, Little Mouse." There was a hint of bitterness in his tone. "You, of all people, know that ain't the truth. Or have you forgotten the way I lied to you?"

"I haven't forgotten."

His tone changed, his gaze growing heated and rolling down my body, lingering on the hem of my nightshirt where it brushed my thighs. "Then why are you here?"

His voice held that gravelly tone that always sent sparks shooting through my body to center at my core.

I'd told myself I'd come in here to thank him for what he'd done. I'd thought I couldn't sleep because he was lying in here, thinking I still hated him, when nothing could be further from the truth.

I was just as in love with Hawk as he'd claimed to be with me. I had been for weeks, and his lies hadn't changed that.

I was still angry.

But I still loved him.

And my body hadn't forgotten the way it felt when I was in his arms.

His growl turned feral as he repeated his question. "Why are you here, Little Mouse?"

Heat engulfed me. Flushed right through my body, head to toe, leaving tingles of pleasure in its wake.

Hawk's gaze hot on my skin loosened my tongue. Brought forth the words I never thought I'd be brave enough to say.

"I'm claiming something you owe me," I whispered. "You said all I had to do was come to your room."

I pulled my shirt off, leaving myself in nothing but panties. My heart slammed against my chest, beating too fast, nerves suddenly taking place of the heat and my own insecurities screaming obscenities for being so bold.

A week in a hospital had done nothing to slim out the belly rolls. My hips were still padded with the fat Josiah had always found disgusting.

But Hawk just groaned at the sight of my naked

breasts. His gaze roamed my body with nothing but the pure lust and desire he'd shown me time and time again in the cabin outside these walls.

"Get over here and sit on my face, Kara."

I blinked.

He chuckled, leaning out of bed to hook his fingers into the elastic of my underwear. "I love putting that look of shock on your face." He tugged on the fabric, forcing me to trot the last few steps to the side of his bed. "But I love the look you get right before you come even more."

He dragged my panties down my thighs.

I reached for the lamp to turn it off, but he caught my hand.

"No. I want you to see how much I enjoy fucking you with my tongue. Want you dripping down my throat, Little Mouse. Open up."

He drew one thick arm around my thigh, guiding me onto the bed to straddle him. Everything I had was bared to him, and he wasted no time in sliding down, positioning himself between my legs.

Mortification shook my thighs, but Hawk didn't give me time for it to last long. He used his broad shoulders to knock my knees out wider, lowering my core so his tongue could slick right through my center.

I moaned loudly and then clapped a hand over my mouth, knowing Hayley Jade was just on the other side of the thin wall.

Hawk reached up and pulled my hand away. "Fuck that. I want this entire clubhouse hearing you moan. Hayley Jade sleeps like she's dead. If she can sleep through Aloha and Gunner watching a hockey game and screaming at the screen nonstop for two hours, then she'll sleep through any noise you make."

He licked my slit again, and despite his assurances, I muffled the cry of pleasure, turning my head to press my mouth against my shoulder.

The rhythm he set was agonizingly slow, his leisurely licks alternated with deep plunges of his tongue and muffled words of how good I tasted.

I fought to keep my weight off of him, grabbing on to the headboard, my arms shaking with the effort of keeping him from suffocating beneath me.

But he nipped at my inner thigh. "Get your hands off that headboard and on your tits."

"I can't!" I protested, legs trembling from how far I had them spread. I wasn't Amber or Kiki, with their toned inner thigh muscles from working out. I'd never worked out a day in my life, and my inner thigh muscles were nonexistent. If I wasn't hanging on to the board my entire weight would be on his face.

He'd said to sit on him, but I really didn't want to have to explain to the police that the dead man in this bed was courtesy of suffocation via vagina.

"Not gonna say it again, Little Mouse. "Hands on your tits. Squeeze your nipples until they're as pink and sweet as your pussy is."

He had no idea how unfit I was. Or how fat. He was used to Amber's skinny legs that he could probably breathe around just fine when he did this to her.

The thought of him doing this to anyone else was horrific, and I shook my head quickly, willing the image away. "I will literally kill you. You need to be able to breathe."

"I need to make you come more."

He speared two fingers inside me, and I gasped, eyes rolling back. But still, I clung to the headboard.

"Do I need to call Chaos in here to tongue-fuck your tits?" Hawk groaned.

Both of us froze.

Like even he couldn't believe he'd said the words.

My core wept at the very thought of being straddled over Hawk's tongue like this, with Hayden licking and groping my breasts, burying his face between the swells, squeezing my nipples while Hawk licked my clit.

"Why would you say that?" I whispered, staring down at him between my thighs. "You hate him."

His eyes blazed with surety. "But you don't. I know because the thought of having both of us has you wetter than I've ever seen you."

I shuddered as his fingers slowly speared in and out of me, hitting that spot inside me that produced new gushes of arousal every time he touched it.

"You want us both, Little Mouse," Hawk murmured between licks. "Tell me you want us both."

He worked me up, getting me closer and closer to the tipping point where all the good feelings swirling inside me would meld into one and explode. We'd done this enough times that I knew what it felt like. Knew what to expect.

He switched hands, plunging his left inside the slick tunnel he'd made of my pussy, the other reaching back to stroke my asshole.

I moaned, giving in to his demands and squeezing my nipples like he'd ordered. My hips rocked mindlessly, on their own path, chasing down pleasure and all the different ways Hawk managed to pull it from my body.

"I want you both," I admitted, not letting my brain think about what that meant for my soul. I was married in the eyes of the Lord. Our religion allowed men to take more than one wife, but never for a woman to take more than one man. She'd be labeled a slut. A whore. Shunned from the community.

Yet, it was accepted here. Rebel and Bliss had multiple men they loved. Children they adored. A community who accepted relationships didn't have to be what the Lord dictated.

My orgasm swirled and built, searching for its release.

While my brain whispered of the dirty, secret things Hayden and Hawk could do to my body if they worked together.

I so desperately wanted to find out what Hayden's touch would be like. If he could make me feel even half of what Hawk did when he was between my thighs.

"If you want us both, I need to get you ready," he murmured. "I want my dick here." He prodded at my rear opening, and in conjunction with the way he filled my pussy and licked my clit, the sensation was mind-blowing.

I rocked some more, greedily taking what I needed and shutting Hawk up in the process. He doubled down on sucking my clit so perfectly I could cry.

The rocking turned into bouncing, needing more friction, and desperate for that plunge of his fingers inside me. I'd lost track of how many fingers he'd added, but each one brought a delicious stretch my body accommodated with complete and utter trust and need.

"Fuck, Kara," he groaned. "You're so wet and relaxed we could both fuck this pussy."

I didn't know why, but the words only turned me on more. The thought of having the two of them inside me so hot I could barely breathe.

When Hawk pressed his finger into my ass, I splintered apart, falling forward onto the headboard and coming on his tongue in an orgasm so earth-shattering I'd never felt anything like it. I gushed new waves of liquid from somewhere deep inside me, Hawk catching it with his tongue and lapping it up like it was pure honey.

I trembled and shook, riding the orgasm out, until Hawk slipped from beneath my legs and knelt behind me, fitting himself to my back and reaching around to grab my breast.

"Hawk," I moaned. He started up a new assault on my nipple, tweaking and rolling it in sharp pinches that would have hurt if I hadn't been so turned on that pain felt like pleasure. "I'm done. I came."

He chuckled into the back of my neck, licking away the fine mist of sweat covering my skin and sucking at the sensitive spots. "You think I missed that orgasm? Not likely. I'm just not done with you yet."

He moved his finger in and out of my ass, gathering up more and more of my arousal with his other hand and letting it slide down between my cheeks.

The feeling was so foreign, the urge to fight back and resist his touch there, but I couldn't deny the feelings it brought forth in me.

"You're going to take his cock so well," Hawk murmured dirtily into my ear. "And mine."

I moaned at his praise, wanting to please him, even though it really had little to do with me.

"I want to fuck you," Hawk groaned. "Tell me I can."

"Yes." I didn't know if he meant my pussy or my ass, but what I did know with all my heart was this man would never physically hurt me, and at this point, he knew my body better than I did.

I'd never touched myself. Never tried to make pleasure spark from places I'd been told were only for a husband.

Hawk's touch had only ever brought me pleasure, and I'd willingly given up all control to him.

If he wanted my ass, then it was his to take.

He pressed a second finger inside me, and I gasped at the intrusion. But then it was gone and his cock was in my pussy, driving home from behind, his fingers digging into my flesh, holding my hips and taking what his body needed from mine, all while giving me more pleasure than I'd thought possible.

Every slam of his hips sent a cry of ecstasy from my mouth until, "Oh, oh, oh," and the slap of his hips against my behind filled the room.

"I want my cum dripping down your thighs in the morning, Little Mouse. I want it wet on your panties all day when you go to his room. I want him touching your pussy and feeling me there and knowing I had you first."

I shivered at the thought.

"Will you do that, Little Mouse? Will you go to him in the morning and let him know that even though I'll share you, you were mine first. Here." He slammed himself inside me. "Here." He rubbed my clit so fast and hard I saw stars. "And here."

His cock still buried in my pussy, he guided me down so I was on all fours and returned his fingers to my rear opening. With two fingers buried deep inside, pressing against the fullness of his dick in my pussy, an explosion of feeling erupted inside me.

I screamed his name, not because I didn't care people would hear but because there was no other choice. The pleasure had peaked and had nowhere else to go.

He slapped my ass, pushing me flat down onto the bed so I could muffle my cries in the pillow while he pumped in and out of me, fast now, his orgasm taking hold.

"Fuck." He buried himself, grabbing my hips again to lift them enough that he could do what he'd promised.

He came hard, his groans mixing with my cries. He pumped into my body several more times before he slowed, his final few thrusts a shuddering shake as he filled me with his seed.

When he pulled out, he held me there, ass in the air, watching it seep from inside me.

Then he found my panties and lifted my boneless legs, fitting the underwear over my thighs and back into place.

He massaged me there, making sure my panties were wet with his cum. And then he lowered his head to kiss my ass. "Go back to bed, Little Mouse. Go back to bed, and tomorrow, you do what I said."

13

KARA

I woke the next morning in my bed, pleasant throbbing between my thighs and slick panties.

Like I'd promised Hawk, I hadn't showered. I'd slept with his cum inside me, the thought keeping me awake until the early hours.

I'd made him another promise.

To let Hayden know Hawk had taken me. That I'd let him mark me, claim me.

That I'd forgiven him enough to welcome him inside my body.

I didn't like to break promises, but I didn't think it was one I could keep, even though my body yearned to hear him praise me. The thought was just too mortifying. Hayden and I had barely even kissed. I couldn't just walk into his room and ask him to put his hand inside my panties so Hawk had bragging rights.

Even if the thought did leave me breathless.

No, Hawk didn't get that satisfaction. Not yet. He'd

ninety-five percent earned my forgiveness, but I wasn't quite willing to give him full control again.

So I got up and showered, put on fresh clothes, and then sat on the end of the bed, wondering what I was going to do with the rest of my life.

The answers came quickly.

Live here.

Get Hayley Jade into school.

Volunteer at the hospital until I had enough knowledge to apply for a paid position there.

Keep Hawk and Hayden from killing each other.

All but the last one seemed fairly doable.

I slipped into the hallway. The clubhouse was mostly quiet, only Ice and Queenie sitting at the bar, though this morning they both had mugs of coffee in their hands instead of beer bottles.

Queenie raised a hand at me. "Morning, Miss Thang. How you doing after your little sexcapade last night?"

I widened my eyes at her.

Queenie burst into laughter. "Yeah, sugar. You're real lucky that girly of yours sleeps so solidly. The rest of us, however..." She took a sip of her coffee, her smile no less evident in the mischief in her eyes. "Gotta say though, until you screamed his name, I thought it was Chaos you were in there with. Pretty sure you weren't going to forgive Hawk that easily."

I faltered, moving over to the bar and taking the mug of coffee Ice poured for me because it was the polite thing to do, even though I didn't really like it. "Do you think I forgave him too quickly?"

Queenie shook her head, the absence of her large hoop earrings jarring, though I didn't blame her for taking those off when she slept. "No, sugar. What's the point in holding on to hate? That ain't going to get you anything good. You forgave him, and look what it got you? A whole lotta orgasms."

Ice just shook his head and stared at the bar top, his cheeks pink.

Queenie ignored his embarrassment and nudged me. "What's your plan for today?"

"I want to enroll Hayley Jade at school."

She choked on her coffee, coughing as she put it down. "No shit? Well, good for you. And for her. That girl needs to get out of this clubhouse for a few hours a day." She glanced at Hawk's bedroom door. "You talk to him about it though? He's gotten pretty protective over that girl, and I don't blame him. She's real easy to love." The tender expression on her face told me she adored Hayley Jade just as much as Hawk did.

My heart filled with love for these people. They'd barely known me when I'd arrived on their doorstep, and yet they'd taken me in and cared for me and my child when I couldn't. I owed it to them to consider their feelings on Hayley Jade's next steps.

"I'll talk to him," I promised her.

Hawk's door opened at the same time, and we all looked over at him.

But his gaze was only for me. The corner of his mouth flicked up, and his gaze grew hot, like he was remembering what we'd done in the dark just hours ago. My pussy clenched in on itself, missing the fullness of his dick.

Hayden's door opened mid throb.

The need there only intensified when he walked out

in black jeans, a black button-down shirt, and with his shoulder-length hair messily tied back off his face with a leather band at the nape of his neck.

I felt like a deer caught in headlights. Like all of them knew how much I was turned on just from being in the same room as them.

Hawk glanced at Hayden, and his smile for me grew. "You do what I asked, Little Mouse?"

Heat flushed my face as all eyes turned back to me.

Queenie chuckled at the clear triangle of sexual tension that had sprung up between me and the two guys. "Oooh, what did he say? Do tell."

I shook my head quickly, my face on fire with embarrassment.

Hayden watched me quietly while Hawk strode to the bar, leaning on the countertop and waiting for Ice to pour him a coffee. He grinned over the top of it at Queenie, making sure his voice was plenty loud enough for Hayden to hear. "Filled her up with cum and sent her to dickhead over there." He jerked his head in Hayden's direction. "Just so he'd know who her pussy belongs to."

"Hawk!" I hissed, glaring at him. "Stop it! I was never going to do that."

He laughed into his mug. "Sure you weren't."

Hayden wandered over, and when Ice ignored him, not offering coffee like he had to me and Hawk, Hayden just reached over the counter and poured himself one. He took a taste, then screwing up his face at the flavor, crossed the space to stand in front of Hawk, the two of them eye to eye.

Nerves sprang to life in my belly, and I cringed, waiting for one of them to throw a punch.

Hawk sipped his drink like Hayden all up in his space was no big deal. He refused to move back though, not conceding an inch.

Slowly, Hayden lifted his mug and poured what was left of the sludgy coffee into Hawk's mug.

Hawk let him, but the smile slowly fell from his face as Hayden leaned in and said loud enough for us all to hear, "If you'd wanted me to taste your cum, Hawk, you could have just asked me to blow you. No need for me to lick it from her pussy." Then he winked at me. "Though for the record, if you'd come to me this morning, even dripping with his cum, I still would have."

Queenie and Ice hooted with laughter, Queenie slapping her knee, her eyes watering at the horrified expression on Hawk's face. Ice got himself under control quicker, turning away to busy himself with dishes that needed washing, but his shoulders shook with silent laughter.

I just wanted the earth to swallow me whole.

Or maybe transport me via secret underground tunnel back to Hayden's room so he could make good on that promise, because just like last night when Hawk had suggested letting Hayden feel how wet I was, the idea turned me hot.

Hayden put the mug down on the countertop and pointed at the coffee machine. "I know I'm a guest around here, but your coffee is shit. I'll bring a new machine home with me tonight."

Hawk frowned. "The coffee is fine. And buying crap we don't need isn't your place—"

Queenie waved him off. "Stop, child. I've seen the man's name on that fancy new restaurant in Providence.

If he wants to be stealing coffee machines from work so we don't have to drink unidentifiable swill, then let him. He's right. The coffee is horrific." She glanced at Ice. "No offense, sugar. You pour a nice whisky, but that's about the extent of your culinary skills."

Hawk looked ready to argue again, but Hayden ignored him.

"I can cook too. I'll probably be working a lot of nights after we open but I can make extras, and someone can come down and pick it up."

Hawk started to protest again, deciding for the entire club that Hayden's services weren't welcome here.

Hayden just stared at him. "War said I need to earn his respect. I intend to do that." He shook his head. "Maybe even yours too. She clearly likes you, so there must be something good about you."

Hawk paused, clearly as surprised at Hayden's words as I was. Then he shrugged. "Aloha is allergic to mushrooms. Gunner can't eat fried shit, his cholesterol is already sky-high."

Hayden nodded. "Okay. Fine. I can work out meals around that."

Hawk crossed his arms and leaned against a wall. "And I don't like pickles."

Hayden raised an eyebrow. "Because they're dick shaped?"

Hawk scowled and jerked his head toward the door. "Don't you have to go to work or something?"

Hayden sniggered. "Actually, I do." His gaze sought mine. "You going to be okay?"

"I want to take Hayley Jade down to the local school and enroll her."

Hawk's mouth pulled into a straight line. "That's not safe. Not after what just happened here, and that was behind our gates. Josiah's people...we underestimated their reach. I never thought for a second they could use our own club members against us, and yet that's exactly what happened."

The funny thing was, I knew all that. I should have been terrified, and a part of me was. Of course it was. My sister had been murdered. Someone had tried to murder me. I certainly didn't want the same thing to happen to Hayley Jade.

But that had happened right here. Behind the perceived safety of the gates where I should have been one-hundred-percent safe.

But I wasn't. I wasn't one-hundred-percent safe anywhere. Nobody was. Most people didn't have their husbands chasing them down in the name of cleansing their sins, but the world was a dangerous place. People walked outside their homes every day and ran the risk of getting hit by a bus or being abducted while on their morning run.

It didn't mean they stopped living.

I had. I'd forced the world to stop turning around me and my daughter in the name of fear, and look where it had gotten us?

She still wouldn't talk, and that was breaking my heart.

The world outside these gates was no more dangerous than keeping her inside it.

I stared at Hawk, knowing I was right but wanting him to feel good about it too. He'd earned that right. He and Queenie both.

"She's never going to get better sitting around here with all of us. She needs school and other kids and a therapist. I want to get all of those things for her."

Queenie's expression morphed into one that was full of pride. "Mama Kara is back." She stood and wrapped her arms around me, hugging me tight. "I'm glad to see it."

I smiled into her soft shoulder, a sense of pride welling up inside me too. I'd been weak when I'd arrived here. Broken. And everything that had happened a week ago should have broken me more.

Except it hadn't.

It had just made everything I wanted clearer.

Hayley Jade healthy, happy, and in school.

Hawk.

Hayden.

The three H's of my heart.

One of those H's was still scowling at me.

Ice noticed too, and cleared his throat. "The other prospects and I could help," he offered. "We can station a guard outside her classroom."

Queenie raised an eyebrow. "And terrify all those kids?"

Ice shrugged. "Outside the school gates then." He glanced at Hawk. "If you want."

Hawk switched his stare to Ice, considering his proposal.

Poor Ice seemed ready to pee his pants under Hawk's intense scrutiny.

I reached over and squeezed his hand encouragingly, while giving Hawk a glare of my own. "I think that's a fantastic offer. Don't you, Hawk?"

He let out a huff, his opinion of the prospects clearly not high.

Ice was like a kicked puppy who still wanted the love of his owner, and it was painful to watch.

"Fine," Hawk said through gritted teeth. "I'd do it myself, but I need to be with you. The other guys all have things going on with the club. But not the other prospects, Ice. Just you. I don't trust any of you fuckers to do a good job, but the others even less than you. Until all of this settles down and we work out something with the school about bringing on extra security, you'll sit your ass outside those gates from nine 'til three, every day Hayley Jade is there. Capiche?"

Ice grinned at his VP. "Yes, sir."

Hawk raised an eyebrow at the formal language.

Ice shrugged. "Yes, boss?"

Hawk rolled his eyes. "Just go get ready, you kiss-ass."

Ice skittered away, clearly pleased with his new role.

I touched Hawk's arm. "You could try being nice to the prospects occasionally, you know."

"I would, if they could try having a half a brain between them."

Queenie let loose a deep belly laugh that I loved. "Don't worry about the prospects, Kara. They know what they're signing up for when they join. All the boys go through it. Makes them better club members in the end."

I wasn't sure I agreed with that. I'd been in Ice's shoes. Where people with more authority than you had full control over your life and you had to be perfect in order to gain their approval.

But then, unlike me and Josiah, Ice had a choice

about whether he wanted to be here or not. He could walk away at any time.

That was not my experience. So Ice and the other prospects mustn't have minded being the brunt of Hawk's bad moods. Even still, I hoped for Ice's sake that they made him a full member soon.

Hawk glanced at his phone. "School day starts in an hour. If we're going to do this, let's do it."

Butterflies picked up in my belly at the thought of leaving Hayley Jade in an unfamiliar place for an entire day, but I forced my feet across the common room and knocked on her door before letting myself in. "Hey, sweetheart. Are you awake?"

She sat on the floor, already dressed and her hair brushed, a book on her lap.

I blinked, surprised she wasn't still in her pajamas. But then I remembered where she'd grown up, and it wasn't actually that unusual she was already capable of getting herself ready in the mornings, even though she was only five.

Shari was a good, Ethereal Eden woman. She'd started teaching Hayley Jade young. Laziness wasn't tolerated, and women especially were expected to rise early in order to bake bread for the man of the house's breakfast.

I'd bet Hayley Jade already knew how to do that.

I knew then I was making the right decision. While there was nothing wrong with a child her age being able to dress herself, or help with the baking, there were other things she needed to know as well.

How to read the book on her lap being one of the biggest.

I knelt beside her and pointed at the words on the

page. "Mr. Crocodile was having a bad day. His tummy was sore."

I paused, shifting so I was sitting cross-legged on the rug with her, facing each other. "Would you like to be able to read those words yourself?"

Hayley Jade looked up, her eyes big with interest.

She didn't say anything, but saying nothing wasn't a no, so that was a start. I was going to have to get her into school whether she wanted to go or not, but her wanting to go, and feeling safe there would make all the difference. "You know how Remi and Madden go to school? I know they've told you about all the fun things they do. Drawing and coloring and singing and playing."

She gave a small nod.

"Well, there's a school you can go to as well. They'll teach you how to read that book all by yourself, and there's other kids there to play with. Would you like to come see it with me and Hawk today?"

Shock spread through me at the giant smile that split her face. It was so wide and full of pure joy that it broke my heart.

She'd wanted this, and I'd been keeping it from her, with my own fears too thick in my head to see what she needed.

I wanted to sink beneath the sense of grief that brought up in me, but I wouldn't.

Like Queenie had said, Mama Kara was back. I didn't want to let her go again.

A middle-aged woman took Hayley Jade's hand and led her into a classroom filled with other kids running about the place and causing general chaos from the moment the woman had stepped outside to greet us. She let out a whistle and then called out, "One, two, three!"

Like a miracle, the kids stopped and chanted back, "Eyes on me!"

Hawk blinked in surprise as the kids all plonked themselves down on a big mat in the center of the classroom, staring up at their teacher and Hayley Jade in interest.

The teacher, Miss Winters, smiled at the students. "Everybody, this is Hayley Jade. She's new to our class. Do you want to know something special? Hayley Jade has a secret superpower. Do you know what that superpower might be?"

The kids gaped and shook their heads.

Miss Winters crouched so she was closer to their heights. "Well, Hayley Jade's superpower is her listening ears. She hears everything we say and understands every word, even though right now, she doesn't speak. Who else has super listening ears? Can you turn them on?"

The kids fiddled with their ears, miming turning on switches like robots.

Hayley Jade did it too, and I smiled from where Hawk and I stood in the doorway, watching on quietly.

"Good job! Now can everyone welcome Hayley Jade to our class?"

"Welcome, Hayley Jade," the kids chorused.

Hayley Jade just beamed at them all, her intelligent

eyes taking in the classroom like it was Disneyland. I supposed to her, it was. There were no classrooms at Ethereal Eden, especially not ones filled with toys and books and educational games like this. It was all brightly colored alphabet posters and kid art.

"Damn, she's an awesome kid," Hawk whispered to me, staring at her with pride in his eyes. "She didn't even cry. And look at her. She's absolutely the smartest kid in that room. She's going to leave all these other kids in her dust."

I couldn't help but smile at him, and then at my daughter as she waved to us, her excitement so clear in her little face.

"I think that's our cue to leave," I whispered to Hawk.

He grunted his disapproval, but I threaded my fingers through his.

"Let her fly on her own wings. She doesn't need you right now."

He made a face. "Don't say that to me. I like her needing me."

I chuckled, pulling him away from the door. "She still does. But just before nine and after three on weekdays, okay?"

He huffed but waved to her and eventually let me close the door.

As promised, Ice was positioned by the front gates, chatting with the school's security guard. Talk of fences and new security systems floated back to me, and if I'd had any last worries I was doing the right thing here, seeing how seriously they were taking Hayley Jade's safety put the last of them to rest.

We'd had a meeting with the school principal and

told her everything. She'd listened calmly and assured us we weren't the only ones in a domestic violence situation and they had procedures in place when it came to the families affected. She'd walked us through every security measure the school had, and even Hawk had admitted he was impressed.

We made our way back to the club van and got in.

Hawk glanced over at me. "What now? We're kid— and Chaos—free until three?" A devilish look crossed his face. "I could—"

I interrupted him before he could suggest something dirty. Which I knew was exactly where his mind was going. "No. No sex. We've done something for Hayley Jade, now we need to do something for us."

His fingers crept toward my leg. "Last I checked, orgasms were for us."

"You said you'd volunteer at the hospital with me."

Hawk groaned, "No I didn't."

But we both knew he had. "I can always go by myself..."

He stared at me.

I giggled. "Then maybe you're volunteering too?"

He put the van into drive. "This is going to ruin my street cred, you know?"

I smiled to myself. So would the way he was caring for Hayley Jade like he was her father, but I didn't mention that.

14

GRAYSON

The free clinic was a madhouse. It was never quiet, but the last few months, with the weather being colder and flu season in full swing, had put a burden on us that was verging on desperate.

It was my personal motto that we never turned anyone away, but there were so many people lining up each week now that I wasn't sure we could continue to keep up.

Cringing at the line out the door, I ran my gaze along the line of waiting patients until it snagged on a familiar face. I strode along the line, smile widening as I approached her but silently watching her for a reason she'd be at the clinic so soon after being discharged. "Kara!"

She jerked and then grinned when she recognized me. "Dr. Grayson. Hello."

My gaze flickered to Hawk standing beside her. "Hawk."

He nodded back. "Doc."

"You gonna hit me again today?" I asked him cautiously. "I just like to be prepared with my makeup kit if I'm going to be sporting a new black eye."

Hawk sighed. "Listen, I'm sorry about that. I—"

I held up a hand to stop him. "Don't. I get it. You're protective. I don't blame you. After everything Kara's been through, I would be the same. No hard feelings." I held a hand out to him.

He stared at it and then at me. "I punched you square in the face. And now you want to shake my hand?"

I shrugged. "Like I said. I understand, and I'm not a grudge holder. I'm a shrink. I've seen what that sort of behavior does to a person's brain, and I'm not down for doing it to my own. Maybe buy me a beer sometime if you see me at a bar and we'll call it even."

Hawk took my hand and shook it. "You're a bigger man than most."

I chuckled. "If only I could find a woman to say the same."

Kara groaned. "And here I was, thinking you were a respectable doctor."

I screwed my face up at her. "Did the glove balloons not give me away earlier?"

She rolled her eyes, but even Hawk's mouth had a slight upward tilt that made me happy. I didn't want to be the regular sort of doctor, who people didn't feel comfortable with. My whole job was getting people to feel as though I was their friend, so they would tell me everything that was bottled up in their heads.

All I'd ever wanted out of this job was to help people feel happy. Maybe the way I did that was classified as unprofessional by my colleagues. But I didn't want to be a crusty old shrink, who was counting down the clock each session. I had my fair share of those patients who just wanted to rant at me, or in the case of some of my married couples, at each other. I had to pay the bills, like everyone else. But that wasn't where my heart lay. I was a better doctor for removing the formality barrier and sharing my own stories with patients so they knew I could relate to their experiences. Even if my colleagues didn't agree.

"What are you two doing here anyway?" I asked them. "I checked your chart before you were discharged and agreed you were all good to go. Did something happen?"

Kara unzipped her purse and pulled out a flyer we'd had posted on the clinic bulletin boards for months, if not years. It was our plea for volunteers, the one we never took down because nobody ever offered up their time and we were always short-staffed. "We'd like to volunteer."

I blinked. "Seriously? Both of you?"

Hawk narrowed his eyes, suspicion etching into his face. "Unless you have a problem with a biker working here?"

I frowned. "Why would I have a problem with that?"

"Lotta people do. Most people are kinda wary about us."

I studied him carefully, knowing all too well the kind of damage feeling shunned by your community could do to a person. "How does that make you feel?"

Hawk laughed. "You gonna shrink me or you gonna sign us up and give us a job to do?"

I chuckled at the realization, clicking the end of my pen so the nib dropped down into place. "Definitely the latter. And sorry, it's a force of habit. Come on, get out of the line. I'll take you out back and get you the paperwork you need." I paused. "There's a police check you need to pass, though…"

Hawk's expression fell, pure disappointment slumping his posture and tainting his tone. "Well, that counts me out then."

In that second, I realized I'd judged Hawk too quickly, and my assumptions had been completely wrong. I'd assumed Kara had dragged him in to help her sign up, not that he actually *wanted* to be here. But the expression on his face said otherwise.

"You kill people for fun?" I asked him.

His eyes widened, and he looked around over his shoulder, but I'd moved us into the doorway of an examination room we didn't have a doctor for. It wasn't private, but there was no one in earshot either. "No."

I nodded. "Okay then. I'm not going to ask if you've ever killed anyone in general because knowing your position within your club, I'm just going to assume you have, and that you had a good reason."

Hawk stuttered. "Okay…"

"You ever rape anyone? Molest a kid?"

The pure disgust on Hawk's face told me his answer before he even said the words. "What? Of course not!"

I moved into the room and searched around on the desk, eventually coming up with the goods. "You just passed the police check. Here. Fill this out, and I'll sign off on it. It's for your ID badges."

I turned to Kara, handing her a form. "I'm going to assume you don't kill people for fun?"

"I don't know if I'm supposed to laugh or be horrified by that question."

I held the paper so she couldn't take it and winked at her. "I'm a pretty good judge of character. I back myself and the years of experience I have. I'm fairly certain you aren't going to deliberately unplug someone's life support."

Kara's mouth dropped open.

"This can't be legal." Hawk's face was full of confusion. "You could lose your license for this, couldn't you?"

I laughed at their shock. "Look, fact is, we would take Ted Bundy's help right now, we're that understaffed. The main thing here is knowing you aren't going to steal drugs, and your access passes won't give you entry to any of the medical supply cabinets, so the police check is bullshit anyway. This isn't Providence. It's Saint View. Around here, we just do whatever we need to do to get by. I've got a very long line of people out there who need help, and I'm not about to turn away able-bodied help."

I shut up as Dr. Tahpley walked into the room, pausing at the three of us standing by the desk. "Oh, sorry, didn't realize you were using the room, Gray."

"Not a problem. This is Kara and Hawk. They're new volunteers, so you'll see them around."

Hawk nodded, and Kara smiled at the older doctor.

"Lovely to meet you. We're excited to help out."

Completely ignoring them, he tossed a pair of gloves into a bin and cracked his neck. "Lunchtime, I think."

Pompous old prick. He did this to the nurses too. Just ignored them because anyone on a lower pay grade was of little interest.

I glanced at the clock on the wall. "It's barely eleven. You didn't start 'til nine thirty."

Tahpley's eyes held a challenge. "Like I said, lunchtime. I'll be back in a couple of hours."

He walked away. All I could do was stare at him.

"What a fucking cunt he is," Hawk muttered.

Kara elbowed him. "Language...but also, I agree."

Hawk sniggered then turned to me. "Her agreeing is about as close to swearing as she's going to get."

I pushed pens at both of them, fighting off irritation at Tahpley shirking his duties yet again. "I'm fine with swearing or not swearing. Trust me, I've heard a whole lot worse. But you see why I'm willing to skip things like police checks when someone comes in and actually wants to help? It's rare. So sign your papers and let's go." I dug deep to find some good humor because we all knew those people out there needed more than scowls and a prescription shoved at them. I grinned at Hawk and Kara, trying to psych myself—and them—up. "We've got lives to save."

It was my way of equaling the balance. While we were in here saving people, my little group of psychopaths would be out there on the streets, ending the lives of others.

15

KARA

The hospital was fascinating. We were given scrubs to change into, then Grayson threw us into the deep end. I'd expected to be rolling bandages or maybe running mail from one department to another.

But Grayson explained that the volunteer program here was more about the emotional support of patients. Sometimes, that meant supervising someone who couldn't be left alone, so they didn't need to be restrained to the bed. Sometimes it meant comforting a child while a parent was seeking help for a sibling. We did some cleaning and other basic admin tasks when the nurses found out we were volunteers and pounced on us with glee.

I worried Hawk would find the whole thing irritating, but when I looked around for him about two hours into our first shift and found an old lady clutching his arm for support as he walked her to X-ray, I saw his expression.

It wasn't boredom.

It was satisfaction. Something I hadn't seen from him when he was at the club.

At two fifty, Grayson called us over. "Well? What do you think? This is generally about the time our volunteers quit. So I totally understand if that's the case."

I gaped at him. "They quit after their first shift?"

He nodded. "More than half. Probably closer to seventy-five percent. So trust me, I understand if it's not for you. This place can be hard. Not just physically, though the vomit and shit isn't my favorite. I don't have to deal with that so much with my regular patients, but down here, there's a lot of it. I think it's the emotional side that gets to people more though. Being around people who are hurting isn't always easy. You both were amazing today, but if you're out, I get it."

"I'm not out," Hawk said quickly. "Not even a little bit."

The determination in his voice was so strong, and pride swelled within me. "I'm not out either."

Grayson's expression switched to thrilled in an instant. He slung his arms around our shoulders. "Really? I knew I liked you two for a reason! Thank you!"

Then he realized he was touching us and jumped back. "Shit. Sorry. That was a bit much. How about a stoic handshake instead?" He cringed in Hawk's direction. "Please still come back. I won't always be this overexcited, I promise. This is just very unusual."

"We'll definitely come back." I swallowed hard and said the words that had been playing over in the back of my mind for the entire shift, even though I'd given it my all. I'd seen Grayson's work today. Saw the way he cared for his patients. It had reminded me there was one last thing on my list of things to do today. "I'd like to make an appointment with you. Two, actually. One for Hayley Jade. And one for me."

If Grayson was surprised, he didn't show it. "I don't have my schedule with me, but your phone number is on the paperwork you filled out. Is it okay if I call you to make a time later?"

I nodded. "Please do."

He glanced at Hawk. "If you ever want to talk…"

Hawk screwed up his face. "Me? It wasn't me who was buried alive." He glanced at me apologetically. "Shit. Sorry. I didn't mean to just bring it up like that."

I shook my head. "It's okay. I think we need to talk about it. Or at least, I do."

Grayson's expression was gentle when he looked at Hawk. "She wasn't the only one hurt by what happened. You love her and you thought you were going to lose her. That's trauma."

Hawk shoved to his feet. "I'm fine. I've been through worse."

Grayson backed off pretty quickly. "I just want you to know I'm here. If you need me."

"I don't."

Gray clapped his hands together. "Great. Then, Kara, I'll call you later. Hawk, thanks for today. See you next shift. Anytime you want to come lend a hand, we'd appreciate it."

Hawk was already walking away.

We both watched him go.

Grayson murmured to me, "Keep an eye on him, Kara. He's not as strong as he tries to make people believe."

I glanced at Grayson in surprise. It had taken me weeks to know the real Hawk, and Grayson had seen through his hard outer shell in the space of an afternoon. "You're really good at your job, you know?" I said to him.

He grinned. "It's the glove balloons, isn't it?"

The next few days, we fell into a routine of sorts. Hayden stayed in his room most of the time when he was at the clubhouse, and the rest of the time he went to work at the restaurant. We all pretended he wasn't working for Luca Guerra, and I fought the urge to go to his room every night.

I'd thought he would come to me, but whether he was respecting Hawk or the club boundaries, I didn't know.

I focused on getting Hayley Jade settled at school and reveling in the happiness and color that had started coming back to her. She'd begun skipping in and out of the building each day when Hawk and I dropped her or picked her up at the gates.

Unhappy people did not skip.

I spent most days at the hospital. The clinic didn't run on all of them, but that didn't lessen the need for volunteers. I liked feeling needed and being helpful. I wished I could do more than hold hands, murmur soothing words, and file papers, but it was a start toward independence, and it was a step in the direction of a life I could see myself enjoying.

Grayson had a new bad joke ready for me every time I passed him in a hallway, and he promised he was working on a new glove balloon camel. I couldn't even imagine how that would work.

On Saturday, I woke up early, just as the sun was rising. I tossed and turned for thirty minutes but couldn't get back to sleep. Next to my room, Hayden's door opened and closed softly.

Nothing had happened between us since we'd come here, and I was beginning to think I'd imagined the make-out session we'd had on the couch in his apartment. As well as the chemistry we'd had when he'd pulled me into that movie theater bathroom. I didn't know where I stood with him after Hawk had blabbed about filling me with his cum so Hayden would know who I belonged to.

Maybe that had been enough to scare him off.

The thought left me breathless. I wanted Hawk.

But I wanted Hayden too.

So I got up, shrugged on a robe, and belted it around my waist. I slipped from my room quietly, finding Hayden alone in the common area behind the bar where there was now a brand-new coffee machine that everyone was loving.

"Could I have one of those?"

He jerked around, hissing when hot milk sloshed over his hand.

I winced. "Sorry. Didn't mean to startle you."

He mopped at the mess on the countertop. "No, it's okay. I didn't realize anyone was awake. I'm overly jumpy around here." He smiled ruefully. "Still kind of half expecting someone to put a gun to the back of my head at any minute."

I sighed, hating he was so on edge. It wasn't fair for

him to live like that. He was a fish out of water here, nobody talking to him, and making it worse by isolating himself, even from me. "You don't have to stay here, you know," I assured him, even though I hated the idea of him going back to his awful little apartment. A thought suddenly occurred to me. "Oh my God. Where are your kittens?"

He bit his lip and then motioned for me to follow him. He went to his bedroom door and opened it a crack.

Three sleeping kittens, who seemed to have doubled their size in the last week or so, were curled up on the end of his bed.

He closed the door again and gave a small laugh. "I snuck them in early one morning when everyone was asleep. You haven't heard them?"

I shook my head. "No, not at all. Hawk said the walls are actually pretty thick."

"Not thick enough to avoid hearing you shouting Hawk's name when you come though." He chuckled, throwing the dishcloth in the sink.

Heat flushed through me, burning my cheeks. "You heard that."

"Everybody heard that."

I buried my face in my hands. "I'm so embarrassed."

He wrapped his fingers around mine and tugged them away. "Why? You were enjoying yourself. Nobody begrudges you that."

"We could have been more discreet." Except I still remember how strong that orgasm had been. How I'd been so mindless to the pleasure that there really hadn't been any stopping the way my body reacted. My breath stuttered at the very thought.

"You're thinking about it right now, aren't you?" Hayden asked softly.

I really needed to get better control of my expressions. "No," I lied, though all I could think about was Hawk filling my pussy, his fingers in my ass, increasing the pleasure and preparing me for the possibility of having two men at once.

I was suddenly boiling hot, my skin an inferno. I tugged at the collar of my pajamas, trying to force the cool morning air down my top before I suffocated. "How's the restaurant going?"

Hayden's heated gaze lingered on me for another long moment. "I want you to come."

I jerked. "Excuse me?" But it was too late. My core was already tingling from thinking about what I'd done with Hawk. It could barely handle the idea of Hayden making requests of it too. Arousal pooled, and I squeezed my thighs together, trying to relieve the building pressure.

Slowly, his gaze locked on mine, he put down his coffee. Closed the gap between us and ghosted his fingers over my hip.

On instinct, I raised my hands to his chest, feeling the hard muscle beneath his shirt and fighting the urge to undo his buttons so I could touch his skin.

I trembled when his fingers found the mid-thigh length hem of my nightshirt and brushed my skin, slowly inching higher toward my panties.

His warm breath coasted over my cheek and neck. If it were even possible, Hayden's voice seemed to get an octave lower. "I meant I wanted you to come to the restaurant, but now I'm a whole lot more interested in what you thought I meant."

Embarrassment rocketed through me again, and I tried to pull away.

He wouldn't let me. He grabbed my thigh and my arm, refusing to let me go. That hand on my leg slipped beneath the line of my panties, still way too far away from my center, just resting on my hip, but the knowledge he only had to move a few inches to be where I really wanted him was maddening.

My breaths got too fast, my pussy throbbing with desire.

His lips ran over my neck and ear. "I can't stop thinking about him fucking you. And how I wish I'd come to his room and joined in."

The sound that escaped my mouth was probably something Hawk would have made fun of me about, claiming I actually did squeak like a mouse.

"I want to know if that makes you wet," he whispered in my ear. "I want to put my fingers to your pussy and know if the idea of having both of us turns you on as much as it does for me. You wet for us, Kara?"

His hand slid between us so agonizingly slowly I wanted to scream. He was giving me every opportunity to stop him, but I just wanted him to get there faster.

"Yes," I murmured.

Hayden groaned into my shoulder, biting the flesh there as he cupped my mound, putting pressure to my clit. It wasn't enough. I ached for more, and I clutched his arms, desperate for something to hold on to because my legs wobbled at the sensation he created inside me.

"Tell me I can make you come." His lips trailed up my neck. "Tell me I can touch you like that, right here, right now, even though I don't deserve to."

I didn't want to think about that. About why he didn't think himself worthy of being with me. I just wanted to feel. Anybody could walk out of their rooms at any minute. Not Hayley Jade, who would be asleep for another hour at least, but there was a club full of other men and women who could see us like this.

But in the moment, I didn't care.

I'd waited so long for Hayden to touch me.

The memory of him and whatever this was between us was all that had kept me going for years, even when I'd thought him dead. It was him I'd see in the darkness. Him I'd thought of when everything around me felt lost. His touch I'd craved when Josiah's cruel fingers had hurt me.

I covered his hand with mine, pressing it deep between my legs, giving him all the permission he sought, even if I was too much of a little mouse to voice how badly I wanted him.

His fingers sank between my folds.

We both groaned.

"So fucking wet. Damn it, Kara." He twisted us, pressing my back into the bar and crowding me in. He drew his free hand down the back of my leg, lifting it up off the floor and wrapping it around his waist.

My eyes closed at the gentle rhythm he worked my core with. In and out, alternating between strokes of my clit.

I let go of him and leaned my elbows back on the countertop. My head fell back, breasts pointed toward the ceiling while he drove my body closer and closer to the orgasm I so desperately wanted from him.

"You're so beautiful." He leaned over me. "Fuck, I

wish you were naked right now. I want to do this slow and sweet, drive you mad until you beg me to let you come."

"I can't wait," I moaned softly, hips rolling to meet each thrust of his fingers. I wanted more too. The idea of him having me naked on the bar was intoxicating. A thrill of forbidden lust shot through me at the very thought.

"I know, sweetheart. I got you. You're nearly there." He pressed against my clit, fingering me until every slide of his fingers produced a moan.

The budding swirl of an orgasm twisted through my lower belly, spiraling down to the place his fingers filled me.

Behind Hayden's back, a door opened.

I jerked my head up, eyes flying open, gaze colliding into Hawk's.

I froze.

Hayden glanced over his shoulder, saw who it was, and turned back to me without hesitation. "Come for me, Kara. You're drowning my hand. I'm not stopping until you're done."

I shook my head desperately, trying to fight the delicious grips of the orgasm digging in tight when Hayden refused to stop. The base of his hand hit my clit every time his fingers filled me, but I couldn't stop staring at Hawk, frozen to the spot, watching me let another man touch me.

Apologies sat hot on my tongue, begging for me to let them loose. My upbringing screamed obscenities in my head about what a slut and whore I was, and that only men could have multiple partners.

That the pleasure inside me was sinful.

Not mine to receive.

And yet Hayden was so hell-bent on giving it to me, I couldn't stand it.

"Hawk." I needed something from him. Anything.

His permission to feel the way I did.

His hand went to the bulge in his sweatpants. He swore beneath his breath, eyes burning as he watched Hayden push me closer and closer to the edge. Hawk's fingers strangled his erection.

"You heard what he said, Little Mouse," he bit out through clenched teeth. "Come for him."

Hayden pushed a third finger up inside me, and I splintered apart, throwing an arm over my mouth so my cries of pleasure wouldn't wake the rest of the clubhouse. I panted through the shock waves of ecstasy that rippled from the place he'd touched me, the orgasm wiping out any doubt or confusion and leaving only pleasure and desire in its wake.

Hayden slowed his movements, letting me coast down the other side of the orgasm and bask in the afterglow.

He kissed me softly, his lips finding mine until the kisses turned hungrier, deeper, that connection between us so magnetic it was impossible to ignore.

I didn't feel complete when he wasn't here. When I wasn't touching him.

My heart swelled with a desire to never let him go.

And yet I had to.

He pulled away all too soon, well before I was ready.

But when he did, Hawk was gone.

16

GRAYSON

Lying out on the couch like a potato, I stared at my phone, trying to find the guts to pick it up and call Kara. I had a good reason to. She'd asked me to make an appointment to talk about Hayley Jade.

The thought had me so nervous it was as if I'd never spoken to a woman in my life.

I'd seen her at work a few times now and had tried to be friendly and as nonthreatening as possible, especially because Hawk was never far away, and I was still pretty sure I hadn't completely won him over. The man had a mean right hook, and I didn't fancy another fist to the eye.

But I was worried if I called her, I'd get to know her better, and then I'd fall in love with her because I was a ridiculous sap like that and a sucker for curvy women with big brown eyes.

That's how it had been with my wife. But the difference was we'd both been head over heels for each other from the first moment we'd met.

Kara already had two men falling at her feet. She didn't need me throwing my hat in the ring just because I was in love with the idea of being in love. If she needed anything, she needed a friend.

I could be that for her. Even if it killed me.

"Just pick up the phone and make the call, Gray. You big pansy-ass chicken," I taunted myself. "You can talk to beautiful women. You are not incapable of being friends with one."

The pep talk didn't help much. I had thoroughly convinced myself I'd come on too strong and she'd think me a creepy weirdo with a fetish for glove balloons.

Why the hell had I made her so many of those? She wasn't a child.

I flipped over onto my stomach and groaned out my embarrassed frustrations into a couch cushion.

An incoming text buzzed, but when I lifted my head from the well of embarrassment I'd created for myself, my phone didn't show any received texts. "Weird," I muttered, only to notice my burner lit up on the bookshelf I'd last left it on.

That couldn't be good.

Someone had broken our code.

We never texted. It was only ever a call that rang three times, signaling a meeting had been called. Worry plaguing every step, I crossed the living room and picked up the burner, using the Face ID to unlock it.

WHIP:

Sorry for the text. I know it's against the rules, but calling would have triggered a meeting, and I didn't want the others to know about this yet. I found a body last night.

I stared at the message, a trickling sense of dread running down my spine.

Another text came in.

WHIP:

A dead one. Not sure if that needed to be spelled out or not.

Despite myself and the situation, I choked on a laugh and texted back.

GRAY:

Figured as much. But this isn't the first dead body you've seen. What makes this one special?

WHIP:

Vic is mid-twenties. Curvy. Brunette.

My blood ran cold.

GRAY:

Strangled?

WHIP:

Wouldn't be texting you if she'd just jumped off a bridge now, would I?

Kara.
Fucking hell.

I snatched up my personal phone from the coffee table and stabbed at the screen until the number I'd saved from Kara's hospital records appeared.

I'd spent days procrastinating on calling her, trying to plan out every word in my head so I would sound charming and sweet and caring. Only to desperately shout her name the second the call connected. "Kara!"

There was a pause on the other end. "Who is this, please?"

I breathed a sigh of relief, recognizing her gentle voice instantly. I sank back down onto the couch.

"Josiah?" she whispered.

I blinked. "Oh, holy shit. No. Kara, I'm so sorry. It's me. I mean. Not me. Grayson, me. Dr. Frederick Grayson. Do you remember me?"

I closed my eyes and slapped myself in the forehead for the babble of nonsense words that were nothing like what I'd planned in my head.

Kara laughed, her voice filled with relief. "Of course I remember you, Dr. Frederick Grayson. We spent half the week together, remember?"

Of course I remembered. I silently banged my skull into a cushion, wishing the floor would just swallow me up whole. There was no way I was going to be able to explain my ridiculous behavior, unless I told her the truth.

She probably needed to hear it anyway.

I flipped onto my back and stared at the ceiling, feeling awful for being glad it was some other curvy brunette who Whip had found dead and not the one on the other end of the phone line. "I'm sorry," I offered. "I was just told of another murder, and for a second..."

I didn't want to scare her by telling her I was so sure there was a serial killer out there who had her in his sights.

Kara's laughter died away. "For a second you thought it was me."

"Yes," I agreed. "I'm really glad it's not."

She sighed heavily. "I am too. Though that poor woman..."

I didn't want to think about the marks on her body. The bruising that would be around her neck from someone putting a cord around it and pulling it so tight she couldn't breathe.

Kara's voice was small. "Does she have a sister too? That's the mark of this killer, you believe, don't you? He kills sisters?"

I nodded even though she couldn't see me. "I don't know yet. It will probably take some time to identify the body. But the rest...the strangulation, the hair color, the body type...they all fit. I know it probably freaks you out to think you could be a target..."

She breathed softly down the line. "I don't even know if it does, you know? I'm already my husband's target. I have to look over my shoulder every day for him. The worst part is the reach he has. He's made me question everybody and everything. I thought I'd recognize his followers, but after what happened, I realize his reach goes beyond anything I'd ever dreamed of."

"Do you still think it was your husband and his people who killed your sister?"

"I do," she said, voice sure but sad.

I shoved another cushion behind my head, trying to

get comfortable. "I still think it's my guy. Do we have any other suspects?"

"The police are still looking at Kyle. He's the guy we traveled here with, who disappeared the same night of my sister's death."

I didn't like the grief that settled into her tone. I wracked my brain for something to say that would distract her. "We could put all their names in a hat and draw one out? Put this to bed once and for all?"

She let out a tiny laugh. "If only it were that simple, huh?"

It was so far from that simple it was laughable. Josiah and his people were all out in plain sight, which was what had me doubting Alice's death was at their hands. Gut instinct told me they wouldn't have made an attempt on Kara's life so soon after, knowing the police were watching them.

The kid they'd been traveling with seemed like an obvious choice, especially because he'd been conveniently missing ever since.

The only problem with all of that was it only lent further weight to my theory.

Trigger would have had no qualms in offing a scrawny teenager before wrapping a cord around a pretty young thing's neck.

Just like I was sure he'd done to my wife and her sister years before.

The day before their deaths had been the last time I'd seen him. He'd been MIA ever since, forever an empty seat at our group meetings.

Anger boiled deep inside me, and I fought to keep it under control, even though there was nobody here to see it. Every time my burner phone rang, I hoped and prayed the meeting that followed would be the one Trigger finally returned for.

So I could kill him with my own two hands for everything he'd taken from me.

For everything he'd taken from Kara.

I forced my fingers to unclench the phone, rubbing away the ache that sprang up inside me whenever I thought about the man who'd murdered my family. "We should talk about therapy," I suggested, trying to force some sort of professional tone, even though my stomach twisted into painful knots just thinking about Kara being next on Trigger's list.

"Oh." Kara sounded surprised, like she'd forgotten I hadn't just called to discuss possible suspects in her sister's murder case and morbidly talk about the dead body my buddy had found.

Not that Whip was my buddy. Whip had no buddies.

Neither did I, for that matter. No true ones I'd actually been able to spill my secrets to.

Except Kara. She was the only person I'd ever told about my wife. Or about the cages.

I put my phone on speaker and switched to the calendar app, scrolling through my schedule. "Do you want to bring her in this week? I'm really booked up, but I could do an early session before school or a late one after it?"

Kara paused. "Is the hospital the only place you can do them? The last time we took her there, she saw Hawk punch you in the face... That's obviously not your fault, but we just have her settled into a new routine, and I'm so reluctant to do anything to upset it. She's still not talking at all, and I just wonder if maybe a less sterile environment might be more beneficial to getting her to open up."

I nodded, scribbling a note about Kara's concerns on a piece of scrap paper I found on the kitchen counter so I could transfer it to Hayley Jade's file later. "I do house calls all the time. Many people feel more comfortable talking in familiar surroundings. What's your address?" I hadn't paid it any attention when I'd grabbed her number from the hospital paperwork.

She paused. "I...um, I don't know if that's a good idea either. I was thinking maybe a park or something..."

I frowned. "I think her home really would be better. If you're worried about me judging your place, please don't. I would never." I truly meant it. I'd lived in some shitholes in my time. Nothing fazed me.

"We're living in an MC clubhouse in the middle of the woods with at least a dozen bikers plus a couple of club women."

I stiffened, my tongue freezing up at the thought of her at one of those places. I knew how they worked. Especially when it came to women. I didn't know why I'd never considered Kara could be living with Hawk, and that if she was, they could be living at a biker clubhouse. The thought made me physically ill.

"Your silence sounds a little like judgment," she said quietly.

"No," I said in a rush, though it wasn't quite the truth. "Just took me by surprise. I'll be there. Five thirty, Friday?"

"That would be great. Thank you."

"Bye, Kara." I ended the call and turned on the TV fast, forcing myself to pay attention to the screen. I'd been five or six the last time I'd been inside the walls of an MC compound, and I had nothing but bad memories of the things that had happened there.

I'd never wanted to step foot back inside one.

But apparently, the time for hiding was gone. And Hayley Jade wasn't the only one who was going to have to face her past.

17

HAYDEN

For once, Sinners wasn't filled with the sounds of nail guns and table saws. There was no sawdust flying all over the place for me to clean up for the thousandth time. There were none of Luca's workmen wandering around, erecting walls or installing appliances. All of that was done, and the only thing left to do before opening night was for me to finalize and print the menu.

Which was proving the hardest part of the entire thing.

Nothing I made seemed good enough. I'd gone through every dish I'd ever practiced after hours in Simon's shitty diner kitchen, and at the time, they'd looked and tasted amazing. I'd been so damn proud of them I'd flaunted them all over my Instagram.

Only now, when I made them again in this state-of-the-art kitchen with all the bells and whistles, they didn't seem enough. *I* wasn't enough and I was in way over my head. Luca was expecting world-class quality from a dumbass street thug from Saint View.

We were days away from opening, and I was going to expose myself for the fraud I was.

I'd covered the kitchen in an array of ingredients I couldn't figure out how to bring together in an edible meal. I'd been leaving the clubhouse at the ass crack of dawn each morning and getting home near midnight, because every waking moment had to be dedicated to getting the food right.

Though it seemed that no matter what I did, I wasn't satisfied.

From the front of the restaurant, someone knocked on the door I'd locked after letting myself in earlier. I probably should have been annoyed by the interruption, but I dropped the tasteless sauce I'd been trying to rescue in the sink. Any excuse to walk away from the mess I'd made and the crushing pressure of knowing I wasn't cut out for this.

Kara waved at me from the street side of the glass door, Hawk a few steps behind her, scowling at the sign with my name on it.

I opened up quickly, gaze devouring her like the oasis in the storm she was. Something inside me relaxed just at the sight of her, and when she smiled warmly and squeezed my arm, it was like dark skies had parted to let her sunshine through, and all of it was focused on me.

I slid a hand along the side of her face and to the back of her neck, leaning in to kiss her cheek. "What are you doing here?"

She shrugged happily. "Day off from the hospital. We

just took Hayley Jade to school. I asked Hawk to bring me over so I could see where you've been spending your time."

I eyed him warily, unsure why he'd do anything for me, especially after the display I'd put on with Kara in the clubhouse earlier in the week. "And he agreed?"

Hawk stared at me. "He agreed to give Kara what she wanted. Because that's the only thing he cares about. She wanted to come here. So he brought her."

I raised an eyebrow. "And does he always talk about himself in the third person?"

He flipped me the bird. "Fuck off. Can I trust you to take care of her for a few hours? I've got something I need to do."

It was on the tip of my tongue to say something smart, but a part of me also realized that though he was asking casually, the request was anything but.

Hawk was in love with Kara. It was obvious to anyone who paid attention to the way he cared for her. Him leaving her safety to me was actually putting a hell of a lot of faith and trust in me. So I didn't give him shit.

I nodded. "Go. I've got her."

He stared at me, and whatever he was searching for in my expression he must have found, because he leaned in, kissing Kara's cheek gently. "I won't be long. A couple of hours max. Call me if he's a prick and you want me to come kick the shit out of him."

She laughed, but I knew he actually wasn't joking.

Kara pushed him out the door. "Go. We'll be fine. See you this afternoon."

I reached around her to lock the door.

She smiled up at me. "I hope this is okay? Just dropping in like this."

I grinned at her. "Are you kidding? You saved me from chopping onions. Plus, I want you to see this place."

Despite the fact I'd had myself convinced just minutes earlier that I was ruining the entire thing, the idea of showing Kara around filled me with pride. I hadn't seen Luca since he'd shown up at my apartment, and other than some texts with plans for opening night, he'd left me to run the place by myself. It was easy to forget he had anything to do with it, and I could pretend it was all mine.

That probably wasn't helping with the pressure, but it did alleviate the guilt sitting heavy on my heart because I'd gotten back into bed with the devil.

Fuck him. I wasn't going to let him ruin this for me. I wasn't going to let my own messed-up head and self-doubt ruin it either.

"You want the grand tour?" I went to the bar and washed my hands in the sink and pulled off my apron.

She followed me, eyes all big for what we'd created inside four walls. "It's amazing. Everything here is so beautiful."

Sinners had almost been fully transformed from a worksite to the upmarket restaurant of my dreams. It was dark and moody, deeply sexy from the dark wood floors, black walls, and red barstools. Black tablecloths covered small, intimate tables.

This wasn't the sort of place you came with a group of friends, celebrating birthdays. Or with your parents when they were in from out of town. This was the sort of restaurant you came to with someone you wanted to get naked with.

We'd provided a place for that just feet away, in the back where my very own little den of iniquity had been erected.

No pun intended.

I pointed around the space. "The maître d' will be positioned just over there by the door, and he'll escort couples to their tables. We've hired a bartender to make signature cocktails and to serve champagne and top-shelf liquor."

She studied some of the bottles on the shelves, ready for drinks to be poured from. "These all look very expensive."

"They are. You want one?"

She squinted at me. "It's not even lunchtime."

"Fair point." I grinned at her. "Come see the rest of the place."

I threaded my fingers through hers, the desire to touch her too strong to be ignored. She followed me through swinging doors that separated the eating area from the kitchen. I bypassed it, embarrassed of the mess I'd made. "Kitchen," I said with a jerk of my head, quickly towing her past.

She dragged on my hand. "Wait, I want to see it."

"Let me show you what's through here first." I pushed through a second set of doors. This set heavier and more elaborate than the first. They were heavy wood, with "Sinners Welcome" carved out of the middle.

Kara frowned at it as I led her through into the darkness beyond. I fumbled on the wall for the light switch, finding it and being careful to only switch on the low lights. The ones we'd use when the club was in session, rather than the bright fluorescent overhead lights that would come on when it was time to leave and for the cleaners to come in.

Kara frowned, taking it all in. Her brow furrowed. "What is this?"

The space had been one big room when Luca bought it. But now walls had gone up everywhere, turning the space into a maze of sorts, with dozens of alcoves for people to indulge in all sorts of different sexual kinks.

"Sex club," I filled her in. "Hawk didn't tell you?"

Her mouth dropped open. "You mean...a club where people..."

She was so cute when she blushed.

"Have sex?" I leaned on a wall. "Yeah. Have your dinner out in front. Dessert out in back." I cocked my head, studying her. "You ever been to one before?"

Her head snapped around so she could transfer her wide-eyed stare to me. "Of course not! Why would you think that?"

I shrugged. "Bliss owns one, you know? Psychos. Not a huge jump to think you might have checked it out. Especially since..."

She frowned at me. "Especially since what?"

I grinned at her. "Especially since you seem to enjoy public sex."

Her mouth dropped open. "I do not!"

I stepped in closer to her. "No?" I lowered my head. "Kara, I had three fingers buried in your pussy right in the middle of the Slayers' compound while Hawk watched. I remember how wet you were. You can't tell me you weren't getting off on him watching."

Pink stained her cheeks, and I gave her an out before she could self-combust. "Psychos is already doing the big open room thing, where everyone can see everyone, cages for performers, yadda yadda. We wanted this to be less of a performance, more of an experience." I pointed at the three different openings to the maze. "So pick a path. Which one do you want to try?"

"Where do they all lead? There's no signage."

I winked at her. "That's kind of the point. It's a surprise."

She indicated to the middle path. "That one."

My dick stirred at the thought of what lay beyond the walls right in front of us. "Good choice."

I led her in the direction she'd chosen.

The same black-and-red theme had been carried through, black padded bed-sized benches scattered throughout the maze for people to have sex on. "Each path starts out pretty chill. They all have these beds for anything people want to do on them." I kept the tone light because I didn't want to scare her, even though all I could think about was laying her out on one of them. "We'll have lube and condoms easily accessible, as well as security in case anyone gets out of hand."

She glanced at me warily as we passed a bed with tie-downs hanging from the sides. "That's very...responsible of you."

I chuckled, leading her deeper through the wide-walled maze.

She stared at holes in the wall. "What are those?"

"Glory holes." When she looked confused, I elaborated. "For men to stick their dicks into and for the people on the other side to reciprocate in whatever way they want. Whether that be with their mouth or some other body part."

She stopped and stared at the holes, like a twelve-inch cock might suddenly appear through one of them. "People just...suck..."

"Or fuck. Depends."

"But they wouldn't even be able to see the person on the other side. What if another man..."

I raised an eyebrow at her. "What if another man gets down on his knees on the other side? Or offers up his asshole?"

Her mouth dropped open. "People...people do that?"

"They do. They will. That's part of the appeal of a glory hole. You don't know what you're going to get. You might get a mouth. A pussy. An ass. But you'll never know who."

"I can't see how anyone would find that a turn-on."

"Not your kink then, sweetheart. Let's go find one that is."

To my surprise, she didn't protest.

"Sex swing," I pointed out, passing one. "Any strong positive or negative feelings about that?"

She shook her head quickly.

"Moving on then." It was strange to be so casually wandering around what would very soon be filled with naked bodies in various stages of sex. But I couldn't deny that when some of these things had been being installed, I thought about bringing Kara here. I wasn't sure she ever would, but even if she didn't, this walk-through would give me an idea of what she was comfortable with.

"Bondage wall." I ran a hand along a wall that had

various tie-downs and restraints attached so multiple people could be restrained at once.

She paused, her breathing a little faster.

"There's no shame in wanting to try something."

"I don't."

She so did. But we weren't there yet. And I'd pushed her buttons about as far as I thought I safely could. There was a vague panic in her eyes I didn't like.

"Hey." I pulled her into my arms and kissed her softly.

She melted, kissing me back. "This isn't what I was expecting when I came here," she whispered. "I'm not sure how I feel about you working here while beautiful women are..." She eyed the bondage wall. "Tied up, just waiting for you to take them in any hole."

I chuckled. "You jealous?"

She shook her head. "Jealousy is a sin."

"Don't know if you noticed, but we're in a club called Sinners. No one is judging your sins here, Kara."

"I don't want other women touching you," she admitted. "I know that's hypocritical of me when Hawk..."

I kissed her again. "No other women are touching me. Not here. Not outside these walls. Nowhere. You're the only woman I want to touch. You're the only woman I've wanted to touch ever since I met you."

"I can't ask you to do that for me."

"You didn't. I haven't been with anyone since I met you. It's always been you I wanted."

"What about Hawk?"

I laughed. "You think I want Hawk?"

The corner of her mouth lifted. "Do you?"

"You've been hanging out with that shrink friend of yours too much, answering questions with questions," I grumbled. But then I looked at her and asked another question of my own. "Do you like the idea of me wanting Hawk?"

She let out a breath and turned away without answering the question. "You still need to show me the kitchen."

I let her go, following her out of the maze, even though I'd barely showed her a quarter of it. I flicked off the lights and resumed the tour. "Bathrooms. They're pretty nice. There's showers in there and fluffy towels and robes. And this is the kitchen. Sorry about the mess."

She didn't pay the spread of ingredients any mind though. Just wandered around the space, poking at all the appliances and running a finger along the countertops. "This is amazing," she breathed. "I would have killed for a kitchen like this back at…" She shrugged, clearly not wanting to bring up the cult she'd been living in for the past five years.

I could barely think about her being held there against her will, and the guilt over doing nothing to help her was eating me alive. "I thought you were happy there. We thought you'd gone home to be with your family. I would have come if I'd known."

She smiled at me and stroked a hand down my face. "I didn't want anyone to know. I'm the only person who needs to feel any guilt over what happened to me." She peered past me to the walk-in storage pantry where we kept all the food. Her eyes widened. "What is that?"

I grinned. "Best part of the whole kitchen. It's like my own mini supermarket." I walked in, hefting up a huge bag of flour I'd left right in the middle. "You can come in." I shifted the heavy weight in my arms and tried to maneuver it onto a shelf, so it was out of the way. "Just be careful not to close the door because the lock—"

The door swung shut behind Kara.

I grimaced. "Wasn't installed properly and we'll be locked in."

18

KARA

*P*anic trickled in slowly, a tiny stream of adrenaline that had me spinning around in the small room and grabbing for the handle that did nothing when I yanked on it.

The trickle quickly became a flood, my chest constricting until I couldn't breathe.

Hayden's arms came around me. "Hey. It's okay."

Except it wasn't. It wasn't at all. My throat felt thick. "I can't breathe."

He tightened his grip on me, lowering his face so his gaze was locked on mine. "You can. You were breathing a second ago before that door locked. The air hasn't changed, and it won't. This room isn't airtight. I already locked myself in here the other day and I was just fine."

But his calm words did little to ease the racing in my heart.

"Women need to be reborn when they have sinned. They need to prove their worth. Prove that the evil can be leached from their souls," I mumbled, fighting the urge to claw at my skin.

Hayden's face paled, understanding dawning in his expression.

I was back in that box.

Back beneath the dirt.

Gasping for air that had run out too fast.

Trembles wracked my body. Darkness surrounded me, blacking out the light, the food on the shelves, Hayden.

All I could smell was dirt.

"Women need to be reborn when they have sinned. They need to prove their worth. Prove that the evil can be leached from their souls," I repeated, Josiah's words burned into my memory, his words scalding my tongue, and yet I couldn't stop myself from saying them over and over.

Hayden's fingers gripped my arms. "Kara!"

It was my fault. The Lord was punishing me for my disobedience.

He always punished me.

"Kara!"

Hayden shook me hard enough, and I opened my eyes.

The pure terror in his shocked me.

"You aren't in that box," he insisted. "You're here. In the kitchen at my restaurant with me. We're locked in but we have enough air. We have food and water, and Hawk will be back soon to let us out."

"I'm going to die," I whispered, a sob building up my throat.

But Hayden's expression was fierce. "Not today. Not in

here. Not on my watch. Look around. Tell me what you see."

I twisted to one side, forcing my eyes to focus on what was in front of my face instead of what was in my head. "Salt. Pepper. Oil."

"Bread," he continued for me. "Honey. Soy sauce."

I tracked down those items, nodding when I spotted them on the shelves. "Yeast. Vanilla extract. Flour." I gawked at the size of the bags. "Why on earth do you need that much flour?"

Hayden laughed, his relief evident as he leaned back on the door and then slid down it to the floor, taking me with him. "I don't know. I got overexcited with ordering last week and now I have enough flour to last a year." He put his arm around my shoulders. "Are you okay?"

I went to say I was, an apology for my embarrassing behavior on my lips. But I was so sick of apologizing for everything I did. What had happened to me wasn't my fault, and I couldn't control how my body reacted when reminded of it. "No," I whispered. "I'm not."

Hayden pressed his lips to the top of my head. "What can I do? I want to help but I don't know how."

I leaned my head on his shoulder, not sure how to answer him either. Until something popped into my head, something that almost had me smiling, despite the situation. "Tell me more about how you like Hawk."

Hayden groaned. "You're really fixated on that, aren't you?"

"It's that or I panic about not being able to breathe." I hid a smile. "It's coming back. You better tell me quick."

"How about I tell you how much I like you instead?" He put two fingers beneath my chin and twisted my face up. "I don't want to talk about Hawk when I could be kissing you."

He lowered his mouth to mine, and all thoughts of Hawk and being locked in a tiny room evaporated from my brain.

All that existed was me and Hayden. My brain narrowed down to the places our bodies connected. Hands. Mouths. Fingers. Tongues. He kissed me until my heart was racing and my breathing was too quick, not because of being trapped, but because of how he wanted me.

We kissed until Josiah's words floated away, and until the kisses became urgent, desperate, our moans of pleasure echoing around the room instead of my screams of panic.

"You're killing me," Hayden murmured over my mouth. "Fucking hell, Kara. I can't keep kissing you like this."

He pulled away, breathing hard, but I dragged him back, demanding his lips this time, instead of just accepting what he wanted to give. I needed him. I needed everything he made me feel and everything he made me forget. I climbed into his lap, straddling his legs and wrapping my arms around his neck, demanding his kisses like they were air I needed to breathe.

His hands traced up my back, skating along my spine and drawing me closer. His tongue found its way into my mouth, and I moaned into him, my core igniting at being pressed against the very noticeable ridge in his black work pants.

"I've thought about kissing you like this so many

times," he whispered. "You aren't real. I had myself convinced I made you up."

I shook my head. "You didn't. I've thought about kissing you too." So many times. I'd lain in bed awake at night for years, believing he lived only in my head, but imagining him breaking down the gates of Ethereal Eden and whisking me away into the night like I was a damsel and he was a knight.

I'd had to save myself. A fact I'd begun to take pride in.

It didn't mean I didn't want a fairy-tale ending with the prince though.

Or princes, if I let myself think of Hawk. Though he would have hated being thought of like that. No good for his street cred.

Hayden drew back slowly, his unfocused gaze becoming clearer. "I need to tell you something."

I waited.

His eyes smoldered in the dim light of the pantry. "I've thought about doing a lot more than just kissing you, Kara."

My breath faltered. Suddenly I was that young woman, lying on her bed, broken by a man who should have loved her but had used and abused her until her soul wept for someone she barely knew. A man she'd thought was dead. Pining for a ghost had still been better than her reality.

I was stronger now, Hawk had built me up until I wasn't just that shell of a woman who'd arrived at the Slayers' compound, fleeing from danger.

But that broken woman inside me who had longed

for Hayden, clung to him as the only safe place she'd ever known, was dying to know what he wanted from her.

And already desperate to give it to him.

"I want you naked," he murmured. "I want to watch you take your clothes off for me."

My breath hitched. It wasn't a demand, the sort Hawk would have made of me. It was gentler. One I could have refused if I'd wanted to.

I didn't want to. "Then tell me to do it."

He groaned, searching my face and seeing clearly what I needed from him. "You're submissive."

I frowned. "I don't know what that means." Not in this context anyway.

Hayden watched me carefully. "You like being told what to do. At least in bed. It turns you on."

Did it? I was just so used to taking orders. Josiah's had certainly never turned me on. I shuddered at the thought of presenting myself to him, face down on the bed so he wouldn't have to look at my face.

But Hawk had made demands of my body that had me tingling from head to toe with just a whisp of memory.

And Hayden's gaze offered more of the same.

I nodded. Letting him know he was right.

He groaned. "Stand up, Kara. Take your clothes off for me. I want to see every inch of you."

I widened my eyes at him. "Here?"

He kissed me deeply, then smiled against my lips. "Here. So every time I come in afterward, I'll remember you standing here, so fucking sweet and naked, waiting for me to touch you."

His lips traveled to my neck, kissing the sensitive spot beneath my ear. "Take your clothes off for me, Kara."

A tremble of anticipation rolled through me as I pushed myself off his lap, leaving his erection to strain against his pants. I focused on it when doubts crept into my head about whether he'd find my body as attractive as Hawk did.

Or as repulsive as Josiah had.

I undid the row of tiny cardigan buttons that ran between my breasts. I only wore a bra beneath, and it wasn't a pretty one, because I didn't own anything sexy.

Josiah had been of the opinion that lingerie attracted the Devil.

But in that moment, I desperately wished for something more attractive. "I'm sorry." My lack of confidence reared its ugly head. "I'm not pretty."

*E*ver so slowly, Hayden moved his hand to the bulge in his pants. He flicked the button on his fly and lowered the zipper.

"Look what you do to me," he whispered. "I'm so fucking hard over how goddamn sexy you are, Kara. Don't ever tell me you aren't pretty again."

His hand slipped inside his underwear, and he hissed, wrapping his fingers around his shaft and pulling it out.

I stared at the thick head of his erection, the rest of him engulfed in his hand. I'd thought Hawk big. His dick more than any I'd seen before him. But Hayden's was bigger again. Probably the same length but thick enough my legs trembled at the thought of how he'd stretch me if he were inside me.

I clamped my thighs together, needing something there to ease the throbbing need building inside me. I stared down at the beautiful man sitting at my feet, well aware he wasn't in my league. "My clothes..." I protested. "My underwear—"

"Will all look best on the floor." He pushed to his feet and took off my cardigan, dropping it by the door. He reached behind me, undoing the wide, unattractive backstrap on my bra and freeing my heavy breasts.

They hung lower than I thought was nice, but if Hayden noticed, his gaze didn't give it away. He just continued undressing me, undoing the zipper at my hip and letting my skirt fall to join the rest of my clothes.

It wasn't cold, but I shivered at being naked for him, his erection straining toward me, but him otherwise dressed. I eyed him, lowering his pants and underwear so I could get a better look.

"Do I scare you?" he asked softly.

I glanced up at him. "You're big. I don't know if I can take you."

He chuckled. "That wasn't what I meant." He placed a kiss on my shoulder. "I have no doubt in my mind you'll take my cock, Kara. I'll get you so wet I'll slide in without a second of resistance from your sweet pussy. But I can only get your body there if you aren't scared of me."

I focused on the buttons of his shirt, undoing them one after the other to reveal the golden skin beneath. "I'm not scared of you." I drew the shirt off his shoulders. He'd kicked off his shoes and socks while I'd been working on his top half.

For a second, both of us just drank the other in. For the first time, there were no barriers between us. His body was all hard lines of muscle with dustings of golden hair across his chest that darkened as it trailed down his abs and met with the patch of hair at his base.

His gaze ran over me in a similar way, trailing across every curve as if committing it to memory, lingering on my breasts and hips and the junction of my thighs. But then he forced his gaze to meet my own. "I didn't protect you when I should have. I kept you against your will. I'm as bad as—"

I silenced him with fingers to his mouth, my voice turning fierce because I knew exactly what he was going to say, and none of it was true. "Don't ever say you're anything like them. Caleb and Josiah and Luca...you're *nothing* like them, you hear me? Not a thing. You've never hurt me, and I know you never will. You're the reason Hayley Jade is even alive. We both would have died in that house if it hadn't been for you. Don't you know you're my hero? One day, you'll be hers too."

He slowly shook his head. "I don't deserve that."

I wanted to argue. Wanted to wipe away the disgust he held for himself for the mistakes he'd made in the past. Except I knew he had to fight that battle on his own. It wasn't one my words could forgive.

He had to find forgiveness in himself. I already had, from the moment he'd placed my daughter in my arms.

I kissed his lips. "Make it up to me then. Right now. Here, in this room where it's just you and me. Make it up to me now and then we never talk about it again."

He trailed a finger down my chest then pressed his hand over my heart, rubbing at the spot, his head low. "I wish it were that easy."

I clasped his hand, moving it lower to my breast. "It

can be."

He cupped me there, squeezing my nipple between his fingers.

A jolt of pleasure erupted at his touch, and I let out a moan to encourage him, to show him I liked what he was doing.

He smiled, then leaned over, plucking a bottle of honey from the shelf beside me. He uncapped it and squeezed a dollop over my skin.

It was cold and sticky, but in the next second it was followed up with the warmth of his mouth, licking me clean. My nipples went hard, aching for more.

"Lie on the floor," he whispered. "I want to put this all over your body."

Heat flared inside me, reminding me I did indeed like when he told me what to do. It took away the awkwardness I felt at being less experienced. It let my brain shut off for just a while, which was a blessed relief considering it didn't stop whirling at a million miles a minute every other hour of the day.

I lay out on a nest made of our discarded clothing, not caring the cold floor seeped through in a couple of places. The heat building inside me at the thought of him licking honey off my body was hot enough to keep me warm.

He balled up his shirt and put it behind my head, then squeezed the bottle, covering my breasts in sticky liquid, pooling it in my belly button.

"Spread your legs, Kara."

Trembling, I widened my thighs, exposing my glistening pussy to him, already wet just from watching him.

Cold honey hit me there, and I cried out in pleasure.

"So fucking sweet," he growled. "I almost wish I hadn't put it anywhere else." He knelt between my legs, bracing himself over me to lick my breasts. He suckled my nipples until they were pink and swollen and clean. Then he trailed his tongue along the soft rolls of my stomach, lapping up the trail of golden liquid.

I laughed when his tongue swirled across my belly button, tickling my skin, but the laughter quickly turned to moans when he kissed and sucked and licked his way lower, over the uneven skin and stretchmarks that had formed when I was pregnant.

His fingers traced the now silver lines reverently, and he gazed up at me. "These were red before."

I nodded. They'd been red and angry and even sore sometimes, when my belly had been swollen tight with the baby growing inside me. But they'd settled over the years. They'd healed to be barely noticeable unless you touched me there, or you were all up close and personal with them like Hayden was right now.

"This is what makes you sexy," he whispered, kissing my belly. "This is what turns me on. Knowing that even after everything you went through, you were strong enough to heal." He kissed my mound. "That's hot as fuck to me, Kara."

His tongue pressed between the lips of my pussy, licking the honey from my core along with a generous dose of my arousal. He didn't stop. He sucked and licked me, cleaning off every trace of honey and whispering sweet words about how beautiful I was in between.

This might have been rough and dirty, on the floor of a pantry, but even if I'd been on a bed somewhere with thousand-thread-count sheets, I wouldn't have felt more like a queen.

He licked me until my thighs trembled with the force of an impending orgasm. He had to be uncomfortable in the tight space, but if he was, he made no complaint, and I forgot all about how small the space was when he slid his fingers inside me, hooking them to stroke the spot that never failed to get me wet.

The orgasm built quickly, fueled by his praises that I couldn't get enough of and the talented way he knew exactly how to put his mouth on me. It shook my core until I clenched down around his fingers and grasped the back of his head, holding him there where I needed him, while I moaned his name as loud as I wanted because there was no one outside to hear it.

He finally lifted his head, with lips sticky and glistening with honey or my arousal, I didn't know which. His fingers were coated in it too, and he wiped them off on his erection. I moaned when he gathered more from my sensitive slit so he was coated in my juices.

Widening my legs, I braced for the thick spear of his erection entering me.

He shook his head, pumping his shaft. "You aren't ready."

"I am," I insisted.

But he wasn't having it. He stared at the opening between my legs, and then at my breasts, his grip on his cock quickening with every stroke. "I want to come on you," he murmured, eyes hot. "Hawk filled your pussy. I want me everywhere else."

My gaze flared, wondering if everywhere else meant my mouth and my breasts and stomach.

Or if it also included my ass.

I trembled, wanting him there but knowing if he didn't think my pussy could take him, then anywhere else would be impossible right now.

Hayden swiped his cock through my folds, not trying to enter me but keeping his shaft well lubricated.

"Hawk has been working my…" I flushed pink. "But I can't… Not yet anyway."

Hayden's dick wept with precum. "Jesus, are you fucking serious? That hadn't even crossed my mind. I just wanted to come on your clit and your tits. But now knowing that…" He groaned. "Fuck, that's so hot. He's not small. If you're working up to taking him…" The look on his face was so full of heat and desire there was no mistaking what he was thinking about.

I flushed, but this time it was with pleasure, liking that he enjoyed what I was doing with Hawk and that he found it as hot as I did.

He brushed his cock over my ass, nothing more than a promise of what could come when I was ready, and then he jerked himself, squeezing his balls with his other hand and made a sticky mess of all the places he'd just licked clean.

19

HAWK

I hit Sinners' doorbell at least four times before I realized nobody was answering it. I stopped the incessant ringing that had really only been to antagonize Chaos. I'd figured he'd come to the door scowling, giving me that look that was so fucking hot it just encouraged further torment. But when me repeatedly playing the too-cheerful doorbell music didn't have the effect of summoning the chef I wanted to badger some more, a kernel of worry lit up inside me.

I peered through the glass, only able to see the front dining area. Everything seemed fine, nothing out of place. But no movement either.

"Kara! Are you and shit for brains in there?" I rattled the doors, but the locks held.

A crash from somewhere deep in the building came, and my worry started up in earnest. "Kara!"

I took a few steps back, contemplating throwing a rock through the front window. But if everything was fine and they'd just stepped out for a smoke or something, Chaos would probably be pretty damn pissed off I'd messed up his window when he was only a few days out from opening the place. It wasn't like Providence was a big town. Getting tradespeople in to fix something in a timely manner wasn't always possible.

Though Luca fucking Guerra probably had connections he could just snap his fingers at. Which only irritated me all the more.

Calling Chaos every name under the sun, I jogged around to the back, finding a rear entrance that only had a simple lock I picked in under thirty seconds.

My old man hadn't taught me much in life, but he'd been a damn good thief, and picking locks had been his specialty.

Of course, that had been a whole lot easier in his day, back when nobody had state-of-the-art security systems like they did these days in Providence.

I half expected one such alarm to start blaring, but all I found was a security door that had been left open. Chaos's truck was still in the parking lot, so unless they'd gone for some sort of romantic stroll around town, they had to be here somewhere.

The thought of them walking around holding hands had me wanting to murder someone.

Only more so when I followed the hallway straight into a dead end...with a motherfucking dildo wall.

I cocked my head, staring at the array of knee-to-waist-height dildos attached to the drywall. "What sort of porno Narnia did I just walk into?" I glanced back over my shoulder just to check I could still see the door that led to the parking lot. Not having anywhere else to go, I went back there and tried the hallway that led in the opposite direction.

My eyes widened as I wandered the dark hallways filled with sex toys and leather benches and—I stared at the huge spa. "Oh, ew. You kinky fucking asshole. You gonna let people fuck in that thing and have their spoof just floating around in it for anyone to get all coated in? Do you have any idea how many germs these things hold in the first place? Let alone when you let people do... that." I gagged, skin crawling at how damn unhygienic a spa in a sex club would be.

Their chlorine bill was going to be through the roof.

"Sex maze," I muttered, turning around at another dead end, this one fully walled with mirrors so you could fuck and check yourself out at the same time, I supposed. "You built a motherfucking sex maze. Unbelievable." Every corner revealed new setups for various kinks, and by the time I made it out the other side, I was vaguely turned on.

That only pissed me off more.

Psychos was my club. I might not have had a stake in the ownership like Bliss and Nash did, but they were my people, so Psychos was too.

I didn't want to be intrigued by whatever fuckface and Luca Guerra were doing over here.

Cranky I already knew a sex maze was going to draw interest and provide competition to Psychos, I slammed my way through a heavy wooden door and found myself outside the bathrooms, the kitchen through the next doorway and a complete fucking mess.

I peered around at everything sitting on the countertops, meat sweating, just waiting to give someone food poisoning. "What kind of a fucking chef leaves everything sitting out like this and goes strolling around town?" I poked at a steak the size of my head. It was probably a one-hundred-dollar cut of meat that was now warm to the touch and most definitely ruined unless you wanted to be sitting on the shitter all night. "Criminal." I picked it up with two fingers and tossed it into the trash.

"Hawk?"

I paused, head swiveling around the room trying to work out where the voice had come from.

"Uh, yeah?"

The pantry door rattled, and Kara's voice came from the other side. "We're in here! In the pantry!"

I peered at the door that wasn't moving, then took a few long strides to yank down on the handle.

Kara and Hayden were on the other side.

Fully dressed but looking guilty as fuck.

I narrowed my eyes at Kara's messed-up hair and Chaos's swollen lips. "What is this? Seven minutes in Heaven?" I crinkled my nose. "I thought this was supposed to be a nice restaurant? But you've got a kink playground out in back, and the two of you reek of sex. Seven minutes in Heaven, indeed."

Chaos smirked at me as he passed. "Was more like seventy minutes, but who's counting?"

Oh, fuck him.

Kara was less smug. She stepped into me, putting her hands on my chest softly. "We were locked in. The handle is broken on the inside."

I gazed down at her. "So you entertained each other in other ways."

Her eyes were full of unspoken apologies. "Please don't be mad at me."

I sighed. "I'm not." It was the truth.

Because the thought of them together...in that tiny space...had he fucked her? Licked her pussy? Had she got down on her knees for him the way she did for me?

It should have made me angry, the thought of her with someone else. But all it did was turn me on, because it was *him*.

Fucking Chaos, walking around the kitchen acting like the cat who got the cream because he'd probably just had my girl bouncing up and down on his cock, her tits in his face.

The room was suddenly so hot and stuffy I couldn't breathe.

But Kara was still staring at me like she'd committed some sort of mortal sin, and I wasn't having that. I dropped my head and kissed her lips, trying to fight off the urge to ask if they'd been around Hayden's dick earlier. "I'm never mad at you, Little Mouse."

It was impossible to not give her whatever the hell she wanted. I was so stupidly fucking in love with her, she could have had the entire town of Providence lining up to plow her, and if she'd promised me that was what she wanted, then I would have stood there watching, making sure each and every one of them made her come as well as I did before they left.

My dick hardened at the thought, the daydream morphing into a club full of people in that maze. Me, Hayden, and other men, all touching her, worshipping her, making her come over and over again while everyone else watched.

I was fucked in the head. I grabbed her hand and towed her out of the pantry, past Hayden who watched me with the smuggest of grins, like he knew exactly what was going on in my brain.

Fuck him.

"What?" I snapped.

He shrugged. "Nothing. Just minding my own business, cleaning my kitchen."

"So you fucking should. It's disgusting. You're going to poison someone."

He leaned on the countertop. "You going to come to opening night?"

I stared at him. "Why the fuck would I do that? So I can spend the rest of the night choking on your poisoned meat?"

He winked at me. "My meat ain't poisoned. I think you'll find it tastes quite good actually."

I flipped him the bird, suddenly sure we weren't talking about steak. "We need to go."

Kara nodded, gathering up her purse. She paused in front of Hayden, glancing at me like she didn't know how to act around the two of us in the one room, especially after whatever the two of them had done in that pantry while I was gone.

But he didn't have any such qualms.

He cupped her face with both hands, tilted it up and claimed her lips, kissing her deep and so passionately I was pretty sure even I felt it in my toes.

I rolled my eyes. "Come on, Kara. Romeo can stick his tongue down your throat some other time."

"Or in your pussy," Hayden countered, his gaze on me.

Kara slapped him. "Hayden!"

He chuckled. "Sorry. That was for Hawk to think about as he drives you home. Me tongue-fucking you, tasting your sweet juices, fingering you, and licking your clit until you scream my name…"

I had to fight to keep in a groan at the very idea.

He knew it too. Prick.

Something passed in the air between him and me. Something hot and needy that had me shoving my hands in the pockets of my jeans so they weren't strangling the erection growing behind them.

"I really hate you," I muttered to him, tugging Kara along with me.

He grabbed my arm, hauling me in so quick I hit his chest. We were pretty much the same height, so his gaze was impossible to look away from.

Until it lowered to rest on my lips.

He breathed out slowly, dragging his gaze back up to meet mine, and whispered words meant only for me.

"Except we both know you don't hate me at all, Hawk. And that when I come to your room tonight, it's going to be unlocked."

20

HAYDEN

With my body relaxed for the first time in months and a secret smile playing across my lips, it only took another hour to perfect the sauce I'd been working on all day. Then one more to turn it into a triple batch so I had enough to feed an entire clubhouse of bikers.

I loaded all the sauce into reheat-safe containers then into my truck, whistling as I drove home to the Slayers' compound with delicious, spicy scents filling the cab.

Queenie leaned on the wall outside, her thick legs encased in the brightest neon-green leggings I'd ever seen, a matching cropped top thing that I had no name for, and a jump rope hanging from her fingers.

"Working out?" I tried to be friendly because she was one of the few people here who gave me the time of day.

Her chest heaved with puffed-out breaths, and she clutched my arm dramatically. "Working out? Sugar, I'm having a goddamn medical episode here. Isn't that obvious? That rope is trying to kill me. I'm minutes from death's door!" She caught sight of the bag full of pasta sauce and straightened. "Oh! Is that what I think it is? Please tell a starving woman you've brought carbs." She waved her hand around, trying to waft the scent from the bags into her nose and inhaling deeply.

I grinned at her. "I have cheese too."

She put the back of her hand to her forehead and let her knees wobble. "You're saying all of my favorite words right now. If there's garlic bread, a girl might just pass away."

I leaned in and opened the bag wider so she could see the long loaves of bread and container of garlic butter I'd brought home from the restaurant.

She made the happiest of noises and shoved me toward the kitchen. "Get to cooking, good-looking."

I left her to finish her workout and trotted into the kitchen, finding Kara and Hayley Jade sitting at the small round table in the corner. Though the Slayers' kitchen was quite large and industrial, nobody really ate in here, everyone preferring to sit on the couches or tables in the common rooms.

Kara glanced up and smiled, but her expression was tired and tinged with worry.

I dropped my bags onto the countertop and wandered over to them, fitting my hand to the back of her neck and squeezing it reassuringly because I wasn't sure if kissing her in front of her daughter was okay.

I waved at the little girl. "How was school, Hayley Jade?"

She beamed at me happily, her teeth all shiny white and cute and tiny.

"She had a great day," Kara said for her. "She brought

home some new art, and we did some homework earlier. She's learning the letters H, I, and J this week. Aren't you, sweetie?"

Hayley Jade nodded.

"That's awesome. They're some of my favorite letters. Especially that H. All the best people have H's in their names. Did you know that? Like, H for Hayley...and H for Hayden."

She giggled and then made a range of pointing motions, trying to explain something with her hands.

Kara squinted at her. "I don't know what you mean, honey. Can you try again?"

Hayley Jade's shoulders drooped, guards coming back into her eyes and her smile fading away. She picked up her fork and poked at the mac and cheese in front of her.

Kara and I both watched her for a minute before Kara tried again. "If you don't like that mac and cheese, it smells like Hayden has brought something else home for dinner."

"I did. Pasta and garlic bread. It won't be long, if you want some of that?"

Hayley Jade glanced over at me, and I held the container of sauce up so she could see it. "Queenie is pretty excited to have hers with cheese on the top."

"Sounds delicious." Kara got up and cracked open the lid on one of the containers. "Smells even better. Do you want to try some?"

Hayley Jade shook her head.

Kara frowned, moving to the cupboards. "Okay, but you need to eat something. You've been at school all day, and the teachers said you didn't eat your lunch either."

Hayley Jade screwed her face up.

Kara paused, interpreting her daughter's expression. "You didn't like it?"

She shrugged.

"Okay. No more peanut butter and jelly." Kara eyed the uneaten mac and cheese. "Clearly not that stuff either, though I can't blame you. Not sure that counts as proper food."

The processed packet recipe definitely didn't appear very appetizing.

Kara pulled out some cans of soup. "What about chicken? Beef? French onion?"

Hayley Jade looked about as enthusiastic as if we'd asked her if she wanted to go to the dentist.

Kara sighed. "She's not used to anything processed, I don't think. We made everything from scratch at Ethereal Eden."

I pointed at the refrigerator, trying to think what was inside it. "I can make anything you want. Eggs? Sausages?"

Hayley Jade shook her head again, this time more forcefully and again made a bunch of points and gestures.

I had no idea what she was trying to say. I glanced at Kara. "Do you know what she means?"

Kara looked like she wanted to cry and moved a few steps away, motioning for me to follow her. She lowered her voice so Hayley Jade wouldn't hear. "No. And it's not the first time. I can't get her to eat anything because I don't know what she likes, and she can't tell me." She glanced past my shoulder at her daughter. "She's already so skinny. It's really worrying me that she's not eating enough."

Hayley Jade made a frustrated sound in the back of her throat, and some more unintelligible signs, clearly trying to tell us something.

I just had no idea what.

And neither did Kara.

Hayley Jade's expression morphed from frustration to anger. She shoved the bowl of mac and cheese away and pushed to her feet so fast her chair fell over. She flinched at the sound and turned big, scared eyes on the two of us, like she was waiting to be yelled at or berated for making a mess.

When Kara simply said, "It's okay," Hayley Jade ran off, her bedroom door slamming closed a moment later.

Kara's face crumpled, and she bent over to pick up the fallen chair. "School has been so good for her. She's really started coming out of her shell. She wants to communicate. I can see it in her eyes."

"But she still won't talk."

"We just need to be patient. I know that. But it's hard seeing her so frustrated." She sighed heavily but drew her shoulders back. "And I get it! I'm frustrated too, but I don't want her to see that. I'm going to go see if she wants to read a story or play a game. I don't want her going to bed upset. I need to fix this. Somehow."

I tugged her into my arms now that we were alone and kissed the top of her head. "You're a good mom."

She breathed into my shirt, some of the fight going out of her posture as she relaxed into my arms. "I'm the worst mom. I don't know how to help her."

"You don't have to know all the answers to be what she needs. Just being there for her is enough."

Kara sniffed and pulled back, forcing a smile onto her face. "I hope that's true. Save me some dinner, please?"

I kissed her mouth. "Sure."

I watched her go, hating she was beating herself up. I put water on to boil for the pasta, reheated the sauce, and baked the garlic bread until it was toasty and golden. When it was all ready, I spread everything out on the countertop, made up a tray for Kara and set it aside, and then went around knocking on all the bedroom doors, rounding up as many people as I could so the food didn't go to waste.

I knocked on Hawk's bedroom door and yelled out that food was up but didn't stick around to see if he came out. I took my bowl of pasta to my bedroom and closed the door.

The kittens pounced on me, only interested because I had food, but I wasn't sharing it with them. I put mine down long enough to squeeze some pouches of cat food into their bowls, and then took mine to my bed, sitting back against the pillows.

Kara had said something earlier in the day that I couldn't let go of.

"Don't you know you're my hero? One day, you'll be hers too."

I couldn't deny that I wanted that. I'd rekindled the connection between me and Kara, but she wasn't the only person I needed to consider if I wanted her in my life.

Her and Hayley Jade were a package deal. From the minute I'd held that little girl as a baby, my heart had expanded to include her. It was impossible not to. She'd been born right into my hands. Taken her first breaths in my arms.

Staring down at her tiny face had altered something in my chemistry, and I'd never recovered from it. Never forgotten her. Never wanted to.

But she didn't have the same connection to me.

I shoved a forkful of pasta into my mouth and chewed it while using the other hand to type on my phone.

Sign language for beginners.

Hundreds of videos sprang up, and I watched some while I ate, setting my bowl down on my lap so I could try to follow along with the way the instructor's fingers moved.

I mastered the letters H and J, though remembering the rest of the alphabet was definitely going to take more than a night's practice. I was on my third video when a particular sign caught my eye.

I smiled at it, practiced a couple of times, making a fist and moving it in front of my mouth and chin. Then took my empty bowl to the kitchen, swapping it for two clean ones. I found spoons and then searched the freezer for the tub of ice cream I knew was in there behind bottles of vodka and frozen peas.

With two loaded-up bowls in my hands, I made my way to Hayley Jade's room and knocked one of them against the wooden door. "It's Hayden. Can I come in?"

The door opened, and Kara gazed up at me, a wobble in her bottom lip. "We're having a bit of a tough night."

Hayley Jade was splayed out on her bed, face down on the mattress. She didn't lift her head when I came in and Kara closed the door behind me.

"She didn't want to play. I've just been reading stories but..." Kara shrugged. "I don't know what to do."

"Can I try?" I whispered.

She nodded quickly. "I'd be grateful."

I cleared my throat. "Hey, Hayley Jade? I've got two bowls of ice cream here. One for your mom...I was going to give you the other one, but it looks like you're sleeping."

Kara took one bowl from my fingers, and we both watched Hayley Jade on the bed.

She didn't move.

Dammit. I'd been so sure ice cream would work, but she hadn't even twitched. I gave it one more shot. "I put all this chocolate sauce on top, but it's okay if you don't want it. I definitely like this flavor so I can eat—"

Hayley Jade's head whipped up. Her big eyes were wide and red-rimmed like she'd been silently crying.

My heart damn near fucking broke. I just wanted to scoop her up and hold her. Rub her back and tell her I was going to make everything better.

I couldn't promise everything. But perhaps I could give her this one small thing.

"Do you want some..." Shifting the bowl to my left hand, I made the sign for ice cream that I'd just learned. It looked very much the same as licking a cone, only the video had said you didn't need to stick your tongue out. I tried to explain it to her. "You don't have to talk if you don't want to. At least not with your mouth. You can talk with your hands. If you want ice cream, you can move your hand like this, and then your mom will know what you need."

Hayley Jade cocked her head to one side.

Slowly, she made the same sign I had.

I handed the bowl over.

She grinned, her eyes saying all the thank-yous her mouth couldn't.

Kara's eyes were shining with tears. "I didn't even think of teaching her to sign."

"I didn't either, until just before when I saw how frustrated she was getting. We can come up with a sign for each of us, but this an H." I showed Kara how to form the letter, while Hayley Jade watched on with interest, ice cream already smeared across her lips. "And this is a J. So at least now, we have the two most important things covered." I winked at Hayley Jade, and she giggled around another mouthful of sugar.

The sweet sound wrapped its way around my heart, mending some of the little cuts I'd put in it over the years. "We can learn some new signs every night. If you want?"

She nodded quickly.

"Thank you," Kara whispered, taking in the sticky smile on her daughter's face.

I kissed her cheek. "I didn't do anything."

I left them happily practicing the letters and slipped back into the hallway.

Hawk was slumped across the couch in the common room, his long legs kicked up on the coffee table while he scrolled something on his phone.

His fingers paused when our gazes met.

Heat flushed through me at the memory of grabbing him at the restaurant earlier, hauling him in against me, and whispering dirty shit in his ear.

I wondered what the sign for cocktease was as I slipped back into my room, knowing his gaze followed.

21

HAWK

After Chaos disappeared into his bedroom with a smug grin on his stupid face, I paced the short length of mine for hours. It was a total of five steps in any direction, and I'd done so many about-faces I was dizzy.

I'd watched the door like a hawk all evening, the lock firmly in place so Hayden could choke on his own words when he twisted the handle and nothing happened.

Sit on that and twist. He thought he knew me so fucking well.

He knew nothing.

So what if I wanted to watch him fuck Kara? So what if the idea of the two of them got me hot? I was a guy. I liked porn as much as anyone, and seeing the woman I found most attractive in the entire world getting railed by a guy who looked like him was straight out of any man's fantasies.

Wasn't it?

War and Bliss fucked around while Scythe and Vincent and Nash watched. We all did it. I'd probably fucked more women in the common room at the clubhouse than I had in my bedroom.

Maybe we all just shared a public sex kink. Or we were all equally messed up in the head.

It didn't matter. Despite what Hayden had promised earlier that day at Sinners, he wasn't coming.

He was full of shit.

When the clock hit midnight, I gave up waiting for my moment of victory and took a shower. I soaped myself from head to toe, scrubbing my skin until it was pink, and then got out, toweling off. Naked, I padded across the room to my bed and got beneath the covers, pulling them up over me.

I closed my eyes and tossed and turned, trying to get comfortable. But every time I did, I ended up lying on my side, watching the door. I screwed my face up, ignoring the urge to stroke my cock.

After another thirty minutes of frustration, I got up and twisted the motherfucking lock to open.

He wasn't coming anyway. So it didn't matter.

It was hours until I fell asleep.

When I finally did, it was with a bitter sense of disappointment.

22

HAYDEN

The promise I'd made to Hawk at the restaurant hadn't been something I'd planned. It hadn't even been something I'd really thought about. He was being a dick, and throwing him off guard just brought out a sick sort of pleasure in me.

He was so up in his head all the time. Guy just needed to chill the fuck out.

He made pushing his buttons too easy, and I was asshole enough to keep hitting them.

I'd had no intention of going to his room.

I knew he'd lock the door, because no matter how much he denied being a homophobe, he was scared as fuck of the attraction between us.

I wasn't scared. Surprised. Intrigued maybe. But not fucking scared.

Until I thought about actually going down to his room. Turning the handle.

And the one-percent chance it might actually be unlocked.

Then a breathless sort of feeling came over me that could have been terror...or it could have been desire.

I'd ignored it all night, staying in my room, giving Hayley Jade and Kara the time they needed together. I tried to read a book, but the words kept swimming across the page, my brain too distracted to focus.

I'd gone to sleep early but had woken up hourly, getting more and more frustrated, until it was damn near three and I couldn't stand lying there a second longer.

I got up and on silent feet crossed the door to my room and opened it, stepping out into the silent, darkened common area. On instinct, I checked Hayley Jade's and Kara's doors. Both were closed.

As was Hawk's.

Not that I was looking at his room.

I was just getting water. Or tea. Or I didn't know fucking what from the kitchen. Something that would make me sleepy enough that I could stop thinking about going to Hawk's bedroom.

Maybe a fistful of sleeping tablets, because I doubted anything else was going to get him off my brain.

I tried to force my feet in the direction of the kitchen. I swear, I told those bastards to go that way.

And yet I found myself moving to Hawk's door, knowing it would be locked, but at least he'd be asleep and wouldn't have the glory of knowing.

My fingers shook, hovering over his handle, and I fought the desire to touch it. "Just fucking walk away, you idiot," I muttered so quietly it was almost just mouthing the words.

If he was awake and saw me try it, I'd never fucking live it down.

And yet, my stupid fingers twisted the handle anyway.

I waited for the stop of the lock.

It didn't come.

The handle turned in my grip, and the door opened.

Holy fucking shit.

Hawk lay in his bed, sleeping. His chest rose and fell, pale moonlight streaming in from the window, lighting up the thick biceps and his bare, chiseled chest.

I should have turned around. Walked away. Taken the silent victory and gone back to my room to sleep.

But I didn't.

I slipped inside the room, closing the door behind me.

Locking it.

Not sure whether I wanted him to wake up or not. I had no idea what I was fucking doing. Only that my dick was hard at the sight of him and I wanted to do this.

He did too, if he'd left his door unlocked.

Fuck.

I stopped thinking. Just let my body take over.

I silently crossed the room, standing over him, watching him sleep for a second. I should have woken him, except the thought of it was painful. He'd open his mouth and say something dumb, and I just didn't want to hear it.

What I wanted was him.

I pulled back the covers, letting out a tiny groan when he was naked, and it was close enough to sunrise that his dick was hard with morning wood.

My own erection stretched my sweatpants, an aching need building inside me. As quietly as possible, I knelt on the edge of the bed, leaning across the open space to where Hawk was sprawled out in the middle of the mattress.

I took his dick in my mouth.

There'd been vague attractions to men in my past, a sneaky kiss and a grope one night in a gay bar I'd gotten roped into going to with a friend. But I'd never sucked another guy off before. So the feel of his thick erection in my mouth was unfamiliar but not unpleasant. In fact, as his cock filled my mouth, my own erection thickened in the same way it did when I went down on Kara.

I had no idea what I was doing, except I knew what I liked when women blew me. So I relied on that knowledge, licking and sucking the head of his cock until he stirred in the darkness.

"Kara," he murmured, his hand coming to the back of my head sleepily.

I froze, not knowing whether I should say something or just keep sucking him off, letting him think I was the curvy woman who was currently asleep next door.

But then Hawk froze too.

The room wasn't so dark our gazes didn't collide when I looked up along his abs and chest to meet his eyes.

He knew I wasn't her. We both fucking knew it.

Just like we both knew he'd left that door unlocked on purpose.

He pushed down on my head, forcing me to take his cock deep.

I gave up any pretense of being quiet and moaned when the tip of him hit the back of my throat. I gripped his base with my hand and then licked up his shaft before plunging onto it again. His fingers tangled in my hair, fisting the shoulder-length strands, and guiding my head up and down, his hips driving up to thrust into my mouth.

My dick ached with the need to be touched. Moisture beaded at my tip, probably leaving a wet patch on my sweats, but all I could concentrate on was Hawk's green-eyed gaze, staring at me while I blew him, sucked him, brought him closer and closer to an orgasm while he lay naked in his bed.

His hips moved faster, so I did too. He tasted like sin and sugar all in one, so fucking different to Kara's sweet honey but no less addictive. I wanted to stroke my dick. Jerk it in the same time he fucked my mouth, but I didn't want to miss the way his eyes rolled back, or the way he hissed in pleasure with every long lick of the thick vein in the underside of his cock.

"Need to come," he bit out in guttural tones that did things to my insides. "You swallow, Chaos?"

For him, I fucking would.

I didn't say anything. Just took his dick deeper, faster, grabbed his balls until he was bucking off the bed, fucking me as much as I was fucking him.

He groaned loudly, coming hard, hot spurts shooting down the back of my throat, taking me by surprise. But I refused to fucking give him the satisfaction of choking. Or spitting, even though the taste wasn't exactly what I'd been expecting either. Our gazes met again as I swallowed him down, licking his cock until every last drop was gone and he was moaning about being too sensitive and begging me to stop.

He lay back on the bed like a starfish, legs spread, one arm over his eyes. His chest heaved, his dick glistening in the moonlight and still wet from my mouth.

He was so fucking hot like that, his body all muscles and tattoos.

I moved for the door, fingers wrapping around the handle.

"Where are you going?" His voice was husky and hoarse.

So damn fucking hot I knew I was going back to my room to jack off over him.

I didn't say anything. What was there to say? I'd snuck into his room in the middle of the night and sucked his dick, just like I'd promised.

Nothing else was part of the deal.

"Go back to sleep, Hawk. In the morning, we'll pretend this didn't happen."

Hawk swung his legs out of bed, and without an ounce of shame over being naked in front of me, he crossed the room, stopping in front of me.

My gaze searched his face, unable to read him, getting nothing from his expression.

All I had to go on was how fucking close he stood. And how he'd participated in that blow job just as much as I had.

"This where you kiss me goodbye?" I asked him. "I'm not your girlfriend. I don't need that from you."

"Good," he said darkly. "I don't need that from you either."

His gaze flickered over mine.

"What then, Hawk?" I whispered. "What the fuck do you want? To punch me in the face? Tell me you don't want me?" I breathed out slowly. "Or for me to sneak in here during the night and secretly blow you?" I swallowed thickly and then let out the truth. It was the middle of the night, and it was dark, and if secrets were going to come out, now was the time. "Because I don't regret what I just did."

His chest heaved with a shuddering breath. "Then stop fucking talking and let me do the same for you."

He dropped to the floor, kneeling at my feet, and groped my erection through my pants.

I groaned, reaching down to give one hard tug on my drawstring, loosening them so he could drag them down my hips.

I was already so fucking hard for him, and he didn't hesitate, opening his mouth and fitting it over my cock.

I groaned at the warm, wet feel of his mouth, and then again when he cupped my balls, playing with them with one hand while his other held my base. He sucked the tip of me and stroked my shaft with solid, regular movements, lubed up by my arousal and his saliva.

"I don't know what I'm fucking doing," he admitted between sucks and licks. "Tell me if it's not good."

I scraped my nails over the cropped hair on his head, pulling it back so he had to look at me. "Your fucking mouth is on my cock. Everything is good. Anything. Just don't stop."

He started up again, plunging his mouth over my dick, stretching his lips wide, taking me deeper with each thrust of my hips. I fought to grab the back of his head, wanting to fuck his mouth fast and hard, but he'd been way more in the closet about whatever this was between us, and fuck me, I didn't want to push him further than he was comfortable with. Despite what he thought of me, I wasn't an asshole.

When he pushed my thighs farther apart and lowered his mouth to lick my balls, I damn near came on the spot.

"Fuck," I groaned, watching his face press between my legs and him suck one ball at a time into his mouth like a goddamn fucking pro. "Fuck, don't stop."

His hand pumped my dick and he buried his face between my legs, sucking my balls better than any woman ever had.

Because he knew what it felt like. He knew how it brought an all-new feeling to a blow job that was already out of this world, just because the person you wanted was down on their knees, letting you have full control over them.

"You gonna swallow, Hawk?" I asked him the same question he'd asked me.

I held the back of his head, encouraging him more than forcing him, but letting him know all the same what I wanted. "I want to come in your mouth."

"Then fucking get it over with," he grumbled between sucks and licks.

I smiled into the darkness, the tone in his voice clear he wanted to do it and I wasn't forcing him.

Even if he was going to pretend he didn't want to know what I tasted like.

"Jerk your cock," I demanded.

"Fuck you," he responded. "Kara might like being bossed around in bed. Doesn't mean I do."

I laughed into the darkness. "Fuck your hand, Hawk. You know you're hard and dripping for me again."

"I hate you," he muttered.

"Try saying that again when your mouth isn't full of my dick."

I shut him up by slamming past his lips, hitting the back of his throat and earning myself a moan.

Despite himself, he fisted his cock, stroking himself in the same rhythm I set on his tongue, both of us getting faster and faster until my balls drew up and I couldn't control it anymore. I came with a shout, his name on my lips, which earned me a filthy look, even though he couldn't say anything because his mouth was full of my cum.

His splashed over my feet, a sticky mess, his groans of pleasure only vibrating around my dick and making my orgasm all the better for it.

I slumped back against the wall and watched him finish, licking me until I was limp in his mouth, completely drained and one-hundred-percent spent.

He rocked back on his heels and pushed to his feet.

We were both sweaty, hot messes, his cum all over his hand.

We stared at each other.

He was the first to speak. "You fucking shot me."

I rolled my eyes. "I also just gave you the best blow job of your life."

He raised an eyebrow. "You think highly of yourself."

"Then tell me I'm not right?"

"You can go now."

I reached for the door. "Oh, trust me, I am."

"I still hate you. This changes nothing."

I sniggered as I left. "You just came twice. Once in my mouth. You want to know what you taste like?"

He closed the door in my face.
I went back to my room with a grin on mine.

23

GRAYSON

The hospital clinic was busy as always, just how I liked it because it meant more and more people within the community were finding out about us and coming in for treatments they so sorely needed. I bustled around, telling Kara stupid jokes whenever I passed her because she always laughed at them, and her laughter was infectious. It brought smiles not only to me but to any of the patients who might have been within earshot of the sweet sound.

I'd heard her repeating the terrible jokes I spent each evening memorizing, and I liked seeing the patients' reactions to the way she told them.

Anything that spread a little happiness around what was essentially a room full of suffering made the time pass easier.

"Doc!"

I drew my gaze away from the pretty brunette, who had an elderly man chuckling over my joke about a donkey and a rabbit.

Hawk waved me over to a patient in the corner of the waiting room.

I made my way through the crowd of people, sidestepping those sitting on the floor because we'd run out of chairs hours ago, and stopped at his side.

He spoke before I could even ask what the matter was. "Female, forty-three. Came in complaining of headache, nausea, and vomiting."

I glanced at the patient and smiled but then turned to Hawk. "Has she been through triage?"

He nodded but then frowned at the woman. "She has, but she downplayed her symptoms, didn't you?"

The woman gave a chagrinned grimace. "I don't want to be a bother to anyone. You all work so hard here, and there's other people in worse condition than me—" She let out a yelp and doubled over, clutching her stomach.

Concern had me crouching in front of her and pressing my fingers to her neck to check her pulse.

Hawk rubbed a hand down the woman's back but focused his attention on me. "You're gonna find her heart rate is sky-high, and look." He pointed to the woman's wrist, peeking out from beneath her sweater. "Rash. I can tell just from touching her that she has a fever. She can't be sitting out here in the waiting room."

"I'm fine, truly," the woman protested, straightening as the pain passed. "I'll wait my turn like everyone else."

I held a hand out to her. "Guess what? It's your turn! Kara will take you into exam room three, okay?"

I'd raised my voice when I'd said Kara's name, and she glanced up, listening to my instructions and scurried to do as I'd asked. Carefully, she helped the protesting patient out of the waiting room.

By the time I turned back, Hawk was already rushing into a cubicle. Vomiting noises came from behind the curtain, mixing with Hawk's deep voice offering reassurances.

"Would you look at that," I mumbled to Willa, one of the head nurses who gave up her time here each week. She followed my line of sight, both our gazes landing on Hawk, who was disposing of the vomit bag.

"He's great," she agreed. "Kara too. They've both been the biggest help the last few weeks. It's a shame they aren't qualified. Because I'd happily have either of them on my staff."

I glanced at her. "Really?"

She nodded, rubbing at the old burn scars on her neck absentmindedly. "Absolutely. Hawk has brought a few patients to my attention, and he was spot-on the money each time. He and Kara both work harder around here than most of the paid staff do. Neither of them ever complains about the shitty jobs we have them do either."

I'd noticed the same, but I'd thought that was because I was paying Kara and Hawk more attention than I would any other volunteer.

I saw another couple of patients and was on my way to collect a third when whistling caught my attention. I did a double take when I realized it was coming from Hawk, scrubbing his hands at the sink.

He noticed my expression, and his quickly turned into a scowl. "What?"

I tilted my head, my curiosity piqued. "Are you...happy?"

"I've spent all morning cleaning out vomit buckets and piss pans. Do I look happy?"

I laughed. "Actually, yeah, you do. You're walking around here smiling and whistling, despite the low-level jobs we've given you to do."

He shrugged. "It's not a big deal. Whatever."

I just waited. "You like this job."

He sighed. "Don't turn a shitty volunteer job into something it's not. Maybe I just got laid. Whatever."

I shook my head. "Didn't need to know that." I glanced at Kara, smiling kindly at Mr. Holdsworth, who came in every week just because he was lonely.

Hawk elbowed me. "Hey. Not her. Fuck off. I don't want her thinking I'm walking around here blabbing about our sex life."

I raised an eyebrow. "But you did get laid. If not her then..." I widened my eyes at him, remembering the man he'd been with when they'd brought Kara to the hospital. "Oh! I didn't realize you and Hayden were actually brother husbands in the biblical sense.."

He sighed, tugging me aside. "It's not like that."

"Isn't it?"

He glared at me. "You're doing that shrink thing where you keep turning it back on me."

"Isn't that why you're telling me though? Because you want advice?"

He shrugged. "I don't know why I'm telling you."

"Do you want me to guess?"

He glared at me. "Do I?"

I sniggered. The answering questions with questions thing was annoying at times, though it was effective, which was why I did it. It wasn't my place as a doctor to push my own beliefs and opinions onto a patient. Only to help them sort out how they felt about a situation. And clearly, Hawk needed to talk to someone. "You don't have anyone else to confide in," I stated. "Either your friends and family wouldn't accept it, or you just think they wouldn't. Third option being it's you who doesn't want to accept whatever happened between you and Hayden."

He thought that over for a minute. "I think I'd rather clean bedpans than talk this over with you."

I nodded, not wanting to rush him. "Fair call. But I'll be over at your place for my first session with Hayley Jade after I finish up here tonight, in case you change your mind."

"I won't."

"Also fair enough." I chuckled, watching him walk away. But then I called him back. "Hawk?"

He stopped and looked back over his shoulder. "Yeah?"

"When are you going to get your GED so we can start training you properly?"

He paused. "Never."

I sighed at his stubbornness. "That's a waste of natural talent. You know that, right? You're good with the patients. Surprisingly good, considering..."

"Considering I'm a biker."

I smiled. "I was going to say considering you're an asshole the rest of the time, but sure, let's go with biker if you prefer."

He scowled and, laughing, I walked past him.

"Seriously, Hawk. Get your GED. I can point you in the right direction after that. Don't be too proud to ask for what you want. I'm in your corner, and I'm pretty smart. I can help."

He glared at me. "Why?"

I frowned. "Why what?"

"Why help me? I'm a high school dropout from Saint View."

"You're more than that."

"You don't know me."

I shrugged. "I don't. But I'm a psychologist. So I pay attention to people, and maybe I see more than you think I do."

"Don't you doctors deal with facts? Sounds to me like you're just doing a lot of assuming."

That he didn't want people to know he was actually a good guy on the inside was what made him so fascinating to me. Despite his assumptions, I had been paying attention, because he was with Kara.

And Kara was damn hard to ignore, even when I'd vowed to just be her friend.

I eyed Hawk and the stubborn set of his jaw. Besides Kara, had he ever had anyone see the good in him? The good I saw every day he worked here? It kinda pissed me off that perhaps nobody had ever seen the potential in him. "You're a man who held a little girl, who isn't his, because it made her feel safe in a scary hospital where people were trying to poke and prod her. You're a man who protected that girl's mother when you thought she was in danger."

"I punched you in the face."

"Sure. I was the perceived danger in that situation, and your intuition was way off, but you did what you thought was right. I respect that, otherwise, I wouldn't be standing here, trying to make you believe you're worth more than you think you are."

Hawk breathed out slowly, giving in to my badgering. "I failed the GED already."

"So study harder and take it again."

He blinked. "Just like that?"

"Sure. Why not?"

"Because I'll look like a dumbass when I fail again."

"Why does it bother you what you look like to other people?"

Hawk groaned.

I held my hands up, backing off. "Sorry, sorry. I'll stop with the questions. But you know I'm right." I grinned at him. "I always am."

He shook his head and went back to his work.

He and Kara left just before three so they could go pick up Hayley Jade from school, but I mouthed the letters GED at him as he left.

Instead of a wave goodbye like I got from Kara, Hawk just gave me a middle finger.

The sun was low when I saw out the last clinic patient and locked the doors for the night. I was normally tired after I finished a shift on the psych ward, but the clinic always left me feeling invigorated.

It wasn't like I didn't believe psychology was important. It absolutely was, and I found people endlessly fascinating.

But there was also a part of me that was a whole lot more satisfied by the work we did with the underprivileged. There was a sense the work I did here one day a week made more of a difference than the hours upon hours I spent listening to married couples fight about stupid shit, or rich snobs from Providence blab about all the problems they'd created for themselves by having too much goddamn money that would have been better spent on a donation.

I left the clinic on the same high I always did, my heart full, my head determined to find a way to do more.

But first I needed to see a little girl who was still refusing to speak. As well as her pretty brown-eyed mother, who had so firmly put me in the friend zone it was sad.

I followed Kara's directions to the clubhouse, taking the winding road through the woods and whistling beneath my breath at the imposing gates at the top of the driveway. The skull figure in the middle with a scythe in its bony fingers was terrifying.

As was the huge tree trunk of a man who stepped from the shadows, a shotgun in his hand.

"What the hell do they feed these guys?" I rolled down the window and stuck both hands out so he would know I wasn't armed. Then louder but with barely more certainty, I called, "I'm a doctor. Kara invited me here to see Hayley Jade."

The tall blond man leaned down and stared in the window at me. "Get out of the car."

"I'd really rather not," I said before really thinking about it.

I changed my mind pretty quickly when I found myself facing down the barrel of the shotgun. "On second thought, it's a lovely afternoon. Maybe I would like to get out and stretch my legs." I reached for the handle slowly and released the lock so the door could swing open.

"That's what I thought." The biker gave me a warning look, as if daring me to run or make any sort of move.

He needn't have worried. I wasn't about to try to outrun a bullet. Plus, I had nothing to hide, which he soon found out as he poked around my car, checking for God knows what.

When he straightened, his expression was slightly less murderous. "You're good to go. Sorry about that. But we had a security breach not all that long ago, and now I don't trust anyone."

I offered him my hand, trying to show I wasn't a threat. "No hard feelings. I totally understand. I'm Grayson."

He took it. "Fang. But you aren't here to exchange pleasantries with me. Go on through. The road will take you straight to the clubhouse. Hayley Jade and Kara are waiting for you there."

"Thanks." I got back in my car and drove it slowly through the gates and down the hill, a big, rectangular building rising from behind the thick trees a minute later.

"Fucking hell." I stared up at the building. Bikes were parked outside the doors, cigarette butts were discarded in an ashtray, and a club jacket slung over an outdoor chair. There wasn't a welcome mat or a cheery front door wreath in sight. The entire place screamed "get out."

I'd promised Kara I wouldn't judge her home though, so I concentrated on just getting myself out of the car.

Because there was a little girl on the other side who needed me to help her.

And because I needed to see for myself that she and her mother were safe here. I still didn't fully understand what had happened the night Kara had ended up in the hospital. The story they'd told about her being partially buried when an embankment had given way was full of holes, but it had been clear that it wasn't Hayden or Hawk who had hurt her. So that had been enough for me and the rest of her medical team to release her. But Fang's comment about there being a security breach a few weeks back rang in my mind, and I couldn't shake the feeling it had something to do with how Kara had gotten hurt.

If that was the case, then I would happily let them search me and my car anytime they wanted.

I forced myself out of the car and over to the door. I rapped my knuckles across it, but when nobody came to the door, I let myself in. "Hello?"

A young woman at the bar looked up, her gaze widening as she took in my suit and tie. "Holy shit. Where did you come from? You lost, handsome?"

I shook my head and smiled at her. "No. At least, I don't think so." I strode across the room and offered her my hand. "I'm Grayson." I held up my medical bag that held the few basic supplies and paperwork I carried everywhere. "I'm a doctor."

She raised an eyebrow and slipped her fingers into my grasp. "Well, well, Dr. Grayson. I'm thinking you are indeed lost, but I'm glad for it. Sit. Have a drink. Ice pours them strong, though..." She leaned in, pushing her fake round tits against my chest. "I'm sure you can handle it though, can't you? I bet you handle a lot of things real nice..."

Her hand traced down my chest and stomach and then lower, trying to grope me.

I pulled away sharply, backing up two steps. "No drink needed. I have an appointment with Kara."

The woman laughed. "Kara?"

I nodded.

The smile fell off the woman's face, and she lost interest in me in the same second. She turned back to the bar and Ice behind it, complaining to him like I wasn't even in the building. "She already has Chaos and Hawk. How much dick does one woman need?"

Heat crept into my cheeks. "It's not like that. We're just friends."

The woman eyed me up and down. "Then you're available? Single?"

I didn't know how to tell her I was single, yes, but there was only one woman I was interested in. And it wasn't her. "Is Kara around?"

The woman sighed. "Kara!"

I winced as the woman screeched down the hallway, but it did have the desired effect of a door opening and Kara's head popping out.

"Hi! You're early. I'm so sorry, I was planning on meeting you out the front, so you didn't have to..."

The woman scowled at Kara. "What? Be accosted by me?"

"I didn't say that, Amber." Kara looked down at her hands.

The woman slid off the barstool, tugging at her short skirt. She strode along the hallway. "Hawk know you've taken a third lover?"

Kara didn't say anything.

Amber glared at her, clearly irritated at not getting a response. She banged on the door behind her, though her gaze never left Kara's. "Hawk! You know your woman has another man out here? How many does that make now?"

The door behind her opened, and Hawk stood framed by the doorway. He reached up to grab the top of it, his gaze sliding to me. He laughed. "Get the fuck out, Amber. He works with us. They aren't screwing."

Kara's cheeks were scarlet.

Even in the midst of her embarrassment, she was still so damn pretty I couldn't think straight. She'd changed out of her work scrubs, and her skirt clung to the curve of her hips deliciously.

Amber shrugged as she passed me. "If you ever do want to do some fucking, *Doctor*, I'm always available..." She shot a dirty look over at Hawk. "Since some people are now getting their needs met elsewhere."

Hawk leaned into the stretch and rolled his eyes. "Jealousy isn't pretty on you, sweetheart."

Amber flounced down the hallway, disappearing into a room at the end of it.

Hawk crossed the room to Kara and put two fingers beneath her chin, forcing her face up and her eyes to meet his. "Hey, Little Mouse. Look at me."

She did.

Something passed between them that didn't need words.

Kara's spine straightened. Her shoulders pulled back.

A soft smile spread across Hawk's lips, and then he lowered his head and pressed them against hers, like I wasn't even in the room.

"That's my girl. Go do your thing with Gray and Hayley Jade."

"And then we'll go to Hayden's restaurant opening afterward?"

Hawk groaned and pressed his forehead to hers. "Seriously? You're going to make me go to that?"

"Please."

He let out a huff. "You know I'll take you anywhere you want to go."

She smiled at him as he dragged himself away, and then she glanced at me, jumping a little, like in Hawk's presence she'd forgotten I was even present. "Oh, sorry. That was terribly rude of me. Let me get Hayley Jade." She hurried toward the door next to Hawk's.

I caught her hand before she could pass by.

Both of us stared down in surprise at my fingers wrapped around her. Her skin was so warm. The pulse at her wrist flickered too fast beneath my fingertips.

I realized I was staring, as well as crossing a professional line. I dropped her hand. "Wait. I like to start by talking to the parent first. Can we sit somewhere and talk privately for a moment?"

Kara cringed. "I was kind of hoping you wouldn't want to do that."

"I need to know what's been going on with her, so I know where to start. Especially because she's currently nonverbal."

Kara surveyed the clubhouse with a critical eye. "It's not exactly very private around here. Do you mind coming into my bedroom?"

I wanted to groan. Refuse to see the place she slept, because I had no doubt in my mind that where Kara was at night, Hawk and Hayden probably were as well. She led me into her room, closing the door quietly behind us, but all I could do was stare at the bed, imagining her naked in it, with Hawk's and Hayden's big bodies sandwiching her between them while they writhed around, pleasuring each other.

This was so damn unprofessional.

I squeezed my eyes closed, irrational jealousy coursing through me that I had no right to feel. She had men in her life. She wasn't available for me to desire the way I did, just because she was sweet and kind and so broken I was desperate to fix her.

There was nowhere to sit but her bed. She perched on the edge and then indicated I could take the spot next to her.

Friends. Friends. Friends.

I pulled my phone from my pocket and showed her the recording app I used during all my sessions. "Are you okay with me taping this? It doesn't get shared with anyone. It's purely for my own notes."

She nodded, and I set the phone to record and put it down between us.

"What do you want to know?" Her hands twisting around each other gave away how nervous she was.

"All of it. Every reason you can think of as to why Hayley Jade might have stopped speaking."

She let out a shuddering breath and nodded.

The story came tumbling out in a rush of words I didn't have a hope of slowing. Like she'd been holding it all together for too long, all of it on the tip of her tongue, the story desperate to be shared in every horrifying detail.

Somewhere amongst the avalanche, Hayley Jade's story became Kara's.

Cults. Forced marriages. Assaults. Hayley Jade's birth. Josiah. Hawk. Hayden. Rebel. Her sister's death.

More trauma than any one person should ever have to endure.

She clutched her stomach, as if setting free the words had caused a physical ache. "All of it is my fault, isn't it?"

I grappled to maintain a professional distance when watching her break down felt like pins being stabbed into my skin one at a time. "No, it's not—"

"I took her back there, Grayson! I stayed for five whole years, convincing myself that her future could be different than mine, when I knew all along she was never going to be safe. I'm a failure. In so many ways. As a mother. A wife. A woman."

I wanted to help, but the doctor part of my brain had completely left the building. All I could focus on was the way her heart was breaking and the pain spilling from it, brimming over, right onto me.

"What do you need?" I asked, voice graveled and choked by the rush of need to protect her from everything hurting her.

She shook her head, but then she laughed bitterly, wiping at her eyes. "I don't know. A hug, maybe? Someone to just hold me and tell me it's going to be okay."

Despite her efforts, tears rolled down her cheeks, silently at first, but then they turned into sobs, her shoulders shaking as her body released the weight that had been sitting on her soul for far too long.

It wasn't unusual. Patients cried in my office on a daily basis.

But I didn't typically feel my own heart breaking

when they did. I didn't normally gather them into my arms and hug them, because the sounds of their sorrow were too hard on my heart to bear it.

"You're not a failure," I whispered back. "Don't ever say that."

I smoothed my hand down her back in gentle circles, not knowing what else to do but wanting to take the hurt away from her in any way I knew how.

I was walking a dangerous line and I knew it.

One of complete and utter unprofessionalism. One I could be reported for, and probably even lose my license.

But in that moment, with Kara staring up at me with big brown eyes and needing reassurance, I would have ripped up my own damn medical certificate. She'd asked for human contact. Touch. Assurance. I wasn't going to tell her no.

"What if she never speaks again?"

It was clear to me that was Kara's biggest fear. That her actions had permanently damaged her daughter. Without even talking to Hayley Jade, I knew it was Kara who needed this therapy more.

Maybe she knew too.

I brushed her tears away with the back of my hand. I wanted to promise her everything would be fine, but I also knew I couldn't make promises I might not be able to keep.

Instead, I just pulled her closer and let her cry.

It had been so long since I'd held anyone like this. Since I'd cared enough about their feelings to feel their pain with them. I hated that she'd been betrayed by people who were supposed to love her.

I knew exactly what that felt like. It cut deep and

never healed, the wound always there, weeping, just waiting to end your life if you let it take hold and drain you dry.

I didn't want Kara feeling that pain the way I had. I didn't want it festering inside her, the way I'd let the pain of losing my wife and my shitty upbringing eat away at me. The places those feelings took you were bleak.

So I held her, murmuring soothing things in her ear, even though it wasn't my place or my right.

The door crashed open, Hawk in the doorway.

Kara jumped a mile, skittering away from me on the bed.

Hawk's gaze landed on me, his eyes darkening. "What the fuck are you doing?"

Ah, shit.

"He wasn't doing anything. I was upset—" Kara's leg bounced, her nervous energy filling the room.

Hawk's anger fed on it. "And what? He thought he could just use your vulnerable state to put his hands all over you?" His gaze went hot with fury. "I fucking trusted you with her!"

Irritation bubbled up inside me. "Settle down." I instantly regretted it. It was probably the worst thing to say, but all the right words had up and left the building a long time ago. All I had left was pathetic attempts at explaining myself. Which truthfully, I couldn't. But Hawk was going to kill me if I didn't try. "I hugged her when she was crying. That's all."

"You hug all your patients like that?" he demanded. "Tucked in tight to your chest, inhaling her fucking hair while getting a hard-on?"

Kara gasped. "Hawk! Stop it! He wasn't doing anything wrong! I asked him to."

"You don't know how men think, Little Mouse. He's been crushing on you ever since we stepped foot in that hospital."

I shook my head angrily. He wasn't exactly wrong, but it pissed me off that he was so wrapped up in his jealousy that he hadn't even stopped to listen to Kara and what she wanted. "Don't do that. Don't dismiss her feelings."

I wasn't even surprised when Hawk launched himself across the room at me.

Or when Kara tried to force herself between us.

What was surprising was the scream of pain that stopped the three of us in our tracks, all of us swiveling toward the doorway and the rooms outside where more shouts and the rushing of feet came.

"Call an ambulance!" someone bellowed from somewhere down the hallway.

It was probably the only three words that could have had both me and Hawk forgetting our squabbles and running in unison from the room to help.

24

BLISS

I'd been ignoring my contractions for hours.

I'd done the same thing with both of my previous labors, and I knew now it was how I coped. I hated a big commotion, everybody staring at me, wincing as each contraction gripped my body. Concentrating on them only made me feel worse, and worrying over everyone worrying about me didn't help.

So I'd gotten up that morning and ignored the tightening of my belly. I'd said goodbye to Nash and Vincent who needed to prepare for the Psychos party happening that night, in an attempt to compete with the Sinners' grand opening. The contractions had been painful but not unbearable as I'd taken Lexa to school and Mila to daycare.

Not wanting to be home alone, I found myself at the clubhouse, seeking the comfort of being near War while he worked and also having the privacy of his clubhouse bedroom. I'd been happily laboring away in private, doing my thing, not bothering anyone.

Until the pain in my back became unbearable and I'd let out an involuntary scream.

I'd never felt pain like that before.

The realization that something was wrong hit me hard and fast, panic rising in my chest and wrapping its way around my throat. I opened the door and stumbled out into the hallway, another wave of pain hitting me, forcing me to lean on the wall for support. I shouted for someone to get me an ambulance.

Ice and War materialized from the clubhouse kitchen, Ice taking one look at me and pulling out his phone.

"I'm calling nine-one-one."

War ran to my side, taking my weight and I turned into the warmth of his chest.

"Talk to me, baby girl. How long do we have?"

I shook my head. I didn't know. Everything suddenly felt wrong, this baby taking a route of his or her own, that differed entirely to the way their older sisters had been born. Where minutes ago I'd felt safe and in control, I was now panicked and terrified and wishing I had gone to the hospital earlier.

Hawk and Kara came rushing from her bedroom, a third man I didn't recognize with them. But in that moment, I couldn't care less who was there. An entire marching band could have popped out of the cupboard and I would have barely noticed.

All I could focus on was breathing through the pain.

War's gaze sought out his best friend's. "Baby's coming."

Hawk gave him a reassuring smile. "Good day to be born. Just in time for Friday night drinks." He moved to my side, peering at my clammy face. "How you doing there, Mama?"

"Something's wrong."

War froze.

Hawk widened his eyes. "What do you mean?"

I groaned, the start of another contraction hitting me squarely in the back. "I've had two babies already. I know what it's supposed to feel like, and this isn't it. That's all I know. Please believe me. Please. Do something."

Hawk nodded as the contraction stole my ability to speak. "I believe you. But I don't know nothing about babies, Bliss. Shit." He glanced over at Ice. "ETA on the ambulance?"

Ice's lips pulled into a grim line. "They're coming, but it'll be twenty minutes."

"Fuck!" Hawk shouted. "Why is this clubhouse in the middle of nowhere?"

I gripped War's hand, trying not to hurt him but having nowhere else for the pain to go. "It's my fault. I shouldn't have come here. I should have stayed at home, in town. Or said something earlier—" Tears dripped down my face.

War shushed me, holding my weight, supporting me, and whispering, "No, baby girl. You did exactly what you needed to do. You're exactly where you need to be."

The familiar possessive growl in his voice soothed the ragged edges inside me, and the next contraction hurt a little less, because he was here, arms around me, whispering in my ear that I was doing everything right, everything perfectly, and very soon it would all be over, and our newest child would be in our arms.

I so desperately wanted to believe him. I clung to his

thick biceps, moaning through my pain, letting his words wash over me until I got a breather.

"Bliss," the man I didn't recognize said tentatively. "I'm Grayson. I'm a doctor. I work with Kara and Hawk at the hospital. I don't deliver babies normally, but I have in the past. I don't think you have twenty minutes before that ambulance gets here. Do you?"

I shook my head miserably, the pain of another contraction making it too hard to speak. The baby's head felt so low and like it would rip me in two.

"Can we get you onto a bed so I can examine you?"

Everyone turned to me for permission, and God, after everything I'd been through in my life, them giving me control over my body and my birth was so gratefully received. But this guy could have been Jack the Ripper and I would have accepted his help. He looked like an angel sent from Heaven. "Please," I moaned.

Permission given, Grayson went straight into doctor mode, barking orders. "I need to get her onto a bed. Do you have any medical supplies here?"

Hawk nodded. "More than you'd think but not much you'd need for a birth."

"Blood pressure cuff and oxygen monitor would be a good start."

"I've got those." Hawk raced away down the hallway.

Grayson got beneath my other arm, he and War practically carrying me back into War's clubhouse bedroom, the one he rarely used anymore because his heart was at home with me, our girls, and Nash and Vincent and Scythe.

The soft mattress felt like a thousand burning spears beneath my back, and I screamed again. Kara followed us in, grabbing my hand, her big brown eyes terrified when I strangled her fingers, but here in silent female support I was grateful for, since Rebel wasn't here to be my person.

"Where's Hayley Jade?" I asked. "I'm so sorry. I don't want to scare her."

Kara shook her head. "Ice took her outside to wait for the ambulance." She gripped my fingers harder. "You scream as much as you need to. Stop worrying about everybody else and do what *you* need."

Grayson grimaced and laid his hands on my belly. "I'm so sorry. This is going to hurt."

I shouted again as he poked and prodded at me. The pain mixed in with another contraction until my vision fuzzed out at the edges. "I can feel the head," I groaned, moving my skirt aside and reaching between my legs to yank at my underwear.

War and Kara dragged it down my legs for me.

Grayson gave a nod. "That is indeed a head."

A little relief spiked through me. "Oh, thank God. I thought she might have been breech."

Grayson knelt at the end of the bed, one hand on my belly. "Definitely not breech but possibly sunny side up."

"What does that mean?" Kara took the words out of my mouth.

"Normal presentation is baby comes out head first, face down." He smiled at me. "I'm definitely no pro at this, but I think your little miss is face up."

"Is that bad?" War asked, a shake in his voice.

Grayson shook his head. "It's not ideal, but it's a whole lot better than breech. That ambulance is going to be here soon, but I don't think she's waiting for it. It's going to be harder than your other labors, but push, Bliss."

Hawk rushed back into the room and fit a blood pressure cuff around my arm and another monitor on my finger, but I barely noticed.

"Vincent and Nash aren't even here," I moaned through the burning ache spreading through me.

War grinned at me. "Just another reason I'm sure this one is mine. Push, baby girl."

Kara squeezed my fingers encouragingly.

Grayson's gaze steadied my heartbeat. "Trust me. Get up on your knees. Use gravity to help the baby's head keep downward pressure. If she's upside down, and we don't have forceps or any other equipment, we're going to need to use what we do have."

There was no option not to. I might have never met the man, but he was calm when everything else felt out of control. I needed to trust someone. Grayson was it.

It was agonizing to move. My muscles all felt locked in place. I screamed as War and Hawk got me up on my knees and gave me their shoulders to brace my weight on. Kara wiped sweat from my brow, quietly telling me I was stronger than I thought I was.

I pushed. The baby slid down, the feeling inside me changing from ripping pain to an odd sense of relief.

Grayson gave a shout from the end of the bed. "I was right! She's sunny side up! One more big push, Bliss. You have this. I'm just here to catch."

I pushed, my screams turning to a guttural groan of determination as my baby slid from my body and into Grayson's arms.

"Not a she after all," Grayson announced.

Oh my God. A boy. I hadn't dared hope for one. All I'd cared about was a healthy baby, and after two girls, the odds seemed on the side of having a third.

We'd all been fine with that. I would have loved a little team of girls to even out all the testosterone that came from living in a house with three grown men.

But this boy would bring us so much joy.

I collapsed against War's chest, completely and utterly spent, my labored breathing the only sound.

The room was so quiet.

The realization was shocking. I twisted sharply. "He's not crying!"

War gripped me tighter. Kara's fingers twisted in the sides of her skirt and she stared at the tiny, vaguely gray-colored baby on the bed.

"Do something!" Hawk shouted.

The room swirled, panic and exhaustion threatening to take me down.

But Grayson spoke calmly, scrubbing at the baby with a towel he must have grabbed from War's en suite. "Give him a moment."

That moment felt like the longest one of my life.

One where my heart stopped beating. My lungs stopped breathing. And all I could do was will for my child to want to live.

His little cry pierced the air, and with his first gulp of air, his tiny body flushed pink.

Grayson grinned and lifted him to my chest, umbilical cord still attached. "Congratulations."

I burst into tears, staring down at the howling baby who, just moments earlier, had me convinced I was never going to get to hear that sweet sound.

War peered down at his son and stroked a thumb across his gunk-smeared cheek tenderly, before placing a kiss to the top of my head. "You're a rock star," he said to the baby. "Just like your mom."

There was a commotion outside, and Ice led the paramedics into the room. They got to work, monitoring me as I delivered the placenta, checking the baby, clamping the umbilical cord.

Hawk and Kara slipped out, and Grayson went to follow them.

I reached out and caught his arm before he could leave. "Thank you."

He shook his head. "No need."

War leaned over and offered his hand. "I disagree. If there's anything me or the club can do for you, just consider it done."

Grayson took his hand. "Just enjoy that baby." He winked at him. "He definitely looks like you."

I stared down at my son, searching his tiny features. He was beautiful and perfect and his little lips were shaped exactly like War's.

25

GRAYSON

With Bliss safely in an ambulance and my heart pounding, I sank down on the battered clubhouse couch and put my head in my hands.

Any trace of earlier hostility gone, Hawk thumped me on the shoulder as he passed me by, his body jerky with leftover adrenaline. "Holy shit. I can't believe that just happened."

I lifted my head to watch him pace the room. "Me either."

He grinned, eyes shining with a high I remembered from early days of my training, when every procedure was new and thrilling. "That was fucking awesome."

I let the anxiety inside me go on a long exhale and sucked up some of his excitement. "You going to get out of your comfort zone and get the GED, so next time you can be the one delivering the baby? I just nearly shit myself. I haven't delivered one since my residency."

Hawk paused, as if he was mulling over the idea, even though it was clear to me he'd been wasting his life, spending it outside of a hospital. If he was this excited by the stress, the bodily fluids, the screaming of someone in pain, especially someone he loved, then there was no denying what he was supposed to be doing with his life.

Maybe he wasn't supposed to be a doctor, but he wasn't supposed to be a biker either.

Hawk needed to be saving lives. Not taking them.

I looked him in the eye. "I meant what I said earlier. I'll help you."

Hawk cracked up laughing and thumped me on the back again. "Deal. And Kara will get hers at the same time." He scooped Hayley Jade up from the floor and tossed her into the air, catching her easily when she sailed back down into his arms. "Won't she, Hay Jay? You'll go to school and so will Mommy and me."

Hayley Jade nodded her little head enthusiastically.

Kara laughed, watching Hawk and her daughter fondly. "I can't think of anything I'd like to do more." She sat on the couch beside me and put her hand on my knee, squeezing it. "You were amazing. Inspiring, actually."

I didn't deserve the praise. My fingers had been shaking the entire time, but half my job as a doctor was reassuring patients and keeping them calm. That was something I did daily. I was damn lucky Bliss's baby had only had a minor complication. Anything bigger and we might have had a different outcome.

It only made me want to get out of psychiatry more. A feeling deep in my gut that more hands-on medicine, the sort I got to do today, and in the clinic, was where I really wanted to be.

But for now, I'd ride the high right through the

weekend and the week of marriage counselling and other mundane appointments I had scheduled Monday to Thursday.

Hawk eyed me. "You need a drink."

I wasn't going to deny that. Delivering that baby had me reeling. Plus, it was Friday night and I wasn't on call. A whisky or a tequila, or both, sounded pretty good right now. "I do." But I wasn't exactly sure where I stood with him now that the rush was over, and Bliss and War were on their way to the hospital with their healthy baby boy. I hadn't forgotten Hawk walking in on me comforting Kara and threatening to beat the shit out of me. "You offering me one, even though you were ready to punch me in the face earlier?"

Hawk studied me, a darkness dropping over his expression. "Whether I punch you in the face or not is up to Kara. She's the one you were all over."

Kara rolled her eyes. "Stop it. If you weren't so dramatic all the time, you would have heard me say he wasn't hitting on me. We're friends. He's my boss, for goodness' sakes."

Sure. Her boss. Friends.

Fucking fabulous.

I shrugged at Hawk, brushing off the rejection of being so firmly in the friend zone. "So...drink?"

He pushed to his feet, brushing his hands off on his jeans. "Yeah. But not here." His gaze rolled down my body, taking in the suit pants and shirt.

I'd ditched the tie and jacket and rolled my sleeves up, but it was splattered with blood and who knew what else after delivering a baby.

"You need a shower. Fresh clothes. Dress up and then meet us at Sinners."

I frowned. "What's Sinners?"

Kara opened her mouth, probably to explain, but Hawk cut her off, sniggering with a smirk. "You'll see. You like to push me out of my comfort zone, Doc. Let's see you get out of yours."

---

*A*s soon as I got home, I googled Sinners and found it to be a new, upper-class restaurant in Providence. The photos of the interior showed a stylish bar and restaurant, and Hayden's name was listed as head chef. Which explained why Kara and Hawk were attending the grand opening.

What I couldn't work out was why Hawk had said it was time for me to get out of my comfort zone. Nice clothes and fancy food weren't exactly out of my norm these days. Though I sounded like a spoiled rich brat, even thinking that.

Which made me uncomfortable. I was no stranger to those nicer things in life now. But it hadn't always been that way. I hadn't forgotten that. I never would. The horrors of my childhood and teenage years were so firmly imprinted in my brain, there was no amount of therapy that could make me forget where I'd come from. Even as an adult, my past had kept coming back to bite me, until it had cost my wife her life.

I showered, finding that for once, my brain switched from memories of Annette to the present day quicker and easier than I ever had before. I'd spent years sitting in my grief over her death, waiting for something to break the spell.

Instead, it had been a someone.

Shame that someone already had two men and only saw me as the friendly neighborhood doctor, who delivered babies in his spare time.

Hawk had told me to dress nicely, so I pulled on a fresh pair of suit pants and a button-down shirt, cuffs rolled to the elbows. I slapped on some aftershave, picked up my phone, and locked the front door.

My phone buzzed on the way down to my car, and when I checked the message on my watch, I stopped.

> Another body came in. Same cause of death. Strangulation. Cops identified her as the sister to the last one. Whoever this guy is, he's escalating. Want to come check it out? I can probably only keep her another day or so.

It was my contact at the morgue.

This time, at least my blood didn't run cold at the thought the victim could have been Kara. I'd seen her only an hour ago, so she definitely wasn't the dead woman lying cold in the morgue with the life strangled out of her.

But it could have been.

If this guy was escalating, how long would it be before he got to her?

I pushed the thought out of my head, reminding myself that for now, at least, she was safe.

And she wasn't mine to protect. No matter how much the urge was there to do so. If I continued to listen to it, it was only going to end with Hawk beating the shit out of me.

I'd probably deserve it.

By the time I parked my car down the street from Sinners, I'd convinced myself I could just be friends with her. Because there was no alternative.

But the minute I walked in the restaurant doors, and she looked up and waved to me from a booth in the back corner of the room, I knew I was full of crap. She had her hair down, brushed out and glossy, just begging for me to twist with my fingers. The deep-blue dress clinging to her tits and then falling softly around her knees nearly had me on mine. She was a world away from the sweet-faced woman who put on scrubs when she came to the hospital and worked her damn ass off.

"I'm so fucked," I muttered to myself, raising a hand in return and pointing her out to the maître d', who waved me on.

"You made it!" Kara stood as I approached. She pressed up onto her toes and kissed my cheek. "Thank you for coming. I know it'll mean a lot to Hayden."

Despite knowing I shouldn't, I took her arm, leaned down, and kissed her in the same spot. "You look beautiful," I whispered gently into her ear.

I knew it was out of line.

But I couldn't help it. It was the truth. The dress clung to her curves so damn enticingly it was impossible not to notice how effortlessly pretty she was. This darkened room, with all its black-and-red interior, low lights, and sultry music, only made me want her more.

I so needed a drink. I hadn't had a crush like this

since high school, and it was getting downright embarrassing.

Next I'd be having wet dreams about her like I was fucking fifteen years old with no control of my dick. Kill me now.

"Thank you." Kara ducked her head, though it did nothing to hide the pink blush in her cheeks.

Had she liked me calling her beautiful?

A tiny seed of hope lit up inside me. One that whispered she noticed me too.

I dropped into the empty seat beside her and reached across the table to shake Hawk's hand, feeling vaguely guilty for the feelings I was harboring for his woman.

He raised his glass at me. "Glad you made it."

"You promised me a drink, so I figured it would be rude not to show."

Hawk grinned and signaled to the waiter. "Can we get another round? Top shelf. Whatever our friend here wants. He delivered a baby this afternoon, so he deserves it."

The waiter widened his eyes. "Seriously?"

I laughed uncomfortably. "I'm a doctor, so it's not actually as impressive as it sounds."

Kara shook her head. "Actually, it was. I was terrified the entire time, but you were so calm and collected. Even when the baby wasn't breathing, you just got the job done. You were amazing."

I swallowed thickly, accepting her praise awkwardly, all while wishing she was calling me amazing for any other reason.

I was a good doctor. I knew that. But I didn't want that to be the only thing she saw.

I wanted her to see me as a man.

But then she turned to Hawk and gazed at him the way I wanted her to look at me, and I told the waiter to make mine a double.

I needed it if I was going to be the third wheel with the two of them all night. Watching him whisper in her ear and her laugh and lean into him suddenly seemed like the worst sort of torture. I struggled to remember exactly why I was subjecting myself to it.

When the waiter brought my drink, I downed it in one and asked for another.

Kara pulled away from Hawk and leaned into me as I set my glass back down on the table. "So we'll have to reschedule Hayley Jade's appointment. Any idea when you might want to do that?"

I stalled on my answer, realizing if I was in agony now, spending more and more time with them wasn't exactly going to help. I couldn't be her therapist when I wanted to be so much more.

I was saved by Kara's gaze flickering to focus over my shoulder. "Hey! They let you out of the kitchen!"

Hawk overdramatically screwed up his face. "Oh, look who it is, here to wreck my mood." But there was a renewed interest in his eyes, and he didn't turn away from whoever was approaching the table.

I swiveled, relieved to be off the hook but then groaning internally at the sight of Hayden strolling across the restaurant in his all-black chef uniform, hair tied back in a messy low ponytail at the base of his neck, and a barely there beard covering his cheeks.

"Jesus Christ," I muttered into my drink. "Could he be any more attractive?"

Hawk glanced over at me and snorted.

Red-hot embarrassment skated down my neck that he'd heard. I cringed. "Sorry. Didn't mean to say that."

Hawk eyed me. "You swing that way?"

I shook my head. "Doesn't mean I'm blind though."

Hawk chuckled quietly, his gaze too all-knowing for me to continue to hold.

Kara eyed us curiously, but then Hayden was at the table, gripping the edge of it and leaning down to plant a kiss on Kara's mouth.

Jealousy surged inside me that both he and Hawk got to do that. Got to touch her all they wanted while everything inside me ached to do the same.

"Everything okay with you all?" Hayden asked. His gaze fell on me. "Grayson, right? We met when Kara was in the hospital. Heard you also deliver babies in your spare time."

"Only on Fridays," I joked lamely, desperate to change the subject. "Great place you have here. Opening night seems like it's going well. Tables are all full. Food smells amazing." I held up my half-empty glass. "Drinks are sweet."

Hayden grinned and tapped the menus on the middle of the table that we hadn't even opened yet because I'd been too busy drowning my sorrows in whiskey. "I recommend the trout."

Hawk grinned across the table at me. "Nice and light. So you aren't too full for...dessert."

"I'm not much of a sweet tooth," I admitted.

Hawk and Hayden both laughed. Kara's cheeks were pink again.

I frowned at her. "What did I say?"

Hawk jerked his head at Hayden, his smirk firmly in place. "You going to invite him?"

"Invite me to what?"

Hayden raised an eyebrow, ignoring me, his question all for Hawk. "He's your boss. You want to see your boss like that?"

"I'd like the earth to swallow me whole now, please," Kara said quietly with a giggle in her voice, making me realize she'd clearly had more than one of the fruity cocktails she'd been sipping on since I'd gotten here.

"I'm not anyone's boss tonight," I assured them, literally no idea what was going on. "I'm not even on call."

Hawk sniggered. "Go on. Give him a ticket."

Hayden shook his head and reached over the bar, saying something softly to the bartender, who handed over a small slip of paper. Hayden thanked him and held it out to me. "Ticket to the after-party. It's held in the room just down the hallway, past the bathrooms. But just be warned, it's not your regular sort of party."

I frowned down at the ticket, not knowing what he meant by that but not wanting to sound stupid either. "Sure. Okay. No problem. Thanks."

Hawk sniggered into his drink again, thoroughly amused with himself.

Hayden tapped the menus once more. "Eat something, it's all on the house. I swear the food is edible. I'll catch up with you all later."

I tucked the ticket into my pocket and turned my attention back to drinking. Hawk eased up on the teasing, and the three of us fell into conversation about work, the patients we'd seen recently, and the treatments we'd given them. It had been a long time since I'd had someone to teach, and it was nice to share what I did, especially with people who were so eager to learn.

But at the same time, it reminded me I never got to do this. I had no one to go home to at night and talk over my day with. I had colleagues, and gym regulars, but no real friends. I was attracted to Kara, but not just in a physical sense. I liked talking to her. She was curious. Asked smart questions, and it was clear her desire to help people aligned with mine.

Hawk was a different breed, perhaps more in it for the thrill, but it didn't make him any less interested.

For the first time in as long as I could remember, I was just having a nice time, enjoying their company and conversation. Drinks flowed, all of us downing more than we probably should have, our conversation and laughter getting loud.

The food came out, and it was mouth-wateringly delicious. Kara moaned at the taste of her first bite, and I nearly choked on my mouthful of trout, drunk enough to imagine that moan coming from her lips because of a whole different reason.

Hawk seemed to have the same idea on his mind. His hand dropped below the table, and I was sure it was headed for Kara's leg.

Or his dick.

The vibe in the room didn't help matters. It was a soft seduction, the music mixing with the freely flowing alcohol and a buzz of anticipation I couldn't quite understand but felt the effects of nonetheless. Our little corner of the room felt private and warm, and when Kara let out a tiny gasp, my brain conjured up an image of Hawk's fingers beneath the tablecloth, creeping up the side of her leg, slipping beneath the hem of her dress and diving between her thighs.

I muffled a noise of need into my drink, but it wasn't enough. I had to get out of here. Dinner had been nice, but the longer I sat here with them, the more I was just torturing myself. "I think I'm going to leave you to it," I mumbled as Hawk leaned in and pressed his lips against Kara's neck, no fucks given that I was still sitting there at the table with them. "Maybe go check out the after-party or something."

If either of them noticed me leaving, they didn't comment, too involved with each other.

The air was slightly cooler in the hallway as I searched for the bathrooms. At the bustling kitchen, Hayden caught my eye and raised a hand in greeting. I returned the gesture but kept moving, the alcohol taking its effect on both my head and my bladder.

I did my thing in the empty bathroom, washed my hands, and then splashed cold water on my face, trying to relieve some of the heat from my cheeks.

I needed to distance myself from Kara. If tonight had taught me anything, it was that. If I considered my behavior from an unbiased therapist point of view, I would have diagnosed myself with a clear case of infatuation.

One that wasn't healthy, considering I was third-wheeling on a date with her and another man, and imagining it was me with my hand between her thighs, making her moan.

I leaned my head on the cool tiled wall of the bathroom and squeezed my eyes shut. I needed to stop this. Stop seeing her. Change my shifts around so I wasn't in the clinic when she was. Recommend her a different therapist because I'd already crossed so many lines with her that we couldn't come back from.

That *I* couldn't come back from. None of this was Kara's fault. It was all on me.

I couldn't stand in the bathroom all night. That was weird when there were guys coming in and out to use the urinals. I slipped from the restroom, gaze catching on the heavy wooden doors at the end of the corridor.

Hayden had said the after-party would be held down here, and there was already a steady stream of people handing over their tickets and slipping inside the doors.

I didn't want to go home and sit in my empty apartment alone. All I'd do was replay every interaction over and over again, and hate myself a little more for every stupid thing I'd said to a woman who was never going to see me as anything more than a friend.

I didn't want a friend tonight. I wanted something more. Someone to take home. Someone who would make me remember there were plenty of other women around.

Curiosity got the better of me, and I followed a loved-up couple to the doors, handing over my ticket to the woman manning the entrance. Her long dress sparkled in the spotlight above her head, a long split up one thigh and another plunging deep between her breasts.

She scanned the slip of paper Hayden had given me, then gave it back, pointing at a number on it. "There's a corresponding locker to your left as you walk in for your clothes and personal belongings. And showers just inside the doors if you want them at any time."

I blinked. Showers? What on earth would I need a

shower for? Lockers seemed like overkill too. I could just hold my jacket if I got hot.

My face must have displayed my confusion because the woman laughed at me. "Are you okay?"

I squinted at her, wondering if I'd heard her wrong. I'd had quite a bit to drink tonight. "I'm just wondering why I'd need a shower?"

She bit her lip, trying to hold back a laugh. "Do you have any idea what you're walking into?"

I shook my head. "I'm starting to think I don't, actually. Want to clue me in?"

The woman leaned in, nipples brushing against my chest, her lips at my ear so she could whisper into it. "It's a sex club, honey. Welcome to the real side of Sinners."

26

KARA

TEN MINUTES EARLIER

*H*ayden's food lit up every taste bud in my mouth. The explosion of flavor was like nothing I'd ever tasted before and made me realize exactly how bland and boring my own cooking was.

I'd offered to cook for this man. How embarrassing. My plain boiled potatoes and slow-cooked stews didn't deserve to call themselves food in the face of this sort of flavor.

But my thoughts drifted away with the fruity pink cocktails I'd been drinking all night, and I moaned, shoveling another mouthful of saucy chicken into my mouth.

Hawk shifted an inch closer, his hand coming to rest on my leg.

I flinched at the unexpected touch, glancing at Grayson, who was eating his meal intently, studying his fish like he might be able to decipher every ingredient used to make it as tasty as it was if he stared at it hard enough.

Hawk leaned in, his lips dragging their way up my

neck to my ear. "That's the noise you make when you come."

I blinked, sure he'd said that way too loud for Grayson not to hear.

"I think I'm going to leave you to it," he mumbled, confirming my suspicions. "Maybe go check out the after-party or something."

His chair scraped along the floor as he pushed it back and stood, dropping his napkin to the table.

I went to say something, but Grayson walked away too quick for me to get a sound out.

"Thought he'd never leave," Hawk mumbled against my skin.

I elbowed him. "Don't be mean. You're the one who invited him here tonight."

"That was before I saw you in that dress and wished I hadn't opened my big mouth."

The dress was one I'd found in the stack of clothes Bliss had donated to me. The old me would have never dared to wear something so...attention-grabbing. But it was a special occasion, and I'd wanted to fit in with the rich women from Providence who had flocked to the restaurant, perhaps because it was the new hot place to be seen...perhaps because they were looking for the spice hidden behind the thick wooden doors down the hallway.

The alcohol swirled inside me pleasantly. I laughed, liking the way Hawk looked at me, the way he touched me, even if he had just made things awkward with Grayson. Every touch of Hawk's fingertips left warmth in its wake. The music in my ears had my hips swaying unconsciously to the beat. Or maybe that was just my body seeking out his. I glanced toward the hallway where Grayson had disappeared, fighting the building urge inside my body to crawl into Hawk's lap.

I forced my focus onto something more mundane. Something more appropriate, since we were in public and Grayson could hit those doors, realize what was beyond them, and turn around and walk back out any second now. "Grayson was amazing today, wasn't he? His stories about the hospital and his patients are so inspiring."

Hawk continued picking at his food with his right hand, but his left inched beneath the hem of my skirt, sliding its way between my thighs. "Sure. Inspiring. But I don't want to talk about Grayson anymore. Open for me, Little Mouse."

I glanced around the room. It was full with people finishing their meals and heading for the party in the back, as well as people streaming in to take their places or bypass dinner altogether in favor of dessert only.

"Not here." I clenched my thighs together, though if I'd given in to the desire inside me I would have done the complete opposite.

Hawk licked a path up my neck indecently. "Do you remember how Chaos made you come while I watched?"

Oh God. If he started talking about that I already knew where this was going to end up.

"Answer me, Little Mouse."

His bossy demands melted me until I was a liquid, flowing to him, no way of fighting it. I could never resist him when he used that tone. "Yes."

"You remember how good it felt? How hard your

sweet pussy clenched around his fingers, coating them with your honey?"

He was trying to kill me and bury me all with one dirty sentence. He knew exactly what to say to have my knees weak and me agreeing to anything he wanted me to do.

Not just agreeing. Wanting it as much as he did. "Yes."

"Let me do it. Let me make you come while others watch."

My breaths turned into pants at the very thought. My thighs fell apart, admitting him access. "Grayson could come back out and see..."

Hawk pressed a finger to my clit. "Grayson is so fucking hot for you he's probably gone out to that party to stroke his dick while he thinks about what I'm doing to you in here."

"What?" I shook my head sharply. "Hawk, stop it. He is not. He's just a colleague."

"He wants you on his cock."

I stared at him. "I don't believe that. We're friends."

Hawk chuckled, stroking the silky fabric of my panties and running his finger beneath the elastic tantalizingly close to my pussy. "Friends don't think about how wet your pussy is right now."

I gasped when his finger slipped inside me. "Hawk..." He was pressing all the right buttons. My eyes wanted to flutter closed so I could ride his fingers without the reminder of where I was until I came. Except I couldn't concentrate. "We have to work with him. You know very well he's about to get the shock of his life down that hallway and will be back out here in minutes. It's bad enough he probably just heard you saying I moan when I come."

Hawk lowered his head so our gazes collided, his eyes studying me while I kept flicking worried glances toward the hallway Grayson had disappeared down.

His breath warmed the side of my neck. "You're dreaming if you're thinking he's too smart and proper to be into what's going on out there. He's probably got some woman bent over a table, fucking her pussy without a care in the world."

The image sent a shudder of desire through my entire body, one I couldn't control. I clenched around Hawk's finger, like I did when I came.

Hawk glanced at me in surprise. "What was that, Little Mouse?"

"Nothing," I breathed. Except I couldn't get the idea of Grayson just feet away behind a door, his dick heavy and glistening, sliding in and out of another woman's body.

Hawk stroked my clit with his thumb. "You're turned on by the idea of him fucking someone." He said it as if it were fact.

I shook my head. "No."

But it sounded weak, even to my ears. Embarrassment coursed through me over the lustful thoughts I had no right to be thinking. What was wrong with me? I didn't even recognize myself anymore. I'd thought that was a good thing. But maybe I was taking it too far.

Grayson was a professional man. My colleague. A well-educated doctor. Not someone to think about in that way. Except now the idea had been planted, I couldn't stop thinking about it. There were so many things he could be doing out there, and I couldn't stop thinking about any of them.

Hawk's lips were at my ear. "Your pussy is throbbing like it wants to be the one he's fucking."

Slowly, Hawk pulled his finger from inside me.

I opened my eyes in time to watch him press it into his mouth and lick it clean. My nipples pebbled beneath my bra, and my core mourned the loss of his touch. All while throbbing at the thought of where Grayson was, and the dirty images Hawk was filling my head with.

Hawk swallowed the last of the liquid in his drink and put the glass down on the table. "I'm not going to ask, because I know it gets you hot when I just tell you what to do. So stand up, Little Mouse. Stand up and go let him fuck you."

I snapped my head around, gaze slamming into his. "What? Hawk—"

"Tell me you haven't just been thinking about him inside you and I'll take it back."

I opened my mouth to deny it, but we both knew it would have been a lie. If I'd been sober, and we'd been anywhere else, where this music and this club weren't stripping away my inhibitions, maybe I would have just lied anyway. But with several cocktails' worth of alcohol in my system, and a heat like nothing I'd ever felt before inside me, I couldn't bring myself to pretend I hadn't just been thinking that very thing.

"Why would you want that?" I asked him, not understanding this man at all who flipped from possessive jealousy to wanting another man to have me.

A smile tipped the corner of his too-sexy mouth. "I'm drunk and horny, and I like the idea of watching. Of you fucking him not just because he makes you hot but because I wanted you to."

He leaned in and kissed me hard, his tongue delving into my mouth and spinning my head even more than the alcohol was.

When he stood and pulled me up from my seat, I didn't say no. I didn't even want to. Something inside me breathlessly demanded I follow him down the hallway and past the doors with Sinners engraved deep in the wood.

Hawk handed over two tickets, and the woman at the door pushed it open, admitting us entry to the den of iniquity beyond.

The maze seemed completely different at night, and I gripped Hawk's hand tightly as he led me to the nearest entrance. The sultry music filled my ears, and my heart pounded to the beat.

Hawk's fingers trailed along a wall of blindfolds, and he picked one off, tucking it into his pocket with a wink at me. "For later, maybe?"

I didn't have time to respond because he was leading me deeper into the room, and the things going on in there stole any words I might have wanted to say. A pretty redheaded woman I'd seen in the restaurant earlier was laid out on a padded bench roughly the size of a king-size bed. People surrounded her, two men sucking and licking her breasts, another slow fucking her between her legs. A second woman alternated between licking the first woman's clit and the man's erection every time he slid out. All of them were in various stages of undress, the licking woman giving us a flash of her wet pussy as she did her job.

I found myself scanning each man's face, checking to see if any of them were Grayson, then berating myself because it wasn't my business what...or who... he was doing in here.

"You want to join them?" Hawk asked in the darkness.

There was a fire burning me from the inside out, but I shook my head quickly, gripping him tighter. He pulled me farther into the maze, past more groups having sex in all sorts of positions. Past women and men on their knees, delivering blow jobs, past a woman on a couch, impaling herself on a thick, black dildo while others watched.

Grayson wasn't any of them.

I wasn't sure why that left me feeling slightly disappointed.

Unfulfilled. Unsatisfied.

The fire inside me, fueled by alcohol and Hawk's dirty words, burned hotter.

"Over there, Little Mouse." Hawk nodded.

I followed his line of sight.

The gasp that left my body felt so loud I might as well have screamed it.

But Grayson and the woman he was with didn't seem to notice. He had his back to us, but there was no mistaking the broad set of his shoulders, even though they were now bare of his usual collared shirt. His back rippled with muscle, tapering down to a narrow waist and rounded ass cheeks I couldn't drag my gaze away from, even though I knew I should.

I forced myself to shake my head. "We should go," I muttered to Hawk. "He'll see us. I don't want this."

Except I did.

Hawk turned and stepped in front of me, pushing me back against the wall and blocking me in with his arms either side of my head. "Ask him to fuck you."

Panic rose in me. "I can't!"

"Why?" Hawk challenged. "You think he won't drop that woman the second he sees you?"

"Of course he won't! Look at her!"

I peered past Hawk at the woman laying herself out on the bed, her legs spread wide, Grayson kneeling between them and looming over her. The woman could have just walked off a catwalk in Paris. She was all blond hair, perfect breasts, and long legs. Not a fat roll or stretchmark in sight.

Hawk caught my chin and brought it back so his gaze bored into mine. "Look at her? Little Mouse, look at *you*."

His words stole my breath, even though the moment was broken by Grayson's woman shouting as he entered her.

I gasped, seeing every second of his slow slide out and then back in. The woman moaned, clutching his back, running her nails down his skin.

Undeniable jealousy bubbled up inside me, mixing with heat so hot I thought I would implode. A whimper of need escaped my lips.

Hawk hiked up the hem of my cocktail-length dress and slid his fingers between my legs. I whimpered at the relief his touch brought me and gasped when he yanked my panties down so they were somewhere around my knees.

Two fingers slipped inside me easily. Hawk glanced over his shoulder, watching Grayson having sex and matching the speed of his thrusts with his fingers.

Grayson and the woman were beautiful together. Her legs wrapped around him as they writhed, both of them taking what they needed from each other's bodies.

Her head tipped back, exposing her long neck, and he fit his mouth there, sucking her and thrusting into her body.

"She doesn't compare to you," Hawk murmured in my ear, watching them as much as I was while he pushed me closer and closer to an orgasm. "Nobody does. He just doesn't know that yet because you haven't let him see you. He hasn't had the pleasure of you dripping down his throat, your thighs locking around his head when you come. He hasn't had you bouncing on his cock while he sucks your tits. If you let him see you like you let me, he'd be on his knees in front of you right now, worshipping your pussy the way I can't wait to get you home to do."

"Yes." I wasn't exactly sure of what I was agreeing to. Maybe it was the idea of leaving this place, getting back to somewhere I felt comfortable, and letting Hawk make good on every dirty promise he'd made tonight.

Maybe it was the idea of Grayson wanting me, if only I would let him in.

I shuddered in Hawk's arms, needing so much more than just his fingers.

"Come for him, Little Mouse. Come watching him fuck her, and then I'll take you home and do it better." Hawk's fingers pressed that spot inside me, stroking it so perfectly.

Just behind him, Grayson moved harder, faster. His hips pounding into the woman who could have been me if only I'd been braver.

The orgasm caught me by surprise, shocking its way

through my system and lighting me up from the inside out. I bit down on Hawk's shoulder, using his shirt to muffle the cry that was partly for him, but mostly for the man across the room who had no idea we were watching.

"God," Hawk muttered into my neck. "I want to fuck you so bad right now. You're so fucking wet I'm tempted to try fisting you. I could make you feel so damn good."

I didn't exactly know what that was, but I could imagine, and I trusted this man enough to know that anything he did to me, I was going to enjoy. I trembled at the thought of all the things I didn't know yet. All the things he could teach me.

He reared back then dove on my lips, kissing me hard, his tongue demanding and sexual, promising me a world of pleasure. His dick was rigid against my stomach, desperate and needy, seeking my body out the same way mine melded into his.

Grayson's woman came with a earth-shattering scream.

Grayson's own moan of completion came a second later.

He would turn around at any second. See us. Know what we'd been doing. I yanked at my panties, fighting against the hold Hawk had on both my heart and my body.

He panted, trying to get himself under control, and then with what looked to be maximum effort, he pulled away, fingers gripping mine. He tugged me around a corner of the maze, leaving me with a final parting glance at Grayson rolling over, his dick still gleaming from being inside someone else.

For a tiny, heart-stopping moment, his gaze caught mine.

Then we were gone, Hawk dragging me out of the maze, stopping only when we got to the kitchen. On spotting Hayden, he strode in like we owned the place.

"Hawk!" I squeaked. "We can't be back here."

But Hawk couldn't care less about my "good girl, always does the right thing, couldn't break a rule" protests. He walked right up to Hayden, leaned in, and said in a voice low enough for only the two of us to hear over the hiss of steam and clattering of pans:

"Finish whatever you're doing here and meet us at home. She needs us both tonight."

27

HAWK

Hayden's expression switched from shock to something white-hot in a split second.

His gaze raked over Kara standing beside me, pink-cheeked and breathless from the orgasm she'd just had watching Grayson fuck someone else, while I'd had my fingers buried in her soaking slit. Her hair was tousled, her nipples straining through the fabric of her dress and just begging for someone to suck them.

When his gaze focused on me with that same burning intensity, all I could think about was the way he'd sucked my cock, deep-throating me until I'd grabbed his hair and come in his mouth.

And how I'd gotten on my knees and done the exact same thing for him.

There was no denying what had happened between us in the darkness.

Or that in that moment, I desperately wanted it to happen again.

I turned, pulling Kara with me, knowing with knee-wobbling certainty that Chaos would follow.

We strode out through the restaurant, past the line of classily dressed men and women still waiting to get inside, even though it was past midnight and the restaurant had closed.

Clearly, word spread quickly in Providence. Whatever Luca and Hayden had done to promote this place, or rather, its after-hour activities, was working.

I didn't let myself think about what that meant for Psychos. If all of Bliss's clientele moved their after-hours partying over here, then who would be left?

That was a problem for the daylight.

Tonight was for sinners.

I opened the passenger side door of the van, letting Kara in, fighting the urge to slap her rounded ass, so damn perfect in that dress I really wanted off her. I jogged around the other side and slid behind the steering wheel, barely able to breathe for wanting to get home and for what I knew was coming.

I backed out of the parking spot and peeled away, down the street, hating that the drive to the compound was more than a few minutes.

Because fuck knows I couldn't wait that long to have her again.

Have him again.

Fuck. I didn't want to think about the erection I got every time Chaos's blue eyes crossed my mind. The way he'd looked in the darkness, the way his mouth had felt, the way I'd wanted to do so much more than just blow him.

I groaned, running my hand over my erection strangled by my pants.

Kara reached across, slipping her hand beneath mine, taking over, unzipping my fly while I drove.

She freed my cock and I hissed in pleasure at her rubbing over the head and the precum beading there. "Don't make me come," I warned her. "I want your pussy, Little Mouse. And your ass."

"But I want you in my mouth."

It fucking killed me when she talked like that. I was so damn hard for her, I could barely stand it.

I dropped my arm, steering with one hand, watching from the corner of my eye as she slid across the bench seat and lowered her head to replace her hands with her lips.

My right hand fell to the back of her head, twisting in her hair while she blew me. Her mouth was warm and wet, and she felt so good, tongue swirling around my dick. My balls ached with the need to come, but I refused to give in to the desperate sensation, concentrating on the road, the only thing keeping me from exploding.

I put my foot down on the gas, knowing if we flew by a cop, I'd be pulled over. If that happened, the cop would be arresting us both for indecent exposure.

There was no stopping now. Not for either of us. The build up to this had been too long. Too sweet.

I needed her like I needed air.

Whoever was on the gate saw us coming and opened it with time for me to fly through without slowing down. I took the road down to the clubhouse, Kara making desperate noises around my cock that only made it harder to concentrate.

At the bottom of the hill, I dragged her up off me by her hair, only hard enough for her to feel the buzz of pleasure in her scalp, because fuck knows I would never do anything to hurt her.

I'd been careless and selfish with women in the past. Not caring about them or their pleasure. She'd brought out something gentle in me that no other woman ever had. All while liking it just as much when I was rough. But I knew the line. Knew where to push her and where to stop.

I loved every second of her giving herself up to me, trusting me to keep her safe.

"Wait for me." I tucked my erection away and did my pants up enough they wouldn't fall off. Leaving the keys in the ignition, I got out of the van and rounded the front, yanking open Kara's door and reaching across her to undo the seat belt.

She sat there waiting for me like the good fucking girl she was.

Her squeal of surprise when I picked her up off the seat was cute as frigging hell.

"I can walk! Hawk, put me down."

"Not a fucking chance. If I stop to put you down, I'm fucking you right here in the middle of the goddamn driveway. There's no way I can watch your sweet ass sway while you walk and not want to pin you down and yank your dress up."

She looked at my face and saw I was dead fucking serious. I was barely keeping it together as it was.

She swallowed hard. "Walk faster then."

I grinned, loving the way she clung to me, knowing in

minutes, I was going to be all over her for the rest of the night.

I'd lost track of the time. The sky was that deep inky black that only showed up well after the sun had set, but still hours before dawn. The clubhouse was its usual blaze of weekend activity, music spilling out, and the common room a full-blown party, despite the fact it had to be at least one in the morning.

Hoots and hollers broke out, the rest of the club noticing me and Kara. Jeers and taunts and sexual innuendos were shouted across the room. Kara buried her head in my neck to hide her embarrassment, but I only needed one thing here. My gaze narrowed in on Queenie, an unspoken question in my eyes.

"Rebel picked her up hours ago, sugar. Remi wanted a sleepover, and I made the executive decision that it was okay when the two of you didn't answer your phones." She winked at me. "Night is yours to do as you please."

"I could kiss you right now," I told her.

"Go kiss your woman instead, hey?" Aloha joked in his jolly voice. "I got Queenie's lips otherwise occupied." He lowered his head to hers, kissing her deeply as she wrapped her arms around his neck.

I strode through the club, pivoting at the last second, not toward my bedroom door, or Kara's...but to Hayden's.

The club went quiet for a single moment, shock punching through the room.

"Uh, you lost, Hawk?" Aloha asked. "You know that's Chaos's room, right?"

Whispers circled around the room, questions of whether something was going on between me and Hayden louder than questions about me, him, and Kara having a threesome. Everyone stared, waiting for me to respond, Amber's questions the loudest. "So what? After all the shit you gave War, now you're gay too?"

I didn't want to care. I wanted to have the balls War had when he'd fallen for Scythe.

I wanted to just say I was into Chaos, but my tongue wouldn't form the words.

I slammed my way into his room and kicked the door shut behind me, without uttering a sound.

Kara stroked her hand down the side of my face gently.

"I'm not gay."

"Okay," she said softly, not a hint of judgment in her tone.

"I only brought you in here because I want to fuck you on his bed. Make sure he knows that even if we're sharing you, you were always mine first."

She nodded.

"Fuck." I put her down on the bed and ran a hand through my hair, knowing my excuses were just that.

Excuses.

I wasn't ready for the entire club to know my business, when even I didn't know my business. One blow job didn't mean I was into him.

Except my heart beat too fast, waiting for the moment he'd get back here and find us.

I groaned, dropping down on the bed beside her. What the fuck had I done? The club might have accepted War and Scythe, but he was the prez. Nobody dared say a word against him.

Maybe as VP they wouldn't say it to my face either.

But they'd talk about it behind my back. Question

everything they knew about me. My authority. My position here. My intentions every time I was alone in a room with them.

I didn't fucking want them all staring at me.

Just like the three sets of eyes staring at me from the corner of the room.

"Oh Jesus fuck! What are those?" I skittered back on the bed.

Kara peered around me and laughed, dropping to the floor to unlock the crate and let the three kittens out. "They're Hayden's kittens."

I squinted at the furry creatures who wandered past Kara and straight over to my legs, winding their way around them and rubbing themselves against the scratchy denim.

Kara grinned. "They love you."

"Yeah, well, the feeling isn't mutual." I shifted my legs to the side, trying to escape them, but they followed, insistently meowing. I stood, moving to the other side of the room, but the little fuzzballs followed. "Yeah, okay, that's about enough of that." I twisted the doorknob with one hand and swept the kittens out into the party with the other, before closing the door so they couldn't come back in.

Kara frowned at me, her white teeth digging into her pink, plump bottom lip.

"What?" I asked her.

"You just sent Hayden's kittens out into a clubhouse full of bikers, half of whom look like they swing cats by their tails for fun..." She stared up at me worriedly. "I don't want—"

I got where she was coming from. But I also knew my guys better than she did. "Just wait." I held up a finger.

Outside, shouts of excitement and squeals of delight lit up the party.

"I claim the black one!" Ice shouted.

"Ginger one is mine!" That was one of the women.

"Oh my God, it's so soft! Hello, sweet baby. Come to Daddy."

Pretty sure that last one was Aloha.

"I presume the kittens have been noticed." I laughed at Kara visibly relaxing. "You didn't really think they'd hurt them, did you? You trust those people with your child."

"I know, but I just thought…because they're Hayden's and nobody here likes him…"

I didn't say anything.

"Except you," Kara said softly.

I lifted my head to meet her gaze, but the last thing I wanted to do was examine whatever the fuck it was between me and Hayden. "I like *you*." I pulled her to her feet so I could tip her chin up and kiss her sweet lips. "I like you a whole fucking lot, Little Mouse. Especially when you take your clothes off and get on your knees for me."

Heat flared in her eyes.

She took half a step back, then bold as I'd ever seen her, dropped the thin straps of her dress down off her shoulders.

I leaned back against the wall, undoing my fly and releasing my newly interested hard-on.

She tugged the bodice down, revealing a strapless bra struggling to contain her full tits. She reached behind her back and unclipped the clasps, slowly drawing away the cups until her pert pink nipples drew my focus.

She went to get down on her knees, but I caught her hand, keeping her standing. "Take that dress all the way off."

"My stomach..."

"Is just one of the places I want to come." I slid my hand across her belly, lowering the dress so it settled around her hips. I'd told her to get on her knees and blow me, but it was me who dropped to the floor and kissed the underside of her breasts, the rolls on her stomach, the curve of her hips. I dragged the damn dress to the floor, taking her underwear with it.

Putting my mouth on her pussy was all too easy, my tongue darting between her folds to flick her little bud of pleasure while she scraped her nails across my scalp. Her thighs were thick and soft, and after a few minutes of me licking her there, she fisted the back of my shirt and pulled it over my head.

Her fingers danced across my shoulders, stroking and scratching my skin gently, until I craved her touch all over my body. I stood, kicking off my boots and toeing off my socks, my jeans the last thing to disappear into the pile of clothes on the floor.

"I want you on his bed," I whispered in her ear, sending a shiver through her body.

She sat on the edge and then scooted back so she was lying. She was so beautiful in the lamplight, the golden glow kissing every inch of her skin, highlighting the desire in her eyes, and the need for me I couldn't get enough of.

I crawled on top, hovering over her soft body so bare

and open for me. I dropped my head, kissing her deeply, and then inch by inch, lowered the rest of me down. I ground my dick between her thighs, brushing against the silky arousal at her core but teasing her there, not entering her, even though she was slick with need.

With my weight on one forearm, I circled my fingers around one wrist, drawing it up over her head. Shifting my body to the other side, I did the same with her right arm, so both her hands were above her head. I kissed her, tongue swirling, moving away to suck her neck and her ear, and then whispering in it dirtily, "On your stomach."

Without waiting for her to move or for her permission, I gripped her soft hips and flipped her over, immediately fitting myself back between her legs and spreading them wide to accommodate me on my knees behind her.

She twisted her head to one side, her dark curls spread out on the pillow, a sharp contrast with the stark white pillow cover.

I grabbed another from the other side of the bed and dragged her hips up just enough to fit the pillow beneath them.

I sat back for a second, palm smoothing down her spine, and then taking two indecent handfuls of her plump ass and massaging the cheeks, spreading them, catching a glimpse of her wet pussy in between her widespread thighs.

Fuck, I wanted her. My dick strained toward her, and I gave in, covering her body with mine and fitting my dick to her pussy.

She gasped when I entered her, but there was no resistance. She'd been so wet in the club she'd been close to taking my entire fist, and the short interlude to now had done little to dry her up. I fucked her slow, loving she didn't feel like she would break beneath me, loving that as I picked up the pace she pushed her hips back, meeting me thrust for thrust with a power of her own.

I used one forearm to take some of my weight and slipped my other hand beneath her to pinch her nipple.

When I told her to put her hand between her legs and the mattress and rub her clit, she did.

"You feel so fucking good, Kara," I murmured in her ear, every word the truth because I was sure nothing had ever felt as good as her body beneath me.

"Harder," she moaned, voice muffled by the mattress and the pillow. "Oh God, Hawk! Fuck me harder!"

My eyes rolled back. I thrust my hips against her ass, riding her pussy, dragging her hips up farther so I could take her deeper and harder.

The door opened.

I didn't stop.

"Hayden!" Kara gasped between slams of my body to hers.

But fucked if I was letting him have her orgasm. I pulled out, sliding my hand along my dick before plunging it back inside her.

I fit my slicked-up fingers to her ass, rubbing it in the way I knew drove her mad. "You come with my name on your lips, Little Mouse."

I took her to the edge, her ass my plaything to control and pleasure as I saw fit. She embraced every thrust. Every squeeze, all while playing with her little bud, just the way I'd told her to.

Such a fucking good girl.

"Hawk!" She shuddered around me, squeezing my dick with her inner walls so forcefully there was no holding back.

I came inside her with slow, deliberate thrusts, her name on my lips. Not the taunting nickname I used so often, but her real name, the name of the woman I was so fucking in love with I could barely see straight. "Kara." It was barely more than a whisp of a sound before I collapsed down on top of her.

She twisted her head back, craning to bring her lips to mine. "I love you," she whispered before claiming them with her own.

Still joined, my dick warm inside her pussy, I whispered back the same, not giving a fuck that Hayden was right there, waiting for his turn.

28

HAYDEN

They were beautiful together. His tight, taut muscles straining and moving as his fucking morphed into lovemaking. Her softness beneath him, every curve, and all of her sweetly flushed skin.

He collapsed down on top of her, the two of them murmuring words I didn't quite catch between them.

A tiny kernel of jealousy erupted at the familiarity they had with each other. At the ease of two people who'd been together before and knew each other's bodies.

I wanted that.

With her.

Hawk's green eyes watched me in the dim light, and my dick kicked at his expression.

Maybe with him too.

He pushed himself off her, his dick still mostly hard, withdrawing from her body and leaving a trail of his cum between her legs

He raised a cocky eyebrow at me, sauntering to the

bathroom en suite, zero fucks given that he was completely naked.

I watched him shamelessly, taking in every tattoo, every scar, the light dusting of hair across his chest that tapered into a trail, then a thatch of darker hair above his cock.

His gaze was no less interested in me, despite the fact I was still fully clothed. But my work pants did nothing to hide the erection growing behind them, my dick needy over his naked body as much as hers.

He wet a cloth with hot water and then tossed it at me, winking as he got the shower running.

I caught the cloth but couldn't let his cockiness go unchecked. I stepped into the bathroom, right into the shower with him, not giving a fuck that it soaked my uniform in a second.

It had the desired effect.

He yelped. "What the fuck, Chaos?"

We were such identical heights, our gazes locked, and I did nothing to hide the way his naked body and his still half-hard cock made me feel. He scuttled back, but I didn't give him an inch, following him in until we were chest to chest, his back to the cold, tiled wall.

We fought a battle with our eyes.

His saying no.

Mine saying I don't give a fuck.

I wouldn't take something he didn't want to give.

And so I waited.

Waited while the water poured down around us. Waited while he battled whatever inner demon tried to deny the chemistry between us. The chemistry that had been there for years, even if he hadn't wanted to admit it.

Fuck, he was beautiful. I flipped the button on my pants.

Lowered the zipper.

I ground my dick against his, feeling him get up again.

He groaned, his breaths increasing until he was panting with need.

His gaze flickered to my mouth, our lips hovering so fucking close our breaths mingled in the tiny gap between.

"Say it," I urged him in a voice barely above a whisper. "Say you fucking want me."

His eyes flicked to my mouth again. His chest heaved beneath the spray of the water, breathless with our cocks rubbing against each other, so maddeningly hot I was sure I'd self-combust.

A war battled behind his eyes. His desire and his cock making it clear what he wanted.

But his brain and his upbringing making it impossible to open his mouth and give me the words I needed.

The moment drew out.

And then passed.

With what felt like superhuman effort, I pushed off his chest and backed away, out of the shower, pressing my lips together and nodding slowly.

"Chaos," he groaned. "I..."

"You what?"

His fingers twitched like he wanted to reach for me, but at the same time, he shook his head.

Too bad.

But I wasn't here to force him. Or to sort his head out.

I stripped my soaking shirt. Dropped it to the tiled floor along with the rest of my soaked clothes.

And left Hawk and his hard-on and his messed-up head alone.

29

KARA

Hayden prowled out of the bathroom dripping wet and without a stitch of clothing on, leaving Hawk behind, staring after him.

They hadn't tried to hide anything from me. I'd seen and heard it all through the open bathroom door. Seen the way they'd touched. The chemistry between them and how close they'd come to kissing.

I saw the hurt in Hayden's eyes when Hawk rejected him, even if he hadn't let Hawk see it.

Hayden crossed the room to me, kneeling on the edge of the bed and crawling across it to where I lay beneath a thin sheet.

"He's not ready," I tried to explain, wrapping my arms around him, wanting to soothe away the hurt in his expression. "It's not you."

He kissed my lips, shutting me up. He kissed me deep, slowly lowering himself down on top of me until he was a delicious warm weight, one I couldn't stop running my fingers all over.

"Tell me you want me, Kara. I need to hear you say it." His voice was deep, sexy, practically a growl of need in my ear. "Tell me you aren't scared when I touch you."

Hawk might not have been able to get the words out, but his problems with Hayden weren't mine. There were no easier words to say when the need for this man had never dimmed, never diminished, not once in the five years we'd been apart.

I'd always wanted him.

He'd always been my hero. My protector. The man who'd loved me without even knowing me, just as much as I'd loved him.

"I've dreamed of this," I whispered to him as he lowered his mouth to my neck and kissed a steady path. "Dreamed of you wanting me the way I've always wanted you." I caught his hand and brought it to my breast. "Touch me."

He shuddered and slid his hand over the swell of my breasts, finding the nipple with two fingers and tugging on it deliciously while he devoured my mouth.

I wrapped my leg around his waist, drawing him into the opening of my thighs. Just like that night at his apartment, our bodies rolled together in unison, fitting together like we'd been made for each other. My heart pounded wildly behind my ribs, my blood starting up a slow beat that spiked with need when he put his hand between us to stroke my clit.

I'd already had multiple orgasms that night, each one mind-blowing in their own right.

Hayden seemed determined to make me have another, fingers slipping from my clit up inside me.

"You're still full of his cum," he whispered in my ear.

I blushed, trying not to moan when he expertly stroked my already sensitive G-spot. "I can have a shower."

He pinned me down. "No."

He glanced over at the corner of the room, and I followed his line of sight.

Hawk sat sprawled in an armchair, threadbare towel wrapped around his waist, doing nothing to hide the erection beneath.

Hayden raised an eyebrow at him. "You just gonna sit there and watch?"

The soft, sweet Hawk I got to see had been buried deep, and the no less sexy, but definitely sarcastic, version sat eyeing Hayden with a smirk. "Fear of premature ejaculation if I do? Performance anxiety happens. Well, not to me, since you've already watched me make her come."

"That a challenge?"

My core throbbed at the thought. I'd already come multiple times tonight. I wasn't sure how many more times it was even possible. "It's not a challenge." I reached up and cupped Hayden's cheeks, drawing his face so he was focused on me. "Ignore him."

Hawk pushed aside his towel and gave his erection one long, leisurely stroke that was clearly designed to show off how big he was. "Hard to ignore when he wants my dick."

Hawk was so insanely cocky when he was in charge of a situation. It was his fallback, his comfort zone.

It was to his detriment.

Hayden knew it as much as I did, and he was nowhere near as polite as I was about ignoring it. He rolled over and opened the top drawer on the bedside table that didn't match the rest of the furniture, all while staring at Hawk. "I already made it pretty clear what I want." He fumbled through the drawer, catching something between his fingers and then tossing it across the room.

Hawk caught it with his free hand and stared down at the object, dropping it quickly. "Oh Jesus fuck, Chaos! Your ass plug?"

Hayden had a challenge in his eyes. "You're so sure I want your cock. Come here and show me. Work my ass until I can take this and then I'll take you."

Hawk said nothing.

Hayden shook his head, getting off me to stand in front of the other man, his erect dick right at Hawk's face height. "Like I thought." He plucked the plug from Hawk's fingers and brought it back to bed. "You talk a lot of shit, Robinson. But at the end of the day, you're just full of it."

I ignored their squabble, gaze focused on the plug, now that I knew what it was. I squeezed my thighs together at the thought of him using it on me.

Both men noticed the change in my breathing.

Hawk took up the slow fisting of his dick again. "It's not your ass I want, Chaos. At least not tonight."

Hayden came back to bed, staring down at me laid out for him, my heart beating too fast at the tension in the air between the two of them. With them unable to resolve it, I somehow knew it was about to be focused on me.

One knee on the mattress, Hayden drew the plug across my chest, circling my nipples and then doing the same to my belly button. The plug had a thick, wide base with a black jewel. The rest was silver, and I shivered as he drew it between my legs, inserting it into my pussy.

"So fucking pretty," he murmured, pumping it in and out a couple of times, coating it in Hawk's cum and my arousal. "Going to look even prettier when this pussy is wrapped around my cock."

He took out the plug, replacing it with his dick.

The noise that slipped from my throat as he stretched me with his rounded knob was so horrifyingly indecent. But I didn't care. I wanted him.

He slid inside me, connecting our bodies, bottoming himself out inside and grinding his pubic bone against my clit in a way that made me see stars.

Before I could get settled, he flipped our positions, rolling us so he was on the bed and I was the one on top.

The one in control.

I braced myself on his chest, feeling wholly exposed and unsure of what to do.

Until Hawk was behind me, one steadying hand between my shoulder blades, pushing me down so I lay over Hayden, my knees and hands taking the brunt of my weight.

And my ass on show.

"Ride him, Little Mouse. Roll your hips and fuck him while he grabs your tits and I fuck your ass."

I let out a shuddering breath so full of desire there was no mistaking it.

Hawk knew exactly what his dirty words did to me. How his bossy commands gave me the confidence to take what he knew my body wanted.

"Lube in the top drawer." Hayden fondled my breasts from beneath me, molding them with his fingers, finding my nipples and pinching them tightly between his thumb and forefinger.

Hawk leaned over and retrieved the small tube. It made a squelching sound when he squirted it onto the plug, and I jumped at the cool gel he slicked between my ass cheeks, searching for entrance.

"Kiss him," Hawk demanded. "Show me that sweet ass of yours."

I bent forward, kissing Hayden's lips, falling into the spell of his cock inside me hitting every delicious nerve ending, his fingers on my nipples, eliciting more of the same, and his tongue in my mouth, a dirty promise of all he could do with it in good time.

I rocked back and forth on his cock, sliding up and down his length, sighing in pleasure when each drive back was met with the touch of the plug going a little farther inside me.

"Oh!" I took more than just the tip inside me.

Hawk's palm slapped across my backside, sending a stinging shot of ecstasy right through me. I glanced over my shoulder and drank in his expression. The look of pure, unadulterated heat as he watched Hayden's cock slide in and out of my pussy and my ass take more and more of the plug, until I was so sure I was going to come undone right then.

Hayden raised his head, taking one of my nipples into his mouth, keeping me still for a moment with my back arched, head thrown back, so full of him and the plug Hawk fit fully inside me.

"I need to come," I panted desperately, "Oh God!"

I'd make my peace with going to Hell. Using His

name in vain was hardly the biggest sin I'd committed tonight.

"Not yet," Hayden uttered between sucks of my nipples and earth-shattering kisses that spun my world on its axis. "Not until we're both inside you." He kissed me hard. "Don't come until then."

He looked over my shoulder at Hawk. "If you fucking hurt her..."

I didn't even need to see Hawk to know he was glaring back. "For her sake, I'm going to pretend you didn't just say that to me."

Were they serious? I was teetering on the edge of an orgasm like nothing I'd ever felt before, desperate to get over the line, and the two of them wanted to have another of their ridiculous spats? Frustration and irritation crashed inside me, the need to explode in more ways than one the only thing I could focus on. "Can the two of you stop arguing for a single minute and just fuck me so I can come?"

They both stopped.

Stared at me.

Slowly, a smile spread across Hayden's face.

Hawk snorted on a laugh.

And then I joined them.

Hayden buried his face in my breasts and laughed. "There's no way the entire club didn't hear that."

"We're never going to live it down." Hawk groaned.

I bit my lip. "I'm sorry but—"

Hawk worked the plug out, kissing my ass, my back, my shoulders.

Need roared through me with every touch, my body on fire with anticipation.

"But nothing." Hayden's eyes were bright with desire. He took my chin between his fingers, drawing my face down so he could claim my lips.

Hawk pushed inside me at the same time, slowly and wet with lube, the feeling of fullness so intense I screamed out a "Yes!" against Hayden's lips, crashing over the precipice and splintering into a million different pieces.

The orgasm gripped me from head to toe, prickling at my scalp, sliding down my spine, tingling through my core, and curling around my feet until my toes scrunched, and I cried out again and again, unable to do anything but hold on while two men delivered the most intense feeling of pleasure I'd ever imagined.

"I can't move." I was completely boneless, flopped down on Hayden's chest.

"You don't need to," he assured me.

Between Hayden and Hawk, without ever breaking the deep, full connection joining the three of us, they maneuvered me onto my side, Hawk behind me, Hayden in front.

While the aftershocks of my orgasm filtered through my sex-soaked brain, they moved inside me. Slowly and out of time with each other at first, until they found a rhythm, both of them pushing and pulling at the same time, leaving me empty, then filling me so incredibly deeply I didn't know where I started and they began.

Another orgasm swelled and built in an instant, my overstimulated flesh too much to bear, but I had no choice when it came to them.

I couldn't deny them any more than they could deny me.

When I looked into Hayden's eyes and he put a hand between us, whispering for me to come with him, I could only obey, the gentle orgasm whisking me away with its waves, his assurances that I was beautiful and perfect in my ear.

Hawk bit down on my shoulder, teeth not breaking the skin but enough for me to feel it deeply and reach a hand back for him. It found his ass, and I pressed into the muscles of his cheek, encouraging him to take me in whatever way he needed to fall over the edge again.

He came with his lips buried in my hair, my neck, telling me how he'd never felt anything more perfect or loved anyone more.

It was a long time before we all fell still.

A long time before they pulled out of me.

The sun was just coming up when we started all over again, all three of us insatiable when it came to each other.

30

GRAYSON

I'd written and deleted so many messages to Kara that hours had slipped by. Nothing I wrote seemed to really sum up the apology I owed her.

"Dear Kara," I mused out loud for at least the twentieth time that morning. "I'm so sorry you saw me fucking some other woman when the woman I really wanted to be fucking was you."

I groaned.

"Dear Kara. All I can think about is how I could only come because I was picturing you beneath me."

Yeah, like I was really going to send that.

"Dear Kara. I want you so fucking bad I can't breathe and I don't care if you're with Hayden or Hawk or the entire Colorado Titans hockey team, I just want to know if there's any chance you *didn't* actually see me screwing someone else and might want to go out for dinner sometime?"

I threw myself onto the couch and wailed into a cushion. "Fuuuckkkk."

I tossed my phone across the other side of the room, knowing I couldn't say any of those things. It made a weird bleeping noise, and I dragged myself over to see what sort of damage I'd done.

There was a message from Kara.

All concerns about the probably broken speaker disappeared. I pounced on the phone, stabbing at the screen, urging the stupid thing to open the message faster, even though in reality it probably only took a few seconds.

> KARA:
>
> I was wondering if you'd like to go to the beach with me and Hayley Jade today?

A familiar sense of unease settled over me at the mere mention of the beach. And yet I found myself typing back in too enthusiastic capital letters.

> GRAYSON:
>
> YES! I'D LOVE TO! I'D ALSO REALLY LIKE TO APOLOGIZE FOR

I cringed at the screen. "Could you actually be any more pathetic, Grayson? Fucking hell." I paused. "Also really lame that you're talking out loud to yourself, so really, is it any wonder this woman is about as attracted to you as she would be her brother?"

I pressed my lips together to keep the rambling inside and deleted the text, trying again.

> GRAYSON:
>
> Sure. Beach sounds great. Pick you both up at twelve?

It was dry and boring, but I clearly couldn't be trusted with caps or exclamation marks or heaven forbid, GIFs. If I didn't watch myself, I'd probably be sending her the love hearts for eyes emoji.

Would it be lame to pack a picnic? Would that seem like I was trying to turn her casual invitation into a date?

I so wanted it to be a date.

"Ah, screw it." I left the house before I could talk to myself anymore. I still had an hour to kill before I needed to be at the clubhouse though, so lame as it might have been, I found myself at the shopping center, pushing a cart around, filling it with anything and everything I thought one might need for a date at the beach.

A *day* at the beach. Not a date. Women didn't bring their children on dates.

Women didn't date men they'd put in the friend zone either.

It didn't stop me taking my cart to the register with it near to full and then packing it all into the trunk of my car.

I made it to the Slayers' clubhouse right at twelve, and Kara and Hayley Jade were already standing in the doorway, waiting for me.

My heart squeezed at the sight of Kara, some of my unease over where we were headed dissipating at a single glimpse of her. Her long dark hair fell loose around her shoulders and down the back of a thick, cable-knit sweater. Leggings clung to her hips and thighs, and white sneakers finished off her outfit.

Last night she'd been a knockout.

This look was cute as hell.

Clearly, it didn't matter what she wore, I found her attractive in anything.

Hayley Jade half hid behind Kara's legs, an adorable pink beanie with a pompom on her head, and a set of Barbies in her hands.

I smiled as I approached them, bending down to talk to Hayley Jade first. "Whatcha got there?"

She didn't say anything, but she did hold out the dolls. I inspected each one carefully. "It's pretty cold out here today. Do you think they're ready for the wind at the beach? Maybe they need sweatshirts like you and I have on?"

Hayley Jade cocked her head to one side and then nodded firmly, spinning on her heel and running back into the clubhouse, presumably to find a warmer wardrobe for her dolls. I straightened, heart thumping at the thought of facing Kara after what I'd done last night and praying she hadn't actually seen me.

Even though we both knew full well she had.

The shrink inside me was shouting about delusions, but I was off the clock, so I told him come back later.

Talking to myself inside my own head wasn't as bad as talking to myself out loud, surely.

I pasted a nervous smile on and rose to my feet.

Only to find Hayden and Hawk standing behind Kara, leaning on the doorway like her personal security squad.

"Uh," I cleared my throat. "Morning. I mean afternoon? How'd everyone sleep?"

Hawk smirked. "We going to talk about last night?"

Heat spread across the back of my neck. "Uh, the part where I delivered Bliss's baby safely and happily into the world? How are they by the way? Did they name the baby?"

Hayden sniggered. "I don't know about them, but I was thinking more about what happened after that."

I cleared my throat, wanting to crawl into a hole and die, even though the two of them were clearly enjoying torturing me. "The food was great," I told Hayden honestly. "Top-notch."

Hawk's laughter was full of pure amusement at my discomfort. "That the only thing that tasted good to you last night, Grayson? When we left, you had your mouth on—"

"Ridge," Kara interjected.

I blinked. "Sorry, what?"

"Bliss called the baby Ridge."

She was throwing me a lifeline.

"Oh, right. Good name. Strong."

Hawk and Hayden were still trying to hold in their laughter. I was *so* giving Hawk bedpans to clean next time we were at the clinic. Asshole.

Hayley Jade ran back with an armful of new clothes for her dolls, and I took the opportunity to escape.

"Ready to go?"

Kara nodded, shifting a beach bag overflowing with things onto her shoulder and stepping out the door.

Hayden caught her by the wrist. "You forgot something." He lowered his head and brushed his mouth across hers.

I averted my eyes but not quick enough to miss Hawk taking her chin and turning her head so he could claim her lips as well.

Hayley Jade stared up at the three of them with a happy smile on her rounded face.

I couldn't say I felt the same, watching them kiss her, knowing they got to do so much more behind closed doors.

Hayden did something with his hands that might have been sign language before he waved goodbye to Hayley Jade, but when the little girl turned her big eyes on Hawk, it was clear there were things she wanted to say, even if whatever part of her she'd locked inside wouldn't allow it.

Hawk didn't seem to need her words though.

He knelt so he was eye height with her and ruffled her hair. "I can't go this time, shortie. I'd love to, but Grayson has promised me he's going to take super good care of you and your mama." He glanced up at me, his expression changing to something fierce. "Aren't you, Grayson? You're going to take such good care of them that I won't have to worry for a second that they're out there without me. Right?"

If there was one thing I could do, it was that. I knew about Kara's past. Knew probably better than Hawk did about others who could hurt them.

I might have been a doctor now, one who threw most of his punches at a bag at the gym. I knew what Hawk saw when he looked at me. I knew he saw me as weak. A paper pusher.

He had no idea I'd spent the first eighteen years of my life in the Saint View ghetto. That I'd grown up in houses where every day was a fight to stay alive.

That I surrounded myself with men who I knew very well could turn on me at any time and end my life. I didn't go to the gym for fun. I practiced with my trainer for the day when one of those men might stop seeing me as a friend and instead decide I was a foe.

I trained for the day Trigger returned and I'd get to take his life as payback for the one he'd stolen from me.

When I stared Hawk solemnly in the eye and declared Kara and Hayley Jade would be safe with me, I meant it with every fiber of my being.

The Providence beach was cold and windy and mostly deserted of people, but the expression on Hayley Jade's face when I helped her out of the back seat of my car was nothing short of priceless. She ran to the short fence that separated the sand dunes from the parking lot and stared out over the ocean with huge eyes.

"She's never seen the ocean before." Kara smiled softly, watching her daughter.

"They kept you pretty sheltered, didn't they?"

She nodded. "That's probably a gross understatement. It was different when I was her age. Before Josiah came along and changed everything we knew." She sat on the rounded log fence next to Hayley Jade and undid the laces on her sneakers, encouraging Hayley Jade to do the same. "Did you grow up around here?"

I shouldered the bags full of food and other supplies I'd picked up at the store and closed the trunk. "Not far." I pointed toward the Saint View end of the beach. "But I didn't get to hang out at this end."

Kara breathed in the deep, salt-laced air. "I'm so jealous. I would come here every day if I could. Hence why we're here now, even though it's too cold to swim."

"Doesn't stop the surfers." I nodded toward the waves a way down the sand, where a handful of surfers sat on their boards in the swell, waiting for the next set to roll in.

Hayley Jade held her socks and shoes patiently, silently waiting until Kara and I were ready. She was such an obedient kid, never making a fuss or drawing attention to herself. Always waiting quietly for permission. I could see why Kara was concerned. It wasn't typical behavior for anyone, let alone a five-year-old who should have been bubbling over with excitement, running around, chattering about everything new her mind was taking in.

"Who wants to race?" My gaze focused on Hayley Jade. "I think there's a perfect picnic spot down there somewhere, and I wonder if anyone is fast enough to beat me to it?"

Kara caught on and put up her hand. "Me! I think I can definitely beat both of you!"

Hayley Jade's smile turned into a grin, and she ran on the spot, little legs pumping like she was warming up for a sprint.

It was amazing to see how she communicated, even without words, and a good sign her trauma hadn't forced her so far in on herself that she couldn't eventually revert back to the way she'd once been.

I rocked on my heels, making out like I was getting ready to sprint. "Okay, then. On your marks. Get set..." They both watched me, poised and ready to run. "Bananas!"

Hayley Jade took two steps and stopped, realizing what I'd said.

I frowned at her. "How come you aren't running?"

She giggled.

Kara hid her laughter.

I grinned, enjoying the sounds of their amusement. "Okay, let's try again. Ready?"

Hayley Jade nodded.

"Set?"

A look of determination came over her expression.

"Peanut butter and jelly sandwiches!"

She shoved her hands on her hips and gave me a stare that clearly just meant, 'seriously?'

I laughed. "Okay, go!"

Hayley Jade took off running, her tiny feet flying across the sand, her slight weight barely making a dent in the surface.

Kara grabbed my shirt and held me back. "Go, Hayley Jade! I've got him!"

God, I loved the sound of Kara's laughter and the warmth of her body as she hauled me against her. Her breasts brushed across my back, and fuck if all I could think about was spinning her around, gathering her up into my arms, and kissing her the way Hayden and Hawk had earlier.

Instead, I howled out in mock frustration. "Cheating! There's some cheating going on here!"

Hayley Jade glanced over her shoulder at us, her excitement clear in her expression.

Kara and I laughed our way down the path after her, both of us sinking into the sand and jostling each other with our armful of bags.

Kara dropped hers onto the sand at the designated spot, and I nabbed the blanket sticking out of one of mine, spreading it out for her to sink down onto. She curled up, tucking her knees to her chest, gaze trained on Hayley Jade, who'd lost interest in the race she'd so clearly won and was busily picking up shells to put in her pockets.

I sat beside Kara, watching her daughter. "She's going to bring home half the beach. You'll be doing shell and sand art for weeks to come at the rate she's finding them."

Kara smiled happily. "I like the sound of that. It's so…"

"Normal?"

She twisted her head, laying it on her knees to face me. "Yes. Exactly that. Normal. Did you do that sort of thing when you were a kid?"

The idea of anyone sitting me down, getting out glue and glitter and paint, and telling me to have fun and be creative was so insanely foreign to me it was laughable. I had no memories like that. Only ones of places my foster parents had ruined for me, the beach being one of them.

While surfers sat out in the water, laughing and joking with each other, and in summer, this place crawled with teenagers and families having a good time, all it represented to me was pain.

My chest got tight as the memories flooded back in. Memories I'd tried to work through in therapy, and when that hadn't worked too well, I'd fought to keep locked tight.

"Food?" I asked her, digging through the bags, pulling out the lunch meats and cheeses I'd brought. "What do you like? I brought chips and sandwiches and juice for Hayley Jade too. Cookies? Candies?" I glanced over at her awkwardly. "I didn't know what any of you liked so I just bought it all."

She laughed, leaning over to rummage through the bag with me. "I can see that. I'm not fussy. It all looks good to me." She picked up some crackers and opened a container of hummus. She munched on a few while we watched Hayley Jade, the crash of the waves the only sound between us.

It drew out so long I had to fill it. "I'm so sorry—"

"I want to—" she started at the same time.

Both of us stopped and looked at the other. She scrunched her face up adorably and squeezed her eyes closed. "Wait. Please. Let me say what I need to say because I don't know if I'll have the guts to say it if I wait any longer. I'm really sorry about last night. I was drinking, and I forgot my place. The whole thing was so incredibly inappropriate of me, and I hope you can forgive me."

I blinked. "You're apologizing to me?"

She widened her eyes. "Of course. What I did... watching you like that when you were..." She covered her face with her hands. "This is officially more mortifying than I even imagined. I swear, I'm not normally like that."

"Like what?"

The question was out before I even really thought about what I was asking.

She peeled two fingers away from her face and stared at me from between them. "I don't normally go to clubs and watch people I know have sex." She covered her face up again. "Please don't fire me from the clinic."

I pulled her hands away. "Kara, you did nothing wrong. I was the one who was...well... you know...naked."

Kara's face flushed red. "You had every right to be. I mean...that's what people do there, right? I shouldn't have...I knew you were in there. I shouldn't have followed."

I paused. "Wait, you followed me?"

She shook her head quickly. "I mean, no! Not followed. Not...exactly. I...we..." She let out a long sigh. "Hawk is probably going to tell you anyway, because he has the biggest mouth known to man. This is so awkward I could die."

"Tell me what?"

She glanced at me. "He thought you went in there last night because you were thinking about me. I told him how ridiculous that was—"

She was so pink with embarrassment. So beautiful. Her gaze was locked with mine, and she was giving me an opening, a chance to say exactly how I felt about her.

I had to take it. "What if I did?"

The wind picked up tendrils of her hair, blowing them around her face. Her voice dropped an octave. "What do you mean?"

Nerves rolled through me, like I was a sixteen-year-old boy asking a girl to prom, desperately unsure of what her answer was going to be but so sure of only one thing: I had to shoot my shot. That I had to ask. I had to hope there was a chance she might feel the same way. "What if I went into that party last night, because the sight of you and Hawk together had me so damn jealous I couldn't breathe? What if I went in there hoping to fuck away the desire I felt every time your leg brushed mine beneath the table. What if I was thinking about you the entire time I was inside her..."

Silence settled between us. Then horror. All mine.

I'd just made this so much worse. "Fuck."

Kara stared at me, shock written all over her face. "Hayley Jade!" she called distractedly. "Not too close to the water!"

I realized instantly how wrong I'd been. How out of line. How everything she'd said hadn't been an opening for me to word vomit about how much I wanted her.

I hated this fucking beach. Nothing good ever happened here. The same crushing feeling I got every time I saw those waves rolling in intensified until my lungs ached. "I'm sorry. This is so inappropriate." I looked away, up toward my car. I couldn't even fucking leave. I'd brought her here, she needed a way to get home. I just wanted the earth to swallow me whole.

"Grayson..."

I held up a hand. "No. Honestly. No need to say anything. I get it. You have Hawk. And Hayden."

"Grayson."

"Just please forget I said anything. I misread the entire situation, and I honestly just want to go throw myself off the bluff. The thought of sharp rocks spearing through the chest, or a shark chowing down on my insides while the waves drown me, actually doesn't seem so bad right about now. Maybe a speedboat could come by and just chop me up with its propellers for good measure—"

"I came last night, watching you with her."

If I'd been able to place a million bets on words that would come out of her mouth, none of them would have been those.

I stared at her. I'd seen her at the club as I'd...finished. Our eyes had locked, no denying on either of our parts what had happened.

But I'd assumed she'd seen me with that woman,

been horrified, and hightailed it straight out of there with only a single, unlucky glance my way that had confirmed it was indeed me she was seeing in that state.

She twisted her fingers around in the blanket. "So you understand now why there is nothing for you to apologize for. It was me who was inappropriate. I stood there, watching you with that woman, and let Hawk touch me —" She looked up and suddenly pushed to her feet, scattering cracker crumbs across the blanket. "Hayley Jade!"

I jerked at the panicked tone in Kara's voice, quickly scanning the sand for the little girl, my stomach sinking when she wasn't picking up shells. I shot up, twisting each way searching for her pink beanie, spotting it as she waded through the shallows, waves splashing up the pant legs she'd been smart enough to roll up to her knees.

"Grayson, that wave..." Kara's fingers clutched me tightly.

The surfers down the beach hooted and hollered, catching the massive swell rushing toward the beach, bigger and stronger than any of the waves we'd seen in the time we'd been here.

Hayley Jade didn't notice us, our shouts to her lost on the wind, zero awareness of the danger hurtling toward her.

The huge swell hit Hayley Jade in the back, the ocean surging and swirling around her, taking out her feet and sending her face first into the white water.

Kara screamed, "She can't swim!"

I was already running, gaze glued to the pink beanie being tossed around. Another unusually large wave hit the sand, pushing her beneath the water again.

I watched in horror as Hayley Jade flailed, trying to

keep her head above water while the ocean drew her deeper and deeper into its depths, the tide sucking her in.

I hit the water at full pace, only to be smacked backward by the third wave of the set crashing onto the sand, freezing cold water filling my eyes and ears and nose.

Instantly I was ten years old again, being held down beneath the water, my foster dad laughing above me while I struggled against his grip.

I couldn't breathe. There was water in my lungs. Fear in my blood. I screamed but didn't make a sound.

"Hayley Jade!" Kara splashed into the water.

The fear in her voice cut through the panic inside me.

I looked around wildly, finding my feet in the churning sea, searching for any sign of Kara's daughter.

I caught the little pink beanie as it slipped underneath the waves.

I dove beneath them, visibility zero, holding my breath the way I hadn't been able to do when I was a kid.

She wasn't fucking drowning in this ocean. I remembered the pain and the terror all too well, and I wasn't letting her go through that.

My hands caught hold of something solid, and I clutched my fingers into the soaking fabric of her jacket, hauling her back to the surface and up into my arms.

She spluttered and coughed, but to my surprise breathed normally, her face white with fear but her lips were a bright pink, not blue-tinged like I would have expected if she'd been without oxygen for too long.

"I've got you." I rubbed her back, encouraging her body to expel any water she'd swallowed.

Kara ran through the shallows to meet us, a worried

expression chewing up her pretty face. "Oh my God. That wave got you good."

"We need an ambulance," I jogged now the water wasn't holding me back.

Kara put her hand on my arm. "What? Why? Is she hurt?"

"She just nearly drowned!"

Kara screwed up her face in confusion. "She was only under for a second. You got to her so quick."

I stopped, confused. "No. She was drowning. I saw..." I stared down at Hayley Jade who looked wet and cold and surprised, but definitely not like she had a lung full of ocean water or had been struggling for air...

The way I had.

Kara put a warm hand on my chilled, wet arm. "She's okay, Gray. Put her down."

I shook my head, blinking away the memories, and dropped to my knees at the edge of our blanket. Kara knelt beside me, quickly finding a towel and stripping off some of Hayley Jade's wet clothes. She wrapped Hayley Jade's slim shoulders and rubbed her arms briskly, warming her up and drying her off. She smiled at her daughter. "You're okay?"

Hayley Jade's teeth chattered, but she nodded, staring at me with big eyes.

I swallowed thickly and tried to smile reassuringly at her, well aware it was now my behavior scaring her a whole lot more than being dunked by a wave had.

Kara shot me worried glances too. "Let's go up to the car so I can get her changed. I brought spare clothes, knowing she'd probably get wet."

I nodded numbly, following her lead, my heart still

racing too fast and my breathing too erratic to do or say anything more. I picked up all the things and trailed them back to the car, packing the mostly uneaten food back into the trunk as the wind whipped around my soaking body, chilling me to the bone.

My head had gone dark.

Memories erupting from shadowy corners and twirling through my brain like a never-ending nightmare parade.

A car door slammed. I jumped, and then Kara was in front of me, undoing the buttons on my shirt.

"What are you doing?" I watched her nimble fingers move down my chest.

"You're freezing."

"Hayley Jade..."

"Is now warm in a fresh tracksuit and watching videos on my phone in the back seat."

"She's really okay?"

Kara nodded. "Really. I should have been watching her more closely. It could have been a lot worse. But you were so quick."

"I didn't feel quick," I admitted. "I thought she went under. A lot. I thought..." I sucked in a breath, but it felt shallow. Like even when I tried to get more air, I couldn't. "I thought—"

The air wouldn't come.

Kara dragged off my shirt and wrapped the picnic blanket around me, which was sandy and a little stiff, but stopped the whipping wind from getting at my skin. She led me to the log fence. "Sit a minute. You're having a panic attack."

I hadn't had one in years, but it felt a whole lot like

dying. With nothing in me left to fight, I did as I was told, sitting heavily. My chest heaved. Stomach churned. I was sure I looked like I was losing it.

Concern radiated from Kara.

I didn't want to scare her. "My foster dad found water torture an amusing pastime." I fought the gut-churning feeling inside me. "Not that he had any of the skills they use on prisoners of war or whatever. He didn't have the patience for anything like that. He just liked to hold my head beneath the water."

Kara stared down at me, horror written all over her expression. "Why? How old were you?"

I shrugged. "Ten, maybe? I don't really remember. Small enough to not be able to fight back." I twisted to stare back at the waves, demon-like in their thrashing, the wind from earlier bringing in dark clouds that made the entire beach feel ominous. "I ran away from home once. Slept just down there, on the beach for two nights before he found me." I rubbed my hands up and down my arms. "He dragged me into the ocean, screaming about what a good-for-nothing shit I was, and how Child Protective Services was going to take away his payments if I wasn't there when they came to check on me."

"He held you beneath the water as punishment?"

"He didn't want to hit me and leave bruises."

"So he tried to drown you instead?" Kara's eyes were round with horror. "Foster parents are supposed to be caring. Nurturing…"

I laughed. "Maybe in Disney movies."

But it wasn't funny. I dropped my head, staring at the ground, hating that this shit still had an effect on me. I'd done so much mental work, trying to get through it, and I thought I had. I even swam now. Regularly. Though only in pools.

But seeing Hayley Jade's head slip beneath the waves while she'd flailed and fought to stay upright had brought it all back, reopening a wound that had defined my entire life.

The laugh turned into a desperate gulp for air, my chest too tight, like someone had a vise around it.

Kara knelt in front of me, her knees on the sandy grass growing at the edge of the paved parking lot. She caught my hand and rubbed it briskly. "Tell me three things you see or hear or smell right now."

My head felt like it weighed a ton. "Why?"

"Someone told me recently it helps calm your nervous system if you focus on what's right here in front of you instead of whatever's going on in your head."

She was right. It was a technique I used with my patients. I drew in a breath that wasn't nearly as deep as I wanted but better than the choking feeling that had me in its grip. "The sky is more gray than blue. That video Hayley Jade is watching is loud enough I can hear it even outside the car." I let my gaze settle on Kara's face.

"One more," she prompted calmly.

"You're beautiful."

She let out a shuddering breath, her gaze dipping to my mouth before dragging back up my face. "Feel better?"

"I feel like I want to kiss you. And I'm so damn scared you're going to say no."

She let out a wobbly breath but didn't turn away. And didn't say no. "I don't understand why you'd want that. I'm with Hawk. And Hayden."

Which was exactly what I'd been telling myself ever since I'd met her.

Except I was selfish enough to not care. To want more, and to ask her if I could have it.

"I still want to kiss you, Kara." I slid my hand to the side of her face, past her ear, tangling it in the wild mess of her hair. "And I think if you're honest with yourself, you want to kiss me too."

She narrowed the gap between us until my mouth hovered over hers, our warm breaths mingling in the cold beach air. I brushed my lips across hers, testing her reaction, buzzing at the feel of electricity when her body connected with mine.

"I don't want to ruin what you have with them. If kissing you will hurt you, I'll walk away." I inhaled the salty smell of her lips.

"I can't have three men, Gray," she whispered. But her eyes closed and she tipped her head back, letting me trail my lips up her neck.

I kissed the spot beneath her ear. "You can have whatever you want. All you have to do is tell me yes."

Her pause was the most agonizing few seconds of my life.

"Yes."

I pressed my mouth to hers, all gentleness gone as she kissed me back just as hard, wrapping her arms around my neck and hauling me in. I stood, lifting us both from the low fence until her ass was on the edge of the hood and we were a mess of tongues and hands, roaming each other's backs, stroking hair, brushing over skin. I ran my tongue along the seam of her lips, loving when she opened for me. The kiss seared, engraving itself in my brain, feeling so damn different than any kiss I'd ever had before.

Until I opened my eyes and caught a glimpse of Hayley Jade in the middle of the back seat.

She covered her mouth, giggling behind her hand.

I threw the little girl a wink and pulled her mother tight, wrapping my arms around her, hugging her close. "We have an audience," I mumbled, smile so wide I couldn't wipe it off my face.

Kara smiled as well, elbowing me. "I thought you were used to that."

31

KARA

Grayson's kisses left my lips tingling. I ran my finger over them absentmindedly, a happy smile pulling at my mouth as I stared out the window. Hayley Jade was still happily occupied in the back seat with my phone and a YouTube video, and Grayson's hand on my leg was oddly thrilling for such a simple touch.

His thumb stroked my thigh, his hand reassuringly warm through the fabric of my leggings, despite his dip in the freezing ocean.

I didn't know what this was. Or how on earth I was going to tell Hayden and Hawk. Maybe I wouldn't. What I had learned from being away from Josiah was that I didn't owe anyone anything.

There was a connection between Hawk and Hayden and me. But they didn't own me the way Josiah had. I was free to make my own choices.

Neither had asked me to be their girlfriend. Hawk hadn't put me on the back of his bike, which I'd been told was the mark of commitment from men from the club.

Kissing Grayson had felt nice. I was attracted to him, and he clearly felt the same.

I'd been tied down so long, I didn't want to cut my own wings.

Maybe Hawk and Hayden had recognized that before even I had. Maybe that was why they'd been so willing to share me.

I didn't want to choose. Not yet. Not now.

I didn't imagine I could be as lucky as Bliss and Rebel and have all of them agree to form a family with me.

I shook my head, rolling my eyes at my own ridiculousness. One kiss from Grayson, and I was already planning to include him in a new family unit? I was completely delusional. One kiss didn't mean anything.

Though the way he rubbed my leg spoke volumes of him wanting to do more than touch me in such a PG manner.

I shivered at the thought.

Grayson glanced over his shoulder at Hayley Jade in the back seat. "She's crashed out."

I blinked, twisting to look at my daughter's sweetly relaxed face, her dark eyelashes fanned out across her pink cheeks in sleep. "I wish I could pass out that quickly," I said enviously. "We haven't even gotten off the beach road yet."

"You didn't spend all afternoon running around."

"Plus she's been at school all week. She's been sleeping like the dead every night. But I think it's good for her."

Grayson nudged me. "You're doing all the right things. You know that, right? You've given her stability. A home. A big family who all love her."

Logically, I knew that. She had safety. Endless amounts of food. Toys and games and the chance to go to school. Most importantly, the club had given her the protection and love of an extended family who doted on her endlessly.

Especially Queenie and Hawk.

I lowered my voice. "But she's still not talking."

"She will when she's ready."

Tears pricked at the backs of my eyes, and I turned away, so desperate to believe he was right.

A red pickup truck caught my eye at the end of the beach lot.

For a second, I couldn't work out why it was so familiar.

Until a lanky young man stepped out of it, stretching his arms above his head and twisting side to side like he'd been inside the cramped vehicle too long and his limbs and joints had paid the price.

My heart thundered.

"Grayson, stop."

He glanced at me. "What?"

We were about to pass the end of the beach lot, and then we'd be on the road up to the bluffs where it would be miles before he could safely turn around.

In that time, Kyle could be gone.

"Stop!"

Grayson stomped down on the brakes, slowing the car enough he could steer us over to the side of the road, a few hundred feet away from Kyle's truck.

I slammed my way out of the car. "Kyle!"

But my voice was whipped away by the wind stirred up by the incoming storm.

Grayson's door closed behind me. "Kara! Who is that?"

I spun around, my chest heaving, heart thumping too fast, and blood rushing in my ears. "The man who killed my sister."

Grayson caught my arm. "Wait, what?"

I yanked it free, terrifying adrenaline filling me at the sight of Kyle. He'd been missing for weeks. Had he been here all along? Still in Saint View? The cops had said they couldn't find him, and yet he was right there in front of me, watching the ocean like he didn't have a care in the world.

While my sister lay dead in a morgue somewhere, the authorities still refusing to release her body because of the graphic nature of her death and their lack of investigative results.

Red hot anger rolled through me.

Alice had been with Kyle the night she'd died. He'd lied to us. Pretended to help us. Only to be the one to pull a cord around her neck and end her life. It was the only thing that made sense to me.

He was Josiah's little errand boy, and it had me so murderously angry I couldn't stop myself from screaming into the wind, cursing him for what he'd taken from me.

I didn't care he was probably still in Saint View because he hadn't finished the job.

He hadn't killed me.

All I cared about was that he go down for what he'd done to Alice.

"You took her from me!" My voice was hoarse from the lump in my throat. "You lured her out of that house and ended a life that had barely begun!"

Kyle turned.

His eyes widened and he rifled through his pockets, pulling out his keys.

"No!" I screamed.

He couldn't get away. I couldn't let that happen. I needed answers. Needed to hear him admit what he'd done. Admit what he'd run away from.

I wasn't going to be fast enough. The gap between us was too big. The distance too far. "No!"

Grayson sprinted past me, barreling across the parking lot at twice the speed I could have even hoped to run, his still-damp shirt open and flying out behind him. "Hey!" he bellowed, then called back to me, "Kara, stay with Hayley Jade!"

I stopped dead in my tracks, realizing he was right, backing up and putting myself between the monster in front of me and the daughter I'd do anything to protect.

Kyle noticed Grayson coming and dropped his keys. He bent to retrieve them, fumbling amongst the grass growing through the sand at the edge of the parking lot, but it was the seconds Grayson needed. When Kyle straightened there was barely a hundred yards between them.

Not long enough for Kyle to get to his car, and all three of us knew it.

He turned and fled down the beach, long legs pumping across the dunes.

Grayson was faster.

A scream of fear caught in my throat as Grayson threw himself at Kyle, crash tackling him to the sand. They rolled, the two of them grappling for the upper hand.

The thought of Grayson being hurt because of me turned my stomach. I knew what Kyle was capable of. He'd proved it that night when he'd lured my sister to a club and strangled her to death. He'd shown, despite his boyish face and age, he had the ability to be a cold, callous killer, leaving Alice's body in a city alley like she was trash.

There was nothing I could do except stand there and watch them fight, terror gripping my throat when Kyle came up on top.

A second later, Grayson switched their positions, pinning him down.

The wind changed directions, as wild as the dark clouds threatening to dump water over the entire beach.

Their shouts filtered back amongst the crashes and thundering of the waves, garbled and unintelligible.

I didn't start breathing again until Kyle let out a scream of pain, Grayson pushing his arm behind his back.

Hayley Jade napped peacefully in the car, zero idea of what was going on outside it, as Grayson hauled Kyle to his feet and dragged him back up the beach.

With every step they drew closer, my head swirled with everything I wanted to say. Everything I wanted to scream.

But when Kyle stood in front of me, forced in place by the vicious grip Grayson had on his arm, words failed me.

I slapped my palm across Kyle's face with all the strength and anger that had been building for all the years Josiah had kept me down. The rage was set free, every hateful feeling exploding from inside me, culminating in the blow I'd delivered to Josiah's disciple.

Kyle's head jerked to the side, Grayson never easing up for a second, despite the way Kyle's shoulder seemed ready to pop right out of its socket.

Good.

I hoped it hurt.

I hoped it hurt even half as much as the pain he'd caused my sister.

"How could you?" I asked Kyle eventually, my voice so broken I barely recognized it. "She thought you were her friend."

To my surprise, when Kyle finally lifted his head to look at me, it was with tears in his eyes. "I was her friend!"

My face screwed up in disbelief. "How can you say that, after what you did? You killed her! You put a cord around her neck and pulled it tight while she struggled to breathe!"

His eyes widened. "I didn't! Please, Kara. You have to believe me. I didn't hurt Alice. I would never. I was in love with her! I still am! Even though she's…"

I scoffed, but his words hit a chord inside me, and I remembered the way he'd gazed at her that day we'd escaped. It had been sweet. Tender. So full of awe and amazement at everything she said and did.

So quickly that sweetness had turned to malice.

"So what?" I accused. "She danced with someone else, and you got jealous? Or was it just you're so ridiculously brainwashed by Josiah that when he told you to kill her, you did it anyway? Killed the woman you loved because you were too weak and gutless to stand up to him?"

Kyle shook his head miserably, wincing when Grayson yanked his arm again. "I haven't talked to Josiah's since we left. I swear it, Kara. I didn't kill your sister. I wanted a life with her. I was going to marry her, if she would have me. That's why I left with you. I would have waited. Waited through as many men as she wanted to dance with, or date, or whatever she wanted. I would have waited for her for a hundred years if that's what it took for her to be ready."

I paused at the depth of anguish in his voice. At the pain in his eyes.

At the truth I heard in his words.

For the first time in weeks, I considered that maybe I was wrong.

"Why did you run then?" Grayson asked gruffly. "If you were so innocent?"

"I was scared," Kyle practically whispered, every inch the man-child he was at nineteen. "I lost track of her in the club. When I couldn't find her, I went up and down the other clubs searching for her, and then eventually I went back to the truck, assuming she'd come back when she was done partying."

A tear slipped down my cheek. "She wasn't partying."

Kyle nodded miserably. "I know that now. I fell asleep in the truck waiting for her. When I woke up, the entire block was crawling with cops. I asked some people what was going on, and they said there'd been a body found, right outside that first club we'd been at..."

"And you knew it was her," I said softly.

"I didn't want it to be." His pain ate up his words, agony in every one. "So I fought my way to the front of the crowd, praying she'd just gone home with someone else because even knowing she was with another man would have been a relief."

"But she wasn't," I filled in for him. "It was her, dead in that alley behind the club."

He nodded miserably. "I watched them put her body into a bag."

The words gutted me, my brain conjuring up images of what that must have looked like. Bitterness crept onto my tongue. "And then you ran." I knew the story from there.

Regrets filled Kyle's eyes. "I knew the cops would blame me, the same way you did. I didn't know what else to do. I couldn't go back to Ethereal Eden. Josiah would kill me on sight for helping you leave. But I had nowhere else to go. My parents have been calling me nonstop since it happened. I haven't answered, but their voicemails are frantic, asking me why the cops keep coming to their home, searching through all my belongings. I want to talk to them so badly, but I don't want them to have to lie for me either."

My heart squeezed at the lost-little-boy expression on his face. He was barely a man. Not even old enough to drink. The terror in his eyes and the tremble in his bottom lip reminded me of the way Hayley Jade had looked when we'd escaped.

Desperate for someone to tell her everything was going to be okay.

"I didn't hurt Alice, Kara. Please believe me. Please *help* me. I don't know what else to do." A sob spilled out past his lips, and his shoulders hunched.

Grayson glanced at me.

"Let him go," I said softly.

Grayson hesitated. "He could be lying. Acting.

Psychopaths are extraordinarily good actors. Trust me, I speak to enough of them to know."

"And do you think Kyle is a psychopath?"

He sighed, letting his grip on Kyle's arm drop. "No. I don't. I believe him."

I did too.

I stared at Kyle, taking in the patchy scruff on his cheeks, his dirty clothes, and now that I wasn't so wrapped up in my anger and grief, I noticed how badly he smelled. I peered past him at his pickup, noticing pillows and blankets stacked up on the back seat. "Have you been sleeping in your truck?"

"Yes, ma'am. Or on the beach if I need to stretch out for a night and I can get warm enough. I stayed at the homeless shelter twice, but I got paranoid the cops would find me there, so it seemed smarter to stay away."

It had been weeks. He was just a stupid, scared, out-of-his-depth teenager who had nobody to turn to. Nobody to care for him.

He reminded me all too much of myself when I'd left Ethereal Eden the first time. How I'd thought myself big and brave enough to take on the world, only to find it quickly chewed me up and spit me back out, a shell of the cocky teenager I'd once been.

I hated Kyle had to learn the hard way, the same as I had.

I glanced back at Hayley Jade, still sleeping soundly on the back seat, and knew I'd do anything in my power to stop her from experiencing that sort of pain.

I sighed heavily. "Get in your truck. Follow us back to the clubhouse. We'll get you cleaned up. Some food and fresh clothes. And then we'll work out where you're going to sleep tonight."

Kyle lifted his head hopefully. "Seriously?"

"Kara," Grayson warned. "I don't know how Hawk and the others are going to feel about that."

I shook my head. "It can't go down any worse than me bringing Hayden back there, can it?"

Grayson seemed doubtful. "I suppose if it all goes pear-shaped I could just announce I kissed you. Then all the murderous rage would turn in my direction."

I patted his shoulder as I passed him on the way to the car. "Maybe keep that one to yourself for now. No need to plan two funerals."

32

HAWK

With War firmly in his little love nest, fussing over Bliss and their daughters and their new baby, running the club fell on my shoulders.

I went through the motions, discussing what we had coming up with the other guys, taking stock of who wanted to go on runs and who was tied up with their day jobs or family lives. It was something my old man would have never bothered with when he and Army had been in this position. They'd been very much of the mindset that club came before all else and that if they said jump, the rest of the club would only ever answer with, "How high?"

But War had changed all of that when he'd taken over. His family, the ones who didn't live here in the clubhouse, were always his first priority, and he'd set the tone for the rest of us.

So Fang spent more weekends changing diapers than hunting down wayward payments with the brute force Army had first recruited him for. Aloha took Queenie on dates instead of sleeping in the back of the van when he drove gun shipments across borders. Gunner went to his grandkids' soccer games instead of overseeing the drug syndicate.

I kept thinking about how I'd rather be riding around in ambulances or helping people at the clinic. But until that was a reality, the black market we'd known all our lives was still the thing that paid my bills.

I leaned back on my chair, poring over the notes Fang was studiously taking as the guys and I decided who was doing what for the next few weeks. Satisfied we were finished, and eager to see if Kara was back yet, I lifted the wooden gavel. "If nobody else has anything to add, I think we're done here." I lowered the gavel toward the table, ready to bang it down, signaling the end of the meeting.

Aloha cleared his throat and raised a hand tentatively. "Boss."

I rolled my eyes. "You don't have to call me that just because War isn't here."

Aloha grinned. "Temporary boss, then?"

I twisted the hammer in my hands, impatient for him to get to the point because I was sure sick of looking at their ugly faces when I could be looking at Kara's.

Or Hayden's, an insidious voice whispered in my head, which I promptly told to piss off because fuck Hayden. What we'd done last night had been all about Kara.

What we'd done in the darkness a few nights before maybe hadn't been, but I could put that down to a lapse in judgement. Chaos was an arrogant prick. He was good as an extra dick when Kara needed one, but that had nothing to do with me.

I wasn't gay.

I might have stopped giving War a hard time about Scythe, but that didn't mean I was heading down the same path. I wasn't about to start plastering the clubhouse walls with rainbow flags because Chaos knew how to suck dick.

The whole situation made me grouchy. And vaguely horny.

Fucking hell.

"What do you want?" I snapped at Aloha. "I need to go get laid."

He raised an eyebrow. "How many times in one day does your dick actually work? Between midnight and this morning when the three of you finally knocked it off, it had to have been put to good use."

I smirked at him. "Works a hell of a lot more times than yours does, old man."

Aloha scoffed. "Says the cocky son of a bitch who's gonna be staring down the barrel of his fortieth birthday in a few years' time."

"Five years," I clarified. "Four years behind you, don't forget."

Aloha chuckled. "Fine, fine. You're the fountain of youth. Don't mind me if I don't drink from it. I'm perfectly content with the idea of a new decade. Gotta catch up to my woman." He sat back, a dreamy expression on his face. "You all don't know what you're missing 'til you've got yourself a cougar."

He growled and swiped his hand like he had claws.

The other guys laughed at his antics, Aloha forever the good-natured goofball who kept this place chill.

I disagreed about the older woman thing, though,

thinking of Kara's sweetly rounded face and the innocence she'd come here with. That I'd promptly stripped away by fucking her in so many different ways and positions, with plans to do so much more with time.

Images from last night kept playing through my head: taking her ass for the first time, feeling Chaos fucking her at the same time through the thin internal walls of her body.

Imagining what it would have felt like if we'd both been encased in her pussy. Our dicks double penetrating her, rubbing all up on each other at the same time.

I dug my fingers into the fleshy part of my thigh hard enough to snap me out of the real-life porno playing out in my head and focused on what Aloha was saying.

He tapped the table with his fingertips. "I want to talk about Ice. I know my opinion don't count for shit, but when are we going to patch him in? He's been a prospect—"

He was interrupted by the static of the walkie-talkie on the table. "Hawk," Ice's voice crackled down the line.

I picked it up, pressing the button so I could talk. "Speak of the devil and he shall appear. Whaddaya want, Prospect?"

Aloha sighed while we waited for Ice to respond. "That's what I've been trying to talk to you about. You get off on making sure he knows he's a pros—"

Ice's voice cut in through the walkie-talkie. "Kara's here with the doc. But there's a red pickup behind them. Kara says they know the driver. Says his name is Kyle."

I exploded up out of my seat, panic flooding my system in a single fast dump of adrenaline that had me racing for the door and my bike sitting outside it with the keys perpetually in the ignition. I slammed my foot down on the kick start, barking orders down the line at Ice, the engine roaring to life. "Do not let him inside those gates, Prospect! You get her and Hayley Jade inside now! If you've ever wanted to prove yourself, now is the time. He doesn't touch one hair on her head, Ice. You hear me?"

I didn't wait for his reply, tossing the walkie-talkie onto the grass, my tires spinning out on the gravel driveway.

I took the winding path quicker than I'd ever dared to in the past, praying for Ice to be useful for once in his fucking life and keep my girls safe until I got there.

If they had so much as a scratch on them, then all hell was going to rain down on whoever had dared to lay a finger on them.

Blind rage fueled me, and I dumped my bike at the open gates, not giving a flying fuck about the screech of rock against metal as the gravel stripped the paint I'd paid a fortune to have done.

My panicked gaze sought Kara out first, only a tiny bit of the rage settling when I found her, Hayley Jade standing beside her, holding her fingers tightly.

I rushed to them, clutching both sides of Kara's face and searching her for any sign she was hurt. "Are you okay?" I reached a hand down to cup the back of Hayley Jade's head. "What about you? You okay, pipsqueak?"

She stared up at me with those huge dark eyes that squeezed my damn heart.

I dragged my gaze back to Kara.

She nodded quickly, fingers twisting in my shirt. "I'm fine. I just—"

I wasn't listening, my gaze falling on the rusted red

truck and the young guy standing next to it looking damn fucking nervous.

So he should be.

"You Kyle?" I stormed the space between us.

He nodded.

"Hawk!" Kara shouted after me.

But I barely heard her, gaze too focused on the young kid who'd done Josiah's dirty work for him.

"He sent you?" I clenched my fingers into fists. "And you had the fucking balls to come here and talk to my woman?"

Kyle shook his head, his hair flopping around his stubbled face. "No. I swear—"

I didn't care what he had to say or why he was here. He was one of them. One of the fucking Josiah worshippers who wanted Kara and Hayley Jade back.

I wasn't giving them up.

They were mine. There was no fucking doubt about it in my head. My brain roared the word, screaming it so loudly it was deafening.

I ran for the intruder, my fist drawn back, ready to connect.

Grayson caught me before I could make contact, deflecting the blow. "Okay, what we aren't going to do is attack someone while Hayley Jade is watching, capiche?"

He pushed me away, putting himself between me and the Jesus lover, holding his hands up to keep the distance.

I breathed out hard. Breath misting in the wet, cold air a storm had brought in.

Grayson eyed me with a raised brow. "We've talked to Kyle. He didn't have anything to do with Alice's death, and he's not in contact with Josiah."

I scoffed. "You believe that bullshit?"

"We wouldn't have brought him here unless we did." Grayson eyed me warily, like I was a bull that might charge him at any moment.

I glanced at Kyle, who was still so shit-scared it was impossible to believe he was anything but a sheltered farm kid who had no idea what he was doing outside the gates of the cult he'd been raised in.

"He's just a kid," Grayson said quietly. "And *your* kid is watching to see how you handle this. Do her and yourself proud and settle the fuck down."

My kid.

Having someone else acknowledge that before I'd even really acknowledged it to myself set my world spinning.

"Your eyebrow is fucking judging me." I turned around to stalk back to Kara. I picked up Hayley Jade from the ground, shifting her up against my chest and supporting her weight with my arm across the backs of her thighs.

She ran her hand over the cropped lengths of my hair, letting the short spikes tickle her palm.

With my other hand, I took Kara's. "Why is he here?"

Kara squeezed my fingers, trying to be reassuring. "He needs somewhere to stay. He's been homeless ever since... well, you know what."

I gaped at her in disbelief of her bleeding heart. "Are you seriously bringing home another stray dog? Wasn't Chaos enough?"

She stared up at me. "You started it by bringing me here."

"You aren't a stray dog," I said gruffly. "And it was Rebel who brought you here anyway."

"It was you who fought for me to stay. You who fought for Hayden. And now I'm asking you to do it again for Kyle."

I glanced over at the lanky twentysomething. Hell, was he even that old? His beard was laughable, patchy like mine had been before I hit my twenties.

I groaned.

"Please?" Kara asked. "I just...I feel like it's my responsibility. He has nowhere else to go. He can't go back to Ethereal Eden. The cops will find him there. If Alice and I hadn't left, Kyle wouldn't be out here on the run. I owe him."

"You don't owe anybody shit, Little Mouse. No one but yourself." I eyed Kyle, staring him down with a glare I hoped like hell portrayed the fact I didn't trust him as far as I could throw his six-foot-plus frame.

I turned to Grayson, sighing, trusting the doc more than anybody else at that moment. "Take them to the clubhouse for me? I'm riding with Kyle."

Grayson paused. "Do I need to remind you that your heart lies in helping people, not hurting them? Or that blood is really hard to get out of upholstery?"

I didn't answer, just clapped the man on the shoulder and trusted him with the only two things in my life I held precious.

I stalked past him, closing the gap between me and Kyle and staring the kid down with a barely concealed distrust. "Keys."

"In the ignition." Kyle's voice was barely above a whimper.

I got behind the wheel.

Kyle just stared at me through the windshield.

I slammed the heel of my hand down on the horn, blaring out a long honk until Kyle scampered for the passenger-side door.

"Get in," I bit out through the open window without looking at him.

He did, pulling his seat belt across his chest like it was armor.

"That's not going to help you if I don't like how you answer my questions."

He nodded quickly, too scared to even peek at me.

I watched Grayson drive through the gates with my girls and waited 'til they'd disappeared from sight before I said anything. "You're going to answer everything I ask you, without question. You're going to tell me the truth. Every word. Even if you think I won't like it. You feel me?"

"Yes, sir."

I screwed up my face. I couldn't remember anyone ever calling me sir in my life, and it was unsettling. But that was beside the point.

"Did Josiah send you here?"

"No, sir."

"Did you kill Alice?"

"No, sir."

"Do you have any way of communicating with Ethereal Eden or anyone in it?"

He pulled his phone from his pocket and laid it on the center console.

I picked it up and pocketed it. "I'll keep that until you earn my trust. Which might be a very long time, because let me be clear, I'm pussy-whipped as all fuck and will do anything for that woman, including taking you in off the streets. But that doesn't mean I ain't watching you every second of every day. If you so much as step a fucking toe out of line, I will come down so hard you will beg me to send you back to your God. You hear me?"

"Yes, sir."

"Stop fucking calling me sir."

"Yes..." He clamped his lips together. "I don't know what else to call you."

I sighed at the conversation I'd had earlier repeating itself. This kid reminded me of all the prospects we'd had come through the gates over the years. Not many of them lasted.

I predicted this kid would be crying into his cereal before the end of the week and begging me to let him leave.

"If you're in, you're in, kid. Do you get that? I can't have you changing your mind and running back to Josiah."

Kyle finally looked me square in the eye, zero hesitation. "I'll never go back there. I can promise you that. I just need somewhere to lie low until Josiah and the cops stop searching for me. I won't cause any trouble."

I could see what Kara had.

The pure honesty in his eyes. The desperation that made you want to help.

Against my better judgment, I nodded and started the engine. "Fine. Is there anything else I should know before I let you in those gates? This is where you tell me anything at all you can possibly think of, because if I find out later you kept something from me, things are going to get heated."

Kyle paused. "Actually there is." He pointed at his phone. "May I?"

"Go on, then."

He picked it up, and to my surprise, after he hit a few buttons, he didn't turn the screen around, he leaned forward and adjusted the volume on the dashboard.

"What's this?" I asked, clutching the steering wheel, impatient to get going now that I'd decided I was letting the outsider in.

"I've been listening to Josiah's podcast," Kyle admitted.

There was a low rumbling growl in the back of my throat.

Kyle hurried to explain. "I just wanted to know what was going on with my parents and to know if Josiah was talking about me or Alice or what had happened to her. I swear, that's all. But there's something you should hear. Bear with me a second."

He skipped the podcast back before letting it play again.

Josiah's smarmy voice filtered through the speakers, filling the interior of the truck. "Now that takes care of this week's sponsors, there's something desperate and disturbing I need to discuss with all of you, members of my Ethereal Eden community. Something I've been keeping bottled up inside that has been destroying me piece by piece every day I keep my silence. On the advice of police, I held my tongue, but I can no longer do that for my heart is broken, a part of it stolen away in the night." Josiah drew in an audible breath, his voice shaking. "If you are listening to this, I need your help. I desperately need your help."

I gripped the steering wheel tighter, a sick feeling washing over me, already knowing where this was going.

"My wife, my beloved, sweet, kind, obedient wife has been taken from me. Forced from her home by men who know not of the Lord's word. Sinners who have turned her good-natured heart against me and our people. The Ethereal Eden family who love and cherish her." He paused and sniffed.

"And the Oscar goes to..." I muttered.

Kyle cringed. "It gets worse."

"Of course it does. The man can't do anything by halves, can he?"

Josiah, apparently done with his fake display of hurt and sorrow, started again. "My wife, my heart and soul, she is but a weak-willed woman. It is not her fault she has been swayed the way she has. She doesn't know any better, but without my guiding hand, I fear for her immortal soul. This is where all of you come in. You listen from all over the country. From California to New York and everywhere in between. If you listen each week, I have to believe you believe in me. That you believe in the work we're doing at Ethereal Eden, and even if you haven't joined us in person yet, you are my brothers. You are my family. And family sticks together.

"So I beg of you. Bring my wife back to me, as well as the child who was stolen with her. She is believed to be in the Saint View or Providence areas, with known ties to the Slayers Motorcycle Club. Retrieving her will be no easy feat. She will fight. She will lie. She will run. But that is the devil inside her! That is what we must overcome so she can take her rightful place by my side. Her captors will fight back, so you must be clever. Take weapons. Use any force you see fit. Because without my queen, my empire is incomplete, and I cannot carry out the tasks the Lord has set upon my shoulders."

I swore beneath my breath. "I'm going to kill him. Slowly and fucking painfully."

"You'll never get to him," Kyle said quietly. "My parents have left me so many voicemails, telling me about all the new security they've put in at Ethereal Eden. Josiah is telling them it's to keep them safe from the men who took Kara and Alice, but obviously that's a lie."

"It's to keep them locked inside."

Kyle hunched over on himself. "They're prisoners and they don't even realize it. But it also keeps Josiah safe within the walls, and this podcast means everyone else is doing his dirty work for him. If you keep listening, you'll hear him offer a one-hundred-thousand-dollar reward and a spot on Josiah's closest council to the person who brings back Kara and Hayley Jade."

I stared at him in horror, turning up the podcast and hearing Kyle's words confirmed in Josiah's voice. "We need to call the police. Have them listen to this. This is a kidnapping threat. They have to get this taken down before it attracts all the fucking whack jobs who need a quick payday."

"I don't disagree, but this podcast has been up for days already. It has hundreds of thousands of listens."

He had to be joking. "You're fucking kidding me? He has that many followers?"

"No, but he has more than you might think. It's something he's put a lot of time and attention into the last couple of years. He calls it spreading the Lord's word."

"But it's really just feeding his own self-inflated ego."

"There's thousands of shares. That's why it has more listens than it should. Word is already out, so even if the cops force him to take it down—"

"It's not going to do any good. Kara is still going to have a merry band of fucking God-loving lunatics after her." I ran my hand through my hair. "We knew Josiah's men were probably lurking around, but a handful of his pod people are one thing. Offering a reward like that raises the stakes to every Joe Blow out there."

"What are you going to do?" Kyle asked.

There was only one thing I could think of. "Kill Josiah."

33

KARA

I paced the clubhouse nervously, gaze flicking to the door every time it opened. Eventually, Hawk and Kyle appeared, Hawk's face like a thundercloud but Kyle's bag slung over his shoulder.

I breathed a sigh of relief as he dumped it on the floor. "You're letting him stay?"

"Until he pisses me off, I guess I am."

I lifted up onto my toes and kissed his mouth. "Thank you, thank you, thank you."

He grumbled against my lips, but then his hand slid to the back of my hair and he deepened the kiss, his tongue sliding with mine. When he drew back, his eyes were warm. "Don't you know by now that I'd do anything for you?"

"I love you." I let him tug me against his chest, cradling the back of my head.

A contented sigh grumbled through him. "Can't get enough of you saying that. Need those words on your lips like I need air to breathe."

"Then I'll keep saying it," I assured him.

He tipped my head back to claim my lips again then reluctantly pulled away. "Can you show Kyle out to your old cabin? We're running out of rooms up here."

"Of course. Hayley Jade is in the kitchen with Queenie making dessert to go with whatever Hayden is bringing home from the restaurant." I noted the time on my phone. "He said he'd be home around now."

"Good."

Grayson glanced over at him. "Did you just say it was good that Hayden was coming home? I thought you two were mortal enemies apart from..." He wriggled his eyebrows.

I hid a small smile at the flustered expression on Hawk's face.

He flipped Grayson the bird. "There is no—" He mimicked Grayson's actions, raising and lowering his eyebrows but without any of the playful amusement Grayson had displayed— "going on with me and Hayden. Whatever you heard—"

"I heard a lot," Aloha called from the couch where he'd clearly been eavesdropping. "A whole lotta moaning, name-shouting, thigh slapping..."

Hawk gave him the dirtiest look known to man. "Nothing happened between me and Chaos. Not that it's any of your fucking business. Don't you have somewhere else to be or something else to do?"

Aloha shook his head. "Nope. Just sitting here waiting for Chaos to bring the food. Same as you. Right?"

Hawk's lips pressed into a tight line at the snigger in Aloha's voice. "Right."

Kyle was a deer caught in the headlights, trying to follow the conversation.

I wondered if that's how naïve I'd looked when I'd first come here.

I was probably worse.

"Come on, Kyle." I touched his arm gently. "I'll take you down to the cabin so you can get settled."

Kyle picked up his bag, adding it to the pile of belongings in his arms.

Hawk jerked his head at Amber. "Go with them."

"Aw, but the food!"

Hawk's tone was no-nonsense and shut Amber up immediately.

I knew better than to argue with Hawk when he was just trying to keep me safe. He was putting a huge deal of trust in Kyle and our gut feelings about him. But if Kyle had to walk around with a shadow the entire time he was here, then that was fair enough.

Trust had to be earned in this club.

So did forgiveness.

The kiss with Grayson played over in my mind. I'd all but forgotten it in all the ensuing drama.

How on earth was I going to tell Hayden and Hawk without one of them, probably Hawk, killing him? Or maybe he wouldn't care? He'd been all for it at Sinners, boldly whispering in my ear to go ask Grayson to...

My cheeks heated at the thought.

"Are you okay?" Kyle asked as I opened the cabin door for him, Amber a few steps behind, smoking a cigarette at the bottom of the steps.

"Of course." But all I could think about was Grayson and Hawk up in the clubhouse, Hayden getting home from the restaurant, and what they would be talking about.

Oh God. I wasn't ready for that conversation.

"Um, bedroom here. Bathroom there. There's not likely to be any food down here, so make sure you come back up to the clubhouse when you're hungry. I'll leave you to it." I jogged back out of the cabin, leaving Kyle with a bewildered and abandoned expression.

Guilt settled in the pit of my stomach, but I rationalized it away, telling myself I wasn't his mother.

And that Hawk and Hayden were probably quizzing Grayson like he was a contestant on *Who Wants to Be a Millionaire*.

Amber chuckled as she followed me back up to the main house. "I'd run back too, if I had those three men fighting over me."

I threw the other woman a look over my shoulder. "They aren't fighting over me. They're…"

"Lining up nicely to plow your pussy?"

Irritation crept up my spine. I didn't want to make an enemy out of her. I wanted to be friends. "You know, where I come from, all the men take multiple wives. Why shouldn't a woman?"

She took a drag on her cigarette. "You know where I come from, we just call that being a slut."

I turned away, reminding myself her words came from a place of hurt and said more about her than me.

But it was hard not to take them to heart.

I wanted Hawk and Hayden.

I'd kissed Grayson.

People would talk behind my back. Call me names.

Maybe not here, where they were used to Bliss and Rebel and their men.

But what was I supposed to do when the other moms at Hayley Jade's school asked about her father? What if she asked? How was I supposed to say her father was none of the three men I was dating?

I wasn't sheltered away from the world anymore. I had to live in it, and the world didn't accept women wanting more than one man.

My quick steps turned trudging.

Amber caught up with me and sighed heavily. "I don't say it to be mean, Kara. But you're delusional if you think you can just have all three of them and there be no consequences. What happens behind these gates isn't the real world, you know? I just don't want to see you hurt."

I didn't really think that true, but when I glanced over at her, her expression seemed sincere, so I kept my doubts to myself. I spotted Hayden's truck in the parking lot and hurried inside, ready to break up the interrogation.

When I entered the clubhouse, Grayson wasn't in the hot seat after all. In fact, the only people in the room were women. Queenie and Hayley Jade sat on the floor coloring. Kiki and Fancy hovered around the closed "church" door.

All eyes turned my way.

That didn't bode well.

I faltered in the doorway. "What's going on?"

"Hawk called church." Fancy didn't spare a look, her gaze focused on peering through the tiny gap between the door and the frame. "Your men are all in there."

I blinked. "Hawk and..."

She raised a thin eyebrow at me. "Don't play stupid, girl. *All* your men."

That didn't make any sense. "But that's church. Members only. Hayden and Grayson can't go in there."

"Whatever was on Hawk's mind was clearly big enough he thought he needed to break the rules." She shook her head. "Never seen that in all my years here."

"Ugh," Amber groaned. "They're going to call a lockdown, aren't they? For fuck's sake. I can't do that again. I'll lose my mind."

"Maybe they're planning a takeover," Kiki mused. "Maybe Hawk wants that prez patch."

"He better fucking not be." Fancy had venom in her eyes at the thought of her son being overthrown.

"Hawk would never," I assured her. But worry bubbled up inside me all the same because something was definitely wrong. I glanced at Queenie, hoping she'd be the voice of reason.

Even she seemed concerned. "Don't worry, sugar. I'm sure whatever it is has nothing to do with you."

Nobody believed that. Least of all me.

A few minutes later, when the men all filed out of the room, nobody appeared very happy. But it was the three men I knew best who I turned to for reassurance.

Hawk's face was a storm cloud. He kissed the top of my head but then mumbled something about needing to do a thing and disappeared into his room.

Hayden made a beeline for his, disappearing down the hallway without a word.

I looked to Grayson, trying to decipher the expression on his face and lowered my voice so no one else would hear. "Did you tell them about the... Do they know? Is that why everyone is mad?" I stared at Hawk's closed bedroom door. Last night he'd been all for me and Grayson exploring the attraction between us, but he'd been drinking, and we'd been surrounded by sex. We'd both gotten lost in it. Was he having regrets? My stomach clenched at the thought of hurting him more than anything else.

But Grayson shook his head. "It's not about you and me. Whether you tell them about the kiss is up to you." He paused, his gaze raking over me. "I really hope you tell them though. Because I want to kiss you a whole lot more."

His words sent a tingle of pleasure down my spine.

I squeezed his fingers. "I want that too."

He breathed out slowly, his thumb stroking over the back of my hand. "Not tonight, though. There's other things going on."

"Why were you in church with them?" My voice was barely above a whisper because I didn't need Fancy or the others poking their noses into my business. "They don't let anyone in there. Not even prospects most of the time."

Grayson's mouth pulled into a grim line. "Hayden's getting changed and then he's going to fill you in." He breathed deeply, inhaling the scent of my hair. "I don't want to leave."

"Then don't," I whispered back.

He shook his head. "I've got some things I need to take care of. Some people I need to check on."

I stepped back, feeling guilty for taking up so much of his time with my drama. "Of course. I'm sorry. You have patients."

"Something like that."

I didn't get to question what he meant because Hayden returned, his work uniform replaced with jeans and a hoodie. His perfect eyes focused on me as he came and fit a warm arm around me. "Need you tonight," he murmured against my hair. "Need you to come with me."

His fingers slid down my arm to tangle around mine.

I stared up at him. "What's going on?"

He tugged me toward the door, his grip tight. "I'll tell you when we're in the truck. Queenie—"

"I'm on bedtime duty tonight. No sweat. Little Miss here has school tomorrow."

I had no idea what was going on, but it was really starting to worry me. Impatient to know whatever it was Hayden was going to tell me, I knelt in front of my daughter, tugging her up onto her feet. "Eat some dinner and don't forget to brush your teeth, okay?"

Hayley Jade frowned, then pulled away, running to her bedroom.

She appeared a moment later with the picture book I'd read to her at least four times before bed last night.

I took it from her fingers and passed it to Queenie. "Queenie will read it for you tonight."

Queenie tapped her long fingernails across the book's cover. "Sure will. This one looks great."

Hayley Jade shook her head, pushing the book back to me.

My heart squeezed and leapt and broke all at once.

She so rarely wanted me over one of the others.

I stared down at the book in my hands. It was about families, the illustrations depicting a mom, a dad, and a young, dark-haired daughter. I couldn't say no to her.

Didn't want to. Especially when she sat so close to my side it could almost be considered a snuggle.

Hayden and Queenie leaned on the wall, watching me read the story, Hayley Jade listening attentively to every word.

I read the short story twice and laughed when she pushed the book at me again, clearly asking for a third round.

"I think I could read this book a hundred times and you'd still ask for more, wouldn't you? How about you come into my bed in the morning and we'll get cozy and read it again then? As many times as you want."

She nodded so enthusiastically, I smiled.

"It's a date. And after, I'll make you some of those pancakes you like."

Hayley Jade's gaze slid to Hayden, her expression turning hopeful.

He chuckled. "Or I could make them for both of you?"

Hayley Jade nodded, and I laughed.

"That sounds like a much better idea." I ruffled her hair affectionately. "Night-night, sweetheart."

Queenie whisked her away into the kitchen, Hayley Jade skipping after her happily at the prospect of Hayden-made pancakes in the morning.

My heart brimmed over with gratitude for the people I'd found here. How we were all raising Hayley Jade together. That was what a true community did.

It was what Ethereal Eden preached but had never actually put into practice. I'd had no support when she'd been a baby. Nobody had been there to help me when she'd cried all night with colic or when I was too sick to take care of either of us. I'd just been told to get on with it. To do my job as a wife because the men had more important things to do.

When Josiah had taken her away from me, not one person had stepped in to stop him.

Not one person had had my back.

Coming here changed everything.

When Hayden held his hand out to me, I put mine in it, knowing my daughter was loved.

And from the expression on his face, so was I.

34

HAYDEN

I hadn't talked to Hawk since our threesome and was happy to keep it that way, since he was hell-bent on keeping every hard-on he got for me some sort of dirty little secret. I had enough on my plate with the restaurant and Kara to give a shit about his rejections.

At least that's what I was telling myself every time his green eyes crossed my mind and I thought about him sucking my cock in the dark, or how much I'd wanted to touch him while he'd been deep inside Kara's body, making her moan.

So when I'd come home from work and he'd given me a single look and jerked his head toward "church," all the smart-ass comebacks I'd been mentally preparing to guard myself with had disappeared.

Grayson had already been inside, and all available club members had filed in after, making it clear something was up.

Fucking Josiah starting a nationwide manhunt for Kara, complete with hefty reward money hadn't been on my bingo card for the day.

Now it was my job to tell her.

With her sitting on the passenger seat of my truck, I drove us out to the bluff while my thoughts tumbled over in my head.

The guys had all suggested calling a lockdown. Possibly even a hard lockdown, where no one came in or out until the threat had passed. It was what they knew. How they'd always dealt with threats to one of their own.

But Hawk hadn't liked that idea any more than I had. Even Grayson had spoken up and made an argument for Kara and Hayley Jade being allowed to come and go as they pleased.

They'd been locked in cages for far too long for us to put them in another.

"What's happened?" Kara asked quietly.

I gazed at her in the early evening darkness. "I don't want to scare you. But I don't want to lie to you either."

She sucked in a deep breath, reaching across the center console and running her knuckles down my arm. "Just tell me."

"Josiah's offered a reward for your return. Yours and Hayley Jade's. A big one. One big enough that the people around here, who are already doing it tough, would easily see a way to make a quick buck. He told them your location. Made it so damn easy for them."

Kara's face fell. Her hand dropped away from my arm, and she sank back on her seat, shoulders hunching, folding in on herself. "I should just go back."

I stopped the car. We were at the bluff parking lot anyway, not in a designated space, but it was late and there was never anybody up here at this time of day, which was exactly why I'd brought her here. "Over my dead body."

She glanced at me. "Don't say that."

"You think I'm letting you go back to the man who abused you for years? You think Hawk is going to let that happen? You want Hayley Jade back with him?"

She shook her head hard enough tendrils of dark hair fell around her face. "Hayley Jade will *never* go back there. I don't care what happens to me, but you have to promise me she'll be safe. That you'll always put her first."

"You both—"

Emotion clogged her voice, and tears filled her eyes. "No! Promise me, Hayden. Promise me she'll always come first. Promise me, if it ever comes down to it, you'll pick her over me."

I scrubbed my hands over my face. "I can't—"

Her fingers wrapped in my shirt, desperately clinging to me, searching for the promise she needed. "Please. You have to. I've already failed her in so many ways."

I stared at her. "Are you crazy? You haven't failed her at all." Anger rose in me. Not at her, exactly, but at the way she thought. At the way she'd been so gaslit into believing that everything that had happened to her and Hayley Jade was her fault. "I was there the day she was born. I watched you bring that girl into this world when you were at your lowest of lows. When anyone else would have given up, you never did."

"That was because of you."

I shook my head. "Stop giving other people credit for what you did. Caleb taking her wasn't your fault. Josiah ripping her from your arms wasn't your fault. Can't you see that all along, you were the victim?"

"Hawk is going to have to call a lockdown."

"He's not. We talked him out of it."

She sighed. "For now, maybe. But for how long? Everyone is in danger while I'm here. If I go back, that all stops." She stared out the window at the night sky. "My life is just one series of prisons after another. I don't want all of yours to be like that too."

Terror rolled its way down my spine. I didn't like the way she was talking. I understood it, but all I could picture was her slipping away in the night, finding her way back to the commune, giving herself up because she was selfless enough to do that so the rest of us weren't targets.

"Please don't," I begged her quietly. "We both know that if you really want to go, you'll find a way. I won't be your jailer. If it comes down to it, Hawk won't be either. You have to be the one to decide you want to stay. That you want us enough to fight."

She didn't say anything.

Just stared down at her hands.

A wave of crushing despair washed over me. Her selflessness was going to be the thing that got her killed.

I couldn't bear the thought of Josiah's hands on her body. Of the things he'd do to punish her.

"Don't be mad at me," she whispered. "You aren't a mother, so maybe you can't understand that this is not a choice. It's all I am. All I have to give her."

I heard the words. Understood where she was coming from. But I was mad. I was mad because she was giving up. Because she wasn't as one-thousand-percent in as I was, ready and willing to do anything to keep us all together.

I was mad because she was going to break my fucking heart.

I stared at the car ceiling, breathing hard. "What do you think is going to happen to that little girl when you leave? What am I supposed to tell her when you disappear in the night?"

"Tell her I loved her enough to give her up."

"Bullshit!" I shouted.

Kara flinched.

Guilt filled me for scaring her, but I didn't take it back. Because someone needed to talk some fucking sense into her. "I'm not looking that girl in the eye and telling her you're gone. She's five, Kara. You know what she's going to hear? The same fucking thing I am. That you didn't love her enough to stay. To fight. To be in her life instead of a goddamned brainwashed cult sacrifice!"

She stared at me, the tears in her eyes melting away, replaced by anger. "How dare you?"

"How dare I? No, sweetheart. How dare you. How fucking dare you come back into my world and turn it upside down? How dare you bring that little girl and make me love her? How dare you sit there, so fucking beautiful and selfless, and then tell me you're throwing it all away because you don't believe in us the way I do? How dare you make me—"

I couldn't bring myself to say it. But silently, my fingers made the sign for, "love you."

I turned away, biting down on my lip.

For a long moment, only the sounds of our breathing filled the air.

"What did that sign mean?"

I wasn't giving her that. I couldn't bring myself to voice the words because it would hurt all too much when she didn't say them back.

Which she wouldn't. Because if she loved me...us... the way Hawk and I loved her, we wouldn't have been having this argument in the first place. "Give us one week, Kara. Give us one fucking week to work this out. To show you that you don't need to do this."

She sighed, staring out the window. "I don't even know how to drive a car."

I blinked, turning back to her. "What?"

She shrugged. "I don't know how to drive. I'm always reliant on you or Hawk or someone to pick me up and chauffeur me around. I can't go anywhere by myself."

It had never even occurred to me. The clubhouse was in the middle of nowhere. It wasn't like there was a bus stop right out front. She didn't have her own money or her own vehicle.

When I stopped and thought about it, it was really no surprise at all she felt trapped.

She was as reliant on Hawk and me and the rest of the club as she'd been on Josiah.

We might not have been abusing her, but in trying to protect her, keep her safe, and give her everything, we'd made her helpless.

Kept her in a cage.

Smothered her independence.

The realization hit me like a sledgehammer, rolling

my stomach until I felt sick. I took the keys from the ignition and tossed them at her. "Catch."

Her reflexes were fast enough to snag the keys before they were lost to the darkness of the floorboard.

She stared down at them. "What are you doing?"

"You said you wanted to learn to drive, didn't you?"

35

KARA

I clutched the keys in my fingers, nervous laughter bubbling up my throat. "I can't drive your truck! What if I crash it? I don't even have a license!"

But Hayden was already out of the truck and rounding to the passenger side to open my door. "There's nobody out here. Everyone starts in an empty parking lot. And we have one of those. We won't go out on the roads."

A swirl of excitement formed inside me. "Really?"

He eyed me. "All you had to do was ask. You want to learn how to drive? No sweat. You want to learn how to make a perfect duck breast with apricot chutney? I can show you. You want to learn how to crochet? Well, I don't know how to do that, but I can figure it out with you." He tucked a strand of hair behind my ear. "I didn't know we were holding you back. I didn't mean to. And I know Hawk didn't either. We just...overdid it. We thought we were protecting you."

"I know." I smiled at him, anticipation spreading through my body. "Better put your seat belt on. You're the one who needs protecting now." I slid out of the seat and trotted past him to the driver's side.

He got in, making a show of putting on his seat belt while I adjusted the seat. My legs were about half the length of his.

"Could you get any closer to the steering wheel?" He sniggered.

"Hey! I have short legs, okay?"

"Fine, fine. I hope you don't crash into anything because the airbags are really going to be painful at that distance."

I glared at him. "Super reassuring."

He laughed. "Put the key in the ignition—"

I was already three steps ahead of him, the engine turning over and rumbling to life, aided by my foot on the accelerator.

Hayden's fingers slid to the handle above the window. "Why do I get the impression you've done that before?"

"I haven't," I assured him. "But I've watched you and Hawk do it enough times to know how." I revved it again, the truck vibrating beneath me. I grinned at the feeling it gave me. "Parking brake off. Gear shift moves to drive. And—" I widened my eyes at the truck lurching forward. "Aaah!"

Hayden tightened his grip on the door. "And you're driving. Don't forget to steer."

I shot him a dirty look, but the reminder probably wasn't in vain. I had taken my hands off the wheel for a second. I clamped them back down, fingers tight on the hard plastic and giving it an experimental tug as we crept along at a snail's pace, just letting it move off its own car magic. My foot was nowhere near the accelerator, too nervous to move it in that direction when having it hovering over the brake felt a whole lot safer.

Hayden's hand landed on my thigh, warm and reassuring. "Relax. You're doing fine. Give it some gas."

At the end of the lot, I dragged the wheel around, maneuvering the truck into a wide U-turn to trundle back in the direction we'd come. Knowing he was there, and he wasn't going to let me steer us off the cliff or into a tree or oncoming traffic, I settled down, even daring to push my foot on the accelerator a little.

A thrill shot through me when the truck responded. We were barely going ten miles per hour, but it felt like flying.

It felt like freedom. Or at least the promise of freedom.

It had been easy to focus on all the bad things the world outside Ethereal Eden's gates offered. But there were simple pleasures here too. Like a man teaching you to drive his truck, just because you'd asked.

All I had to do was ask.

We drove around the lot for twenty minutes, practicing the very basics of driving. I even reversed at one point, though that was kind of terrifying.

Breathless with giddy excitement, I stopped the car.

Hayden glanced at me, watching me put it into park. "Had enough?"

"For tonight."

"How'd it feel?"

I grinned. "Like freedom."

Like a reminder of everything I'd be giving up if I went back. Josiah would have never let me drive his truck.

I wouldn't have dared to ask. It would have ended in a punishment for forgetting my place.

I was as guilty as Hawk and Hayden. The boundaries I had here weren't only of their making. I had a role in them too.

They weren't mind readers, and I no longer had to let a man make every decision for me.

I could ask for what I wanted.

What I needed.

Hayden rubbed the back of his hand over his mouth, not doing a good job of hiding the satisfied smile tugging at his lips. "Good. How about I drive us home though? It's getting late."

I could ask for what I wanted. What I needed.

And what I'd always needed was him.

"Not yet." I crawled over the center console and settled myself on his lap, knees either side of his legs, not caring that it wasn't terribly comfortable. "There's something else I want first."

His hands settled on my hips, and he laughed. "You know, most people pay their driving instructors with cash…"

I ran my nose up the side of his neck. "Do they? One small problem with that. I don't have any." I kissed the spot beneath his ear.

His fingers tangled in the back of my hair, pulling it enough that my head tipped back, exposing my throat.

"No?" he murmured. "I suppose I could call this a free first lesson then…"

The stubble of his short beard scraped over my skin, tantalizingly different than the softness of his lips and tongue as he worked his way from my chin to my collarbone.

"I think I'd rather pay in another way."

He pushed the neck of my shirt aside so he could kiss my shoulder. "Okay, if you're really intent on paying, I accept cash, check, or sex in my truck."

I laughed, slipping my hands down his chest and then underneath his hoodie. I ran my fingers along the ridges of his abs and flicked the button on his jeans. "What if someone parks beside us?"

He unbuttoned my shirt. "Then I'll put my mouth over your nipple so nobody sees it."

I looked past him as he pushed aside my shirt and groped my breasts through my bra. "Oh no. Someone's coming."

There wasn't a hint of sincerity in my voice. The bluff was as empty as it had been ever since we'd come up here.

Hayden chuckled into the swell of my breasts and dragged off my bra straps, flipping the cups down and kissing his way across my skin. "Oh no."

His tongue rasped over my nipple, sending a shiver of pleasure down my spine. He switched to the other side, tending to that breast as sweetly as he had the first, building my nipples into stiff, needy peaks that begged for more.

He delivered. He raised my breasts to his mouth, alternating between long licks and sucks with his mouth, and tweaks and pinches between his thumb and forefinger.

Like they had a mind of their own, my hips rocked over his, and I leaned back, supporting my weight by holding on to his knees, offering him better access to my body.

He groaned at the sight of me like that, face and breasts pointed toward the roof, hair dangling down my back, hips slow winding, a sensual tease of what was to come. "You're always beautiful. But fuck." He kissed the soft, flabby skin across my belly that was deeply scarred with the evidence of having carried a child. "Confidence looks good on you. I don't think I've ever seen you as sexy as you are right now. Lift your skirt, sweetheart. Need to feel your hips move like that while I'm inside you."

I moaned at the thought of him penetrating me. At the thought of the long, slow slide into my body while his heated gaze burned a path across my skin.

I raised myself up, all weight in my knees, craning my neck so my head didn't hit the roof.

Hayden dropped the passenger seat all the way back so it lay almost flat. He watched me intently as I raked up my skirt so it bared my thick thighs and all the cellulite I'd tried to hide. I didn't care anymore. Not tonight.

He wanted me just the way I was. He always had. Hawk, too. It had been me who'd had the problem with it.

Hayden's fingers brushed the inside of my thighs as he undid his fly and dragged his jeans and underwear down low enough to expose his cock. He was already hard, thick, and straining toward me, like his dick knew where it was supposed to be and what it was supposed to do without any guidance from his hands.

I tugged my panties to one side, knowing it would be too hard to get them off in the confined space.

I couldn't wait.

I wanted him.

I'd always wanted him.

I swiped the head of his cock through the wet arousal pooling between my folds. Coated him in it while he hissed in pleasure.

"Ride me, Kara," he groaned, fingers digging into the flesh at my hip. "Sink your sweet, wet pussy down on my dick and ride me before I fucking come all over myself just staring at you."

He didn't have to ask twice. I was already on my way.

We both shouted when I dropped down onto him, his dick a thick spear of pleasure inside me, stretching me wide at the base. I rocked my hips, getting some friction for my clit, grinding over his pubic bone, feeling the delicious scratch to his hair, before rising up to sink back down deep.

I slid my hands along his stomach and chest, taking his hoodie with me. I didn't bother taking it off him, it was too difficult in the cramped space, and it wasn't necessary for what I needed. But I delighted in the hard ridges of his abs and pecs, so completely different to the softness of my thighs either side of him.

I kissed his mouth, tangling my tongue with his, and sliding up and down his erection. His hands trailed from my back to my ass, holding on tight, not controlling or even guiding my movements because tonight was mine.

Mine to control. Though I doubted I was suddenly about to become dominant in the bedroom, I liked the expression on his face, the sweet agony where he was barely inside me, the torturous wait before I plunged back down, offering him relief from the need building behind his eyes.

He kissed every inch of me he could get his mouth to, craning into odd positions to touch and suck my breasts, his lips trailing hot, sweaty paths up my inner arms. Every now and then his hand grasped the back of my neck, hauling me down so he could kiss my mouth. Stealing my breath in passionate kisses that would have fueled my dreams for a lifetime if I didn't have him right there beside me to act them out in person.

Every time he did that, he loosened his grip on my neck, like he'd remembered that tonight, he didn't get to be the one calling the shots.

At least not all the shots.

I was there for those deep, drugging kisses as much as he was. They connected a part of me to him that wasn't physical. They cemented that feeling that had always been there between us.

The one that felt like coming home when I was near him. That felt like peace and calm when the rest of the world felt out of control.

It was him I needed tonight. Him I needed while my clit sang the pleasures of friction, sending an orgasm ripping through my body. I shuddered and shook around his erection buried deep inside me. My inner walls clamped down on him, holding him as tight as the fingers I had tangled in his hair.

He groaned into my mouth as his orgasm took hold. His fingers bit into my flesh in the most delicious way, and he whispered all the sweet words I'd spent years dreaming of hearing him say.

That he saw me.

That he wanted me just the way I was.

That I was his.

I pressed my face into his neck, licking his warm skin, tasting him and committing it to memory. My hips slowed their pace, but neither of us stopped completely, our frantic thrusts to get off turning into agonizingly slow glides that were sweet torture to us both.

I sighed into his neck, so content in his arms I didn't want to remember there was a world outside.

One that wanted me hurt.

One that wanted us apart.

"Please don't leave, Kara," he whispered.

He didn't ask me for a promise.

Because we both knew it was one I couldn't make.

36

KARA

The next few days, everyone was on edge. Hawk hovered around, stressed to the eyeballs and seeming like he wanted to call a lockdown at any minute. Every time the men disappeared into church, the other women and I held our breaths, waiting for their decision.

I wrung my hands nervously, hating their lives could all be severely impacted because of me. Kiki and Amber told stories of the last lockdown they'd had and how they'd hated every moment of it. Queenie was too sweet to say anything, but the dirty looks Fancy threw my way told me nobody was very happy with me for bringing this to their doorstep.

But each time the men came out, it seemed Fang and the others had talked Hawk off the ledge.

I was glad for it. Not because I was selfless. Lord knew I'd been more than selfish a time or two lately. But because the fact was, nothing had happened.

The police had come by, and Hawk had yelled at them for a good hour, while they assured him they were investigating the kidnapping threats and that they'd issued an order for Josiah's podcast episode to be removed.

That hadn't been enough for Hawk, and Hayden and Grayson had sat by quietly, not looking too happy about it either, but nobody could get a word in around Hawk's ranting.

He'd taken me to his room that night, and we'd had slow, sweet, lovemaking sex. The kind I doubted anybody but me knew he was even capable of.

It had been full of fear and love, and it broke my heart to see him the way he was.

Hayden had the restaurant, and Grayson had his job to distract them.

But in the absence of War, who was still holed up in his love nest with his family and new baby, Hawk's focus was solely on keeping not only me but the entire club safe.

The toll was beginning to show.

But the world didn't stop turning because we had problems.

Hayley Jade kept going to school because keeping her sheltered from the threats and happy was my main priority. She was thriving in the company of other children. She got herself up every day and was dressed and ready hours before we needed to leave. Once or twice, though she still didn't make a sound, I caught her lips moving as she tried to read the simple, two-or-three-words-per-page books the school sent her home with.

I volunteered at the hospital more than I ever had.

Partly because I loved it. Partly because wherever I

went, Hawk went, and if anyone needed to be in their happy place right now, it was him.

The hospital was truly turning out to be that for him. He and Grayson bantered back and forth every time they found themselves in the clinic together or on the same ward on days the clinic didn't run. I didn't miss the way Hawk asked him questions any chance he got, comfortable enough with Grayson or Nurse Willa to show interest in something, even if they were the only two he did that with. He still curled his lip at the doctors who acted like nurses and volunteers were so far beneath them they didn't even get the courtesy of a hello. I couldn't blame him. Some of them were horrible.

The Friday free clinic rolled around, and Hawk actually whistled beneath his breath, despite the fact the parking lot was unusually full and we had to walk farther than normal.

I nudged him. "You're in a good mood."

He shrugged. "I like it here. I like feeling useful and like I'm doing something that actually matters." He glanced at me. "I think we should enroll for the GED classes."

Excitement lit up inside me. "You do?"

He slung an arm around my shoulders and kissed the top of my head. "I can't exactly keep pretending I'm only here as your bodyguard." His gaze strayed to the ambulance sitting in the ER dock and the paramedics milling around it, restocking supplies and marking things off on their checklists. "I want that."

"The rush of treating patients in an emergency situation? Or the paperwork?"

He chuckled. "I'm all about the action, Little Mouse.

Hopefully, my partner will be better at crossing T's and dotting I's than I am."

I put my arm around him and squeezed. "You'll be an amazing paramedic." I meant it with all of my heart. I didn't think my future was there beside him in an ambulance. I didn't thrive in high-pressure environments like Hawk did.

But as I walked inside the clinic full to the brim with waiting patients, too poor to go to a doctor at any other time, my heart settled into something that felt a lot like happiness.

If someone had asked me in that moment what I wanted to spend my life doing, I would have easily answered, this. I didn't know if that meant becoming a nurse, or maybe a physiotherapist or a dietitian, but I knew all of that started with just getting my high school equivalency so I could begin.

All my years of studying the Bible weren't going to help me here. And I couldn't wait to learn something more than scriptures. Something inside me craved it as much as Hayley Jade did. I smiled at the thought of getting up early with her every morning, her practicing her reading while I studied before the breakfast Hayden would make in the kitchen. Hawk joining us with books. Grayson looking over our shoulders and offering help while he fit his tie around his neck, a day of work stretching ahead of him.

I bit my lip at the daydream, knowing I was crazy to think it could be that easy.

Except it felt like it might be.

When Grayson was the first person we saw as we entered the hospital through the staff entrance, my heart lit up and a tiny voice whispered inside my head that he was the thing in my life that could make it complete.

"Hi!" I said a bit too loudly, nerves suddenly fluttering around my belly at the sight of him in fitted suit pants and a button-down shirt rolled to his elbows. His forearms, thick with corded muscle, drew my gaze, and it lingered there, while my stomach did backflips at how attractive he was.

I didn't know how I hadn't seen it earlier.

But ever since that night at Sinners, and since he'd kissed me at the beach, I was struggling to think of Grayson as a friend.

I wanted him to be so much more.

His warm gaze settled on me, and I breathed out slowly, trying to calm my nerves.

Hawk pulled me in so his lips were to my ear. "Settle, Little Mouse. I can practically smell you getting wet over the sight of him."

I was sure my cheeks went bright red.

I hadn't told Hawk or Hayden about the kiss on the beach but I had a feeling they knew something had changed between me and Grayson.

"Morning, Doc," Hawk drawled. "What's on the agenda today?"

Grayson jerked his head toward the waiting room. "It's already crazy here. We're so busy. Which in a way is good. I've been pushing the hospital board to extend the clinic's hours, because clearly the community needs it. One day a week isn't enough. They disagreed, but after this turnout, they have to see that we need more resources. More time. More everything."

I peeked around the corner at the waiting room, and

my mouth dropped open. Every seat was full. People stood around the edges. Some had taken up seats on the floor, like they'd been there for hours and were too tired to stand any longer.

Grayson grimaced. "Willa was here early. She said they were lined up around the block, waiting for the doors to open."

Grayson's phone rang, right as a voice from the examination cubicle behind me called my name.

All three of us glanced over.

Hayden sat on a bed, legs dangling over the side, his work uniform still on but his hand bandaged with thick white strips of cloth. He waved the injured limb pathetically.

"Oh my God!" I rushed to his side. "What are you doing here?"

Hayden shrugged. "Small kitchen injury that wouldn't stop bleeding. I just need a couple of stitches—"

Hawk followed close behind me, immediately going to Hayden's side and picking up his hand, unwrapping the messy bandage to examine the wound. "So you came here instead of coming to me? That's fucking insulting. Do you have any idea how long you'll wait here for someone to throw a few stitches in that?"

Hayden huffed at him. "You and I aren't exactly besties lately."

It was true. The two of them had been mostly avoiding each other since the night of the infamous threesome that was apparently never to be repeated, because Hawk and Hayden were too busy trying to one-up each other.

Hawk pressed his lips together and then drew the

curtain. "I'm still perfectly capable of stitching up your finger." He lowered his voice. "Even if I didn't want to fuck you."

Hayden watched him carefully. "You wanted to fuck me. You still do. That's the whole problem, isn't it?"

Hawk paused in rifling through the supply stand for a suture kit. "Do you want your finger fixed or not?"

Hayden held out his hand with a sigh. "Just stitch it, you know-it-all."

Grayson stuck his head around the curtain, gaze landing on what Hawk was doing. He half covered his eyes with his hand. "I'm going to act like I don't see you doing that, unlicensed, in a hospital."

Hawk didn't lift his gaze from where he was taking great delight in spraying Hayden's cut-up finger with some sort of stinging antiseptic that had Hayden flinching. "We were never here, Doc. You saw nothing."

Grayson didn't seem convinced. He glanced over at me. "Stitches are one thing, but please don't let him attempt any open-heart surgeries while I'm gone. I know he's confident, but some things actually do require proper training."

I chuckled. "I'll do my best."

"I'd rock an open-heart surgery," Hawk muttered, his entire attention focused on his work.

Hayden just rolled his eyes. We all knew Hawk's arrogance was out of control. But it was also something I kind of loved about him. I wished I had half the confidence in myself. I had no doubt in my mind that if someone had actually desperately needed heart surgery, and Hawk was the only one there to do it, he would have at least had a go.

I shook my head. "I need to get out there. Willa will be run off her feet, no doubt, and begging for some help." It suddenly registered that Grayson had said he was leaving. "You aren't actually leaving are you? The clinic..."

Grayson cringed. "I know. But I just got a call and I need to run home. I'll be as quick as I can."

Hawk glanced over at him finally. "You ditching us like your stuck-up doctor friends who think they're too good to help the people who really need it?"

Grayson gave him a dirty look. "You did not just lump me in with Tahpley and his crew. I think you know me better than that by now."

Hawk eyed him, then nodded. "Fine. Go. Don't know what's so urgent it can't wait 'til five, but whatever."

Grayson's mouth pulled up at the corner. "That attitude is what'll make you a great paramedic. Don't lose it." He turned to me. "Tell Willa I'm sorry and I'll be back as soon as I can."

I nodded, watching him break into a run as he made his way down the corridor to the exit, swiping his staff card on the box by the door so they would let him out.

The noise from the waiting room was reaching a swell, and the nurses trying to keep the peace out there floated back to me. It was a job I could do for them, freeing them up for the actual medical procedures. At least the ones Hawk wasn't stealing from them. "I need to go. Will you two maybe manage to be civil to each other while I'm gone?"

"Can't make any promises like that, Little Mouse." Hawk stuck his tongue out the side of his mouth and stabbed a needle into Hayden's finger, pulling through a length of cord and neatly closing the slice mark in

Hayden's skin. "But I won't kill him. So go on out there and do your thing. I'm nearly done here. Once I send old butterfingers here back to work, I'll come join you." He made another stitch. "Honestly, how the hell do you cut yourself this bad? Aren't you some sort of hot-shot chef? Don't you have any knife skills?"

Hayden ignored him and turned to me. "I'm fine."

"You sure?"

"Absolutely. See you tonight. Unless Hawk here has given me a staph infection and I'm back here in a few hours with a raging fever and gangrene."

Hawk glared at him. "Sometimes I really wish I'd just left you to bleed out on the side of the road, you know?"

"Sometimes I wish I'd aimed that gun higher than your leg."

I sighed. "And sometimes I wish the two of you would just admit you want each other and kiss, but hey, we can't all get what we want, can we? I'm going out to help some people who aren't in the middle of using an argument as foreplay."

Hawk stopped his sewing and stared at me. Hayden's mouth dropped open in shock.

I snorted on a laugh and left them gawking.

Men were idiots. At least the two of them were.

Stupid, sexy, lovable idiots, who really needed to get on the same page because I hadn't stopped thinking about being sandwiched between their naked bodies.

I really wanted it to happen again. Even if I wasn't going to admit that to anyone but myself.

Maybe Grayson could join in too.

I was suddenly glad he'd left because my cheeks

flushed hot, and I was sure the images playing on a loop behind my eyes were wanted by no one but me.

Dirty, sexy, foursome images, just rolling around in my head, blinding me to what my reality actually was. But for a sweet moment, as I made my way through the waiting room to where Willa sat behind the nurses' station looking frazzled, I let myself have the fantasy.

I'd later blame that for not noticing that the number of people in the waiting room had doubled since my first peek. I didn't notice the swell of voices when I entered, the volume getting loud, so I couldn't pick out overall words until they were shouts.

"That's her! I'm sure of it! Josiah's wife!"

The mention of my husband's name sent a chill of fear down my spine.

A swarm of men, men who I'd thought to be patients, stood from their chairs, all spinning in my direction. One glared at me with a hate so startling I took a step backward, hitting my hip painfully against the nurses' desk.

I shook my head fast. "No," I lied. "I don't know what you're talking about."

"Kara," Willa asked behind me, concern filling her voice. "What's—"

"You must repent!" A man lunged for me, his expression twisted in hateful devotion to the man who'd made my life a living hell for the past five years.

I screamed, his fingers wrapping in the sleeve of my shirt and yanking.

The sound of tearing fabric cut through the sudden din in the waiting room, at least a dozen men swarming me, forcing me back farther and farther as they came at me with hate in their eyes.

Hate Josiah had put there with his words. His podcast. His insane reward I knew these men would never see a dime of because that was just how Josiah rolled. He'd think nothing of offering money to have these people do his dirty work for him, knowing all along he had no intention of paying.

I yanked my arm away from the man, backing up until I hit a wall.

"Someone call security!" one of the nurses shouted.

But I already knew security would be too late.

The room spun. I tried to suck in air around my panic, more and more people spilling into the waiting room, a planned attack in progress that I'd been stupid enough to walk straight into.

"Get back!" Willa shouted, her and two other nurses putting themselves and chairs and anything else they could find in the path of the mob who had me in its sights.

"Repent." A low chant started. "Repent. Repent."

More and more voices added. One of the nurses screamed when a man grabbed her, shoving her roughly in order to get to me.

The voices grew louder, people not involved fleeing in fear and furniture crashing to the floor in their haste to get away. But the mob outnumbered everyone else, and they enclosed on me like hungry sharks.

"Stop!" I yelled. "Please! He's not what you think! He's a liar. He's not giving any of you any money! This is a hospital. There are sick people here. Just stop!"

"Repent. Repent. Repent." They pushed forward again, fights breaking out amongst each other as they tussled to get me.

At the back of the room, I caught a glimpse of Hawk and Hayden, but they were quickly swallowed by the crowd between us.

"The Devil has control of her tongue!" the ringleader shouted.

"Cut it out!" another replied.

"She's worth a hundred K! Get the fuck out of my way!"

My blood ran cold.

I'd listened to the podcast. Josiah had asked for me back in one piece. Unharmed.

These men didn't care. Their gazes were wild with the hunt, and a brand-new fear unlocked inside me, swirling up my throat until it felt like I couldn't breathe.

Willa flung her nurses' pass at me. "Get back behind the security doors!"

I stumbled, another hand catching me, sharp fingernails cutting into my skin. A scream ripped from my throat as I dragged myself away.

"Kara!" Hawk and Hayden's bellows of my name were simultaneous.

But I couldn't get to them, and they couldn't get to me. We were separated by an impenetrable wall of people.

Willa shoved me through the security doors, falling in after me, a doctor rushing in from behind to yank the doors closed.

Willa scrambled to her knees, groaning in pain but her gaze all for me. "Are you hurt?"

I shook my head. "No. I don't think so. But—"

Pounding came from the other side of the door. The wood rattled, and Willa and I both got to our feet, preparing to run.

Through the tiny glass window, we watched in horror at the pandemonium on the other side. An all-out brawl had broken out, men running at the door and barging it with their shoulders, trying to break it down.

"Call a code nine," Willa urged the doctor, staring through the windows, terror in her eyes at the patients and staff we'd left on the other side in order to save ourselves.

The doors weren't going to hold.

We both screamed as something solid hit them. They were using a chair as a battering ram.

"Kara!" Willa shouted. "Run. They're going to be in here any minute!" She grabbed at my arms, my hands, trying to pull me away.

But through the doors, Hayden's gaze met mine.

I signed Hayley Jade's name, my fingers moving fast.

Hawk appeared beside him, breathing hard, a cut on his face dripping blood, showing me he'd already been fighting. I signed it again, this time screaming her name along with the sign.

Because I wasn't the only one Josiah had wanted.

This mob would be at her school too.

"Go!" I screamed at them through the door, tears streaming down my face, sure they couldn't hear me but unable to keep the word from ripping straight from my soul. "Go to her!"

Hawk's expression was pure anguish. His soul clearly torn between staying here and fighting for me.

Or leaving to save the little girl he'd so obviously fallen in love with.

"Hawk, please! Go!"

He let out a bellow of anguish that was torn from

somewhere so deep inside him I was sure he might never recover. He spun on his heel, the crowd swallowing him up and jostling Hayden so roughly I lost sight of him for a second.

The crack of breaking glass splintered through the chaos.

"Kara! We have to go now!" Willa screamed. "If they get through those doors, there's no telling what they'll do to you!"

But I couldn't leave until I told Hayden the one thing I should have already said.

When our gazes locked through the crowd, I made the same sign he'd shown me in the truck.

The one I knew in my gut meant I love you.

He silently mouthed the words back at me.

Hayley Jade was the last thing I signed, praying he would go to help Hawk, as the locks gave way and a mob full of men hunting me down stormed through the doors.

37

GRAYSON

My burner phone buzzed incessantly from my briefcase, sitting on the passenger seat. I fumbled one handed with the locks while I drove, cursing beneath my breath when I couldn't get them open in time to answer the call.

Like it always was, the number was blocked and I had no way of knowing who'd been the one to call an emergency meeting. Only that calling twice meant something big was going down, and I was sure I wasn't going to like what.

By the time I got back to my apartment, I half expected the four of them to be sitting in the hallway outside my door, but it was empty of any and all psychopaths, unless I included myself.

Which I did not, despite one doctor's ill-thought-out diagnosis in my early twenties.

The guy was a quack and had no idea what he was talking about.

I got to work, giving my apartment a quick tidy up,

though it was pretty clean to begin with. I pushed the couch to one side and pulled the dining room chairs from beneath the table, setting them up in a circle.

I didn't expect to have time to worry about food. I'd taken too long to get out of the hospital, and the first call had come in at least an hour ago now. Though nobody had shown up yet, so clearly I wasn't the only one who'd been in the middle of something.

They'd all come eventually, they always did. We were a family more than ever after Trigger's disappearance. We showed up when one of us needed the others.

Despite the fact I didn't kill the way they did, I still included myself in the family we'd built here.

It was the only one I'd had after my wife had died.

I listened for the door while I rummaged through the refrigerator, searching for anything to feed four fully grown men. There were some cold cuts and cheese. I always had a loaf of bread in the freezer for toast, since these meetings were generally held in the early hours of the morning.

It was odd for one to be called at this time of day, which only made me more nervous about whatever was going on.

As did the fact nobody had turned up yet.

I sat, eating a ham and cheese sandwich like the sad kid at school, who invited the whole class to their birthday party only to have no one show up. The clock ticked, but nobody came to the door. I didn't understand. I hadn't imagined those calls. I'd checked the log on the phone twice to be sure.

I'd been gone from the hospital maybe an hour when I decided I couldn't wait any longer.

And that something was very wrong.

They never didn't show. If they weren't here now, there had to be a reason.

I called the numbers I had saved for each of them, not bothering to check my caller ID was turned off because this wasn't me calling a meeting. There was no need to respect our anonymity code when I was calling to make sure they were all alive.

If they were all breathing, I wanted those return phone calls.

But something churned in my gut, a deep-set knowledge I wasn't going to receive them.

"Fuck it," I said to the empty apartment, picking up the keys and shoving them into my pocket. I dragged the door shut behind me and ran down the stairs, making my way into the garage where I'd left my car.

Preoccupied with worry, I slid behind the wheel and drove deep into Saint View.

Whip's house was at the rounded top of a dead-end road. The street in the worst part of Saint View only had a dozen houses still standing, the rest in various states of demolition, either by an actual wrecking crew or by bored street thugs with nothing better to do than be destructive in an area where everyone turned a blind eye.

Whip's place was probably the nicest on the street, but that didn't make it nice. It was a shithole by anyone's standards. The porch steps creaked beneath my weight as I pushed myself up them to the front door that didn't quite close properly. Moisture had swollen the wood until it no longer fit.

It left gaps big enough for bugs to crawl through.

And for a muffled scream to filter out.

"Well, that's not fucking great." I slammed my fist against the door. "Whip! Stop whatever the fuck you're doing in there and open up."

A curse, one a lot louder than the one I'd uttered, floated back, but then Whip's heavy footsteps pounded down the hallway.

The door opened a crack, but to my surprise, it wasn't Whip's sharp blue eyes staring back at me.

"X?"

He smirked. "Doc. Fancy seeing you here."

I raised an eyebrow. "Since when do you hang out at Whip's place?"

He shrugged with a fake nonchalance that wasn't fooling anybody, let alone me, the man who'd studied all his odd behaviors and quirks for years. "Just dropped around for a cup of tea."

Another muffled scream filtered back.

I gave X a pointed look. "Are you boiling Whip in the kettle along with the tea bags? Because it sounds like someone back there is in pain."

He rolled his eyes, flinging the door open dramatically. "Fine! You busted us. You better come in."

I followed him inside the run-down shack of a house, made oddly homey by knick-knacks and photos on the wall. If I'd had more time, I would have liked to stop and take a poke around, see what those items told me about the man who'd been in my group for longer than either of us could remember.

It had started with him, me, and Trigger. We were the originals.

"Whip! Doc is here."

I paused in the living room, taking in the big man sprawled out across it. "You're here too?" I asked Torch.

"Apparently." He took a long draw on a smoke, the end burning red in the dim light, all the blinds drawn and the sunlight only peeping around the corners. "Ace is getting some food together in the kitchen if you want a sandwich or something."

With the blood-curdling screaming coming from one of the bedrooms, eating was the last thing I felt like doing.

Whip appeared from a room somewhere down the hallway, wiping his hands off on a grubby cloth. A plastic apron with flowers all over it covered his clothes.

It also happened to be covered in blood, not that anybody but me seemed fazed by that.

"That's..." I pointed to his chest.

Whip glanced down, his eyebrows rising like he hadn't even noticed the blood spray. "My granny's apron. Don't give me shit about it. It does the job."

Right. Got it. Not exactly what I'd been hoping for an explanation on, but okay then. I cleared my throat, ignoring the moans from the back room and the way X picked at dried blood from beneath his fingernails.

I perched on the arm of the couch. "I guess you all got too tied up to attend the meeting."

X sniggered. "We ain't the one's tied up, Doc."

I cringed as the person who was being held in a room down the hallway let out a helpless scream that didn't even register on the expressions of the other men. So I tried to school my features into the same blank stare, even though my heart beat too fast.

I knew them. Knew what they did. I'd heard all their stories. All their secrets.

I just hadn't seen it in person. Heard it. Smelled it. God, there was a stench I related to torture. Piss. Shit. Vomit. Blood. Fear. All of it combined together to produce a smell I had spent years in therapy attempting to forget.

I swallowed thickly, trying to focus on the reason I was here. And not the pure evidence right in front of me that these men were dangerous.

"What meeting?" Whip asked.

I frowned. "One of you called for a meeting. Twice. But then didn't show. I got worried when none of you answered your phones..."

Torch leaned over and picked up his phone from the coffee table. "We were...busy." He turned the phone around so I could see the screen. "I didn't get a call for a meeting though. Only the call from you about fifteen minutes ago."

Whip went into the kitchen and pulled his phone off the charging cable. "Nothing on mine either."

Ace called back that he had nothing either.

We all looked at X.

He was tossing Froot Loops into his mouth one by one, stopping only when he realized we were all staring at him. "What? I don't even know where my phone is right now. Wasn't me who called for a meeting. I'm good. *Real* good. Got my friends. Got sugar. Got a guy tied up in Whip's spare room that we're thoroughly enjoying messing with. Who needs a meeting?" He wandered to my side and slung his arm around my neck. "Do you want to come meet Jones? He's number forty-seven on the list. Fresh outta jail for beating his grandmother nearly to death for the measly three grand she kept under her floorboards."

"I needed the money for drugs, and the old bitch wouldn't give it to me! It wasn't my fault!" Jones shouted from the bedroom. Then tacked on. "Help me, please! Call the police!"

X snorted on his laughter, yelling back something I didn't catch because my mind had only just caught on to something else.

"Wait." I held up a hand, interrupting X tormenting his victim. "Are you honestly saying none of you called me for a meeting?"

Whip clapped me on the shoulder, his hand heavy and reassuring. "We've all been here since last night when we picked Jones up off the street. Nobody's had time to call a meeting. Though we'll probably all need one when we're done here." He glanced at X. "Some of us are having a little *too* much fun."

As the oldest of the group, he was the unofficial leader. The others followed his lead during group times, and it was clear to me now it was the same when they were "working."

"But if none of you called the meeting..." My words were quiet, catching all of their attention. I jerked my head up in horror.

Whip said the words all of us were thinking. "Only one other person has that number."

X chuckled like the maniac he was. "Trig's back!"

38

KARA

Willa and I ran through the hallways, her leading the way because she knew the rabbit's warren better than I did.

But the mob of men who'd made it through the door were relentless, held back by security staff only long enough to give us a head start.

"Here!" Willa slammed her security pass against a scanner.

"Open, open, open," I muttered to the automatic doors, throwing a glance over my shoulder, fear racing down my spine as the first of the mob broke away from the hapless security guards.

"Wait there, Jesus bitch. Time for you to go home and for me to get paid!" It was the big guy, the one who'd demanded my tongue be cut out for speaking the word of the Devil.

His eyes gleamed with pure malice and evil, the kind I'd grown up being warned about.

I'd dismissed all of Josiah's teachings, but the eyes

being a window to one's soul rang in my ears, and in that instant, staring at that man and the obvious intent in his eyes, I renewed my belief in evil, if nothing else.

My head flashed with nightmarish images of what would happen if a man like that got his hands on me. A lifetime with Josiah might have been more humane.

The door sprang open, and I grabbed Willa's hand, dragging her through with me. On the other side, both of us spun in unison, pushing the door shut, the sound of the locks reengaging the sweetest thing I'd ever heard, apart from Hayley Jade's little voice.

We were outside the hospital, the door we'd taken one that wasn't in regular use. I glanced around, trying to get my bearings as to which part of the hospital we were in.

The first thumps of the men trying to get through the door had both of us backing away quickly, our tiny reprieve clearly over.

Willa breathed hard, her chest rising and falling from the exertion of running. "The door won't hold long." She spun around, starting up a jog because neither of us had another sprint in us. "My car is just over there."

A vehicle felt like a beacon of safety. But... "Keys..."

Willa jingled the lanyard her security pass hung from. "A nurse is never without them. We still need them for many of the older parts of the hospital, as well as some drug storage and our lockers. I keep my car key on here too, because Lord knows I lose one set of keys often enough, I'd be a disaster with two." She pushed the tiny button on the side of one key, and a car to my right lit up, the doors unlocking.

"I can't drive." My single lesson with Hayden definitely didn't give me the skills to get behind a wheel unsupervised. Terror coursed through me at the thought of trying to get away alone, knowing it would only be minutes before those men found a way out here.

Willa gave me a look like I was insane. "Girl, you think I'm leaving you? You clearly don't know me too well at all."

I breathed a sigh of relief and scrambled into the passenger seat, giving the doors to the hospital one last fearful glance as Willa gunned the engine. "They're holding."

"Maybe the external doors are stronger than the internal. The windows are shatterproof because you probably wouldn't be surprised to know how many people try to break into hospitals, being that's where all the good drugs are. But it won't be long until they find another way around." She smiled at me reassuringly. "Don't worry, we'll be long gone by then. My son, Colt, always tells me I have a lead foot. Though he's one to talk."

True to her word, Willa put her foot down hard on the accelerator, and we jerked out of the parking lot, pausing only long enough for her to swipe her security card again so the boom gates would lift to allow us to exit.

I raised the lever on the side of the seat and lay it right back as we rounded the front of the hospital, not trusting any of the people milling around out there.

"They could just be patients and their families. It's a popular place to smoke," Willa tried to reassure me.

I stared at her from my horizontal position.

She grimaced, even though I hadn't voiced my worries. "Yeah, okay. I don't trust any of them either. Just stay down until we get out of here."

She didn't have to tell me twice. I stared at the ceiling of her car, counting silently in my head to try to distract myself from the reality of my situation.

I should have just gone back to Josiah when I'd had the chance. I was almost certain he would leave Hayley Jade alone if I returned.

It was me he wanted. Me who'd betrayed and embarrassed him.

But it was too late now. I couldn't go back. But I couldn't stay here either.

They would keep coming. They would never stop. No one I loved would ever be safe while I was around.

"Where do you want me to take you?" Willa asked gently once we were speeding through the streets of Saint View. "I don't think you should go home."

I agreed. If those men had tracked me down at the hospital, they would know about the clubhouse for sure.

"Your daughter's school?" Willa asked.

"No. Hawk will be there making sure she's safe." And hopefully Hayden.

Willa glanced in the rearview mirror and sped up a few miles. "Good. Because that plan is out of the question anyway. I think there's someone following us."

I jerked upright, twisting around to peer out through the back window. Willa took a corner, and behind us, two other cars did as well. Fear swallowed me up at the idea of leading any of those men anywhere near Hayley Jade. I couldn't see who was driving the vehicles, but in my mind's eye, it was the big man with the devil in his eyes.

I was suddenly glad it was me he was following. The thought of him even setting his sights on my daughter was incomprehensible.

I mumbled a silent prayer, not knowing who I was praying to when I no longer believed in whatever God Josiah preached about. But it was habit, so I prayed in my head to the universe, to whatever powers there were, for all of them to protect Hayley Jade.

And the two men I'd sent to save her.

I would save myself.

Willa took another turn, but the cars didn't follow.

She breathed a sigh of relief. "False alarm. We're good."

Except we weren't. What was done was done. The people chasing me weren't suddenly going to stop because I'd gotten away once. They would come back. Again and again.

Until the inevitable happened.

I had to leave.

My heart squeezed at the thought of leaving Hayden and Hawk. At realizing those moments in the middle of chaos had been our goodbyes. A tear dripped down my cheek. I already missed the feel of their arms around me.

But I'd known all along we were living on borrowed time.

They'd look after Hayley Jade. They'd explain to her that I'd gone not because I didn't want her, but because I loved her enough to leave so she could have a normal life. One away from the evil that followed me everywhere I went, no matter how hard I tried to shake it.

If I believed in Josiah's God anymore, I was sure he'd say I was a cursed woman.

Cursed from loving two men. By kissing a third. All while married in the eyes of the Lord to a fourth.

I needed to say goodbye to Grayson.

To write a letter for Hayley Jade that he could take to her.

I needed a minute to catch my breath and work out where I was going, without a cent to my name or any way of getting there.

Grayson was the one place Josiah's podcast hadn't mentioned. The one place that might be safe for me right now. But my phone was lost somewhere at the hospital, so I couldn't even call and ask him. "Do you know where Grayson lives?" I asked Willa.

She nodded. "I went to his housewarming party. He's literally the only doctor I'd do that for. The rest can go to hell. But he's one of the good ones."

"Could you take me there, please?"

Willa didn't ask questions. Just steered us to some nice apartments in Providence, and stopping outside the doors. "I don't know the security code to his building, but his apartment is the penthouse. You can buzz him to be let in."

She reached across the center console and squeezed my fingers. "I wish I could tell you to go to the police. I wish I could assure you they'd protect you from whatever it is you've gotten yourself into. But I know from firsthand experience they're more likely to hurt than to help." She smiled sadly at me. "I have a feeling you aren't coming back to work, are you?"

I so desperately wished I was. I'd have given anything to turn back time to a few weeks earlier, before Josiah had set his dogs on me, when it felt like I had everything I wanted and needed for the first time in my life.

I wished I'd known to savor it a little longer. To cherish it a little more.

The memories would be all I had to take with me, and that was a crippling sort of pain, one I knew I would never come back from.

I pulled away from Willa with tears in my eyes, thanking her for her help but knowing I couldn't sit there another minute, or I might cave in and ask her to take me back to my daughter.

I dragged myself from the car, and with a heart that felt like it was breaking, pushed the intercom button on the penthouse apartment. There was a click when Grayson answered, but he didn't even get a word out before I burst into tears and a babble of sorrow. "I need you," I choked into the intercom. "I don't have anywhere else to go."

The door buzzed, unlocking the door, and I leaned on it, entering his fancy building. I made sure the door locked after me, just in case anybody did make the connection between me and him and made their way here. Then took the elevator to the top level, the doors opening into a tiny hallway that only had one door. I practically fell onto it, giving in to the silent desperation and guilt and shame eating me alive.

The door opened.

Strong hands grabbed me before I could slide to the floor.

"Well, well, well," a voice that wasn't Grayson's purred in my ear. "Here I was, expecting my son of a bitch brother. Instead, I get his pretty little wife replacement."

Fear turned my blood to ice, my head swirling. I scrambled to get away from the hulking man, but his fingers were tight around my arms, nowhere for me to go. "Who are you?" It was on the tip of my tongue to explain

Josiah was never going to pay him a cent when his words registered through the confusion.

Grayson's brother.

He chuckled, dragging me inside and kicking the door shut with his foot. "The look on your face is kind of insulting. He never talked about me then? Surprising. He used to love to tell everyone all about how I killed his wife and her cunt of a sister."

Shock stole my breath.

Grayson had spoken of a serial killer, warned me he thought there was one who targeted sisters. Confessed he believed that killer to be his wife and her sister's murderer.

He'd never mentioned the murderer was his brother.

The man pulled me tighter and inhaled the scent of my hair deeply. "What a brother he is, bringing me another, just like the first. Has he ever told you how much you look like her?" He ran his tongue across his lips. "Or how pretty her face was when I put a cord around her neck and strangled her?"

The end...for now.

The story continues in the final Saint View Slayers Vs. Sinners book, Three to Fall.

Visit www.ellethorpe.com for bonus scenes, merch, and special editions.

ALSO BY ELLE THORPE

Saint View High series (Reverse Harem, Bully Romance. Complete)

*Devious Little Liars (Saint View High, #1)

*Dangerous Little Secrets (Saint View High, #2)

*Twisted Little Truths (Saint View High, #3)

Saint View Prison series (Reverse harem, romantic suspense. Complete.)

*Locked Up Liars (Saint View Prison, #1)

*Solitary Sinners (Saint View Prison, #2)

*Fatal Felons (Saint View Prison, #3)

Saint View Psychos series (Reverse harem, romantic suspense. Complete.)

*Start a War (Saint View Psychos, #1)

*Half the Battle (Saint View Psychos, #2)

*It Ends With Violence (Saint View Psychos, #3)

Saint View Rebels (Reverse harem, romantic suspense. Complete)

*Rebel Revenge (Saint View Rebels, #1)

*Rebel Obsession (Saint View Rebels, #2)

*Rebel Heart (Saint View Rebels, #3)

Saint View Strip (Male/Female, romantic suspense standalones. Ongoing.)

*Evil Enemy (Saint View Strip, #1)

*Unholy Sins (Saint View Strip, #2)

*Killer Kiss (Saint View Strip, #3)

*Untitled (Saint View Strip, #4)

Saint View Slayers Vs. Sinners (Reverse harem, romantic suspense)

*Wife Number One (Saint View Slayers Vs. Sinners, #1)

*Torn in Two (Saint View Slayers Vs. Sinners, #2)

*Three to Fall (Saint View Slayers Vs. Sinners, #3)

Dirty Cowboy series (complete)

*Talk Dirty, Cowboy (Dirty Cowboy, #1)

*Ride Dirty, Cowboy (Dirty Cowboy, #2)

*Sexy Dirty Cowboy (Dirty Cowboy, #3)

*Dirty Cowboy boxset (books 1-3)

*25 Reasons to Hate Christmas and Cowboys (a Dirty Cowboy bonus novella, set before Talk Dirty, Cowboy but can be read as a standalone, holiday romance)

Buck Cowboys series (Spin off from the Dirty Cowboy series. Complete.)

*Buck Cowboys (Buck Cowboys, #1)

*Buck You! (Buck Cowboys, #2)

*Can't Bucking Wait (Buck Cowboys, #3)

*Mother Bucker (Buck Cowboys, #4)

The Only You series (Contemporary romance. Complete)

*Only the Positive (Only You, #1) - Reese and Low.

*Only the Perfect (Only You, #2) - Jamison.

*Only the Truth - (Only You, bonus novella) - Bree.

*Only the Negatives (Only You, #3) - Gemma.

*Only the Beginning (Only You, #4) - Bianca and Riley.

*Only You boxset

Add your email address here to be the first to know when new books are available!

www.ellethorpe.com/newsletter

Join Elle Thorpe's readers group on Facebook!

www.facebook.com/groups/ellethorpesdramallamas

ACKNOWLEDGMENTS

There's an ever growing group of people who make these books possible and they all deserve the hugest thank you.

Thank you to the Drama Llamas. You guys make my days fun. If you aren't already a member, it's a free reader group on Facebook where I share all sorts of stuff. Come join us, everyone is welcome. www.facebook.com/groups/ellethorpesdramallamas

Thank you to Montana Ash/Darcy Halifax for writing with me every day and being the best office buddy/work wife ever.

Thank you to Sara Massery, Jolie Vines, and Zoe Ashwood for the constant support, friendship, and book advice.

Thank you to the cover team:
Emily Wittig for the discreet covers and Michelle Lancaster for the photography.

Thank you to my editing team:
Emmy at Studio ENP and Karen at Barren Acres Editing.

Dana, Louise, Sam, and Shellie for beta reading. Plus my ARC team for the early reviews.

Thank you to the audio team:

Troy at Dark Star Romance for producing this series. Thank you to Michelle, Sean, Lee, and E.M. for being the voices of Kara, Hawk, Chaos, and Grayson.

And of course, thank you to the team who organize me and the home front:

To Donna for taking on all the jobs I don't have time for. Best admin manager ever.

To my mum, for working for us one day a week, and always being willing to have our kids when we go to signings.

To Jira, for running the online store, doing all the accounting, and dealing with all the 'people-ing.' Not to mention, being the best stay at home dad ever.

To Flick and Heidi, for helping pack swag, and to Thomas, who refuses to work for us, but will proudly tell everyone he knows that his mum is an author.

From the bottom of my heart, thank you.

Elle x

ABOUT THE AUTHOR

Elle Thorpe lives in a small regional town of NSW, Australia. When she's not writing stories full of kissing, she's wife to Mr Thorpe who unexpectedly turned out to be a great plotting partner, and mummy to three tiny humans. She's also official ball thrower to one slobbery dog named Rollo.

When she's not at the office writing, she's probably out on the family alpaca farm, trying not to get spit on.

You can find her on Facebook or Instagram(@ellethorpebooks or hit the links below!) or at her website www.ellethorpe.com. If you love Elle's work, please consider joining her Facebook fan group, Elle Thorpe's Drama Llamas or joining her newsletter here. www.ellethorpe.com/newsletter

Made in United States
Cleveland, OH
23 August 2025